Underneath the Killing Tree

MARIJKA BRIGHT

Copyright © 2017 Marijka Bright

Marijka Bright has asserted her right to be identified as the author of this work under the Copyright, Designs and Patents Act, 1988.

All rights reserved. No part of this publication may be reproduced, stored in a retrieval system, or transmitted in any form or by any means, without the prior written permission of the author.

This is a work of fiction. Names and characters are the products of the author's imagination and any resemblance to real persons, living or dead, is purely coincidental.

ISBN-10: 1545434484
ISBN-13: 978-1545434482

For Anja

1. TWO BIRDS, ONE STONE

Emlyn Quinn was never much one for parties; which was why, when she slipped away quietly from the revelling crowd, she knew that no one, including her husband Malcolm, would think anything of it. He might have played the role of her keeper more often than that of her husband, but even he knew there were limits to her civility and that there were times when it was better to allow her the space she needed, rather than to push her beyond her threshold.

"Tiresome vultures," she mumbled to herself as she traversed the terrace and came to rest her weary body against the cold stone of the balustrade.

Living in a small town, which some would classify as quaint, had started to get the best of her, and from the very moment that Malcolm had suggested hosting a party on the grounds of their estate, Loxley Hall, she had dreaded being on the receiving end of all the attention from the small minds and the big mouths of the village. One could not sit in the shade long in such a town without the wheels of gossip beginning to turn, and now was not the time to be inviting the crowds into their inner sanctum.

She had pleaded with her husband to postpone the affair, however Malcolm Quinn had always been a man who did as he pleased and her protestations over the party had fallen upon deaf, if not uncaring ears.

She gazed out across the gardens, admiring the dew drops, which glimmered in the well-manicured lawn, refracting the rays of the mid-morning sun. It gave the impression of a sea of diamonds scattered amongst the blades of grass. She inhaled the cool, fresh, morning air deeply into her lungs and closed her eyes as she tried to banish her anxious thoughts from her head. Some distance behind her, muted voices and laughter floated on the early autumnal air, punctuated by the clinking of glasses.

A touch as light as a feather brushed her shoulder. Addie, her Lady's maid, came to rest on the balustrade next to Emlyn and placed a long, fringed shawl around her Lady's shoulders.

"You've been ill My Lady – you don't want to go making it any worse; standing out here in the cold with bare shoulders like that," Addie said, as she made some minor adjustments to the shawl's final resting place. "Master Quinn is looking for you; shall I tell him that you're unavailable?"

"Leave my husband to me, dear Addie – it's not him that I'm worried about right now anyway," Emlyn replied, closing the shawl more tightly around her shoulders, a shiver pulsing through her body.

"Yes, it seems that the vultures are already circling – looking for any morsel of gossip to peddle about town, especially after the reception held here for Captain Hope last week," Addie said.

Emlyn stared out towards the embankment at the back of the property and replied, "It's not really them that I'm so concerned about either, although they do make my life particularly uncomfortable." She ran her finger along the cold stone of the railing and turned to face Addie; her voice lowered and asked, "Have you been able to contact him?"

"You mean Captain Hope?"

"Yes. Have you been able to find him?" Emlyn repeated.

"No My Lady, I haven't and his mother hasn't seen him either; not for at least two days."

"And no word from him?"

"Nothing."

Addie's response hung in the air between them for a few moments.

Emlyn sighed and said, "He has only just returned to me and now he has disappeared once again. I hope he hasn't become suspicious. I need to get to the bottom of all of this before my husband figures out exactly what I've been up to." She inhaled deeply and continued, "Well, our Baden Hope has always been a man of his word, so I'm sure that the meeting will go ahead as planned. Is everything prepared?"

"I've done everything that you've asked," Addie answered confidently.

"Good. Now, I'd better go and see to my husband – did he say what he wanted?"

"The men are preparing to leave on the hunt and he wanted you there to see them away."

Emlyn reached into her dress pocket and pulled out a small, apricot coloured envelope. She handed it to Addie, who nodded and walked purposefully across the terrace and out of view.

Emlyn returned to the drawing room, where the morning's revelries had begun. The room was now emptied of the shrill and watchful wives of the men, who would be accompanying Malcolm on his hunt. She picked up a champagne flute from the silver tray which lay upon the table and drained it of its contents. Emlyn was going to need many more of those, before this day was through – she just knew it.

"We've been missing you at the party," Malcolm said from the doorway behind Emlyn, giving her a start.

She picked up a fresh glass and turned to see Malcolm striding through the open doorway, his rifle slung on his shoulder and a riding crop hanging lazily from his left hand. His eyes scanned her from head to toe.

"I'm happy to see that you decided to cooperate and participate in today's festivities. Your dress is rather sufficient," he said.

"Well, you have Addie to thank for that," Emlyn replied shortly.

He walked to her, hooked his arm through hers and escorted her towards the rest of the group.

"I know you didn't want this party, but I just need you to see out this one day, and then you will have all the time you need to rest. And remember, I won't tolerate any misbehaviour in front of Lord Southby," he said.

If her plans came to fruition, it would be more than misbehaviour that Malcolm would have to fret about that afternoon. But for Emlyn, there was still so much more to do. She was close – but she needed the final pieces of her complex puzzle to fall into place.

She nodded up at him and said, "I'll do as you ask, as it is my duty."

Malcolm eyed her suspiciously and in an unconvincing tone he said, "That's the spirit, my love."

They rejoined the guests who were now in the front courtyard, where the horses were waiting to be mounted. The women were clucking like a gaggle of tipsy geese, who were more preoccupied with the cut of each other's outfits, rather than wishing their husbands any kind of fortune on the hunt.

For a man of middle-age, Malcolm climbed atop his horse with ease, and the men trotted off towards the tree line just beyond the stables, each with their very own rifle strapped upon their backs and each with the intention of taking at least one life that day.

*

Time dragged for Emlyn that morning. Every instance that she looked up at the time piece, which sat in all of its glory above the mantel, it was as though time had barely moved at all. On a couple of occasions, she would have sworn to it that the hands of the clock had moved backwards. She kept drifting in and out of the conversations adding platitudes and niceties wherever it seemed appropriate, all the while contemplating the coming meeting with Baden and the plans to finally confront her husband that afternoon.

This situation was entirely new for her. She had never been the type of person to care about anything. She had her duty to her family and to the household, but other than carrying out those basic functions, she had never taken up any kind of cause. The compulsion had never struck her; however, this time it was different.

Emlyn was one of the last people to have seen little Cecil Watson before he vanished. She felt responsible and if Baden or Malcolm had something to do with the disappearance, then *she* was going to get to the bottom of it – even if she didn't quite understand the evidence which she had uncovered so far.

The clock struck quarter to eleven and moments later, Winnie the housemaid, cluttered noisily through the door. She held a tray of canapés in one hand and an open bottle of champagne in the other. As Winnie turned towards her, Emlyn made a movement to take one of the devilled eggs from the tray and with a discreet swish of her hand, she knocked the champagne bottle out of Winnie's grasp and directly onto her own lap.

The champagne splashed from the bottle, covering her blue chiffon dress in a fractal shaped splatter. In the ensuing chaos and rush of apologies spewing forth from Winnie's mouth, Emlyn stood, excused herself and made for the door under the pretence of going to '*tidy herself up*'.

"You can't just go off and leave all your guests," Emlyn's elderly Aunt Bett trilled, swirling her champagne glass in Emlyn's direction.

"You can't expect me to sit here wreaking like the town drunk," Emlyn retorted. "Anyway, I'm sure that you are more than capable of keeping everyone entertained in my absence, my dear Aunt Bett," she added, realising that her initial tone required some tempering.

As though the gaggle had only just noticed her presence in the room, they turned their beaks towards Emlyn.

"So, what are you going to do about the return of that delicious Captain Hope? I hear that he was your suitor before he left for the Great War," asked one.

"If I were a few years younger, I'd be after him myself," giggled another.

"Surely, you're not encouraging my niece to commit adultery?" Aunt Bett chided – facetiously waggling her finger at them both. "I'm the only eligible lady around here, and I have my sights set on someone much more regal," she continued, drawing the cluck of the crowd away from Emlyn.

She used this distraction to excuse herself once again, walked across the hall to the sewing room and locked the door behind her. The window was unlocked, as Addie had promised. Emlyn hesitated for a moment, running through the directions which Addie had given her late the night before; she was to slip around behind the greenhouses, to be out of view of the terrace and the drawing room windows, to get down the embankment unseen.

It was as easy as Addie had described. Beyond the greenhouses, the vast gardens began to slope away from the house and in no time Emlyn had arrived at the agreed upon meeting place – on the worn, wooden bench, underneath the old linden tree, hidden by the embankment at the far end of the grounds. She felt like a criminal, sneaking around her own estate, but she couldn't risk the scandal of being seen alone with a man who was not her husband; not if she wanted her allegations to be taken seriously.

She thumbed open her golden snuffbox and admired the mother-of-pearl which lined the inside as it glinted in the sunlight. She took a pinch of snuff between her thumb and forefinger, raised it to her nose and snorted the powder deeply. The effect was instantaneous and she lay back upon the bench and enjoyed the lightness of her mind and of her body.

The moss-laden branches of the linden tree reached upward like tentacles being drawn towards the water-coloured sky. The light breeze caused the rustle of a million leaves and she listened to the sounds of nature which surrounded her.

The toll of the church bells began in the distance; four dim rings to signify that the hour had arrived – one ring for each quarter represented. She stood and straightened her dress; the champagne had already dried. Without much thought, she started to pace. She had hoped that the party had not scared Baden away. They had planned this tryst before the party had even been considered and Emlyn had not been able to get in contact with him to reschedule – so eleven o'clock that morning it had remained.

As the distant bells began their steady toll, quiet footsteps approached Emlyn swiftly from behind.

Clang; she froze, closed her eyes and awaited the kiss to brush the side of her neck – the way that Baden used to always greet her. It was one concession she could give to him knowing that the last time they had met he was starting to get impatient with the entire situation.

Clang; she cocked her head to the right, her blond ringlets fell from her shoulder to reveal her long, slender neck.

He was close now.

Clang; his hand shifted her hair from her neck and he took it back as if he were tying it up. The coolness of the air danced across the nape of her neck; the anticipation of Baden's touch caused her skin to tingle.

Clang; his breath warmed her neck as the goose bumps rose across the small of her back. It had been so long since Malcolm had touched her, that her knees felt weak at the caress of another. She thought for an instant that maybe she had made a mistake. How could Baden be involved in any of that sordid business?

Clang; his lips swept passionately across her neck, the part where the neck itself meets the shoulder. She felt the moisture of his lips on her skin and in that moment her entire body quivered. It felt so good. It felt different however, softer. Maybe the time he had been away had made him a gentler, more caring lover.

Clang; breathless, she felt compelled to turn around and kiss him as she used to all those years ago, but as she tried to turn her head, her hair was yanked back hard, so ferociously that her neck was jolted and fully exposed. A gloved hand clamped itself tightly over her mouth. Her heart thumped and she struggled against the strength of her attacker, unable by the circumstance to breathe. She reached both of her hands backwards; clawing and scraping to find any point of weakness. Try as she might however, her arms were not long enough.

Clang; her head still felt light from the snuff and her body was weak from her illness. She mustered her determination and threw her body weight backwards with one mighty shove of her feet. Her flailing arms were able to grasp the top of her attacker's head; she gripped at it as hard as she could. But all she felt was the fabric of a hat as she wrenched it off the top of his head. Unadulterated panic burned through her.

Clang; she dropped her knees and made him carry her weight. It was harder for her to breathe and the veins in her forehead began to swell. In a last ditch effort, she tried to bite the arm that was holding her captive, but the grip that was imposed upon her was too steadfast for her weak, ailing body to fight.

Clang; something thick and rough slid over her head, abrading her nose and ripping at her lip as it scratched along the length of her face, over her chin and down around her neck. The attacker loosened his grip and her hands reflexively shot up towards her neck to protect it from the rope which now encompassed it, but she was too late.

Clang; she felt the violent jolt which took her sailing upward and her feet could no longer feel the safety of the ground beneath them. She tried to cry out for help, for salvation, but the only sound which came was the gurgle of a desperate woman. A second and more vicious jolt caused an intense pain to shoot through her entire body, radiating from her neck down to the very tips of her fingers and toes as it raised her up higher and she could feel her eyes bulging, trying to escape from their sockets. She let out her final, staggered breath as the last of her hope evaporated and she realised that this was her final moment and there was nothing else that she could do.

****

Royal Trudeau was falling into the most marvellous of dreams, in which he was about to become the first ever person to cross over the Einstein-Rosen bridge, when his slumber was rudely interrupted by the sharp ring of his phone. Dazed and confused, he reached his hand towards the noise and swatted at it like a fly. After a moment of sleepily wondering why his actions were not quashing the sound emanating from his bedside table, he came to his senses enough to realise that it was his work phone ringing and that it wasn't going to answer itself.

"Trudeau here," he said drowsily into the phone.

"I didn't wake you up, did I?"

Royal could hear the wind blustering in the background as he recognised the voice of his old friend, Detective Inspector Andy Bliss, and he knew that this wasn't going to be good news for his slumber and he would have to put his Nobel Prize winning dream back onto the shelf.

He had already risen as he replied, "My subconscious and I were about to venture beyond our solar system and make contact with other civilisations, actually."

"Well, you'll just have to reschedule your space travel for some other time. We've got a messy one for you here on Earth; and you know what? You're never going to guess who it is!" Andy exclaimed.

Royal was half dressed and trying to button his shirt with one hand as he answered, "You're way too enthusiastic about a dead body; especially at this time of the morning."

"I know I am Royal," Andy replied, "but it's John Quinn."

"Oh God – it wasn't you, was it?" Royal said, suddenly feeling much more awake.

"You got me, case solved. How do you do it?" Andy jested.

He gave Royal the details and then they rang off. Royal wondered exactly how John Quinn had met his end and he was certain that however it had eventuated, it would not be punishment enough for what he had done; especially to Andy.

Royal watched the kettle boil and then filled up his thermos. He was getting older and these middle of the night wake up calls were not getting any easier. However, being able to keep one eye on Andy was motivation enough for him to keep coming back for more.

He arrived at the scene, took out his ID card and showed it to the officer, who was assigned to guard the outside of the factory. There was already a small crowd gathered out the front, mostly workers who had arrived to start their morning shifts from the way that they were dressed.

'*Good, no media; yet,*' he thought to himself.

The officer held out the card in front of him and looked from Royal's face, to the card and back again.

With a furrowed brow he said, "This doesn't look much like you." And he shook the card at him.

"Well, yes – I've cut my hair and lost some weight since that photo was taken," Royal replied, irritated that the young officer didn't already know who he was talking to.

"Some weight?" the young man said with his eyebrows raised. "Look, I can't let you in here, until I verify this with the Inspector."

He wandered away from Royal, said something into his radio and awaited a reply.

"You should really get this updated, Doctor Trudeau," the officer said as he handed the card back and waved him through.

"Just tell me where it is," Royal snapped.

"Through that door, to the left and then down the stairs – you won't be able to miss it," the young officer said as he turned his back on Royal and continued with his watch dog duties.

The scene that met Royal's eyes was not a pretty one. The brightness of the spotlights made the stainless steel surfaces glimmer and the blood pools and spatters shined with great contrast to the dull and bluish face of a man once very familiar to Royal. Dried blood was encrusted on John's clothing and his white, protective smock was now smudged with differing shades of brown.

"We haven't touched a thing; just taken photos, so you're free to move whatever you need," boomed Andy's voice from high above him, on a walkway which looked out upon the factory floor. "We're just checking through his office now. You know, you should really get a new picture – that's the third time this month that you've caused a stir," he continued.

Royal dismissed Andy with a wave of his hand, positioned his leather briefcase, proceeded to put on his green coveralls and set about his work.

He extracted his scalpel, approached the body, careful not to step in any of the blood and he made an incision into the top of John's thorax. He needed to use some extra force to get the probe into position, but with the condition of the body, it wouldn't make much difference.

He studied the place where John's arm had once been and examined the exposed section of the humerus which was protruding from the shredded flesh. With his small, pocket camera he took some pictures of the wound. Royal then looked into the machine. Flesh and bone were still clogged in the sharp teeth of the mincer.

He took a few more samples and photographs and then called out to an officer nearby, "Where's the SOCO?"

"Oi, Benny, you're up!" the officer shouted across the factory floor to a man who looked more like the drummer in a heavy metal band, with his long, black hair and his long, black beard, than a Scene of Crime officer.

Benny walked across the floor, already in his coveralls, tying his hair into a bun and covering his head with the hood.

When he reached Royal, he stuck out his gloved hand and said, "Doctor Trudeau, it's such an honour to be working with you."

Royal sidled past his hand and placed his samples methodically into the allotted sections of his bag.

"Benny is it?" he asked over his shoulder.

"Yes, Sir," he replied.

"I've got everything I need from here. The scene's yours. I need you to organise the body for transport and get that machine to my lab after you've taken the prints. You know where my lab is?"

"I do," Benny answered.

Royal made his way up the stairs and found Andy sitting behind an oak desk in an office with panoramic views of the entire factory floor. Andy looked pale and drawn out, but his eyes shone with the same brightness that Royal had admired since their days at university together.

"What can you tell me, Roy?" Andy asked, a serious look on his face. "Is it just an accident or do we have a case here?"

Royal took his thermos out of his bag and poured out two mugs. He handed one to his friend and asked, "How are you?"

Andy rubbed his eyes and replied, "I'm fine. Actually, I couldn't be better now that John Quinn is dead."

"You don't look so good – have you been drinking?" Royal asked.

"For your information, this is what I look like when I haven't been. I'm dry and I intend to stay that way," Andy answered, taking a sip of his coffee.

"You know I only ask because I care," Royal said.

There was a knock at the door. A petit woman in a powder, blue suit and immaculately groomed hair – especially for such an ungodly hour – stood in the doorway.

"Pridis," Andy said with a smile. "Did you manage to get them?"

"That's the thing Inspector; they're all gone – not even the CCTV from the areas surrounding the factory. It's a black spot – from about 11pm until 4 o'clock this morning. Why are we wasting our time on a work-place accident anyway?" Pridis asked.

"An accident?" Royal interrupted, unable to hide his dismay at the officer's impertinence.

"You two haven't been properly introduced, have you?" Andy turned to Royal and said, "This is Detective Sergeant Diane Pridis my new partner," and he turned to Pridis and said, "This is Doctor Royal Trudeau, a Medical Examiner of the highest order, talented scientist and my long-time, best friend."

Pridis took a step forward and began to offer her hand, until Andy gave an obvious shake of the head and she stopped and stood at ease at a point almost equidistant from the two men.

Royal looked at Andy and then at Pridis and pronounced, "This was no accident – John Quinn was murdered."

2. THE STATE OF PLAY

Detective Sergeant Diane Pridis studied her reflection in the mirror. Despite the harshness of the fluorescent lights hanging in the bathroom, she looked as she always did. Neat, well-groomed and as though she had it all worked out. But she knew better. Upon closer inspection, there were the many tiny imperfections that only she could see. Actually, the imperfections were not so small – but she was working hard on them and it would only be a matter of time before the real Diane Pridis would be a true reflection of the mask that she adorned herself with every single morning.

She turned on the faucet and splashed some water across her face. The shock of the icy coldness caused her to shudder and she felt her focus sharpen immediately. She was beginning to feel the effects of such an early morning, and her determination to get through it without any help was beginning to waiver.

She had received the call from Inspector Andy Bliss at around 5am that morning and with her routine now whittled down to a fine art, she was up and out of the house fifteen minutes later. Not that she'd been asleep – sleep was a foreign concept to Pridis at the moment and she was holding onto the reason why in her left hand. The elliptical, blue tablet shone on her palm.

'One more couldn't possibly hurt. This is the case that I've been waiting for. It

could make my career; Vicki will just have to understand.'

She quickly pushed the thought of Vicki and the discussion that they had had about the ramifications of a relapse, out of her mind. Thoroughly convinced by the little voice which had been gnawing away at her for the entire morning, she threw the oval-shaped pill into her mouth.

She was about to scoop up some water from the running tap, when there was a knock at the door and Inspector Bliss' silky voice called through it, "Pridis, are you in there? We need to get started on the briefing."

The mirror reflected her guilt back upon her. She looked at herself with utter distain at her lack of self-control as her eyes implored her to give in to that one last hit. She spat the pill into the sink in sheer disgust.

"Oh bollocks," she muttered to herself and to Inspector Bliss she called, "I'll be out in a sec."

She wiped her face with some paper towel, rinsed the now sodden tablet down the drain and straightened her hair, which in the space of a few minutes had become, in her opinion, a flyaway mess on top of her head.

What on Earth was she thinking? Why had she even brought them with her? All of this was a part of the habit and it was these things that she needed to break. She rifled through her bag, picked out the rest of the Adderall pills from within and cast them away angrily into the nearby receptacle.

With the pings of the tablets against the bottom of the metal bin came relief. She rested her hands on either side of the basin and looked deeply into her pale, green eyes. She promised herself that she wouldn't let that voice get the best of her again and gave a sharp, resolute nod of the head.

Inspector Bliss was leaning on the wall of the corridor flipping through a thick and tattered file. Pridis wasn't sure about him yet. She still had the warnings of her colleagues swimming around her head and true to their words, she couldn't be sure from the looks of him, whether he was sober that morning or not. But she had needed a fresh start, with a new partner and according to the Superintendent, it was Inspector Bliss or nothing.

He still wore the edges of the smirk, which had been plastered across his unshaven face since she had met him at the crime scene earlier that morning.

"What are you so happy about anyway?" Pridis snapped, surprised by the notes of irritation in her own voice.

Inspector Bliss peered up at her from the file. If he was surprised by her tone, he didn't show it.

He replied, "Well, I wouldn't say that I'm happy exactly – but to have John Quinn off the streets brings me a great deal of satisfaction; even if I'm not the one who removed him from them."

She tried to catch a whiff of him as they entered the briefing room, but all she could smell was his aftershave. That was a good enough indication for her that he was still sober. He set the file down on the table at the front of the room and began to sort through the pages that he had marked with pink and orange Post-it notes.

"Do you have your notebook with you Sergeant?" he asked as he continued to shuffle through the file.

"Yes Inspector," Pridis replied, as she extracted it from her bag.

"We have a few minutes before the team comes in. Can you run me through the circumstances around the missing CCTV?" he asked.

She quickly scanned her notebook and replied, "I spoke to a bloke called Rory Hicks. He's the supervising night guard for the security company who looks after the factory."

"There was a guard on duty last night?"

"Well, yes and no," Pridis answered still referring to her notes. "The security company sends a guard around three times a night to inspect the area – you know, make sure that there's no funny business going on. Between these patrols there are cameras installed throughout the factory and the grounds which are remotely monitored from Hick's home office."

"And this Hick's fellow; works alone, does he?"

"No, not usually. Normally, he watches the cameras and he has another guard," she flicked through her notes again, "a Jürgen Sampson, who does the night runs, which takes him past the seven factories that make up their zone. But get this, last night Jürgen didn't show up for his shift and no one's been able to get a hold of him since. I've had one of the DCs trying to track him down all morning – no luck yet though."

"Let me know when you get him in – I'd like to speak to him as soon as possible," Inspector Bliss said, adding a nod of encouragement for Pridis to continue.

"Right so, Hicks couldn't find a replacement on such short notice, therefore he spent the entire night, I quote, *'Running around London like a right git, trying the fuck to cover off these factories, while leaving my poor, infirmed mum to keep an eye on the screens.'*"

"And have you spoken to his mother yet?" he asked.

Pridis felt her left leg tremble and a wave of nausea swept through her as she replied, "Hicks said that he came home after the second run at about 4am to check on his mum and the monitors had all been switched off, the cameras were off-line and every bit of footage from the shift had been deleted. On top of all that his mother was fast asleep in her own bed. She's not able to do that by herself and when he asked her how she'd gotten there, she told him that her husband had helped her to bed. The thing is Inspector, her husband has been dead for 15 years."

"Although her reliability as a witness is questionable, I still think it's worthwhile talking to her. See what you can get – you never know, we might luck out and get a few moments of lucidity. But make sure you don't push her too hard," Inspector Bliss instructed.

Pridis dabbed at the small pool of sweat which had collected on her top lip as she noted the instruction in her notebook. She took a deep breath and steadied herself. She hoped that Inspector Bliss had failed to notice her blushing cheeks, yet another unpleasant symptom of her withdrawal.

"I've got our tech guys out at Hick's house working on it as we speak. They're trying to retrieve the data, but it doesn't look too promising."

"And it's the same for the CCTV around the factory?" he asked.

"That's the worrying thing. The cameras covering all entry and exit points to the entire area have been wiped – and these are the ones that are run by us. So, whoever's involved certainly has some kind of reach," Pridis replied. She added hesitantly, "Do you want to know what I think?"

"It's a bit too early for theorising, isn't it?" Inspector Bliss said, eyeing her over the rims of his reading glasses, like a patronising school teacher.

"I'm sorry Inspector, I didn't mean to jump the gun, it's just that..."

"No, no," Inspector Bliss interrupted, waving his hand to silence her.

The way his hand swept through the air, as if it was sweeping her and her value as a detective and even as a person aside, stirred a feeling of resentment deep inside of her. She had always struggled with authority, but over time she had learned to keep her emotions in check.

But this time it was different. It wasn't about his position of power; as a police officer, she had long ago abandoned her need to always be in control. It was about the expectations of this new partnership with him. Yes, it was a partnership fraught with potential problems, given his status as New Scotland Yard's whipping boy, but after the way her last partnership had gone, she was hoping it would be something better. But with this one dismissive motion, her hopes and expectations had been flung hopelessly out of the window and were replaced with disappointment and despair.

The silence thickened the air between them and what could only have been seconds seemed like minutes piling upon each other like unwanted little reminders of each of her own insufficiencies.

Inspector Bliss straightened his back and said, "There's no need to apologise – maybe there's a learning opportunity here about holding off on your responses until I'm finished – but we can work on that. I was going to say that, yes, it's a bit early, but you don't need my permission to have a theory or an opinion. In fact, I encourage it."

In that moment, she felt her doubts and insecurities subside, but they didn't fully dissipate and she wondered whether these unfamiliar feelings were a side effect of her withering addiction or whether her intuition was picking up on something more sinister.

She forced a smile, the one that she was so used to relying upon – especially at family functions – the one which caused her nostrils to flare ever so slightly, and asserted, "The way these cameras have all been handled and the callousness of the crime itself – I have a strong feeling that this could be a professional hit. I think this John Quinn was involved in organised crime or at least he pissed someone off who is. To me it looks as though they were trying to torture something out of him and when they got what they wanted they finished the job."

"I don't disagree with you on that Sergeant and there is definitely more to John Quinn than meets the eye," Inspector Bliss said tapping the thick file which lay in front of him. "And now we've been handed the perfect opportunity to expose him once and for all."

Pridis knew that Inspector Bliss' file held the notes from the case which had ruined his career all those years ago. She had heard all the stories of his obsession with John Quinn and his gradual descent into alcoholism and general chaos when he couldn't make the case stick against him. It didn't help, that Inspector Bliss had been the one to lose the Crown's only eyewitness to the alleged crimes. But Pridis had to admit, finding John Quinn murdered in such a manner, did make her suspicious. But of who, she was not yet sure.

There was a knock at the door and Pridis swung around expecting to greet the rest of the team arriving for the briefing, but instead she was met by the harsh features of the Superintendent's secretary.

Redvers O'Dell was a burly man in his early 50s. Pridis found him particularly intimidating which was probably part of the reason why the Superintendent had kept him on as her secretary. In his day, he had made a very formidable police officer. It was out on the beat where he had sustained his conspicuous limp and it was the reason why he was no longer an active member of the force.

"What can I do for you Red? Looking to get back in on the Quinn case?" Inspector Bliss called from behind Pridis, who was still facing the room's newest entrant.

Redvers had an awkward look about him and he avoided any eye contact with Inspector Bliss as he replied, "I would have loved to have had a crack at that bastard myself. Shame someone else got in before me."

"You better watch what you say old man, I might have to bring you in for questioning," Inspector Bliss jested.

Redvers sighed and continued in a flurry, "Look Andy, the Super wants to have a word with you."

"Now? But what about the briefing?" Pridis interjected.

Redvers furrowed his brow and addressed himself directly to Inspector Bliss, "She wants you in her office now Andy. She's got a bee in her bonnet about something and there was nothing I could say to stop her."

"The briefing shouldn't take more than half an hour Red, it's imperative that we get started as soon as possible – she knows that as well as anyone. Are you sure you can't hold her off until then?"

Redvers shook his head and with his eyes planted squarely on the greying carpet as if transfixed by some pattern that only he could see, he said, "There isn't going to be a briefing today Andy – not one run by you anyway."

Pridis swung around sharply to face Inspector Bliss, "The Super can't do that, can she?"

"She already has!" came the triumphant exclamation of a woman's voice from behind the burly frame of Redvers.

Pridis was immobilised by the sound of the horribly familiar voice grating at her from behind. It was a voice she had hoped that she would never have to hear again, and it was the next six words which delivered with them such an overwhelming sense of dread, that her thoughts flashed abruptly to her little, blue saviours lying helplessly at the bottom of that bin.

"Dee, you've been reassigned to me," Inspector Teri Tilman said as her high heeled footsteps click-clacked from the corridor, into the room.

"But..." Pridis breathed, furrowing her brow at the intrusion and dreading being partnered back up with the woman who she had been so eager to escape from in the first place.

Before Pridis could finish, Tilman replied, "Don't worry Dee, it's only temporary – we won't be getting our little partnership back together for long, only while your precious, new Inspector is off on his little break."

Pridis stole a look at Inspector Bliss, whose appearance mirrored her own confusion and then she felt the tight clasp on her arm; long nails digging into her flesh through the thick sleeve of her suit jacket.

As she was hauled towards the door and out of the room Pridis shook her arm free from the grip of her subjugator and said, "I'll be with you in a moment Inspector Tilman; I just need a quick visit to the Ladies room."

***

"What the fuck are you playing at?" Andy thundered as he burst through the door of the Superintendent's office.

His fists were clenched and his chest was tensed to the point that he thought his muscles might actually explode.

"No one knows more about this case than me. No one knows John Quinn better than I do!" he exclaimed, his face running hot.

Andy Bliss glared at his superior, who was sitting in her high-backed, leather desk chair, with the telephone handset raised to her ear, calmly listening to the person on the other end of the line. Instead of retaliating or showing any kind of emotion, she composedly signalled to Andy to sit in the chair opposite her.

Andy looked at the telephone and thought for a moment about the satisfaction he would feel if he were to pick it up, rip its cord from the wall and throw it as hard as he could through her office window. He took an instinctive step towards the Superintendent's desk, but in lieu of grabbing the phone, he thumped his fists down hard. His blood pulsed through his veins and the rush of adrenaline made his heart leap into his throat.

He pounded his fists down once more, this time so hard that it caused the skin on the little finger of his left hand to split open. He awaited her reaction and when, after a few seconds, he saw that there wasn't one forthcoming, he leaned forward, snatched the phone out of her hand and slammed it back down on the receiver.

"What the hell do you think you're doing Inspector?" the Super demanded, her voice faltering.

Superintendent Daria Zukowski was not an easy one to unsettle and so Andy felt a sense of gratification at causing her discomfort, especially in the wake of what had just transpired in the briefing room. Not only had she taken away the one thing which would finally bring Andy some closure on a case which had haunted him for the last four years and at a stretch had caused the breakdown of his marriage – but she had given it away to the one person who he knew was responsible for the case against John collapsing the last time they had the chance to nail that self-righteous son of a bitch to the cross.

"What am *I* doing?" Andy asked incredulously. "That's a good one." He let out a high, fake laugh and continued, "*I'm* the one here who's trying to do my job and *you* seem intent on standing in my way."

He picked up the nearest thing from the Super's desk, which happened to be an ornamental bell in the shape of a Bobby's hat, and he threw it hard against the wall; a fitting emphasis to his point.

The noise of the bell itself, in conjunction with the loud thwack that its momentum ending impact into the wall produced, had the effect of rousing the resting giant from his desk, and within an instant, Redvers stuck his head in through the still open doorway and inquired, "Everything all right in here?"

He didn't specify to who his comment was directed, but Andy knew where Red's loyalties lay and he was certain that it wasn't with him.

The Super looked at Andy as if waiting for reassurance from him that he'd finished his tantrum and after Andy gave her a nod, she said to Red, "Thank-you Mr. O'Dell, I don't think I'll be needing your protective services today."

Redvers closed the door behind him and Andy finally took the seat that had been offered to him by the Super when he first arrived. He took a moment to compose himself and with the fire still burning in the base of his stomach he began to reaffirm his already stated position. But before he could come out with more than his initial counter arguments, the Superintendent cut him off.

"Inspector, you know that I would love to have you working this case. Your knowledge of all the major players would certainly create plenty of efficiencies and make the job a hell of a lot easier. But with your, shall we say, chequered history with the Quinn case, coupled with the trouble that you had with his wife the last time – I can't see any alternative than to give the case to someone else."

"But does that someone else have to be bloody Teri Tilman," Andy spat; he could feel the rage beginning to rise from the pit of his stomach once again. "It was her incompetence that fucked up the case against John Quinn last time!"

"We've spoken about this before – there's no proof that Inspector Tilman was the one responsible for losing that witness. Tilman said it was on your watch and I'm inclined to agree with her. She's my best detective, and quite frankly, Inspector, your work has been in decline for quite some time now," the Super rebutted.

"Tilman's toxic and you know it. She was my partner for long enough for me to see exactly what kind of person she is and it's not pretty – she'd throw her own mother under a bus if it made her look good and probably her own children, if anyone would be sick enough to take that woman to bed," Andy said with a shudder.

The Superintendent gave Andy a steely glare and said in a strong, even tone, "I won't have you talking like that about any of your fellow officers, Inspector. Anyway, the decision's been made and ratified by Chief Superintendent Wilcox; you're off the case and there will be no further discussions on the matter and if I find you anywhere near it – you'll be suspended."

She relaxed her shoulders and continued, "Look Andy, we're not investigating John – there was no tangible evidence back then and I'm sure that there would be even less now. I know that you want to find out about those missing girls, we all do, but this case is about finding John Quinn's murderer; not drawing and quartering a dead man."

Andy knew that there was nothing he could say to change the decisions that had already been made but he countered anyway, "Maybe the murder is connected with John's own indiscretions – it couldn't hurt digging into the past and having a look. Think about the families of all those missing girls – think about the closure that they would finally get from this too."

"You'll just have to trust that Tilman is up to the investigation – she was your partner on the Quinn case four years ago. And she's got Pridis with her too. I'm certain that Pridis will keep things moving in the right direction. You must've noticed by now, how switched on she is – I've got that one ear-marked for great things," the Super said.

Andy was still beyond angry, but he'd been on the force long enough to know that it was pointless to keep trying to shovel this shit up the hill. He was defeated for now and he started to gather himself together to leave.

The Super motioned for him to stay and said, "When was the last time you had a break?"

Andy thought for a moment and replied, "Yesterday – I had a crumpet at about quarter past seven last night."

"I meant a real break – like a holiday. You do remember what one of those is, don't you?"

"Not that long ago," Andy said defensively.

The Super picked up the folder which sat in front of her and said, "According to your file, it's been just over four and a half years, which I'm sure is against union policy. I've spoken to HR and I'm putting you on leave for the next four weeks – go on a holiday, visit your family, find yourself a hobby, do something – just stay away from the Quinn case. You haven't taken a holiday since before Jarmila left you and I can see that it's taking its toll."

At the mention of his ex-wife's name, Andy felt the all too familiar surge of guilt penetrate his chest. He couldn't help but think about the last time he had seen her and the way that things had ended. Lies, sorrow, Andy in a drunken rage – his memory of that night of four years ago left in tatters by the pile of whiskey bottles lying empty in the corner of his bedroom.

But the one thing from that night which remained clear in his mind, was his flying right hook and his wife's tooth clattering to the floor and her blood spattering the wall behind her.

He felt sick. He needed air. He stood up and without another word he stumbled out of the Super's office. He burst into his own office and found Pridis sitting in there looking like an enthusiastic puppy. He ignored her, reached into his desk drawer, pulled out his bottle of Chivas and poured out two fingers into his mug.

"What are you doing Inspector? It's half past eight in the morning!" Pridis exclaimed.

"I've been up since God knows when, and anyway from this moment I'm on holidays; so it's really none of your business," Andy snapped.

He drained the whiskey from his coffee cup in one satisfying gulp. He poured another and shot it down, picked up his jacket from the back of his chair and without another word, left Pridis sitting alone in his office once again. As he left the building, he felt a weight being lifted from his shoulders and for a brief moment he felt free.

3. AN UNEXPECTED ARRIVAL

The sound of the wooden-spoked wheels came to a crunching halt outside the great gates of Loxley Hall. Mary Loxley rifled through her trouser pockets for the correct change to give to the driver. Her cigarette dangled casually out of the side of her mouth, and she blew a great stream of smoke to accompany her hand, as she tendered the driver his fare through the small trapdoor behind her head. He gave her a reproachful grunt and showed no inclination to dismount and help her with her bags.

The old badger had had a look of disapproval etched on his face from the very moment he had picked her up in his hansom cab from Sheffield station. He and his cab had seen better days and since the arrival of automobiles, which were now commonplace, his obsolescence was only a matter of time. If he wasn't desperate for the money, she was sure that he would have rejected her fare altogether.

Mary unloaded her small suitcase and travel bag, turned to the driver as he prepared the cab for departure and stated, "Our external drapery does not maketh the person, my dear sir. But if it did – you would indisputably be a sewer rat!"

The cabman gave her a look of indignation, flogged the horses, and without a word, trotted away in the direction of Sheffield, some 5-miles back down the road.

Having lived in France since the end of the Great War, Mary had not had to put up with the disapproving stares and murmurs of those who were prim and proper and whose upbringings had told them that a lady should not wear such things or behave in such a fashion. If only their upbringing had included the bestowal of better manners. The contrast with her home of the last 2 years was astonishing to her still. If she had wanted to wear trousers and a cloche hat through the streets of Montpellier, then that was her business and hers alone.

"As outdated as his antediluvian cab; silly old sod," she mumbled under her breath as she watched the dust puff into the air from the wheels of the cab, now off in the hazy distance.

Mary dragged on her cigarette, inhaling as deeply as she could, before stubbing it out on the sandstone wall as she passed through the pedestrian gate. It had been a long time since she had called Loxley Hall her home and she had mixed feelings coursing through her as she walked through the vast gardens up towards the house.

She followed the path, whose shape resembled more a wisp of smoke than a means of getting efficiently from one place to the next, admiring the forest of trees, which she remembered fondly from her childhood. She had always loved the adventure that the seemingly infinite gardens of the estate had constantly promised her.

Around the final corner, the crenellated roof of Loxley Hall overshadowed her. She hadn't thought about this place in such a long time and receiving Emlyn's letter almost a week ago to the day – so out of the blue – had brought with it, not just memories of a past better left behind, but also an intense feeling of unease.

When Mary had been handed the letter by her live-in companion, Rosaline Stern, she had recognised the handwriting on the small, apricot coloured envelope immediately. She had flipped the envelope over and over in her hands while she contemplated all the reasons why her sister would be writing to her when she hadn't heard from her since the day she had left Loxley; and not one of her postulations were positive.

Rosaline had become impatient with her as she declared, "It isn't going to read itself, now is it?"

She handed Mary the letter opener that had been sitting on the table, beside the Chaise lounge, upon which Rosaline had been reclining, beckoningly upon. She slid the blade along the sealed edge of the envelope and retrieved the letter from its cosy resting place inside. Rosaline stood behind her, resting her hands on Mary's shoulders and her lips pressed lightly on the top of her head. Mary unfolded the sheet of paper and held it so that they both could read it.

"What in God's name is all of that supposed to mean?" Rosaline exclaimed abruptly.

Instead of answering, Mary strode across to the bookshelf and extracted her copy of H.G Wells', 'The Sleeper Awakes', ensuring that she had taken the 1910 edition from the shelf and then returned promptly to her seat.

"It's a book cipher my Lovely; now if you would just write down the words I call out to you, then we'll have the code cracked in no time."

For Emlyn to feel it necessary to write in their special code, set the alarm bells ringing and when the words *hostility, disappearance, treachery* and *danger* all appeared in quick succession, Mary didn't need to read the letter in its entirety to know that strange things were afoot at Loxley Hall and somehow Emlyn was right in the middle of it all.

It was very much unlike Emlyn to go off on an investigation, especially a dangerous one; that was more Mary's cup of tea. It was this fact which had concerned her the most as she had made her journey back to Loxley Hall.

With heavy legs, Mary crossed the gravelly courtyard towards the front entrance, wondering exactly what she was about to walk into. She reluctantly climbed the stone steps, reached for the majestic, lion-headed door knocker and knocked as hard as she could. In the same moment, a gun blast drowned out the sound of her own blow.

She dropped her bags and sprinted towards the stables. The sound of crunching footsteps pursued her. They were getting further and further away as she hit her stride and ran at her top speed. Her side ached and her lungs burned as they tried to suck in more air than they could hold, but she didn't stop running. Her thoughts were on Emlyn and of the dangers her letter had foretold.

The stable door was wide open and a pair of feet protruded, motionless, from one of the stalls. The horses squealed; especially Emlyn's dark-brown mare, Truffles. She leapt against the stall door, ears pinned back and her eyes wild. She was an old horse now, going on fourteen, but she still cut quite an imposing figure.

Mary approached the feet and peered cautiously into the stall. A boy, who would have been no older than Truffles, was sprawled on the ground. A rifle lay next to him and blood dripped from his mouth and nose. Relieved that it wasn't Emlyn, Mary immediately set to work. She checked his pulse and his pupils and concluded that he had been knocked unconscious.

She tucked the rifle under her arm and settled the horses. At the back of Truffles' stall a bullet hole pierced the wall.

Behind her, the boy groaned and asked in a groggy voice, "What happened?"

Mary swung around and said, "You were trying to murder this horse and if it wasn't for your inexperience and ineptitude, you would have been successful."

She pointed the rifle threateningly at the boy, who remained seated on the ground.

"I'm not inexperienced, I've been on loads of hunts," the boy said indignantly.

"Watching others shoot and shooting the gun for yourself are two very different propositions. Taming recoil isn't as easy as it looks; I had to attend to many of these kinds of injuries during the war. Although most of the soldiers weren't stupid enough to hold their rifles directly in front of their faces," Mary said as she watched his face drop and his ears turn pink. "We will see what the police have to say about all of this."

The boy's eyes widened at this new threat and he tottered sideways. He tried to answer, but he was cut off by a man who had entered the stables and was just a shadow standing in the brightness of the open doorway.

"The boy was only doing as he was ordered."

As soon as Mary's eyes adjusted to the light she lowered her weapon and asked, "Godfrey, is that you?"

"Yes. And who might you be, to come in here and accuse my son of murder?"

"It's me, Mary. I thought the war had gotten you!" she exclaimed. She looked over at the young boy, "And Granville…. I haven't seen you since you were this big," Mary said waving her hand around hip height. She thought for a moment and then added, "What the devil is going on here?"

Godfrey didn't answer her question, instead he approached Mary. She surveyed the man who was now standing in front of her; war had not been kind to the poor, old butler. He had a strong limp which favoured his left side terribly and scarring around his hairline and down onto his neck. She had seen this pattern of burning many times before; mustard gas exposure.

"Oh Mary it is you; I mean My Lady; I am sorry I didn't recognise you. I'm so glad that you're here. It's been a difficult time for us all here at the Hall and I was afraid that things were starting to get out of hand."

"I'd say that they already are. For one thing, your son was trying to kill my sister's most prized possession..." Mary started.

"But Master Quinn ordered that the horse be shot," he interrupted, momentarily forgetting his place.

"Emlyn would never allow such a thing. She loves that horse more than anything. It was our parents' present to her as a consolation when I left for boarding-school."

"She's not really in a position to protest, now is she?" Granville said carelessly.

Godfrey raised his hand to quiet Granville. His eyes immediately dropped to the ground and he shuffled his feet.

"What do you mean by that?" Mary demanded.

Her line of questioning was interrupted by the entry of a young girl whose uniform suggested that she was the housemaid.

She said with an airy tone, "I saw the front door open and thought I better come and make sure that everything is all right in here."

The young housemaid froze. Her eyes flashed from Granville's face, to Truffles and then landed squarely on Mary, who still held the rifle.

Her initial look of confusion quickly dissolved into anger, but before she could react, Godfrey said, "Winnie, can you take Granville inside and see to his injuries and then prepare the blue bedchamber in the west wing? Our Lady's bags are next to the front door."

At the orders from Godfrey, Winnie swooped in ever so efficiently to rescue Granville. With her arm around his shoulder, she helped him up and they moved towards the door.

"The nasal fracture hasn't displaced the septum, so if you clean him up and put a cold compress on it, he should be as good as new within a few days," Mary directed.

Winnie nodded submissively and both her and Granville shuffled away. Once they had left, Mary returned her gaze to Godfrey and asked once again, "What did Granville mean?"

Godfrey's face turned serious. Mary stood perfectly still. She waited for the answer – but deep down inside she already knew what he was going to say.

Godfrey swallowed and said in a quiet voice, "I am so sorry Lady Mary; your sister is dead."

*

Mary Loxley was never the type for overt displays of emotion – even if that was what the situation had called for. Other than the passion that she was prone to show when in the heat of a disagreement, she would never outwardly display what her internals knew so well. So, when Godfrey's words confirmed her innermost fears, she didn't fall in a heap, wailing and crying ruefully about the unfairness of it all.

Instead she had a few moments where her mouth and throat became dry, her stomach rolled and she could not breathe, before logic and practicality resumed control.

"How was she killed?" was the first of the many questions that were zooming around Mary's head to bubble to the surface.

Godfrey looked horrified as he replied, "My Lady, I think it would be better if you could wait to speak to Master Quinn. He can give you the answers that you are wanting."

"I'd much rather hear it from you," she replied, placing a consoling hand on his shoulder.

"Maybe it's best if I just show you."

They walked slowly from the stables, towards the embankment at the back of the property – the stunted pace due mainly to Godfrey's gammy leg. Mary carried the rifle firmly under her arm; she had no intention of letting it back into the hands of the young and impetuous Granville.

So many thoughts and questions spiralled through her mind, but before she could collect them, Godfrey said, "I know how much you loved Lady Emlyn. I'm sorry that we had to meet again under such circumstances, My Lady."

Mary did love Emlyn. Even though they had never had anything much in common, they had always found a way to keep their relationship close and their bond tight. She had missed Emlyn terribly – leaving her was the hardest part of leaving Loxley – but she knew that Emlyn understood why she had to leave. Mary had asked her to come to Montpellier, but the responsibility of being the eldest sister, even if only by a year, weighed all too heavily on Emlyn and she stayed out of loyalty to their dead parents and to the estate.

Mary had never quite understood any of it. It wasn't because she was selfish – no, not at all – she had given just as much as everyone else, especially during the war – but it was the fact that there was so much more to life than just aspiring to be somebody's wife.

They reached the top of the embankment and Godfrey pointed to the old linden tree and said, "She was found hanging from there; ruled it self-murder, they did."

"A suicide? But that's ludicrous!" Mary exclaimed.

"It's a hard case to argue against when it was Master Quinn, accompanied by the town magistrate, the town doctor and Lord Southby, who discovered her. Master Quinn insisted that she'd been feeling quite ill, both physically and mentally for some time now and with Captain Hope's sudden return, that was the final straw. He blames himself for not seeing the signs for what they were and for not doing more about it all," Godfrey sighed.

A quick study of the tree revealed the place where the rope upon which Emlyn was hanged had been affixed. There were clear markings on the lowest branch, which was at least eight foot above the ground, where the friction from the pull of the rope had caused the mossy covering to be disturbed in two distinct rings.

Mary said more to herself than to Godfrey, "Unless Emlyn trained to become a circus acrobat in my absence, she could not have catapulted herself from that bench and strung herself up from that tree."

"Sergeant Markson saw it the way of Master Quinn and the others – and I don't see him changing his conclusions anytime soon," Godfrey replied.

In the early afternoon sunshine, a glimmer caught Mary's eye. She approached the base of the tree and picked up, what she knew to be Emlyn's snuff box.

"I'm glad to see they did a thorough search of the area," she said, waving the box at Godfrey. She placed it into her pocket and said, "I will go and talk to this Markson fellow and see what else he decided to leave out of the investigation."

"Very good, My Lady," he replied, although he sounded quite dubious about it all. "Shall I relieve you of the rifle?" he added.

"I think I'll keep it with me for now," she replied, ignoring the irritated look which flashed across Godfrey's face.

Mary turned to take a final look at the tree. She had been away far too long to truly know Emlyn's psychological state, but knowing her penchant for avoiding all things which involved manual labour or any corporeal activity, she knew that this would not have been the way upon which her sister would have settled to kill herself; much too much work and planning. She was certain that if it ever came to such an extremity, Emlyn would have chosen a much more sedentary way to go; most likely an overdose of some kind of pharmaceutical concoction.

This led her to two conclusions; either Emlyn had an accomplice to her own suicide – or the theory that seemed to be most coherent with the evidence – that Emlyn was murdered; and she, Mary Loxley, was going to get to the bottom of it all.

***

Louise Ellis' day had gone from bad to worse. That morning, she had found out that the Earl – Lord Southby – would be staying on at Loxley Hall for at least another week. This meant double the normal workload in the kitchen, as Malcolm and that old battle-axe Aunt Bett, loved to put on a show of prosperity for the belted Earl.

It was Malcolm's way of showing that although he wasn't of noble blood, he could still maintain the required airs and graces and appear as one should to such a crowd. This made the life of the staff of Loxley Hall much more difficult, however they knew that it was only on very rare occasions that nobility visited the Hall, and without Emlyn, it would quite possibly be the last of these visits.

To make matters worse, Louise's kitchen was now awash with the blood of the young footman of the house and filled with the noise of the housemaid, who was clearly in love and in a panic at the boy's injuries. Louise had told Malcolm that the child wouldn't be capable of killing that damned horse, but he hadn't listened and now she had to find other meat to prepare for the following evening's banquet.

This wasn't her only concern either. Winnie had also brought with her the news that Lady Mary had arrived, just in time to witness the calamitous events in the stables and it was she who had put a stop to the death of the horse.

Why was Mary even there? Louise knew for a fact that no one of the house had written to her upon Emlyn's death – by order of Malcolm – and she couldn't imagine that Mary showing up was by chance. She had spent so much time away from the house, avoiding any of the responsibility of helping to run Loxley Hall and living a wicked life in France with that little, piece of French toast of hers, that her actions didn't correlate to any such sudden coincidences.

"It was that blasted Captain Hope," Louise blurted out loud upon deciding that it was he who had summoned Mary.

"What did he do ma'am?" asked Winnie as she held a damp cloth to Granville's bloodied nose.

"Oh nothing," Louise muttered continuing to chop her vegetables. "Can you take his bleeding nose away from the dinner?" she demanded as an afterthought, pointing her knife towards the door.

"But I can't stop the bleeding and this is the closest place to water that both Granville and I can fit into, without taking him into the upstairs," Winnie protested.

"With Lady Mary here, you'll need to make up her chamber. I'm sure Granville is man enough to handle a small knock on the nose," Louise commented in the hopes of at least halving the crowd that was taking up the space in her kitchen.

"Of course I can," garbled Granville through the cloth that was being held to his face. "If that woman hadn't come when she did, I would've done that horse in easy. Who does she think she is anyway? She told me I don't know how to shoot," Granville complained "She's only a woman – just because she wears trousers doesn't make her an expert on guns," he added fiercely.

"I may not like her and I certainly don't agree with her choice of fashion, but she knows what she's talking about. She served on the frontlines in the Great War," Louise said as she performed the sign of the cross and turned her eyes to the heavens.

"Yeah, but only as a nurse," Granville retorted with acid streaming through his voice.

"Without the feats of many of the nurses and the women doctors over there, who knows how well Britain's plight would have gone," Louise defended.

"Oh, poppycock!" Granville exclaimed; a mirror of his father when he didn't have a sufficient rebuttal to an argument – they had all heard Godfrey use that expression many, many times before.

"Maybe you'd sound more intelligent if you watched your mouth before you spoke," Louise snapped.

"I hope you're not speaking to Miss Louise like that, Grannie," Martha, Louise's sister who was also the assistant cook, interjected as she entered the room.

"He's had a knock to the head, so I think we can forgive him for it. Only for today though," Louise answered with a smirk on her face. "Had some trouble with the rifle, did our young footman," she added still smiling.

"What have we to prepare for the banquet now?" asked Martha.

"I was just about to ask you to go on an errand to pick up a side of beef from Mr Myers'," Louise answered, referring to the local butchery.

"I guess it's that, or we could roast up young Grannie here – considering it was he who cost us the dinner," Martha chortled.

"Too skinny," Louise argued, reaching across the bench and pinching his bony shoulder.

"Yes, wouldn't get much off him," Martha agreed – the two sisters cackled in unison like two plump and hardy wicked witches.

"That's not funny," Winnie objected as she gathered herself to leave.

"Where are you off too, Win? We were just teasing; we'd never eat your boyfriend!" said Martha.

"He's not my boyfriend!" Winnie protested, and then added, "I'm off to the blue bedchamber to prepare it for Lady Mary."

Winnie hurried out of the kitchen, after giving a final concerned glance towards Granville – who had made to move himself towards the servants' chambers, still clutching the damp cloth which he held firmly to his nose.

Once the two sisters were alone, Martha said, "Lady Mary's here? At the Hall?"

"Yes. Strange coincidence, isn't it?" observed Louise.

"Yes, quite," replied Martha. "You don't think Addie had anything to do with it, do you? She's been acting quite erratically lately – especially since the…. unfortunate incident."

"She could have – although I wouldn't look too far past that Captain Hope. He's caused nothing but trouble since his return. He should have just stayed vanished."

"I will speak to Addie, just in case. I want to make sure that we don't have anything to worry about from her. That's the last thing we need right now," Martha decreed.

"Like a hole in the head," Louise agreed.

She put down her knife and shuffled across to the counter.

She took two schillings from the canister which stood against the window sill and said to Martha, "You better get off to Mr Myers', before all the best cuts are gone – remember it's for Lord Southby."

Martha took the money and exited the room with a spring in her step, whistling a merry tune as she went on her way.

Louise set her sights back on to the chopping board which lay in front of her. She continued to cut the carrots with a lot more energy than was necessary. She felt sick to the stomach at the thought that she was going to have to continue working in that darned kitchen for God only knew how long – pretending that none of this was beneath her.

Her day had not gotten any better. She placed her hand on her stomach and caressed it gently.

"Don't worry, it's only a small set-back; not much longer, little one," she whispered.

***

Betty Clovely had never thought herself to be a transient woman, however all this staying in the one place seemed to be having an invariably negative effect on her life. She had always been a traveller. Her first husband, who died in 1907, was in the ambassadorial services and if they had ever been posted somewhere for any length of time, it was most usually somewhere exotic and interesting. Not that she had ever given up her very British ways and her love of tradition; but she saw it as her duty to spread England's civilised ways to the uncivilised masses.

When she had arrived at Loxley Hall a fortnight or so ago, she had arrived with thoughts of a party. A party so grand that it would take her mind off the misfortune that she had suffered at the hands of the Admiral in Constantinople. She had been hopeful once more of finding an appropriate replacement for her late husband; namely a baronet and the newly appointed Admiral of the British Navy. A man who would be able to keep her in the kind of life that she had grown accustomed to over the years. However she was unsuccessful in her endeavours and had come to Loxley Hall to forget this latest rejection. She had only planned on remaining in Loxley for the length of a long weekend – but her plans had gone awry after the death of poor, sweet Emlyn.

Death had made a habit of impacting upon Betty and her plans in recent years, and she was beginning to consider that maybe it was a curse. Firstly, it was the death of her husband, which put an abrupt end to her glamorous life on the road. Then, her sister and brother-in-law had died in that terrible accident, causing her to have to come to Loxley Hall to look after their orphaned, adolescent children, Emlyn and Mary.

That episode stole two years from her concentrations on her own life and it was during that time which she had found the perfect suitor for a young Emlyn. She had encouraged a courtship which resulted in Emlyn's marriage to Malcolm Quinn some two years later; and it was in her old friend's study which she was standing, watching the younger man pour her a glass of sherry.

"How could she have found out Mal?" Betty demanded, picturing the moment she saw Mary saunter across the front courtyard from her position upon the window seat, high above in the sitting room.

He turned to her, glass outstretched in offer of peace, and replied, "The news of Emlyn's death was all around the village – anyone could have sent news."

"Yes – but how many knew of Mary's whereabouts? No, I'm certain that you have some questions of loyalty from somewhere within your household. You need to squash their spirits, before you have a full-blown mutiny on your hands."

"I can deal with the staff. The question that I need assurance on is can *you* deal with your niece?" Malcolm replied.

Betty took a sip of sherry. She could feel the trail of warmth, seep from her throat down into her stomach and she took a moment to consider her answer. Her mind drifted back to Mary's unexpected arrival and her own instinct to spring from her chair and run from the house. But Betty had her own plans and she needed more time to put them into action.

She replied, "Don't worry about me Mal, just you worry about getting Lord Southby on side. I can handle Mary if I must. Otherwise I think avoidance is the best policy."

"Quite," Malcolm answered, nodding his head in agreement.

She stared out of the study window, taking another sip of her sherry. In the distance, Mary emerged with that stupid, old fool, Godfrey, from the embankment at the back of the estate – the place where the body of poor Emlyn had been discovered swinging in the breeze, like a piece of meat in the back room of a butchery. She couldn't quite make out what Mary was holding, but from where she was it seemed to be the long, steel barrel of a firearm.

Betty's mind shifted to the thought of her bags, which were now sitting neatly in a row on her bed and she strongly considered her position. All that she knew for sure, was that she couldn't possibly run into Mary – not now. She was certain that if she did, her demeanour, coupled with the way that she wouldn't be able to look Mary in the eye, would give away the fact that Betty Clovely knew that she, herself, was the one who was responsible for Emlyn's death.

4. OF ENEMIES AND FRIENDS

They had lived quite separate lives for a long time now. Each going through the motions of a relationship long since dead, buried and on the cusp of full decomposition. They had reached a place in their 12-year marriage, where they were entangled to the extent that it was far easier for them to stay together and live side by side in a static kind of misery, rather than go through all the associated difficulties and upheaval that a divorce would have invariably caused them. Yet none of this reduced the shock that John's death had caused to Alex Dewill's system.

She sat there inspecting the same patch of the dust-ridden coffee table which she had been staring at for the last half an hour. It felt as though her brain had switched off or had somehow left her body completely and she was hovering somewhere beyond the realms of this reality. She reached around in the depths of herself, grasping for the right emotion; the kind of emotion which would match the situation that she found herself in. But plumbing the depths of a deep, dark void, was a sure way to come up empty handed.

She wondered how long it had been since she had spent any real time in this house. It felt so foreign to her. She had moved out of the house and of the relationship a long time ago. She ran her finger over the coffee table and examined the dust which now sullied her fingertip.

She speculated about when the last time it was that anyone had cared enough to dust the house, let alone the table, and she pondered who had even been around to create so much dust to begin with.

Both she and John were so focussed on their individual careers and on their own lives, that their marriage had boiled down to a brief greeting in the mornings, which was always coupled with a mechanical peck on the lips, and an even more mechanical fuck on the last Monday of every month – and if Alex didn't insist on it, then even their monthly copulation went begging.

"I suppose I'll have to make some kind of arrangements," she said in a detached voice. "And then there's the business too – I guess I'll need to do something about that."

"Don't worry about all of that stuff now," came the quick response from the kitchen.

The kettle whistled, sounding as though it were calling from a distant land. Alex could hear the crash of cups, saucers, spoons and the like being juggled noisily around the kitchen by her visitor, which made it exceedingly obvious that he had yet to be fully domesticated.

"Milk?" came the questioning call from the kitchen.

"And sugar," she replied flatly, feeling nauseated at the thought of taking anything into her stomach.

Alex studied the man who returned from the kitchen carrying a tray holding the necessary accoutrements for a Devonshire cream tea. Matthew Bowman was all arms and legs and he knew it. His self-consciousness made those around him feel awkward just watching him. When they worked together in the kitchen, she always had the feeling that he was only seconds from disaster at any one time – yet in the seven months that Matthew had been her apprentice pastry chef at the trendy, French restaurant, Céleste in Soho, he was yet to put a foot out of place.

Matthew set the tray on the coffee table that stood between them, sending a wisp of dust particles into the air. Alex watched the dust float blissfully through a beam of sunlight that was slicing through the semi-darkness of the room from around the edges of the valanced curtains.

Matthew sat down heavily on the chair opposite her. He looked at her with mournful eyes. It was hard to tell whether he was being empathetic, or whether he was taking John's death much harder than she was.

"You didn't have to come over," Alex said as she watched Matthew pour out two cups of tea.

"I wanted to," he replied looking up at her.

"I don't really know where this leaves us," she said as she raised her hand to her head, which was pounding.

"Us?" Matthew asked.

"The restaurant, I mean."

"Oh. None of that matters right now," Matthew said reasonably. "You've just lost your husband; we don't have to talk about any of this. If you like, we don't even have to talk at all."

Matthew leaned forward again and added milk and sugar to each of the cups. He then began to place scones onto each of the plates and divvy out the strawberry jam and clotted cream.

"I couldn't possibly eat anything right now," Alex said raising a hand to stop him.

"You need to eat something; you don't want to faint – especially when you're about to spend the morning with the police."

"I feel as though someone has punched me in the stomach. If I eat now, I'd be more than likely to throw up on the police and I don't think they'd take that too well. Knowing them, I'd probably end up locked in a cell, charged with assault," Alex replied.

Matthew smiled. "They're not that bad. And anyway, this time you're the victim – I'm sure that it won't be anything at all like the last time."

"As long as I don't have to see that idiot Inspector again," Alex retorted, clutching at her aching forehead.

Matthew reached across the table and put his hand on her knee. "Are you feeling all right? How's your head? Do you need your pills?"

Alex shrunk away from Matthew's hand.

She waved in the direction of the stairway, "My Fioricets are in my bag; somewhere up there – if you could bring them to me..."

Matthew bumbled around upstairs. Alex could only imagine how his elbows and knees were trying hard to knock over everything that they met. She put her hand on the place where Matthew had touched her and she sighed.

Alex knew that she was swimming in dangerous waters when it came to Matthew. Over the last month, she had noticed that his demeanour had changed markedly in her presence. He had become moody and even more nervous than usual. And whenever he thought that she wasn't looking, she could see him in her peripheral vision eyeing her hungrily.

In the enclosed spaces of the kitchen, she felt the intensity of his misplaced affections burning through the air between them and if she hadn't known better, she would have thought that Matthew had been the one to shove John's arm into that mincer, just to get the chance to have her all for himself.

It wasn't unnatural for co-workers to develop feelings for one another, especially when they worked so often together, in such an inter-dependent environment and in such close proximity – bonds were bound to form – but if she was nothing else, she prided herself on her loyalty and she would never have betrayed John, not even in the midst of their failing union. But now John was gone and she wasn't sure how long she had before Matthew's feelings would get the better of him and he would inevitably attempt to take John's place.

It's not that Matthew wasn't a good person, and he was certainly a good-looking man; his potent, green eyes in contrast to his shining black hair was quite something to behold, but it was the way that he carried himself which made it obvious that he could never be the kind of person that ever stood up for anything, let alone himself. And it was strength that Alex needed more than anything right now.

She picked up the photo frame which sat on the small, side table, next to her and examined it closely. She felt a fleeting moment of guilt wash over her as she scrutinised the subjects of the photograph; their two smiling faces staring back up at her. At some point, John did have the power to make her feel; she had even loved him with what she thought was all of her heart, once.

She used the corner of the nearby cushion to wipe away the thin film of dust which had accumulated on the glass and frame. This was her favourite photo of John – it was a Polaroid from the night that they had met and she had always marvelled at the fact that someone so handsome had fallen for someone like her. John used to always say that she was more beautiful than she knew, but she could never see what he was talking about – not even now.

Pale, average height, skinny, and breasts which resembled bee stings, she was anything but voluptuous; and her perfectly straight, long, brown hair caused more of an imposition for her work in the kitchen than anything else. The only reason that she didn't cut it all off was because of John. She guessed now it no longer really mattered.

She heard a bang emanate from the direction of the stairs and then, "Don't worry, I'm fine," shouted out a couple of seconds later as Matthew emerged holding her canister of migraine medication.

She took two tablets, easily swallowing them without any liquid – and was contemplating taking an unprescribed third, when there was a sharp knock at the door. Matthew made a move to answer it, but Alex stopped him in his tracks.

"I don't want the police to see you here – God only knows what they'd make of it," she whispered urgently.

"They just want to ask you a few questions and get an official ID on the body – I'm sure they don't think you had anything to do with it," he replied.

"You don't know what they're like – last time they didn't leave John alone for months. And look at how that turned out – they didn't have any evidence and they still kept coming at us. I don't want to give them an excuse."

"All right then – but I'll be back to check on you later."

To her relief, Matthew headed in the direction of the backdoor. Alex knew how the minds of the police worked and seeing the 'grieving' widow with such a good-looking house guest on the morning of her husband's death would automatically spell suspicion. No, she wasn't stupid; she wasn't going to get herself involved in any of their games – and she certainly wasn't going to get herself caught in any of their childish traps. Alex Dewill was way too smart for any of that.

She heard the backdoor close, waited a few more moments, to ensure that Matthew had cleared the dustbins, and then she opened the front door. In a flash, she felt the force of the heavy wooden door throw her backwards, pain stabbed through her face and body. She tried to regain her balance, but her momentum was too strong and her head struck the wall behind her, hard.

The greyness radiated into her periphery. The room spun and as her surroundings became blurry, all she could make out were two figures dressed from head to toe in black and the shining, silver barrel of a gun.

****

Mary Loxley hid her newly acquired rifle under the mattress in the blue bedchamber. It wasn't the most unique of hiding spots – but there wasn't time to go gallivanting around the house in search of a more imperceptible resting place. It was fast approaching supper time and she wanted to interrogate Sergeant Markson before the day's end and before she ran into anyone else who was under her net of suspicion; which included everybody at Loxley Hall and everyone else in the village.

She rummaged through her case and gathered her note-pad, pencil, a book of matches and a brand-new packet of Wills' Goldflakes. She opened this last item, shook out a cigarette and lit it.

There was a quiet knock on the door.

"Who is it?" Mary called.

"It's Winnie My Lady, I've brought you some refreshments after your long journey."

Mary opened the door and said, "Come in then. I never can turn down freshly prepared sustenance."

She inhaled the smoke deeply into her lungs, feeling the satisfying rush of relief flow through the muscles of her lower back. She hadn't wanted this interruption, but seeing the stack of sandwiches which were now laid out in front of her, had made her realise how hungry she was.

Mary sat on the velvet vanity chair which stood in the alcove, adjacent to the window and motioned for Winnie to join her.

"Oh no, My Lady, I couldn't possibly sit up here with you – it's not proper," Winnie protested.

"There's enough food here for the both of us, I can't possibly eat it all myself. And anyway, I have a few questions that I'd like you to answer for me," Mary reasoned.

"Only for a minute; I still have to help with the dinner and I also have Granville to attend to," Winnie replied, concern passing across her face as she sat in the chair opposite Mary.

Mary placed her cigarette into the groove of the ash tray, picked out the ham and pickle finger sandwiches from the platter, and arranged them in a neat fan pattern on her plate. Winnie poured out the tea and Mary encouraged her to take some food. Once they each had their preferred beverages and sandwiches in front of them, Mary asked the one question which had been bothering her since she had seen where Emlyn had died and the question which Godfrey was unable to answer.

"Why was Emlyn down that embankment, when she was supposed to be hosting a party?"

Winnie's mouth lolled open as though she were in a stupor. Returning to her senses, she picked up one of the sandwiches from her plate and nibbled on its edge. She looked like a lost, little bird, who was starving and had found a crumb, but couldn't decide whether or not it was poisonous.

Winnie placed her plate upon the table and looked earnestly at Mary.

She cleared her throat and said determinedly, "I don't know what you've heard My Lady, but Lady Emlyn was killed by her own hand and when you're not thinking right, you tend to do odd things, don't you?"

"Do you really believe that my sister committed self-murder?" Mary questioned.

Winnie mulled over the question – taking the opportunity to gulp down her tea.

She replaced her empty tea cup onto the saucer and replied, "I don't want you to think that I'm an eavesdropper or nothing, but I did overhear Master Quinn telling the policeman that Lady Emlyn had been in a deep depression. But I didn't see any of that – if anything she seemed happier – especially since Captain Hope returned. I mean, she had been taken ill in the week before she died, but other than that, I never saw her unhappy at all."

"Did anyone find a suicide note?" Mary continued.

"I don't know nothing about a note; but there is something else that I heard."

Mary nodded in encouragement, taking a bite of her own sandwich, enjoying the contrast between the saltiness of the ham and the sour tinge of the pickle. Still chewing, Mary leaned forward to amplify the clandestine nature of their meeting and to reiterate the fact in Winnie's mind that anything said in the confines of this room would be kept solely between the two of them.

Taking the cue from Mary, Winnie continued in a hushed tone, "It's just that I overheard the Ellis sisters talking a few days before Lady Emlyn died and they were saying that Captain Hope was going to meet her on the morning of the party, underneath the very same tree where she was found, you know........swinging."

"You think that Baden may have had something to do with it?" Mary questioned.

"I can't say for sure, but it does seem odd, doesn't it? He was supposed to meet her, right there in that very spot and on that very day, and then she turns up dead. And I've been here in this house for almost two years and Lady Emlyn has never seemed sad to me. I can't say that I spent every waking hour in the same room with her, but during my time here we became close enough and she never told me of any troubles; nothing worth killing herself over anyway," Winnie explained.

"Thank-you Winnie – you've been more than helpful. And I do agree with you, I think there are some things here that don't add up," Mary said.

As Winnie left the room amid the clatter of cups and saucers balanced unevenly upon the tray, Mary regathered herself to leave, and although she didn't truly think it possible that Baden could have hurt Emlyn, she couldn't shake the feeling that Baden Hope was somehow involved in her murder.

****

"The bitch had her face right against the fuckin' door – what the hell was I supposed to do?" Sparks grunted as he lowered himself back down into the car.

He ripped off his balaclava and used it to wipe the spattering of blood from his hands.

Kevlar Gold chewed on his cheek, which was a bad habit from way back when and calmly answered, "I'd say for starters, you probably shouldn't've kicked her door in. She was already opening up for us."

Sparks sighed at his father and replied, "Well it was you who told me to be intimidatin'. I was just tryin' to add a bit of drama."

"We're not in a fuckin' movie, son, we've got a payin' client and now I'm gonna have to call him and tell him that we've balls'd it up again."

"It's not that bad Dad – I left a note for her, for when she wakes up. And I'm sure she won't be forgettin' that broken nose in a hurry," Sparks insisted.

Kevlar lit his cigarette and assessed his son, who was now struggling to take the gun out of his pocket, and wondered whether the family business really was the right place for him.

"Careful with that kiddo; I don't want any holes in me car or any blood on me new upholstery," Kevlar growled, tipping the ash of his cigarette out of the window.

"Don' worry, I know how to use a gun dad; you've been teachin' me since I was a kid," Sparks panted as he managed to rip the gun out of his pocket and wave it at his father's head.

Kevlar swatted the gun out of his face and retorted, "You still are a kid, mate."

Ignoring Sparks' protests as to his maturity levels, he revved up the engine of his car and they started their long commute back across London. Kevlar had high hopes for his son, but he wasn't sure if he was cut out for the job. It was his fault that they were in this situation in the first place. Their client, Luke, had wanted them to collect the money that was owed to him from this John Quinn guy, and then use their highly renowned stand over tactics to convince him to sign some papers that this Luke had sent them; *'easy as fuckin' pie, right?'*

Wrong. This was the kid's first official job and it was the jumpy bastard who had leaned against the control panel when John was reaching his arm into that machine as they came up behind him. Kevlar should've known. The kid was bouncing all over the place from the moment he found out that he was finally going on a proper job.

Kevlar couldn't remember a time when he had ever seen so much blood, or heard such a bloodcurdling scream – and he didn't think he could ever forget the crunching sound of the bones being splintered by those metallic teeth.

But being a professional, even after such a disastrous beginning, Kevlar tried everything to get the poor bastard to sign the papers or at least tell them the code to the safe so that they could get at the cash, but they couldn't make heads nor tails of anything he said.

They were never supposed to harm him, let alone kill him and at first when Kevlar called through to the client, Luke was enraged. But after Kevlar used his best negotiating and problem solving skills, they came to a new agreement and their client offered them the opportunity to redeem themselves.

This second job was not about collecting the debt that was owed; all they had to do was intimidate this bitch enough and then the client would take care of the rest. As Kevlar drove his Mustang back towards their own neighbourhood, doing his best to avoid the bulk of the morning London traffic, he hoped that they had done enough. He figured that being attacked on the front door step of her own home would be frightening enough – Kevlar just hoped that the client wouldn't be too annoyed about the bird having a rearranged face. Regardless of anything else, Kevlar Gold knew that Luke had bigger plans for this Alex Dewill woman, and from what he'd heard and seen of him so far, Kevlar certainly didn't envy her position.

5. WHATEVER WILL BE, WILL BE

During his short 25 years in this world, he had been exposed to so much darkness, so much hatred and despair, that he had thought there was nothing left that could touch him any longer. Nothing that could throw him back into the depths of desolation which he had found himself wading through at the end of the Great War. Nothing which could surpass the torture he had put himself through every single day for the last two years, for sending so many other young men to their violent and decidedly anonymous deaths from the trenches. But all that was war – this on the other hand was something so unexpected, so much out of the blue, that Baden Hope could no longer see any meaning to life; not any of it, none at all.

She was his only reason for still being alive – he had carried the hope of her in his heart all the way through the war. Even when he had received news of her impending nuptial to some stranger – he knew in his soul that Emlyn still loved him. She was the reason he had eventually pulled himself out of the mire and had returned to Loxley from his self-imposed exile. He had returned determined to take back what the war had taken from him. And now that she was gone, she was the reason that he was finally going to set himself free from the tribulations this life had thrown at him.

"We will be together again soon my love," Baden mumbled to

himself as he finished securing the end of the thick rope to the base of the tree.

He wanted to double himself over and scream and squeeze and twist and contort until he could wring all of his rage, all of his feeling out of himself. But he had been doing that for the past week and none of it had worked, and although Baden still felt the fire of emotion searing through every fibre of his body and of his soul, he knew that he had made the right decision. The decision which he had already made peace with many years before.

For someone called Hope, he was certainly running in short supply of it.

He hadn't washed; not for a week. He could smell it – but he didn't care. Nothing mattered anymore. He looked up at the branch, the one where she had chosen to put an end to their twisted fates. He picked up his rope and he flung it through the air so that it wrapped around the branch twice. It hung like a python awaiting its prey. He took the end of his rope and he stepped up onto the old, wooden bench. It was a place so familiar to him. It was the place where he and Emlyn were, and it was the place where they would forever be.

He tied the hangman's knot and then slid the noose slowly over his head, letting it rest heavily upon his broad shoulders. Standing in the exact same place where she had been, he thought only of her and what she must have felt in her final moments. He had loved her; he still did. But this love was no longer a source of any kind of comfort. Pain stabbed at his heart and anguish burrowed relentlessly into the pit of his stomach. He wanted to vomit. He wanted to rip open his insides and pull them all out, bit by bit, and be free from all of his sorrow.

He yearned for her; he wanted nothing more than to be with her. How could he have ever considered any kind of future without her?

He uttered, "The hand is past, the time has come," as he collapsed away from the safety of the bench.

As he began his deathly swing through the air towards his final salvation, a desperate cry rang out from somewhere behind him, but he was beyond all of that now.

Time slowed in that moment and he could feel every sensation coursing through his body. The coolness of the breeze against his skin, the strong beating of his heart, the coarseness of the rope which had tightened around his neck and the freedom that only a dying man can possibly know. And then the pain – excruciating pain.

***

"She gave me the envelope, but I threw it away; just like you told me to," Addie insisted as Martha interrogated her from the open doorway of the maids' chambers.

"If that's so, then how come Lady Mary is here now?" Martha repeated for the third time, her voice elevating with each repetition. "Of all the times that she could pick for a surprise visit, you're trying to tell me that she just so happened to choose this particular week?"

"All I know is that I didn't send it and I haven't sent anything since. It must have been Captain Hope, there's nobody else left in this town who would want to see Lady Mary return, not after everything that she's been up to in France," Addie replied.

"Well that may be the case. But let it be known that if anything does come of this – it'll be on your head. I won't have any attacks of your conscience, leading us all to the gallows," Martha said pointing her finger accusingly at Addie.

Addie's face ran hot as she retorted, "And you'd do well to keep your voice down. Half the household will hear you if you're not careful. I haven't gone through all of this, only to back out now – and you tell that sister of yours that I'll have what's owed to me; sooner rather than later."

"Oh, don't worry, you'll get everything that you deserve, my dear Addie," Martha replied and she spun around, exiting the room as abruptly as she had entered it only a few minutes before.

Addie tried to return her focus to the pile of socks which sat in front of her, each with its own hole for darning, however her mind was running with a million thoughts and her hands were trembling irrepressibly. She laid down the needle and thread, and rubbed her fingers across the coarseness of the thimble.

All of this had started off innocently enough, she reassured herself, but Addie was becoming more and more aware that her involvement in this entire situation was spiralling beyond her control and that was the one thing which scared her the most. Having her fate held at the mercy of the capricious Ellis sisters was a most unpleasant state of affairs indeed.

She wondered how she had managed to get herself so deeply involved in the first place. Granted, it was wartime back then, and there were things that needed to be done. Everybody had their fair share of tasks which fell upon them that they didn't want to do – or would have even found abhorrent under normal circumstances. But those times – those most unusual and uncompromising of times – called on her for the most uncomfortable of measures. And it was the last two years of the Great War when Addie's fate had shifted into the hands of others.

But Addie wasn't in all of this alone and she had something that she could hold over Martha and Louise Ellis' heads too – if it came down to it – and she was not afraid to use it. If Addie was going to go down for anything, she was well prepared to bring the rest of the inhabitants of Loxley Hall down with her.

Her thoughts were interrupted by a sudden commotion coming from the direction of the kitchen and then a flustered sounding Louise Ellis shouting out, "This isn't a damn hospital – not anymore anyway." And adding, with a long enough pause to indicate that it was most certainly an afterthought, "My Lady."

There was a loud bang, and Addie, wondering whether it would be wise to render some kind of assistance, arose from her place on the bed and walked tentatively towards the open door. As she peered around the corner, she almost ran head first into Granville, who it seemed had been standing next to her open doorway waiting for her to emerge.

Both of his eyes were blackened and his nose, which was normally the size of a thruppence, had swollen to the width of two pennies.

"What on earth have you done to yourself?" Addie asked, without much thought for the answer.

Her attention was still drawn to the din coming from the open door of the kitchen and she found her gaze following in that same direction.

Granville, apparently having noticed this fact, didn't answer her question and instead said, "Captain Hope's done himself a mischief and that know-it-all Lady's in the kitchen fixing him up; Miss Louise is having a heart attack," he added with a cheeky smile – which revealed a chipped front tooth.

"Lady Mary's in the kitchen?" Addie asked, a surge of panic pulsing through her.

"Yeah, and she's causing a right stir. I don't like her all too much – but I do enjoy the way she's getting up the Ellis sisters' noses," he replied, still smiling.

Addie took a final glance at the kitchen doorway and then she turned and re-entered the maids' chambers. She sat next to her pile of socks – which seemed so much bigger than when she had started her mending. She looked up at the sound of footsteps, surprised to see that Granville had followed her inside.

"You'd better not let Mr Godfrey catch you in her Grannie, my boy, or we'll both be in trouble," Addie said.

"Dad's off in the other wing of the house – some problem with the Earl and his chamber pots," Granville replied. He took another step into the room and said in a hushed voice, "I heard you and Miss Martha having an argument – is everything all right?"

"You'd do well to forget you heard anything," Addie answered.

Granville advanced yet another step and said, "I couldn't help hearing about that envelope you dropped the other week. And I...." he hesitated.

"I didn't drop it – I threw it away. And what's it got to do with you anyway?" she asked feeling irritated, more about Martha and her bluster, than about poor, misguided Granville.

"Well, I thought that you'd dropped it, and I didn't want you to get into any trouble and so I picked it up and sent it off for you before anyone found out about it."

"You did what?"

"I was only trying to protect you."

"I don't need your protection."

She stood up from the bed. Adrenaline had begun to coarse through her and her mind had started to take flight. It was only her body which now needed to catch up.

"You'd be doing yourself a favour not to tell anyone that you sent that letter and I mean anyone. You really don't know what you've done," Addie said as she pulled a small case from the cupboard and started to remove her meagre possessions from her bedside table and place them carefully inside.

"What are you doing? You can't leave –….I, I….," Granville stuttered.

"You what? Come on, spit it out."

"Nothing," he said, his shoulders drooping.

"You didn't see or hear anything; got it?" Addie snapped and she turned her back on him.

She heard his footsteps retreat down the corridor and set to work. There was no alternative other than to pack her bags and run. If the Ellis sisters ever found out that the letter she was supposed to destroy, had found its way into Lady Mary's hands, she would suffer the consequences and she was none too keen to test out how genuine Martha's threats were.

It was now only a question of getting her hands on the money that had been promised to her from the very beginning. It was not a sum that someone in her position could afford to walk away from and it would be more than enough for her to have a fresh start in Sheffield or even in London. However, what would the money be worth to her if she somehow ended up in jail, or stone-cold dead and swinging in the breeze?

***

"What's the point? None of it's going to change anything; nothing is going to bring her back," Baden argued, wincing as he hobbled beside Mary.

"But don't you see – she couldn't have done it herself, and you've just proven it for us," Mary said enthusiastically as she tucked the notebook, where she had made a study of the scene which Baden had created, into her trouser pocket.

"You should have just left me there."

"Where?" Mary questioned exasperatedly. "Flailing around on the ground with a fractured wrist and from that limp of yours, I'd say a severely bruised coccyx?"

Mary had appeared over the embankment just as Baden had leapt haplessly from the bench. She had gone there with the intention of sketching the area and henceforth illustrating that the entire scenario of Emlyn's suicide was complete and utter balderdash. But instead, she had managed to find herself living proof, that if someone had wanted to hang themselves from that branch, using that bench, it was a sheer impossibility; and she was now in the process of escorting that living proof directly to Sergeant Markson.

"I asked her to run away with me, you know?" Baden said in a resigned tone. "At the reception they held for my return – I asked her to leave Malcolm and come with me back to Borneo."

"Emlyn in Borneo? I can't even tell you with much certainty as to whether she had ever ventured beyond the comfort and safety of the front gates of Loxley Hall," Mary said with a hint of amusement seeping through her voice.

"You'd be surprised about some of the things your sister and I got up to while you were away at that fancy boarding school of yours," Baden retorted.

"But still – could you honestly see her living in a hut, bathing in a river in front of the natives and fighting off insects the size of cricket balls?" Mary laughed.

Baden gave her half a smile and said, "I guess we'll never find out."

"I suppose not," Mary replied. "There are a lot of things that we will never find out about her now and we will never get to see the person that she was going to become. But what we can do, is find out who killed her and why," she added determinedly.

Mary appraised the man who was now striding a little more comfortably next to her. Baden's wrist, which before she had realigned it, had looked more like an oddly shaped banana, was now wrapped neatly in a bandage and held fast by a splint. Mary hadn't seen Baden since before the war and she could now see in the late afternoon sun that he had been hardened by his time in the trenches. He had the gait and posture of a soldier, and the boyish good looks which he had been blessed with as a teenager, had matured into a robustness that could only have come through exposure to the elements and an abundance of hard work.

"You were the reason why she was down the embankment that morning; she was there to meet with you, yes?" Mary asked.

Baden nodded.

"We had set a meeting for that morning at 11am. She was to give me her answer to my proposition – but I couldn't make it."

"It seems a little odd, wouldn't you say, that you would miss such a life changing rendezvous. If I'd just asked my long, lost love to run away with me, I'd be sure to get their answer; I wouldn't be so blasé about it all." She paused, more for effect than anything else and then added, "Are you sure you didn't meet Emlyn that morning and when she gave you an answer that you didn't like, you killed her?"

Baden stared at her in silence.

Mary continued, "Maybe the scene that I walked into today was set-up just for me. You knew that I had come back and you knew that I'd come looking for the killer and so you played the poor, little boy who lost his soul mate. Or maybe, you were punishing yourself for something that you did in the heat of the moment; trying to appease your guilty conscience?"

"You're right," Baden replied, his voice sounding defeated.

"I am?" Mary said.

She had only been goading Baden, in an attempt to get a reaction out of him – anything to bring him back from the edge of the precipice that he had been teetering on the edge of since his failed attempt at suicide. But she hadn't expected this. She had been ready for him to try and punch her, out of anger, out of sheer disgust at what she was suggesting – but with those two words, he delivered a blow which was so much stronger than anything that he could have physically thrown.

War changed people in so many different ways – but she had never expected that Baden could ever hurt anyone that he cared about so much.

"So you murdered my sister when she rejected you?" Mary said, this time with much less certainty, her hand tightening around the pencil in her pocket – ready to strike at his jugular if necessary.

"I may as well have," Baden replied downheartedly. "If I'd just been there; if I hadn't gone to London, then none of this would have happened and Emlyn and I would already be half-way around the world from here."

"What does London have to do with all of this?" Mary asked, getting frustrated with Baden's round about manner.

Baden looked up at her. He had a singular tear rolling down his left cheek, but his face was a picture of stoicism.

"I was called away urgently to London and I couldn't get word to her before I left. Believe me, I tried. I even passed a note along to Addie. At the time, I didn't think that she would mind me standing her up, not once she had heard my explanation. I took the first train to London that morning and by the time I had arrived back into Loxley in the late evening, the town was awash with the news of her death," Baden explained.

"And what was so pressing in London, that you couldn't wait until you had received Emlyn's answer? You could have both gone there together."

"You wouldn't understand," Baden replied, staring straight ahead.

"Why don't you give me the opportunity to try?" Mary asked.

"I received word that one of my Lieutenants had taken a turn for the worse and had been hospitalised in London. The letter made it sound dire and he had requested specifically to see me before he died.

Since the war I have remained in contact with my company men; not that there are many of us left now. I had to go. But when I got to the hospital, my Lieutenant wasn't there and when I tracked him down, he was in perfect health."

"What did the hospital have to say about it?" Mary questioned.

"No one there had heard of my Lieutenant or the doctor who had signed off on the letter. It was on the hospital's own stationery, but the letter wasn't sent by the hospital."

"Someone wanted you out of the way," Mary reasoned.

"But no one knew about our meeting. I can assure you, that I didn't tell anyone about it," Baden said confidently.

"I can name at least three people here who knew about it – all staff – and with the way news travels around Loxley, I'm certain that there would've been more. Do you still have the letter? Maybe I can run a few tests of my own on it."

"I can get it for you – it's still in my day bag," Baden replied.

They had now progressed beyond the front gates of Loxley Hall and were proceeding down the slight incline, towards the township of Loxley. Mary took out her packet of cigarettes, shook out two, put them both in her mouth and lit them with the same match. She puffed on them a few times, to ensure that they were sufficiently lit, and then she proffered one to her companion. He accepted it with an expression of thanks and they continued their walk in an uneasy silence.

From the information that she had garnered from Baden, the sender of the letter was most assuredly involved in the murder of Emlyn. But finding the sender, was not an easy proposition and she needed a place to begin. She needed a clue as to who would have wanted Emlyn dead, and other than the letter she herself had received from Emlyn, Mary was already staring at a dead end. Emlyn's letter had spoken of a conspiracy, but she had not given any more information other than the fact that it involved a disappearance.

Mary sighed. Given that since she had last called Loxley home, at least half of the town had disappeared – either lost to the war, or otherwise departed – she had very little to work with. She took a final drag from her cigarette, smoking it all the way to the butt as she always did, and then threw it to the ground and pulverised it into the dusty pathway with the toe of her leather boot.

They had now reached the main street of the town, and in the late afternoon sun, most of the shopkeepers had begun their nightly closing rituals. They passed Mr Myers' Butchery, where the proprietor was hosing down the floor behind the counter – his display case emptied of its wares. The next shop along was Mr Nansy's Fine Confections, where he had placed an array of brightly, coloured, cellophane wrapped sweets on display in the window; and two stores along there was Mr Courtney's Apothecary, where Mr Courtney himself was standing out the front, in deep conversation with two middle-aged women.

As Mary and Baden approached, their conversation became hushed and the three of them gave Mary sideways glances. Noticing this, she extracted Emlyn's snuff box from her pocket and took a pinch, snorting it as loudly as she could manage. Mary enjoyed the satisfaction of both the light headedness caused by the snuff and the noises of dissent which emanated from the now close knit circle. Baden smiled at Mary as Mr Courtney and the ladies shook their heads disapprovingly.

The elder of the two ladies, the one who was the most animated in their discussion, turned to face Mary and Baden.

She tilted her head to one side, and with a simpering voice, much akin to a condescending schoolmistress, she said, "Homosexuals and those who fraternise with self-murderers are not welcome in this town; I don't care who your ancestors are."

Mary could feel the tension rise from Baden's body next to her, but he didn't move. She on the other hand was about to respond when she saw something which caused her to hesitate. It was not this contemptuous cow who interested her, it was her acquaintance – a quite unremarkable woman – who was attempting to shrink into the ground behind this lady; and she would have been successful had it not been for the sunlight gleaming from the frame of the cameo brooch pinned proudly to her lapel.

"And where did you get that?" Mary questioned, pushing her way through, so that her face was now level with that of the unremarkable woman's.

Her hand travelled instinctively to the brooch and then she dropped it away just as quickly.

The other lady, with surprising strength, swung Mary back around to face her and said, "It's none of your business where Mrs Watson makes any of her purchases, young lady – if I can call you that."

She gestured towards Mary's trousers and screwed up her face.

Mrs Watson spoke from behind Mary with a mild-mannered voice, "It's all right Ethel; she has a right to know."

Mary turned around to face her and Mrs Watson continued, "Your sister, Lady Emlyn, she gave it to me – a few days before she died. She was a very good woman, your sister."

Ethel clucked from behind, wanting to add a dissenting voice, but Mrs Watson raised a hand to quieten her.

"Emlyn would never give away that brooch – it was our mother's and she's never been a day without it, not since the day our parents died."

Mrs Watson put a consoling hand on Mary's shoulder and led her a few paces away from the others and said, "Lady Emlyn told me that she had some information that would help me."

"Help you how?"

"This isn't the place to talk about it, but if you can come to my house tomorrow we can discuss it then," Mrs Watson whispered.

"What exactly are we talking about?" Mary asked.

"Lady Emlyn was looking into the disappearance of my son, Cecil."

6. WATCHING THE DETECTIVE

Alex Dewill felt as though she had a heavy weight attached to the very front of her face, stretching her nose down towards her chin. She had been given pain medication and her nose was now packed full of gauze, but she still felt the uncomfortable pressure of the swelling of her facial injuries, and her eyesight was impeded by the distension of the tissue surrounding her eyes. According to the paramedics, who had attended to her at the scene, the break wasn't a serious one. The inflammation would subside over the next few days and her eyes would remain blackened only for a week or so. She was given a colourful selection of four medications to take in differing amounts at different times of the day.

'*Only a week*,' she thought to herself. Those paramedics didn't have to walk around the streets of London with a hastily mashed potato for a face.

The seat was uncomfortable, just like the rest of the drab and greying interrogation room. Alex had a sudden pang of regret at the thought that she'd told the paramedics not to take her to the hospital. She hadn't wanted to go and they couldn't force her to either. But now that she was sitting in the heart of Scotland Yard, her body feeling as though it had aged a hundred years, and confronted by this twitchy, little detective in the powder, blue suit – she realised that the hospital was the better option.

Alex stared across the table at the officer, trying hard to forget about the dull ache in her shoulder from the secondary impact she had with the wall behind the door. The officer had introduced herself as Detective Sergeant Pridis when she had entered, and since they had been sitting in that soul-destroying room, she hadn't stopped fidgeting. Pridis had rifled through her bag a hundred times, taken out her notepad and pen and repositioned them as an obsessive-compulsive child rearranges her peas. And her leg; she wouldn't stop bouncing her bloody leg and it was beginning to drive Alex crazy.

Alex didn't know what this Pridis woman was playing at and she was getting sick and tired of waiting. This was another one of *their* tricks — she just knew it — and she wasn't going to get suckered into being the one to begin the conversation. She was determined only to give the coppers the answers to their questions and nothing more.

The door swung open and a tarty looking woman in high heels entered. Alex recognised her immediately and realised that her initial assumption was correct: *This was not going to be pleasant.*

The room's newest entrant sat down next to Pridis and laid out a browning file, littered with Post-it notes. She leaned forwards and put a consoling hand across the table towards Alex and said, "I'm Detective Inspector Teri Tilman and this is my Sergeant, Diane Pridis."

"I know exactly who you are. Don't think that four years is long enough for me to forget what you put us through. Where's that partner of yours? I don't want him anywhere near me."

Tilman smiled at Pridis and replied, "If you're referring to Inspector Bliss — you can rest assured that he'll be nowhere near this case — or the Yard for that matter."

"Did they finally come to their senses and sack him?" Alex asked hopefully.

"Not yet," Tilman replied. "But he won't have any involvement in the investigation at all."

"He's on holidays," Pridis added.

Alex was relieved. After the case against John had fallen through,

Inspector Bliss had begun to turn up everywhere. She and John never had a moment's peace. At one point, he came to her restaurant and barged his way into her kitchen. He had been drunk and unintelligible, but she had ascertained that he had wanted her to testify against John. But there was nothing to testify about. There had never been any indication that he had done anything wrong, other than being a failure as a husband – and that was not a crime. John had just been in the wrong place at the wrong time.

Tilman said, "I know it's been a very difficult day for you Ms Dewill, so I'd like to keep this as short as I can. We just have a few questions and need some details clarified so we can move forward with our investigation."

"I don't know how I can help you," Alex replied. "John and I have been living quite separate lives for a long time now."

"Why don't we start with what happened to you this morning? Do you remember any detail at all? Anything that might be able to help us catch who did this to you and potentially your husband's murderer?" Pridis asked.

Alex found it difficult to speak through her broken face. The pain killers were beginning to wear off and she felt as though her head had been squashed by a steamroller.

"Can I get a glass of water?" Alex asked, indicating towards the pills she had in her bag.

Pridis left and returned with the water.

Alex swallowed her tablets and then said, "I've already told the constable who brought me here that I don't want to press charges. All I did was open the door and then whack – the next thing I know, I woke up on the ground with my neighbour hovering over me. I didn't see anyone, nothing was stolen and I don't know why anyone would want to hurt me – or John for that matter. I'm sure it was just a couple of kids."

"On the same morning your husband was murdered, you think that some kids randomly decided to kick in your front door? That's some coincidence, Ms Dewill," Tilman said.

"I've never been known for my good luck," Alex answered.

Her hand moved instinctively to her pocket. She could feel the piece of paper folded delicately in there; the note which she had awoken to find attached to her chest. She had already decided not to show it to the police. Alex wasn't going to let this turn into a witch hunt for her dead husband.

The note tied her attackers to John's murder, but if she gave it to the police, they would find some way to blame everything on John. Alex had been caught in their web before and she wasn't going to put herself in that position again; even if it meant that she would have to break the law in doing so.

"I don't know why you're wasting your time talking to me. You guys are detectives – why don't you go out there and detect?" Alex snapped, feeling emboldened by the powerful painkilling medication.

Tilman cleared her throat and said, "I've sent someone to your house to see if they can lift some fingerprints and to have a look around the front porch. If you want, we can organise for a locksmith to repair your front door for you, before you return."

Alex hadn't considered what she was going to do when she returned home. She hadn't even thought beyond that interview. Her day had so far consisted of a series of events, each of which had required all of her concentration and energy in the moment they occurred. The future had become a far-off, hazy dream, that hadn't required her contemplation – not until now.

Her door still hung from its hinges – the constable having done a makeshift repair job on the spot. And then there were the senders of the note; the message which had cost her the use of her nose and the look of her face. Had they really given her a week's respite or would they return, next time in the night and do to her as they had done to John?

"A locksmith would be great," she replied, her mind still in a desperate fog.

She wondered if she should show the note to the detectives. She couldn't be sure of her safety and they did seem to be more sympathetic to her needs than she had anticipated.

Pridis noted something in her notebook and then asked, "Did your husband have any enemies? Did he owe anyone money? Did he gamble?"

"No. Never. He was always at his factory," Alex answered.

"Were you aware that John's company was having financial difficulties until about two months ago?" Pridis continued.

"John didn't say anything to me – but I was never involved in his business – just as he wasn't involved in the way I ran my kitchen. If you think this has something to do with John's factory, shouldn't you be talking to Robert?"

"Robert who?" Pridis asked, picking up her notebook once again.

"Robert Leung – he's been with John since the very beginning. He'll know what's been going on with the business," Alex replied.

Alex wondered what kind of detectives these two women were, considering that they didn't even have Robert, who was the second in charge at Quinn's Meats, on their list of people to talk to. She removed her hand from her pocket and away from the note.

"He's not on the employee list I picked up from the secretary there," Pridis said to Tilman. To Alex she asked, "Do you have a number for Robert Leung? It'll save us some time."

Alex fumbled with her phone and pulled up Robert's number. She showed it to Pridis, who wrote it in her notebook.

There was a short, sharp knock on the door and another officer, one who looked like he was born to wear the uniform, entered.

He said, "Excuse me Inspector, but there's a Marcus North here, he says that he wants to speak to his client."

Tilman looked across at Alex and said, "An attorney? You don't have something to hide, do you?"

"I didn't call him," Alex said, shrugging her shoulders.

"Shall I let him in?" the officer enquired.

"If it's all right with Ms Dewill," Tilman simpered.

Alex wasn't sure what Tilman was playing at. She had let her defences down for just a moment and now somehow, she was playing their game, but she didn't know the rules. Alex couldn't see how Tilman would benefit by bringing in John's attorney.

Alex shrugged and said, "Fine, why not?"

The officer left the room. Moments later, Marcus North, a slender man, aged somewhere in his mid-forties, entered the room.

"Ladies," he said in greeting, nodding at Tilman and Pridis. He sat down next to Alex and said, "Can I have a few moments alone with my client?"

"She's not under arrest, Mr North. We were asking her a few questions about this morning's attack and of course her husband's murder," Tilman said. "She's got time now anyway, I'm sure she wouldn't feel comfortable sitting at home alone, before the locksmith has had a chance to fix her front door."

"And what are *you people* going to do about my client's safety? How are *you* going to protect her from these thugs when they come back?" Marcus questioned.

"If they come back," Tilman retorted.

"We'll put a car out the front of your house, for now, and they can keep an eye on you. But there's not much else we can do for you right now – unless you can tell us something more about them," Pridis said raising her eyebrows slightly.

Alex thought for a moment and replied, "I didn't see a thing; I wish I had – but there's nothing I can say that could help you."

"Do you have any family that you can stay with?" Pridis asked.

"There all dead," Alex replied. "Maybe my friend Matthew….," she trailed off, talking more to herself than the others.

***

Tilman and Pridis left the interview room, walked along the corridor and stepped into the observation room next door. Through the one-way glass, they could see into the room they had just left. Alex and Marcus were having an urgent discussion.

"I think that went well," Tilman said, touching Pridis on the arm.

Pridis cringed at both the sound of Tilman's grating voice and at the unwanted contact between them. Why did they have to be put back together again? It was hard enough for Pridis to escape from Tilman in the first place, and now here she was, right back where she had started – at the mercy of this manipulative cow.

"She gave us nothing and I'm sure she's lying about the attack," Pridis replied, still painfully aware of the grip Tilman had on her arm.

Tilman had a smirk on her face – like a toad that had just had its fill of fly carcasses as she said, "I think you're about to get the full story."

She flicked the switch near the door, which turned on the loudspeaker. Voices, which had before been muted, now filled the room.

"That discussion's privileged – we can't listen in," Pridis said.

"Oh, grow up Dee; she's not his client and she's not under arrest," Tilman said. As she opened the door to leave, she added, "And take some notes, would you? I want a full report on everything you hear."

***

"What do you mean Robert has disappeared?" Alex said in a rush.

"I mean exactly that. He didn't show up for his shift and no one has seen him since he left his house early this morning," Marcus answered.

"You don't think he had anything to do with it, do you?" Alex questioned.

"I wouldn't think so. They may not have been good friends, but they certainly trusted one another," Marcus replied.

"Maybe he's dead too," Alex postulated. "I mean, if these guys are serious about collecting the money, then maybe Robert is involved too. Why else would they have come after me?"

"What money? Ms Dewill, do you know something that you're not telling me?"

Alex hesitated. She hadn't wanted to involve the police, but here was a man, who John had trusted enough to keep on a retainer for the past 7 years – and considering that John was a man who found it difficult to trust anyone, that was certainly saying something. She had to tell someone, and Marcus North was the man with the reach and resources she needed.

She slid the note, which had been left earlier by the intruders, across to Marcus.

She didn't need to read it again to remember the words which had been scrawled across the page in ink as red as blood.

"£250,000 by this time next week or we'll crush you. Your husband's debt is now your debt. Don't run, we're watching."

He considered it for a moment and then said, "And you didn't show this to the police?"

"No, I didn't; and I have my reasons not to. The point here is Mr North; can you help me?"

"Two hundred and fifty thousand pounds is a lot of money to procure in such a short space of time, but given that you have the country estate, I should be able to use that as collateral for a loan. I'm surprised John went to a loan shark in the first place considering the resources he had at his disposal."

"What do you mean country estate? Everything we had went back into John's business – we couldn't even afford our own house repayments."

"John didn't tell you? He's been the owner of Loxley Hall since his parents died when he was 19. Now that he's dead and he didn't have a will – its ownership falls directly to you. His relatives live there; they run a retreat."

"Relatives? But John said that he didn't have any family left. That lying son of a bitch. What else has he been hiding from me?"

"I for one, had no idea about the loan shark," Marcus replied.

Alex was too tired to be angry and at least John had left her something other than a worthless meat factory, that was a being run into the ground. She thought for a moment and then added, "I should let John's family know about the funeral. Do they even know he's dead?"

"Don't worry about all that for now; they won't release his body until they find the killer and I can handle the family. You know, maybe you should stay up there at the Hall until we sort all of this out – it might be safer than staying in that house of yours," Marcus suggested.

"But the note says not to run," Alex insisted.

"As long as they get their money by next week, I'm sure they won't bother with you. It's just an intimidation tactic. They won't even know that you've gone. And the Hall's only up near Sheffield – it's not as though you're leaving the country."

"Can you organise it?"

"Of course I can; I've dealt with John's family often enough over the years. I'll make all the arrangements."

Marcus walked to the door, said, "I'll be back," and he left Alex sitting there alone.

She had always known John to be a secretive man, but to hold the title of a country estate and to hide his own family from her, was an entirely new level of deception. Alex didn't know John Quinn as well as she thought she did. But she still knew that as many secrets as he may have wanted to keep and as many other women as he may have wanted to fuck, he was definitely not the man that they all thought he was.

"*I'm his wife, surely I would have noticed something out of the ordinary*," she thought to herself.

***

Pridis had her phone out of her pocket and had already dialled the number. Something about Loxley Hall didn't sound right to her. It was more of a gut feeling than anything else, but she couldn't shake the thought that there was more to it than just being an old inheritance. John had lied to his own wife about its very existence and he had borrowed money from a loan shark, when his own solicitor had suggested that Loxley Hall would have been more than sufficient collateral for a loan of the size he had required.

The phone clicked and the voicemail of Detective Inspector Andy

Bliss played through and then a beep rang out.

Pridis said, "Look Inspector – I know you're off the case, but what do you know about a place called Loxley Hall? It's up near Sheffield and John Quinn was the titled owner – a fact that he never shared with his wife. I don't know what it is about it, maybe it's nothing, but for some reason it doesn't sit right with me. I thought that it might give you a little something to do on your time off. I hear that Sheffield is lovely at this time of the year.

"And one other thing Inspector – it turns out that John had some big debts with a loan shark and now they've threatened the wife. Looks like this murder could be underworld related after all."

She rang off and as soon as she had hung up, her phone vibrated in her hand. She looked at the screen expecting the caller to be Inspector Bliss, but there was Vicki's smiling face staring back up at her from her phone. Pridis rejected the call. She didn't want to speak to Vicki, not yet anyway. She had already let her down in so many different ways that day, that she had begun lose count.

It was Vicki who had saved her from the psychologically damaging relationship that she had with Tilman and it was Vicki who had helped her with her battle against her Adderall addiction. And within the space of this one day, she was back on the road with Tilman and she had already taken more Adderall than she had in the past month combined.

The Adderall certainly did enhance her performance on the job by giving her the extra energy and concentration that she needed, but it also took away from other aspects of her life. However, Pridis was fast coming to realise that being a detective meant that realistically, there wasn't any time or space for a life other than the work.

She rifled through her bag and took out the last of the four pills she had salvaged from the bottom of that bin. She swallowed it without water, and felt an instant rejuvenation of her focus.

"If I'm going to get through this then I'm going to need some more," she mumbled to herself.

She flicked through her contacts and hit the call button.

The line was picked up quickly and she said, "Hey Benny, where are you?"

"I'm still with Doctor Trudeau – I haven't heard from you for a while. You're on the Quinn case, yeah?"

"That's why I'm calling. I need another bottle," Pridis admitted.

"I thought you told me that you were done with those."

"That was until I landed this case and I have to work with Tilman," she replied.

"I see. Well that makes sense. I'm gonna be here all day; Trudeau's got me running a few interesting tests on the mincing machine in his laboratory, but I've got some stuff in the back of the van, if you're able swing by," Benny explained.

"I'll be there in half an hour – I have some questions for Doctor Trudeau anyway," Pridis said.

"See you soon Dee," Benny trilled, in a perfect impression of Tilman.

"Don't you start calling me that too or I'll have to break your fingers," Pridis replied and she hung up.

***

Marcus North found a quiet corner and he dialled the number which for the past 8 years he had longed to forget. It had barely rung before a man's smooth voice answered with a hello.

"I've done it. I've convinced her to go up to the Hall," Marcus said.

"Good," the voice at the other end of the phone answered with a satisfied purr.

"Is that all you wanted? Does this finally make us even?" Marcus pleaded.

"If everything goes to plan, then yes," replied the man.

Marcus felt some of the tension release from his body – but he was still in a precarious position. He knew that his blackmailer wasn't an easy man to please.

"I'm certain it will go to plan – Alex seems to be a very reasonable young woman," observed Marcus. "I just have one question though," he added.

"Yes?" said the man.

"She won't get hurt, will she Luke?" Marcus asked. "Not like John did?"

"That will depend on her," Luke said and then he hung up the phone without another word.

Marcus stood there for another minute, absent-mindedly staring out of the nearby window. His gaze floated around the courtyard below as his mind drifted back to his office and to a photo that he had sitting upon his desk. It was a picture of his yacht, a yacht which he used to love, but which now had the potential to get him into a lot of trouble. He wondered how Luke had found out about his little secret all those years ago. He thought he had been so careful. It was a secret which he had now paid for time and time again with what felt like the remainder of his soul. But he couldn't take that kind of risk with his life or even his career and he could now see the light at the end of the tunnel.

He certainly had doubts as to whether his decision was the right one. But he couldn't think about Alex right now – there were more important considerations at hand. Whether he had done the right thing or not, it was too late now to stop what he had started.

What was the worst that could happen anyway?

7. THE SINS OF THE FATHER

Lord Timothy Southby had never had the compulsion to see what went on in and around the servant's quarters in any of his own houses, let alone those in the downstairs of Loxley Hall; he was always merely the happy recipient of all their hard work. He had never been interested in *them* as people or indeed as anything else, however, this day had been different. Southby had needed to speak to Godfrey, but he hadn't seen or heard from him since the earlier disturbance with his chamber pots and his attempts to summon him had thus far proven to be unsuccessful.

Over the years, Godfrey had been a thorn in the side of the Southbys and the Earl's current stay was no exception.

Southby knew that his father wasn't perfect – not by a long stretch – but for his father, the previous Earl, to be told in no uncertain terms to stay away from Loxley Hall, by *the Help*, was just not dignified. And so, for the last fourteen years of his life, his father had obeyed Godfrey, and had not once set foot in the Hall. Southby himself rarely visited during that time, and when he did, he avoided being alone with Godfrey. It was usually easy, given that Southby's visits tended to coincide with events which catered for a great many people.

However, that morning when Godfrey was tending to Southby's chamber pots, avoidance was impossible, and Godfrey had taken his opportunity. He was bent low, after extracting one of the pots from under the bed, when he looked up at Southby and said, "I don't want to have to remind you – as I did your father – that you've got no business touching things that aren't yours."

At the time Southby was taken aback. He wasn't used to the staff taking such a tone with him and he was unsure as to what the Butler was talking about. It wasn't until later, when he had seen Lady Mary walking in the distance with Captain Hope, that it had dawned on him. But he was nothing like his father. Not in that respect anyway. Yes, there may have been an incident or two in the past, and maybe one of those had involved Lady Mary, but he certainly was not his father.

Southby had decided therefore, to visit Godfrey in his quarters – it was the only way. He knew what the staff were like at the Hall and he couldn't afford his reputation to be sullied; especially not in the lead up to his thirty-fifth birthday. It was a pivotal time in the scheme of his life, and he wasn't going to let some meddlesome servant ruin things for him with pure innuendo and rumour.

This, however, had proven to be a fruitless plan and he had only found the Footman lying somewhat depressed and downcast on Godfrey's bed, with two shining, new black eyes and a nose the size of a tennis ball. Southby knew better than to ask any questions and he was certain that the young boy must have deserved his beating – he did look like a little upstart.

Southby turned and hurried along the cramped corridor back towards the narrow staircase. He felt claustrophobic and yearned for the fresher air of the house itself. Near the base of the stairs which led back up to the safety of the world he knew so well, he stumbled upon the kitchen. It was then that a brilliant idea struck him.

He sashayed in through the doorway and leaned against the nearest bench, crossing both his arms and feet. He observed the two cooks, the elder with blazing orange hair sticking out from underneath her cook's cap, carving away expertly at some kind of meat and the younger of the two staring glassy eyed at a pot boiling upon the stove, stirring it rhythmically to the point of hypnosis.

Neither paid him any attention and so he cleared his throat in order to gain their notice.

Without looking away from her task, the orange headed cook shouted, "Just leave it on the table." And she waved her knife wielding hand nonchalantly in the air.

Not used to being treated with such disregard, Southby cocked his head to the side and considered the two women before him. He wasn't exactly sure of what to make of this situation – he was so used to being at the centre of everything and although he was in their domain, that didn't lessen his importance, did it? He cleared his throat once again.

"I told you to put it on the table," repeated the cook still not looking in his direction.

"What is it exactly, you expect that I should be putting on the table?" Southby asked.

There was a clatter; the younger cook had dropped her spoon and it had clanked noisily against the stove top. The other had frozen, knife suspended in mid-air, her gaze fixed steadily upon Southby.

'*Now that's more like it,*' he thought to himself and he smiled.

"Sorry My Lord, I thought you were the delivery boy," the orange headed cook apologised.

"Never you mind about that; you can make it up to me however," Southby replied.

"Yes, of course Sir, what can we do for you?" the younger cook asked.

"I want my apéritifs in my room this afternoon and I want you to ensure that Godfrey brings them to me," Southby ordered.

"Yes, My Lord. Mr Godfrey is out at the moment, but as soon as he returns, we will send him up to you with your beverages," the orange headed cook answered subserviently.

"Very good. I see that you are both considerably busy; I'll let you get back to your work."

As Southby climbed back up the stairs, he heard raised voices emanating from the kitchen. He didn't much care for what they were saying, he had gotten what he wanted and that was all that mattered.

Their petty disagreements were nothing to him. He had much more important things to worry about, the most urgent being the task of securing his inheritance – which had been locked away from him until his thirty-fifth birthday and came – thanks to his dead father – with a web of strings attached to it.

Southby exited the downstairs area and inhaled deeply. Was it his imagination or was the air much easier to breath up here? He made his way as quickly as he could – while keeping up the appearance of good grace – to his room to prepare for his confrontation with Godfrey. As he was about to enter his room, a door from further along the corridor opened and Malcolm emerged.

"Can I speak with you for a few moments, Lord Southby?" Malcolm asked.

"I have some affairs to attend to before dinner; can it wait?" Southby replied.

"What I have to say will be of some interest to you – I may have found a solution to your problem," Malcolm offered.

Southby reluctantly entered Malcolm's office and he sat down on the leather wing-backed chair, as Malcolm poured out two tumblers of whiskey.

"Which problem are you referring to?" Southby inquired as Malcolm handed him the glass.

"Why, how many do you have?" Malcolm asked.

"Not as many as you, I suppose," he replied. "I gather then that you are referring to the problem of my inheritance?"

"I'd say that's the most pressing, wouldn't you?"

"Yes quite," Southby replied.

Southby took a sizable mouthful of his whiskey and appraised Malcolm over the rim of his glass. He wondered how such an old and decidedly unattractive man had been able to land such a young and vibrant beauty as Lady Emlyn. And now that she was dead, God rest her soul, Loxley Hall had landed squarely into his lap. It had gone from sixth generation Loxley to first generation Quinn in the blink of an eye and Malcolm didn't seem the least bit perturbed by any of it; not by the untimely death of his wife, nor by the manner in which it had occurred.

Southby finished his whiskey and indicated that he would have another measure. Malcolm obliged and Southby said contemplatively, "Tell me something, Malcolm. Did you ever really love her?"

"You know as well as I do that marriage is a business proposition. When was the last time you met anyone who'd married for love?" Malcolm sipped his whiskey, turned to face Southby and continued, "But over time, I did grow very fond of Emlyn and I will miss her. It may not seem like it, but everyone grieves in their own way."

"I always thought I would find someone with whom I enjoyed spending my time – but alas, it has yet to happen and now my time is running short," Southby uttered.

"Yes, well, as I said, I think I may have found a solution to your problem," Malcolm reiterated.

"All right then. I'll listen – what do you suggest?"

"Betty Clovelly," Malcolm replied, setting his glass down heavily upon the table.

"She knows of someone?" Southby questioned.

"No, I mean; Betty Clovelly – she's the one. She can give you what you need, in the required timeframe and everybody gets what they want," Malcolm answered.

"Not quite everybody," Southby said downheartedly. "And what would everyone think?"

"What would everyone think if you were thrown out of your castle and de-belted?" Malcolm rebutted.

Southby drained his glass, stood up and made to leave the room. He stopped at the door and said, "Let me think it over. I will give you my answer within the next day."

How had he allowed it to come down to this? Was he really so desperate?

'*My damned father – still causing me supreme discomfort from well beyond the grave*,' Southby thought to himself.

He closed the door to Malcolm's office behind him and sauntered back towards his room, lost in his thoughts. It wasn't until she was almost upon him that Southby noticed Lady Mary in the corridor.

He had not seen her since Malcolm's wedding, 5 years prior, and her beauty had grown to a level that was even higher than before.

She strode towards him, looking confident and womanly, even in her trousers. Southby actually found her unusual fashion oddly arousing. He moistened his lips and faced her completely. He had the sole intention of apologising for his minor indiscretion the last time they had met. It was a rarity for him to apologise, but even he had to admit that he had been wrong.

Before he could speak, however, Lady Mary stepped up to him, their bodies touching, her face right up to his. He could smell her; so sweet. His instincts cut in. A fire burned through him. Maybe she had forgiven his drunken mistakes. He put his hand on her back and pulled her close into him. He thrust his groin against her, to show her how much he wanted her to be his. Her eyes shined blue and as he leaned in to kiss her he felt a sudden and agonising pain.

"You're just as bad as your father – although at least he had the decency to stay away from here after what he did," Lady Mary said in a deadly whisper into Southby's ear.

The pain was so strong now that it felt as though his entire abdomen had been slashed open and his entrails were spilling out onto the floor.

"If I feel *this* near me again," she said as she twisted and squeezed his groin even harder, "you will lose *it*," and she let go of her grip.

Lady Mary continued her walk along the hallway as if nothing had happened. Southby hobbled into his room and fell sideways onto the bed, clutching his groin. He had to admit that she was one hell of a woman. He had heard of some of her feats during the war and he was not surprised that she was so formidable. No one had ever challenged him as she did and it disappointed him that he would never possess her.

Southby sat up on his bed and took his shoes off – the picture of Lady Mary still strong in his mind and his groin still smarting. He knew he deserved it – he deserved it even more than Lady Mary knew.

There was a knock on the door and Godfrey entered carrying a large tray with an assortment of bottles and glasses. Southby was well known for his drinking prowess and Godfrey had been sure to cover off all of the bases. He sat up straight and took a deep breath.

He said, "I'll start with a Vermouth."

"Very good Sir," Godfrey answered as he set the tray down on the nearby table, opened the corresponding bottle and poured.

"I don't know what you've heard about me Godfrey, but I want you to know that I'm nothing like my father," Southby said.

"No Sir, I don't think that you are; I think you're much worse," Godfrey replied, still casting his gaze across the tray full of drinks.

Southby was speechless. He knew what his father was capable of and he had never imagined that anyone could think him to be like that.

"I've never touched a child," Southby retorted.

Godfrey handed Southby the Vermouth and looked him directly in the eye, "The way I see it, is that your father had a sickness, a disgusting one, but a sickness all the same. You on the other hand, knew what was happening and you did nothing about it – that makes you a monster. If I didn't know any better, I'd say it was you who was responsible for Lady Emlyn's death."

Southby's hands were shaking. He was fighting hard to supress his rage and hold on to the last part of decorum that he had left. Who was this servant, to be telling the Earl anything?

"Get the hell out of my chambers," Southby spat, as he felt the muscles tighten throughout his entire body.

"Very good Sir," Godfrey replied as he limped towards the door.

"If I were you, I wouldn't go repeating that to anyone – if you know what's good for you," Southby threatened, standing up from the bed and using his height advantage as a means of intimidation.

Godfrey stepped towards him and sneered, "What are you going to do? Kill me?"

"There are far worse fates than death Mr Godfrey," Southby declared as he snatched up the bottle of Vermouth and poured out another shot. He drank it down and as Godfrey left, Southby whispered, "Yes, plenty worse fates, old boy."

***

The adrenaline was still coursing through Mary Loxley's veins as she spread her gaze over the grounds of the place that she used to call her home. She hadn't seen Southby since that fateful night of 5 years earlier and she had hoped that she wouldn't have to again. However, having the opportunity to finally put that man back in his place, had been worth it.

'Self-entitled, good for nothing Prat,' she thought to herself as she fumbled through her pocket looking for Emlyn's snuff box.

"Drink?" Malcolm called from the opposite side of his office.

She held up the snuff box and said, "No, I'll stay with this thank-you."

She'd been feeling unwell since her excursion into town with Baden, and she couldn't possibly stomach anything stronger than watered down tea.

"Emlyn had one just like that," Malcolm said as he joined Mary at the window, a tumbler of whiskey held firmly in his hand.

Mary pinched some of the snuff between her thumb and forefinger and inhaled.

"It is Emlyn's. I found it out underneath the linden tree. I'm surprised that it wasn't discovered during the police investigation. I was going to speak to Sergeant Markson about it today, however he wasn't in when I arrived at the station house," Mary replied.

"Yes, he's not particularly bright – but we are left with him for the moment. He's getting along in age however so we should be blessed with a replacement sooner, rather than later," Malcolm said.

"Bright or not, I'll be visiting him tomorrow and I just wanted to let you know that I'll be requesting that the investigation into Emlyn's death be reopened," Mary said.

"To what end, Mary? I know that it must be difficult for you, but your sister, my Emlyn, killed herself – there's no two ways about it. We all saw her hanging from that tree – it's a picture that has been branded on my mind forever and I will never forgive myself for not being able to save her."

"She didn't kill herself," Mary stated matter of factly. "It's not possible."

"You didn't see her sadness. Maybe if you'd just written to her once in the last years you would have known; you would have noticed that she had been lowering herself into a very dark place. She had been digging a hole and was burying herself deeper and deeper every day. I just wish that there was something more that I could have done. I didn't recognise it for what it was until I saw her hanging from that infernal tree. I didn't know that she would take it to such an extent."

"Regardless of her psychological state, Emlyn could not have killed herself. Not without help, and I intend to find out exactly what happened," Mary declared.

"Let's say that you are right; who exactly do you think would want your sister dead?"

"I don't know yet. Maybe the same person who took Cecil Watson," Mary replied.

"Cecil Watson? What does he have to do with any of this?" Malcolm asked sounding exasperated.

"That's exactly what I am going to find out."

Her mouth was feeling dry and her head was light. She moved from the window and sat on the corner of the nearby divan. "I think I will take that drink Malcolm," she uttered as she lit a cigarette.

Malcolm moved across the room to prepare her drink. He said, "I can tell you one thing – it couldn't have been the same person who took Cecil Watson."

"Why not?" Mary asked.

"Because he went to the gallows for it back in 1917; I was the one who captured him," Malcolm replied. "I'll never forget it. I felt so responsible. I wish that I had handled the entire situation differently. But it was wartime and we had so much going on here on the home front. I know that it can't possibly compare with what you were facing out on the front lines; but running the convalescence hospital here at Loxley Hall was no easy task and getting those soldiers, back up, fit and ready to fight came with its own challenges.

"For one of those soldiers to be responsible for kidnapping and murdering that little boy – I should have seen it sooner. I should never have let that Watson woman bring her son into the hospital that day. We all live with regrets."

"That we do," Mary agreed.

Malcolm handed her the glass and she took a sip as she stared pensively at the wall behind Malcolm's desk, where a stately painting of him was hanging, albeit crooked. She wondered whether she was on the right track after all. If what Malcolm was saying was true, then there was no mystery surrounding Cecil Watson's disappearance and pursuing it was just a cruel exercise in raising the hopes of some poor woman, who had lost a child before his time. Not that they weren't a dime a dozen since the end of the Great War – most mothers had lost children and husbands for that matter.

Emlyn must have discovered something – she certainly wasn't the type to go stirring things up just for the sake of it and to give Mrs Watson their mother's Cameo brooch would have been on more than just a whim. No, Emlyn was onto something and it must have been important, and Mary was determined to figure it out. She was to meet Baden at the Watson's the following morning and she could hear about it first hand from them, but for now, she had other business to attend to.

She said, "I just crossed paths with Southby – is there any reason that he is staying on at the Hall? I know he and Emlyn were never close, I'm surprised that he's here at all considering he and his father's history."

"We have some business to attend to; nothing for you to worry about," Malcolm said.

"But that's just it Malcolm, I do worry. I worry quite a bit, now that my sister's dead and I am the last Loxley. This is my family's legacy and I don't want it twisted in with the Southbys."

"You've never shown one iota of interest in the running of this place; and regardless of anything else, Loxley Hall is now mine and there is nothing more to say of it. If you must know, the business with the Earl has nothing to do with the Hall and everything to do with your Aunt Bett. If you have anyone to blame for his attendance here – you can blame her," Malcolm replied.

"Aunt Bett is here?"

"Yes. She was here when the unfortunate business with your sister occurred. The poor dear was so upset that she didn't leave her room for a good three days; like a daughter to her, Emlyn was."

"And you; how many days did you stay in your room grieving? If I didn't know any better, I'd say that things for you are carrying on around here as usual."

"Somebody has to keep things up and running," Malcolm retorted. "And it's not as though I can count on you for any help and support with that. You ran away from your responsibilities after the war – you don't have a right to march back in here and tell me how to run Loxley Hall."

"You're right – I don't have any authority here anymore. I never really liked it much here anyway. It's just with everything else that's going on, I didn't expect to see Southby – you of all people should understand that," Mary replied.

"The sins of the father are to be laid upon the children," Malcolm uttered.

"Shakespeare knew what he was talking about," Mary replied.

She finished her drink and said, "I'm going to lie down before dinner; I'm feeling tired after my journey."

"As is your will," Malcolm replied. "Please stay as long as you like; it's been difficult here without Emlyn – it'll be nice to have you around," he added.

"Thank-you; your hospitality does mean a lot to me." She stood up and made her way to the door. "Just one last thing; How do you know that you caught the right person? How do you know that it was the soldier who took Cecil Watson?"

Malcolm looked her directly in the eye, his nostrils flaring and his face turning red as he said, "We found him with the boy's arm, he was clutching it like it was some kind of damned trophy."

***

Malcolm Quinn sighed as the door swung shut after Mary exited the room. He hadn't expected to hear that name again so soon. Why did people keep bringing up that blasted boy?

Malcolm had wanted to go to war, however he had failed his medical and that was the end of it, until he was asked to head up the operation of a wartime convalescence hospital at Loxley Hall. It was Malcolm's opportunity to contribute to the war effort and he grasped the chance with gusto. His hospital had been one of the most successful and it was something for which he felt extremely proud. Everything that he had done there had been for the good of Britain and he couldn't help but feel satisfied that he had played his part in the success of the allied forces.

His only mistake; the only thing which detracted from his self-satisfaction, was Cecil Watson. If Cecil hadn't come to Loxley Hall that day, then he would still be alive instead of haunting Malcolm at every turn. Emlyn had started to ask questions a few weeks earlier and now here was Mary doing the exact same thing. When was he ever going to hear the end of it? Everything that Malcolm had done during that time had been for the greater good and he wasn't going to tolerate anyone coming in there, trying to tell him anything different.

He took his keys out of his top pocket and opened his desk drawer. He looked at the neat stack of 27 files which he had kept locked in there since the end of the war. He had tried to burn them after Emlyn's body had been found – but he couldn't bring himself to do it; each of them had their own special meaning to him and it just didn't feel right.

He ran his fingers across the top of the pile; the paper felt smooth and cool to the touch.

"Am I disturbing you?" came a voice floating in through the now open door.

Malcolm slammed the drawer shut, locked it and put his keys back safely into his pocket. He looked at the elderly woman who had just entered, over the top of his half-moon glasses.

"You couldn't possibly disturb me, Aunt Bett," he replied with a smile breaking out across his face.

"Have you spoken to Lord Southby? Did he accept my proposal?" she asked eagerly.

"I did speak to him and he said that he will give me an answer within the next day – however I think the outcome will be favourable," Malcolm answered.

"This is wonderful news; exactly what I needed to hear," she replied with excitement. "And what about our other piece of business?" she asked.

"It will all be taken care of," Malcolm replied.

"Excellent – you've been such a perfect nephew, my dear Mal. I certainly chose well," Aunt Bett replied. "Now, I'm going to prepare myself for dinner, I have an aristocrat to impress," she added and she left the room as abruptly as she had entered.

Malcolm picked up his glass and emptied it of its contents. He had had enough of all of these people, with all of their interruptions. He just wanted them gone, so he could get on with living the life that he wanted, the way that he deserved; and now that Loxley Hall was finally his, he was on the cusp of having his freedom and his very own fortune for the first time in his life.

8. SECRETS AND LIES

Detective Sergeant Diane Pridis knocked sharply on the redwood door. The corridor in which she stood was dark, except for a flickering light, which emanated from underneath the door in front of her. Pridis had never worked a case with Doctor Trudeau and so she had never been introduced to his unusual working space. She had heard about it, of course – the Yard had a way of making even the smallest of morsels, a meal for the masses – but she had not yet seen it for herself.

The door burst open and in front of her stood Doctor Trudeau, wearing red rimmed glasses, with an orange cravat sticking out from beneath his white lab coat. Pridis was thankful to remember his earlier aversion to shaking hands, as he had patches of a grey substance covering the length of his arms and caked unattractively under his fingernails.

"Ah, you; good, come in," Trudeau said, stepping back from the doorway and allowing Pridis the space to enter.

Pridis nodded in greeting and proceeded inside. The first room she encountered was empty other than a fluorescent light in the corner, which was switching on and off at intervals and pointed directly at an exotic looking plant.

"An experiment; it's a Grevillea," Trudeau elucidated. "For a poisoning case in Australia," he added, as he ushered Pridis along into the next room.

In contrast to the last, this room was bright white and full of light. Benny was hunched over the mincing machine – also known as the murder weapon – on the opposite side of the room. He was trying, with all of his might, to pull something out of it. He was tugging and tugging. Pridis had a sudden flash in her mind to the look of horror she imagined would have been on John's face as he had tried to rip his own arm away from that machine. It was very much like the look that was set on his face as he had died – pallid, with his mouth wide open as though he was screaming in sheer pain and terror.

Pridis winced and cleared those thoughts from her mind. She gave her attention to Trudeau, who was standing at the bench in front of her and kneading a greying dough.

"I hope you're not going to eat that," Pridis remarked, as she thought back to the one time she had tried to bake bread, unsuccessfully.

"My dear girl; I sculpt," Trudeau replied, swishing his arm to the corner of the room, where there was a table full of greying rocks. "Helps me to think. I'm having an exhibition next month if you want to come. In Dartmouth though," he added as he picked up his lump of clay and smashed it into another large mound on his left.

Pridis smiled. If these 'sculptures' were anything to go by, then there was no way that she would even contemplate going to his ridiculous exhibition.

"Sounds interesting," she replied. "You'll have to give me the details."

Trudeau was still elbow deep in his clay when he said, "I wish that I had some better news for you – but I've got nothing. I can tell you, with great confidence, that he died sometime between 1am and 2am, but other than that," he sighed, "not a fingerprint, not a fibre – not yet anyway. I'll keep looking and I'll let you know as soon as I find something."

"I don't know if you've heard, but Inspector Bliss is off the case," Pridis said as she leaned against the nearby bench.

"Yes, he came past earlier – already into the booze," Trudeau said shaking his head.

"Well, you can't blame him – everyone at the Yard knows how the Quinn case affected his career," Pridis replied.

"He was obsessed; but with good reason. I worked that case with Andy and I can guarantee that John Quinn was not a good man. And anyone who spoke to the witness knew that she was telling the truth," Trudeau replied.

"I've read the files, but can you tell me about the original Quinn case? I'd like to get a feel for what everyone was thinking and how you reached your conclusions," Pridis asked.

"If you've read the files, then you must know the bulk of it. Emily Baribel was working the streets that night. John Quinn picked her up and paid her to have sex with him at a hotel. He then ordered room service – they ate, and then the next thing she knew, she woke up loosely tethered in the back of a van. She broke free of her binds and the next time the van stopped, she made her escape," Trudeau recited.

"But she didn't see who was driving the van, did she?"

"She could only assume that it was John driving. He was her last customer, he was the one to order the food – but she never saw him behind the wheel. I checked the room that she insisted he had taken her to and there was no evidence of him ever being there. Given that she was a drug addict and a prostitute, nobody took her seriously, except for Andy. He believed her and after taking the time to talk to her, so did I," Trudeau said.

"If Emily Baribel was telling the truth, then why did she run off just before she had to testify in court?" Pridis questioned, sounding like the detective that she was.

Trudeau looked up at her from the clay, which had so far held most of his attention and he replied, "She didn't run off – Emily Baribel went missing four years ago and nobody has seen her since."

"But the report said……" Pridis began.

"I know what the report said," Trudeau snapped, "but it was Tilman who was supposed to be protecting Emily that night, not Andy;

he had his own problems to deal with and so Tilman had covered for him. She said that she left her post for a few minutes – and when she returned, Emily was gone. Tilman swore that Emily must've left of her own accord; but I checked the scene for myself and I found two drops of blood and there were imperceptible signs of a struggle.

"But there was nothing we could do; we couldn't find Emily and we had no other witnesses, no proof, nothing. Andy knew that it was John – John even had the nerve to taunt him about it after the case had fallen through, but we didn't have anything tangible – not after Emily disappeared.

"I've known Andy for a very long time; we started at medical school together and I've never known him to take a backward step. And I don't expect him to now either."

Trudeau shifted his weight towards Pridis, bent himself low, so that his face was level with hers and said, "I want to know right now – whose side are you on?"

Pridis instinctively stepped backwards, running herself hard into the bench behind her. She could feel her brow furrow. Her heart beat rose and she was ready for anything. Who did this man think he was?

She could feel anger rise in her as she exclaimed, "What the hell are you talking about?"

"I want to know if you've got my friend's back or not, because if you're not with us, then you're against us. I know you used to work with Tilman; I want to know where your allegiances lie," Trudeau shouted.

Benny had raised his head from the machine and Pridis could see that he was trying hard to eavesdrop.

She took a deep breath and tried to calm herself. She didn't want to be the hysterical one in the room – she'd leave that to Trudeau.

"I may not have worked with him for long, but Inspector Bliss is my partner – I'm on his side. If he wants to investigate on his own time, I'm not going to get in his way. If you want evidence of my loyalty, speak to Inspector Bliss; I've already called him with a tip."

"What sort of tip?" Trudeau asked.

"About a place John Quinn owned called Loxley Hall – it's out near Sheffield and John's wife didn't know a thing about it until their lawyer told her today," Pridis replied. "I suggested that Inspector Bliss should pay them a visit – Quinn's family runs a retreat. Inspector Bliss gets his holiday and he can look into John Quinn at the same time."

"I'm sure Andy will be happy for the distraction," Trudeau said. He walked back to his clay and dug his hands into the enormous mound as if nothing had happened. He added, "Well, I'm glad that we sorted that out; Tilman has everybody over at the Yard fooled. I'm glad to see that she hasn't fooled you."

"Tilman is a lot of things, but incompetent isn't one of them. She plays games. I just wonder if losing Emily Baribel wasn't one of them," Pridis wondered aloud.

"What do you mean by that?" Trudeau asked.

"I'm not sure yet," Pridis replied.

Her line of thought was interrupted by the ringing of her phone. She excused herself and answered. It was DC Crocker, who she had charged with the task of locating Robert Leung. So far, he had come up empty handed and he wanted to know if she had any other leads or advice that she could give him.

"Just keep looking; Robert Leung must be somewhere – let's just hope for his and his family's sake that he's not lying on the bottom of the Thames," Pridis said and she hung up.

Trudeau was still semi-submerged in his clay, sculpting what appeared to be a demented cat. It certainly looked more promising than his other works – but still not enough to warrant a trip to Dartmouth. Pridis walked across the room to Benny, who was still pulling away at something in the machine.

"Can we get the stuff, I'm in a hurry?" Pridis asked impatiently, thinking that she should probably get back to the crime scene sometime before midnight.

"It's in the back of the van, in the compartment to the left; where the tyre jack should be," Benny said. "The keys are in my pocket."

He shook his hips and the keys jingled. She reached in and extracted them. From where she stood, Pridis could now see that Benny was wearing a blood-spattered smock and he was trying to pull a pig cadaver – which had had its front quarter wedged into the rotors – from the grips of the machine.

"Their ligaments have a similar tensile strength to ours. The Doc wants me to pull it until it rips off. I've been timing, and so far, it's been 13 minutes," Benny explained excitedly.

"Great," Pridis replied, hoping to forget the image she had just seen. "I'll leave the keys in Trudeau's letter box." She paused at the door and called to Trudeau, "There is one thing that I would like to know the answer to; if you can give it to me, that is."

"What's that?"

"How did Inspector Bliss conclude that John Quinn had taken all those other girls, the ones that he attached to the file?" she asked.

"It was me; I came up with the connection. There was a pattern. Thirteen women, all missing from the same area, with similar traits; each one disappearing in April of the previous thirteen years. Actually, it was Andy's brother, Edris, who wrote the algorithm so that we could search the databases. He's a bit of a computer whiz. It's a shame his talents are wasted – he's into petty crimes."

"Family isn't always easy," Pridis replied and she left back through the front room and headed out to Benny's van and her little, blue saviours.

***

"Time always seems to go so much faster when I'm with you," Andy Bliss said as he watched Carla arise awkwardly from the bed and pull on her dress.

"I need to use the bathroom," she replied without giving Andy a second look.

She disappeared for a few moments and returned looking a little less dishevelled. Her mascara was still smeared across her temple, but that gave her extra appeal.

"The money is on the table," Andy said as he propped himself up against the pillow and rubbed his eyes. "Do you need help with that?" he added as he watched her struggle to reattach her prosthetic leg.

"Do I ever?" she replied tersely.

Andy sighed. The last thing he wanted to have right now was a confrontation with Carla. She was his escape; she always had been; no questions and no responsibilities – but now it seemed that she wanted more than that and it was something that Andy wasn't willing to give her.

She stood up again from the bed; this time with a firm foundation, and she walked towards the door.

"I don't want your money," Carla said, the light capturing a glittering trail down her right cheek as her hand rested on the door handle.

"Don't spoil a perfectly good afternoon with this. We've talked about it already Carla; just take the money and go," Andy said.

"You just don't get it, do you?" she replied the door now standing ajar.

"If I don't pay you, then what the hell does that make us? You know I can't have a girlfriend – you know what happened with me and Jarmila and I can't offer you anything more than this."

"It's my leg, isn't it? You don't want me because I'm not complete," she accused.

Andy had never asked her how she lost her leg and he had never really cared. It was always Carla who brought it up and it was always Andy who reassured her. Well this time he had had enough. He wasn't going to placate her – maybe it was because of his constant reassurances that she had formed such an unwanted attachment to him anyway.

"You know what? You're right – you would be a hassle and it's a hassle that I don't need; especially now."

"Fuck you," she shouted as she kicked his table with her plastic leg, breaking the table's leg in half.

She slammed the door and Andy could hear her bustling along the narrow corridor.

He arose from the bed and picked up the table. He propped it up precariously against the wall. *'Fucking bitch,'* he thought to himself angrily. What on Earth could she possibly want from him? He picked up his whiskey bottle, uncapped it with his teeth and took a swig. He felt bad about Carla, but what else was there to do? He couldn't keep on with her – not now that it had come to this. It was a shame – he had been seeing her since before he'd even met Jarmila – but she was nothing but a prostitute, a one-legged one at that – and they were a dime a dozen around here; he'd just have to find himself another, suitable replacement.

He picked up the two fifty pound notes, which had fluttered onto the ground from the broken table and he reached for his phone, which had bounced beneath the adjacent shelf. He had yet to call his father – he'd been putting it off the entire day – but now was the right time. He pressed the button; it was dead. *'Stupid battery'* he thought to himself as he plugged it into his charger.

His phone immediately sprung to life and beeped at least five times. He had missed three calls and there were several text messages. He contemplated unplugging it and returning to his uncontactable bliss, but his need to know got the better of him.

He listened to the messages – it was all much of the usual. Superintendent Zukowski called to make sure that he was actually gone from the Yard and she gave him the number of a travel agent which she had used many times before and was very reliable – *'Travel agent? Hasn't she heard of the internet?'* he thought as he deleted her message.

Trudeau called to tell Andy to hold off on his 'substance abuse' until the evening, when he could come out and join him. Andy knew that Royal hated drinking and he hated pubs, but he had known Andy long enough to know when he was on the cusp of an almighty bender; and Royal was always on hand to help pick up the pieces. He had always been there and Andy knew that he forever would be, despite all that had happened in the past. He took another swig of his whiskey as he determined that he would go back past Royal's lab and check in with his old friend on his way to visit his father.

The third message was from Pridis. He still felt bad about the way he had left her at the Yard that morning – sitting expectantly in his office and he, casting her aside like a dirty, old piece of rubbish – it was not the way he had wanted their new partnership to progress.

He was about to hang up when he heard her harried and rushed voice asking about John Quinn and a place called Loxley Hall.

He searched his memory banks. Nothing. No Loxley Hall. Nothing about Sheffield. And then she hit him with the loan shark. It didn't make sense to him at all. Why would John need to go to a loan shark? Andy had looked into John's finances over the years and although Quinn's Meats was not a booming business, it seemed odd that he would suddenly turn to an element so far out of his own control. It didn't sit right with Andy, it was not in John Quinn's nature to do something like that.

He tried to call Pridis back. No answer. He moved across the room to his laptop and he switched it on. He typed in Loxley Hall and found a simple website for it. It was located on the outskirts of greater Sheffield and it was billed as some kind of religious retreat.

Andy weighed it up for a moment. He had planned to go and visit his father with his enforced time off. Andy hadn't seen him for over year and he was starting to feel guilty. There was that nagging feeling in the back of his mind which every adult child feels when they neglect their aging parents. But his father was weak. He always had been and it made Andy sick to the stomach to see him every time he visited. So the visits had become fewer and fewer until they had stopped altogether.

He had always used his job as an excuse and he knew it. And now his job was giving him a reason to back out once again. It was not as though he had let his father know that he was coming; he hadn't been man enough to pick up the phone and face his responsibilities. But this was a chance to find out more about John Quinn and to see if he could finally put an end to all of this.

The needs of the 13 families, of those 13 missing girls outweighed anything his father could need. And to be honest, Andy's father had put himself into a position where neither of his sons could stand to face him. His mind was made up. He clicked on the link and he made a reservation at the Loxley Hall retreat for that afternoon.

Andy snatched up his overnight bag – which he always had prepacked and ready, picked up his hipflask and his car keys and walked out of the front door. He was on his way to Loxley Hall and hopefully to the answers that he had spent the last four years of his life, searching for.

***

Alex Dewill had just finished attaching her new front door key to her key chain when there was a knock at her door.

"I told that fucking Constable not to let anyone through," she muttered to herself. "What's the point of having a watchdog if they're fucking useless?"

She peered out of the window at the side of the door. She sighed and opened it partially, keeping her face in the shadows.

"What are you doing here?" she asked.

"I told you I'd come back to check on you, so here I am," Matthew replied.

"I'm tired – you should go home."

"I want to be here. What's wrong with your voice, you sound different?" he asked stepping towards the door. "What the hell happened to you?"

Alex hadn't been quick enough. She had stepped back as he approached, but he had already seen her mangled face.

"Just an accident. Nothing to worry about," Alex replied.

"Nothing to worry about? You look as though you've gone ten rounds with Evander Hollyfield. Come, sit down, I'll fix you something to eat," Matthew said as he ushered her back inside and into the living room.

"I'm not hungry," Alex replied as she sat on the couch. She picked up the Polaroid that she had been studying earlier and placed it face down on the coffee table.

"Food makes everything better," Matthew said, reflecting the sentiments of any good chef.

As he walked into the kitchen, Alex called after him, "Good luck finding anything in there."

Matthew poked his head back out of the door and said with a smile, "You'll see – I'm the master of improvisation."

He disappeared again and in no time, she heard all the familiar sounds of cooking; the banging of pots and pans, running water, the hiss of the gas stove top, the scraping of a metal knife against the wooden grain of the chopping board, and then sizzling. It was comforting. It didn't take long for the aroma of garlic, onion, beef and all manner of things to permeate the room. Alex's stomach growled. She hadn't realised how hungry she was until that moment.

Matthew emerged from the kitchen holding a bottle of red wine.

He handed it to Alex and said, "Can you open this? It should complement what I'm cooking nicely."

Alex took the wine glasses from the shelf, found the bottle opener in the drawer where it had lay untouched for the last few years, and opened the bottle. She allowed the wine to breath and then poured out two glasses, filling hers to the brim.

'Not a bad drop' she thought to herself.

Alex set down her glass and trudged wearily upstairs. In the bathroom, she found her pills. She swallowed the two which were to be taken with food and then checked the boxes. As she suspected they both warned her not to take them with alcohol – but Alex was never one to take recommendations from boxes.

She walked into the bedroom and looked around. There were little reminders of her husband everywhere and she didn't want to deal with it. Not now. She opened her closet, lifted down her travel bag and started to pack. She had just zipped it up, when an idea struck her. She entered John's wardrobe, pushed past his suits, knelt, pulled back the carpet and lifted the floor board.

She sighed in relief. The red, metal box was still there. She had never been happy to have a gun in the house, but John had always insisted and now it would finally come in handy. Alex took the gun out of its case and the carton full of bullets. She wasn't sure how it worked exactly, but she had seen it in the movies enough times. She tentatively pressed the button on the side of the handgrip and the magazine sprung out. Her hands shook as she loaded one bullet at a time, and once it was full she locked the magazine back into place.

The gun felt heavy in her hand. She contemplated returning it to its box and burying it back in the depths of John's wardrobe, but then she reminded herself of the attack on her that morning and the threatening note. She ensured that the safety was on and then shoved the gun into the side pocket of her travel bag and zipped it up hastily. She wasn't going to be caught unprepared again.

Alex picked up her bag and carried it downstairs. Matthew was already sitting at the table with wine glass in hand and two plates full of spaghetti laid out on the table.

"Where are you going?" he asked between sips of wine.

"I'm going away tomorrow, for a few days; I don't want to stay here – not right now anyway," Alex replied.

"Where to?" Matthew asked.

"I'm staying with John's family in Sheffield; they run a retreat," Alex answered.

"I thought you said he had no family."

"It's a long story."

"Well, I've got all night."

Alex sat down across from Matthew. She picked up her wine glass and drank.

She said, "To be honest Matthew; I wouldn't know where to start."

They ate in silence. The food tasted good and it was nice to have Matthew's company. After they had finished he cleared the table, and when he returned music played loudly from his phone. He reached his hand out towards her.

"When was the last time you danced?"

"I don't want to Matthew. I can barely breath right now and I'm getting tired," she replied.

"I'm serious; when was the last time you danced?"

She thought about it and then answered honestly, "I can't remember. It feels like never."

Matthew took her by the hand and led her to the centre of the room. He held her in his arms and they danced. She felt warm and safe and she allowed herself to get lost in the music and in his arms.

He lightly kissed the top of her head and then he whispered, "I'm coming with you. I wouldn't know what to do with myself in that kitchen without you. And I know that your face was no accident, Alex – I won't let anything happen to you."

***

Royal Trudeau had been standing with his hands immersed in the cold clay for at least the last fifteen minutes. He hadn't moved since Pridis had been there, deep in thought about what he had overheard. He shouldn't have been surprised, but somehow the thought hadn't crossed his mind that morning when he had made his way to the meat factory.

His thoughts were interrupted by Benny, who had come over to him, holding the head and shoulder of a dead pig.

"It took 32 minutes. What do you want me to do now?" Benny asked.

"The machine records the data as to the time it became jammed – if you could extrapolate the data you have just gathered from your experiment and correlate it with the machine's data, we should be able to come up with an exact time of death," Trudeau replied, still semi-distracted.

"All righty, Doc," Benny replied and he wandered back to his corner of the laboratory, still carrying the pig like a scientific badge of honour.

Trudeau extracted his hands from the clay; they were numbed from the cold. He rinsed them thoroughly and walked into the front room.

The fluorescent light was still flickering – Trudeau found the repetitiveness of it somehow comforting. He took his phone out of the top pocket of his lab coat and he dialled the number which he had memorised four years earlier.

"Dad?" came the questioning voice of a teenaged boy.

"No, Finn; it's Royal – I need to speak to your Mum," Trudeau replied.

The boy's voice altered from one of concern to outright aggression.

"You're not supposed to call here," he barked. "Not after what you did!"

"This is important Finn – can you put your mother on?" Trudeau replied gently.

"She doesn't want to speak to you."

Royal could hear a scuffle and a woman's voice came on the line, "Who is this?"

"Before you hang up on me Jo, you need to hear me out," Trudeau said in a rush.

"And why should I do that, Royal?" she replied, her voice a mirror of her sons.

"Because it's about Robbie."

"You don't get to call him that. Haven't you done enough to this family? You need to stay away from Robert and stay away from us," Jo answered.

"The police think he could be involved in John's murder; I just wanted to warn him. If he knows anything at all, he should come forward, straight away. The people who killed John mean business and I don't want anything to happen to him. I still care Jo," Royal said.

"What happens to Robert, is no longer any of your business. Leave us alone," Jo scowled and she hung up the phone.

Royal wandered back into his lab. Benny was hunched over the machine again and his lump of clay stood as it had done. He had tried to warn Robbie, that was all that he could do. Jo was right, Robbie had chosen his family over their relationship and it was no longer any of his business what happened to him. At least he had tried.

He dug his hands back into the clay and tried to shake the terrible feeling that sat like a stone in the bottom of his stomach; the feeling that Robert Leung was already resting somewhere buried in his own watery grave full of clay.

9. THE BODY OF THE SON

The drive to Sheffield had been a pleasant one. After escaping from the incessant traffic of London and advancing steadily along the M1, Andy Bliss had begun to enjoy the scenes of rolling countryside which peeked through the occasional breaks in the embankment. The vast green and yellow fields and the fresh, cool air had an immediate effect upon his mood. So long had passed since Andy had been outside of London, that he had forgotten how much he actually liked it.

'Maybe this retreat will do me some good,' he thought to himself as he uncapped his silver hipflask and took a mouthful.

It was nightfall by the time Andy pulled up out the front of Loxley Hall. The imposing, wrought iron gates towered before him. He rolled his car slowly along the meandering driveway and as he rounded the final bend, Andy could see the crenallations silhouetted against the darkening sky.

"This isn't a country estate; this is a fucking castle," he uttered as he parked the car.

The front door swung open before he had a chance to knock.

"You must be Mr Bliss. We've been waiting for you," an elderly woman said in a quiet, rasping voice.

She stepped back from the doorway, allowing him entry. She ushered him into a room just off the entrance hallway and indicated for him to take a seat in front of a large desk.

Her fastidiously groomed white hair shined in the light. She did not seem to be as old as her frail, skeletal body portrayed and one of her eyes was as blue as an early summer's sky. Her other eye however, was cloudy. It was difficult to discern exactly where she was looking at any one time and when she began to speak, Andy didn't know if it was to him or to someone standing in the corner.

"I have some papers for you to sign before we begin," she said, sliding them sharply across the desk towards him.

Andy perused the document.

"Why do I need to sign a liability waiver?" he questioned as he came to the third and final page.

"It's the standard form – nothing to be concerned about. We just want to be protected against any change of heart – you understand. You will find that our methods have been tried and tested over a number of years and we have an almost perfect success rate."

Andy had no idea what she was talking about, but he didn't want to portray his ignorance and get himself thrown out of the place before he had his chance to snoop around. He signed the papers and slid them back towards her.

Behind the desk, hung a stately painting of John Quinn wearing an old-style suit; a golden medal pinned to his chest. It was just like that self-centred son of a bitch to display a painting of himself.

"Owner of the place?" Andy asked casually, gesturing towards the painting.

"Oh no, that's not my nephew; a good likeness though. That painting is almost 100 years old. Malcolm Quinn – my grandfather. He was a war hero. He inherited Loxley Hall after his wife, a Loxley herself, committed suicide," the elderly lady explained.

"I see, Mrs Quinn," Andy replied, thinking how alike John was to his ancestor.

"I'm no longer a Quinn – not since I was married – but you can call me Vanessa. Familiarity over formality these days," she replied. She made her way towards the door and continued, "I'll just go and fetch my son Mark, he can show you to your room. I've left some supper up there for you. You'd do well to get a good night's sleep – we have an abundance of God's work to get through tomorrow and we want you fresh and ready for it first thing in the morning."

"Yes ma'am," Andy replied politely, wondering exactly what work the old bat thought that God had in store for him.

"We're happy that you've chosen to come here. I'm sure we'll be able to help you to find the fresh start that you need," Vanessa rasped as she exited the room.

"Thanks," Andy replied, contemplating what the new day held for him and hoping that he hadn't just inadvertently signed himself into rehab.

****

Mary Loxley stretched out on her bed. Surrounded by the colour blue, she felt a sense of calm transcend the strain of her situation. The blue bedchamber had been her mother's room, and Mary could still smell the faint odour of her frangipani perfume. The chiffon drapes, which hung down lavishly from the four-poster bed, resembled a waterfall reflecting the rays of the early, morning sun. A picture of the Brighton foreshore, which she had painted for her mother during a semester of art at Roedean, hung on the wall directly in her line of sight.

Mary's head was caressed gently by the pillow and she fought the urge to be consumed by the comfort and fall asleep. It had been a long day so far and there was still so much of it to come. She felt sick and tired, but she had to remain alert. There was much that she didn't know and she still couldn't be sure as to exactly where the danger lay.

She mumbled with a hint of irritation, "Why couldn't Emlyn have been more specific in her letter?"

She rose from the bed and opened her carry bag. She emptied out her clothing and distributed them appropriately between the wardrobe and the chest of drawers, laying everything neatly in its place. As Mary hung up the one dress which Rosaline had managed to sneak past her, her foot kicked the front panel of the wardrobe. It sprang loose and with it, so did a memory.

As children, she and Emlyn would often play hide and seek around the house. One day when Mary went to hide inside this wardrobe, she tripped and broke the front panel. Emlyn found her attempting to repair it and promised not to tell anyone – a promise that Emlyn had kept to her dying day.

Mary thought for a moment; Emlyn's letter had mentioned that she had acquired some hard evidence – something which was of great importance to her investigation and that she had wanted Mary to help her verify. Surely Emlyn would have hidden it in a place that only the two of them knew.

Mary lowered herself to her knees and reached her hand into the darkness of the hole which now gaped in front of her. Towards the very back and diagonal from her position, her hand hit something rectangular, wrapped in fabric. She opened the parcel and staring back at her was an old notebook, the cover a faded shade of maroon.

The handwriting was Emlyn's and she could tell from the first few dated pages, that it was her diary. As uncomfortable as she felt, immersing herself in the pages of a dead woman's most intimate thoughts, she turned to the last entries.

The final entry was dated a few days before her supposed suicide and the tone was anything but downhearted. It spoke of Emlyn's joy at the unexpected return of Baden, who everyone in Loxley had presumed dead, and the fact that she was going to accept his proposal to run away with him to Borneo – although he would have to wait until she concluded her investigation into the disappearances and ensured that Baden himself wasn't somehow involved.

Mary scanned the previous entries and found nothing in reference to Cecil Watson or any other disappearance for that matter; however, Emlyn's consistency for reporting in her diary left a lot to be desired and the evidence which Mary had hoped to find, was nowhere to be found. If Emlyn had uncovered anything, then she had hidden it somewhere else.

Mary's thoughts were interrupted by a scraping sound outside her door. Her hand fell instinctively to the barrel of the rifle she had tucked away underneath her bed. A piece of paper appeared beneath the door. Mary sprung to her feet, burst through the door and peered into the hallway – but she was too late, the deliverer was already gone.

She picked it up and examined the unfamiliar scrawl. It said: *'Meet me underneath the linden tree tomorrow at dawn. I know who killed your sister.'*

The corridor was silent. If Mary wanted to know who had sent the note and what they knew, then she was going to have to be down that embankment early the next morning, in the exact same place that her sister was murdered. It could be a trap, but she had something that Emlyn didn't have on that fateful morning and she moved across to the bed, picked up the rifle and checked that it was loaded.

****

"This is your room," Mark uttered as he placed Andy's bag just inside the doorway.

He stood, blocking the door for a moment by leaning against the doorjamb, looking at Andy expectantly. Mark was much taller and his frame filled the space quite imposingly. Andy wasn't sure if he was waiting for a tip, but either way, his wallet was in his bag and he didn't think that Mark had done enough to earn one just yet.

Mark leaned forward and said, "I bet you've got a big cock."

"Sorry?" Andy replied.

"You, big cock," he said in a stunted manner as he reached towards Andy's groin.

"I don't see how that's any of your business," Andy retorted, swatting Mark's hand away just before he made contact.

"Good man. You passed the first test. Mother will be pleased," Mark proclaimed.

He shouldered past Andy and marched back down the hallway from whence they had come.

Andy entered the room, still shaking his head. The last time his penis had been the subject of such speculation, he had visited a queer establishment in East London with Royal, and Andy had to admit that their conclusions weren't as complimentary as Mark's had been. He locked the door behind him and sat on the bed. He wasn't sure what had just happened, but given that these people were John Quinn's relatives, Andy was not surprised by their odd behaviour.

The walls were a light shade of blue, a contrast to the faded, royal blue curtains. Over one of the posts of the four-poster bed, draped a singular piece of worn, material. There was a small cross perched on top of the bedhead and hanging over a small chest drawers was a textured painting of a seafront landscape. It was so faded that it looked as though it had been painted over a hundred years before. A large wardrobe filled the space next to the entry way. It was antique and Andy was certain that it would have been worth a lot more had there not been a small panel missing from the front of it.

He opened the wardrobe; inside was a painting. It was a painting of the crucifixion of Jesus Christ; but not the usual representation. This painting seemed to go beyond faith and into the realms of an obsession with the excruciation of Jesus' death. It was so bone-jarringly realistic that Andy could see the exhaustion, the torment and pain in the whites of Jesus' eyes and hiding in the shadows were the four horsemen of the apocalypse laughing.

He flipped it over and wasn't surprised to see that it was signed, *John Quinn, 1997'*.

'Twenty years ago and he was already a sick fuck,' Andy thought to himself.

He put the painting back into the wardrobe and locked the door. Andy wasn't superstitious or religious – but something as grotesque as that painting, didn't deserve to see the light of day. He extracted his hipflask and took another nip. He wasn't hungry, which turned out to be a good thing, as the supper Vanessa had left, was dry and unappetising.

Andy kicked off his shoes, lay on the bed, and closed his eyes. He could still see the visions of that painting etched on the backs of his eyelids. He thought about his plans for the following day and how he was going to find out the information he yearned for. And as his mind wandered, he finally turned his back on his difficult day and let the waves of slumber wash steadily over him.

****

The sky was a deep shade of purple, lit only by the glow of the sun which had yet to peer over the horizon as Mary reached her destination underneath the linden tree. The cool morning air was enough to wake her and the mist rose from her mouth with each exhalation. She stowed the rifle safely under the bench and sat down. She had spent a good part of the night trying to figure out who had sent the note and had come to only one conclusion.

Addie was more than just a Lady's maid to Emlyn; she was a friend and a confidante, and if anyone knew what had happened to Emlyn, it was her.

Mary reclined on the bench and lit a cigarette. She soaked in the first rays of the rising sun and watched the wisps of smoke vanish, as they dissipated into the cool air. The shade of this tree had always been a place of tranquillity and safety, however this day, it felt desolate and she had a strange feeling, as if the tree itself was giving her a sense of foreboding; its branches reaching out to consume her as it had her sister.

Mary dispelled her feelings as silly and superstitious – two things which she was most definitely not. She stubbed out her cigarette on the flat earth beneath the bench. The sun was now above the horizon and she sat forward waiting for Addie to appear.

Time marched on; Mary heard the church bells in the distance, first ring eight and then later for the quarter. She was becoming impatient; she had even started to carve a figure eight into the wood of the bench next to her leg, using the sharp edge of Emlyn's snuff box.

Again, the bells tolled – it was half past eight. Mary had her appointment at the Watson's at nine and she couldn't possibly be late.

Mary trudged back up the embankment. She swept the house and gardens with her gaze one last time before she headed towards the front gates of Loxley Hall. Addie could wait until later – it was time to find out exactly what the Watsons knew and what had launched Emlyn onto this dangerous track in the first place.

****

Andy settled himself onto the bench he had discovered, after fighting his way through the weeds and long grass which surrounded Loxley Hall. The bench was down a sharp embankment and in the shade of an ancient linden tree.

He was thankful for the solitude. The morning had been harrowing to say the least. It had started with a dry piece of toast, which ended up being the highlight of the morning's proceedings, and ended with a 'debriefing session' where Vanessa had attempted to ascertain which of Andy's family members had abused him as a child.

"It's the reason you're the way you are," she had explained.

"I wasn't abused," Andy had insisted repeatedly.

"You're suppressing the memory; let it be free and you will be released," Vanessa had insisted back.

This conversation seesawed back and forth for much of the morning and it had left Andy feeling violated.

'How is this shit still legal?' he wondered to himself.

He took out his trusty hipflask and unscrewed the cap. Its level was already waning and Andy had started to formulate a plan of escape so he could get a refill. Vanessa had confiscated his car keys that morning and it was a stipulation of his treatment that he remain within the grounds; however, there was no way he was going to last more than a day of intensive conversion therapy without at least a quart of whiskey up his sleeve.

He leaned back. All that Andy could hear was the sound of the wind in the leaves and he enjoyed the warming sensation that the whiskey provided him. The trunk of the tree twisted upward from the ground in front of him and it had thick branches promulgate out in every direction. Moss grew around the trunk, like a shear green dress, stretching only partially up one side like a low cut back.

His hand found a pattern, carved long ago into the bench and as his fingers traced the figure eight, quiet footsteps approached steadily from behind.

****

Mary was ankle deep in mud by the time she had trudged her way to the end of Black lane, where she found Baden perched upon the Watson's front doorstep. He was in a much brighter state than the day before and he had taken the time to bathe.

She had worried about leaving him on his own the previous afternoon; but if he was so determined to take his own life then he would have found a way, whether she had stayed by his side or not. It was heartening, all the same, that he had made an effort and that his eyes were no longer deadened to the world around him.

"You're early," she said offering him her hand.

"I'm eager," Baden replied, lending his great mass to Mary's outstretched arm.

"It's hard to see more than two people living in this place," Mary said in reference to the small cottage in front of them.

"It would be difficult for you to picture, given the size of the house you were brought up in – but us common folk, we find a way to manage," Baden answered.

Mary was preparing to defend herself, when a broad smile broke out across Baden's face.

She slapped his arm and said, "I don't know how Emlyn ever put up with you."

"It was love; pure and simple," he replied

Baden knocked on the door and Mrs Watson opened it. Her dress was fit for a royal visit and she still had the cameo brooch pinned to her chest.

"Do come in," she said courteously.

She directed them inside, to the small sofa and table clustered compactly in the corner of the room. A pot of tea stood on the table; the steam swirled into the air.

"Mr Watson wanted to be here, but he couldn't miss work. They've had a shortage of workers in the factory since the end of the war."

They all sat down around the small table, "Tea?" she offered.

"Thank-you," Mary replied.

Mrs Watson poured out three cups.

"It's a lovely home you have here, Mrs Watson," Mary said as she sipped her tea.

"Thank-you my dear; but you're not a very good liar. My husband and I haven't cared for it much. Not since we lost our boys. We haven't seen the point," she replied.

"I'm sorry, I didn't know you had any other children," Mary said.

"Our son Clive. He died fighting in the war," Mrs Watson answered, her voice trailing off as if she were stuck in some worn-out memory.

"I went to school with Clive," Baden said. "I'm sorry for your loss."

"Our losses are no greater than those of all the other families around here. Your family are lucky to have you back Mr Hope. We all thought that you were lost to the war too; your name is still on the town memorial."

A dark look crossed Baden's face and he sank backward into the sofa.

Mary took another sip of her tea and then she said, "The war stole from all of us. Everybody lost something; whether it be family, friends or even parts of ourselves – but to lose a child at home, an innocent being, who didn't choose for any of this; that is worth more than the others. They all chose to be a part of something bigger than themselves, but Cecil, he was only a child and I'm so sorry that you had to go through it.

"I'm not sure what my sister was doing for you or what she had found, but I want to help you too – I want to finish what she started.

If you could just tell me exactly what you told her, then I can follow her path and hopefully we can all get the answers that we're searching for."

"Bless you my dear," Mrs Watson said as she put her hand upon Mary's. She took a deep breath and said, "It's all my fault really. I took Cecil into the hospital that day – my father was too ill to look after him and Master Quinn needed me to cover a shift. The hospital was overrun with sick and wounded soldiers and we needed as many nurses on hand that could be spared and so I asked Master Quinn if I could bring Cecil in and he told me that I could – as long as he stayed out of the way.

"It only took my little Cecil about an hour to cause a stir. I was seeing to my rounds, when I heard a ruckus coming from the special ward. I found Cecil in there, grappling with a patient.

"Ignatius Finch had been in a stupor since he had been admitted a few weeks earlier and he was left most days sitting in a wheel chair off to the side of the ward. I wouldn't have believed it if I hadn't seen it myself. That evil man gripped my Cecil's arm so hard, that by the time I had prised him off there were the beginnings of a bruise. Lady Emlyn saw it too.

"My Cecil was so afraid, that he ran away. Lady Emlyn and I searched and searched and we couldn't find him. It was Master Quinn who brought him back to me – Cecil had fled into the kitchen and was found by the Ellis sisters. I brought him home after that.

"He awoke in the night, crying. He told me that he knew what was happening to the missing soldiers. I didn't know what he was talking about – but he insisted that he had to show me something important. Cecil always did have such a vivid imagination. He always made up such lovely and elaborate stories. He could have been anything."

She stopped for a moment; a tear in the corner of her eye.

"I awoke the next morning to find Cecil gone. I went to the police and they spoke to Master Quinn, who told them about the troubles on the ward. They went to question Ignatius and he was gone. Before that day no one had seen him move a muscle, not even blink. But I know it was that wicked man who came in here and took him that night. If you ask me, I'd say he was possessed by the devil.

"They found him clutching my baby's arm, in the middle of the field just beyond Loxley Hall. They tried to question him; to find my Cecil's body, to bring him home to me – but it was no use – he didn't respond. They hanged him the next day. We searched for Cecil's body for a while afterwards, but with the war still raging, interest was lost fast and in time it was just me and my father out there searching the fields.

"We never found him. Part of me still doesn't really believe that he's gone."

"Did my sister tell you why she had a sudden interest in all of this? It can't have been easy for you having to relive it," Mary asked.

"She told me that Master Quinn had had a nightmare. He had cried out Cecil's name so desperately that it had frightened her. That was why she came to me in the first place – to hear my story. Then, a couple of days before she died she returned. She said that she had found some files that could help – that maybe we could find my Cecil's body. She didn't say anything more; she told me that she didn't want to cast aspersions before she had all the proof – but Lady Emlyn insisted that she was close.

"I'd do anything to find my little boy's body. Clive was lost to the war – I can accept that – but my little boy's body is out there, somewhere close, I can feel it and all I want is to give him the burial he deserves, so my Cecil can finally be at peace."

****

"I see you've found my fortress of solitude," came a decidedly camp voice from behind Andy as he felt the sharp pain of a splinter enter his finger from the pattern he was tracing on the bench.

Andy swung around, biting his finger, trying to dislodge the small shard of wood now embedded in its tip.

"No need to gnaw your hand off; I've been here for ten days already and they haven't broken me yet," the man said as he sat down heavily next to Andy.

Andy surveyed the man who took out a packet of cigarettes and offered him one. He had a strong jaw line, inquisitive eyes and his hands told Andy that he wasn't afraid of hard work. His broad shoulders and thick set frame were a stark contrast to his effeminate voice and mannerisms. Andy accepted the cigarette and the man lit it. He took a drag and felt his head spin straight away. He hadn't had a smoke in about 10 years, but he figured that he deserved one after the morning he had just endured.

"I'm Jordan," the man said, his hand outstretched.

"Andy," he replied, taking another drag on his cigarette, while he shook his new acquaintance's hand.

Jordan held onto it and examined the finger which Andy was chewing.

"Ah, a splinter, I have just the thing."

He removed a manicure set from the inside pocket of his jacket and took out the tweezers. Andy felt a white hot pain and within seconds Jordan had extracted the culprit and returned Andy's hand to him.

"So, you want to cure yourself of your gaydom?" Jordan asked, staring down his nose at Andy in disapproval.

"Yep," said Andy not wanting to blow his cover.

Jordan rolled his eyes and said, "I didn't think I'd find anyone coming willingly to this antiquated torture house. You're not serious, are you?"

"What are you doing here, if not to change your ways?" Andy asked.

"Gunning for my Pulitzer prize; but don't tell," Jordan replied, with a wink. He pointed to the linden tree and said, "They call this the 'Killing tree' you know? The townsfolk say that when this place was a war hospital, the tree would call to the soldiers and they would come out here and hang themselves from its branches; like a siren's song. I didn't find any evidence in the records about soldiers, but they did find a woman hanging from it, her head was almost severed too."

"Really – when?" Andy asked, his interest piqued.

"A hundred years ago," Jordan replied. "But there are rumours of other things that have gone on out here too," he added conspiratorially.

"Like what?" Andy asked.

Jordan sprung to his feet. "Oh shit, I hate dogs!" he exclaimed and he jogged up the embankment. At the top he turned and said, "I'll see you in shock therapy," and he disappeared over the hill.

Andy turned back to the tree. There was a small terrier digging at the base of it. Andy smiled. The dog picked up a stick and trotted towards him.

"Here boy," Andy said and the dog came nearer.

Andy grabbed the stick from him. He was just about to throw it when a beautiful lady came running into his view.

"Oh thank goodness you found him," the lady said taking the dog by the collar and attaching his lead. "He's just so stubborn sometimes."

Andy was so struck by her shining red hair and her pale blue eyes, that he forgot about the saliva covered stick he was holding in his hands.

"It's fine. Anytime," he said blankly.

She smiled at him and then walked away, her dog following reluctantly behind, now tethered by his lead.

Andy called after her, "We should have a drink sometime."

"Come to the pub down the street – I'm there most nights," she replied.

"I will," Andy said and he waved at her with the stick.

She disappeared through the trees and Andy was left alone once again. He was about to throw the stick away when he caught a proper look at it. It wasn't a stick at all; it was a bone – and from his brief time as a medical student, Andy knew that it was the femur of a child.

He strode over to the place where the dog had been digging. There he saw the edges of a pelvic bone. He knelt and gently brushed away the soil. Lying in a shallow grave was the skeleton of a one-armed child.

He picked up his phone and dialled, still staring blankly at the bones in front of him.

"Trudeau here," came the answer from the other end of the line.

"Hey Roy, it's me. I've found something."

"I'm almost there," Royal answered.

"What do you mean you're almost here?"

"Tilman had me removed from the case – so I thought I'd come and check out this Loxley Hall with you," Royal replied.

"Removed?"

"I'll explain when I get there."

"I don't think you'll like it here," Andy countered. "You do know what this is, don't you?"

"I saw it on the website. Don't worry, it'll be like camp. Plus, it would take a whole lot more than a bunch of religious nutters to convert me, old boy," Royal said.

"It's a crime scene now anyway – I'll have to call it in," Andy said, wondering how he was going to explain this to the Super without losing his job.

"What did you find? Not our missing girls?" Royal asked, his voice betraying his excitement.

"No – I've found an old skeleton. It's a kid; but it's the foot in John Quinn's door that we've been waiting for," Andy replied.

"Perfect – see you soon," Royal said.

"Oh, and Roy, bring whiskey," and with that Andy hung up and sank down to his knees.

He looked at the small, fragile skeleton which lay in front of him.

He bowed his head and said, "It is the darkness of the blackest night that has brought you under this tree and it is with the sorrow and torment of a thousand broken hearts that have mourned your passing – but with the light, comes salvation and I will find your justice and you will finally be able to rest in peace."

10. IN THOSE WE TRUST

Diane Pridis massaged the crick in her neck as she sat in the cluttered lounge room of the Leung residence. She had fallen asleep at her desk late the evening before, trawling through files of known standover men and loan sharks in the London area and trying, by some work of miracle, to link any of them to John Quinn. It was a sign of the times that the number of loan sharks on file had more than doubled over the last few years and it didn't make Pridis' job any easier.

Mrs Leung sat with both her arms and legs crossed, staring plaintively at the wall in front of her. She appeared childlike in her oversized, cream-coloured, cardigan. Beside her lay an empty box of tissues. The air of the room felt heavy and sad. Pridis sensed that she was talking to a woman who already knew the worst had happened and that finding her husband's body was a mere formality. They had been going around in circles and Pridis had decided that this interview was a waste of her time.

"I don't know what else I can tell you," Mrs Leung uttered not lifting her gaze from the wall. "Robert left the house yesterday at the same time he always does. Then I got a call from the secretary telling me that John had been killed and that Robert was nowhere to be found. I tried to call him, but his phone was switched off and it's been off ever since. It's not like him to disappear like that. You are looking for him, aren't you?"

"Yes, of course we are," Pridis replied. "He's very important to our investigation. Did he ever talk to you about his work at the factory? Did he mention the finances at all?"

"John would have had his head if he did. He made him sign a confidentiality agreement and Robert never broke it. I had no interest in the business and Robert was always so busy. I don't know what John wanted to hide – he was a very private man."

"Why don't you ask that pervert you work with?" came the defiant voice of a teenaged boy from the doorway across the room.

"Finn, go back to your room!" Mrs Leung snapped.

"No, I want to hear what she has to say. Did you tell her that he called here yesterday?" Finn said.

He entered the room and crashed down onto a seat at the table. He fumbled through his pockets, pulled out a packet of cigarettes and lit one quickly, taking in a strong, prolonged drag.

"Put that out!" Mrs Leung shouted. "Since when has it been okay to smoke inside this house?"

"Since you couldn't keep a reign on *your* husband. First, he fucks that scumbag and now all of this," Finn snapped, drawing back on his cigarette again and then stubbing it out in the middle of the dining table. He looked directly at Pridis now and said, "You tell that pervert not to call here again and if you see my father, tell him that he's no longer welcome here either."

Finn breathed heavily, his eyes burned with an anger that Pridis had seen many times before in the process of making an arrest. He stood; his chair flew backwards and he stormed out of the room.

"Don't judge my son on that performance. He really is a good boy," Mrs Leung said. "Finn hasn't been coping well; even before all of this happened. He still hasn't forgiven Robert for cheating on me – especially with a man. I knew what I was getting myself into when I married him, but Finn can't choose who his father is."

"But what does any of that have to do with me?" Pridis asked.

Mrs Leung sighed, "Royal Trudeau. He wasn't like all of the others;

Robert was going to leave us, for him. He'd never been so serious about another man before; it had always been about experimentation for him – until Royal. He ingratiated himself into our lives and even spent time with Finn. Then when Robert told me that he wanted to move in with Royal, I couldn't take it any longer. It was unavoidable that Finn found out about his father and from there everything fell apart. I blamed Royal for it all; but really it was my fault. I should never have tried to change Robert."

"So it was you who got Doctor Trudeau thrown off the case?" Pridis asked.

"I was angry. I know that Royal was only trying to help and I know I shouldn't have reported him to Inspector Tilman, but it's too late now," Mrs Leung replied.

Pridis rose from her position on the patch-worked couch and made her way across the room. She handed Mrs Leung her card and put a hand on her shoulder in comfort.

"Thanks for your help. Let me know if you hear from him – we're doing all we can to find your husband," Pridis assured, thinking that getting Trudeau off the case was the worst thing Mrs Leung could have done for her husband.

The air was fresh outside and Pridis was happy to be in the wide open space of the street. The Leungs hoarded trinkets and knick-knacks and sitting in their house gave the distinct feeling of being constricted. Half-way along the street, Pridis could see Finn hurtling away at a great rate of knots on his skateboard.

'*Poor kid,*' she thought to herself as she closed the car door behind her.

Pridis knew all too well how hard it was to get entangled in your own parents' relationship troubles and she felt sorry for young Finn. Her phone rang and she answered.

"I was just about to call you Inspector," she said. "Leung's wife was a bust."

"Don't worry about her now – let DC Crocker handle the Leungs from here; I've got something else for you," Tilman trilled.

"What is it?" Pridis asked rummaging through her bag for her notepad and pen.

"I got word that a pair of loan sharks were involved, in both the attack on Ms Dewill and John Quinn's murder – I want you on it straight away," Tilman instructed.

Pridis suppressed a grunt. She was hoping for something new – she tucked her notepad away. She hadn't bothered to tell Tilman about overhearing the information about the loan sharks the day before and she hadn't had any success in locating the right ones so far.

"Where did you get your information from?" Pridis asked.

"I've got my sources and they're more than reliable," Tilman replied.

"Did your source happen to give you anything else to go on – there are thousands of loan sharks in London alone?" Pridis asked.

"In the words of Ms Dewill – you're a detective, go out there and detect," Tilman chirped and she hung up the phone.

'As helpful as an acupuncturist's cat,' Pridis thought to herself.

Before she had a chance to turn the key in the ignition, her phone rang again.

"Inspector, I was just about to call you," she said.

"Your Loxley Hall tip was a good one," Inspector Bliss said.

"You found something?" Pridis asked.

"The skeleton of a one-armed child."

"You think that Quinn was into little boys?" Pridis asked instinctively.

"These bones are a lot older than John Quinn – but they've given us an in. I just need to speak to the Super – she's the next on my list of people to call."

"Good luck with that – do you want me to soften her up for you first?" Pridis asked.

"No; I can handle Daria," he replied. "How are you going working with the Kraken?"

"I would have gone with the Banshee, but the Kraken does have a better ring," Pridis said.

Inspector Bliss chuckled.

"I've been following up on the loan shark angle; without much luck though – do you have any suggestions?" Pridis asked.

"I have an informant who mixes regularly with that kind of element. I'll give him a call and see what I can find out," he offered.

"Thanks Inspector – and if you need anything, let me know." She paused for a moment and then said, "Have you heard that Tilman threw Doctor Trudeau off the case?"

"I did – he's up here with me. It seems that he was in need of a holiday too," Inspector Bliss replied.

They rang off and Pridis smiled. Although she was having difficulties in the here and now, she couldn't help but feel hope for her future and her partnership with the much-maligned Inspector Bliss.

***

Andy Bliss searched through his phonebook. It wasn't very often that he used this particular source, but this time he could come in very handy. He hit the contact and the phone dialled the number. The voice on the other end of the line answered:

"What's up bro, running out of criminals on your end of town?"

"Edris, always a pleasure my brother," Andy replied.

"You've got one minute Andy; I'm on my way to complete some very important business."

"And what business might that be?" Andy interrogated.

"Tut, tut, you know we don't talk about that, my brother. What do you want? Clock's ticking."

Edris Bliss was Andy's older brother by two years. When they were teenagers, Edris became involved with the Clover Street Crew, and he hadn't looked back from a life of petty crime ever since. Granted their home life was less than ideal – their mother incarcerated constantly because of her out of control kleptomania and their father working long hours in the factory – but Andy could never understand Edris' choice to abandon his family for a bunch of hoods.

Now into his thirties, Edris was heavily involved in small-fry organised crime and Andy knew that these low-life, loan-sharking thugs, were just the kind of people that his brother was involved with. He was a wasted soul; charming, intelligent, exceptionally talented with computers; but Edris insisted that these criminals were his family and that he was exactly where he belonged.

"I need you to look into the world of loan sharks for me," Andy stated.

"That's a pretty big scene there, bro. What, you need some money? Coppers not paying you enough?" Edris asked.

"A loan shark stuck a guy into a mincing machine, fucked him right up. We just want to stop it from happening again," Andy replied.

"What's the name of the dead guy? It'll help when I'm out there doing your job," Edris asked.

"John Quinn."

"Isn't he that clown who got away with trying to abduct that woman and dragged you through the mud a few years back?" Edris asked.

"The one and the same – but I assure you, as much as I would have loved to, I didn't do it," Andy said a smile breaking out across his face at the thought of it.

Edris laughed and said "OK, I'll look into it – but only for you little brother. By the way, time's up," and he hung up the phone.

It was always hard for Andy to speak to his brother. Edris had always been good to him, even though they had taken very different routes in their lives. But now that they were both at opposite ends of the scale, Andy very rarely saw his brother and when he did, it was usually for some kind of favour. They never just spent time together being brothers, Edris always had his tough guy façade up. He kept up the act just to hurt their parents – but he had been hanging out with that element for so many years, doing what they do, that it seemed he was no longer pretending to be a gangster and a criminal; Edris had finally become one himself.

***

Robert Leung sat alone in his hotel room wondering what the hell he had gotten himself into. He closed his eyes and rubbed his temples. His head had ached incessantly since the morning before and he couldn't help but think that he was a dead man walking.

He took off his jacket and rifled through the pockets for his paracetamol. He freed two capsules from the blister pack and gulped them down with a mouthful of Carlsberg from the mini-bar. He rubbed his temples again with his free hand.

Quinn's Meats had been steadily leaking money since the meat adulteration scandal had rocked the entire European meat industry and although they had regained much of their credibility they were struggling to keep the creditors at bay. Robert, who was known as a financial whiz, had tried several cost-cutting measures, but nothing seemed to work. The entire industry had been tarred with the same brush and although Quinn's Meats had never once used horse meat in any of their products, they had to claw themselves out of the mire like everybody else.

John said that he had tried. He had always been the face of the company and the public relations hinged upon him and his customer contacts – but Robert could see that even he was losing it. Then one morning a couple of months back John came in with a briefcase full of cash. The sudden cash injection had been more than enough to cover the wages and suppliers bills in their greatest time of need and that was all that mattered; the wolves had been kept from the door.

Robert didn't ask where the money had come from and at the time John hadn't told him. In reality, he didn't want to know. *'What he didn't know couldn't hurt him,'* had always been his motto and he wasn't going against that anytime soon. But his time of ignorant bliss was short lived. A few weeks later John had forced him to come to a meeting with a man called Kevlar Gold. That was when Robert understood exactly how much trouble John had gotten them into.

Gold wanted his money and he wasn't afraid to demonstrate to them exactly how serious he was. He showed John a video of his wife and assured him, that Alex would be the recipient of a face full of acid if Gold had any problems with the repayments.

"250,000 pounds John? What were you thinking?" Robert had yelled at him after the meeting was done and Kevlar Gold had driven away.

"Don't worry about it Robert. I've got it covered," John had replied.

"It's not you who's going to get their face melted off if we don't come up with the money," Robert had shouted, unable to calm his nerves.

"Get a hold of yourself," John had yelled and they had left it at that.

"Stupid son of a bitch," Robert mumbled under his breath, taking another sip of his Carlsberg and looking out of the hotel window at the Hong Kong skyline.

What had John been thinking? All he had achieved was to get himself killed and now Robert found himself in hiding. He wasn't going to come to the same end as John. His mind flashed to the horrors of the morning before.

He had arrived at work as per usual and changed into his smock. Thursday morning was his only early morning of the week and it was a trade-off as John always went through the machine checks on a Wednesday night. He had found it odd that the lights were left on, but with John's car still in the carpark, he had assumed that John had found a problem with one of the machines and was trying to fix it.

It wasn't until he had walked out onto the factory floor that he saw him. He had never seen so much blood – and the look that was etched on John's face, contorted with pain – was something he would never forget. Robert knew immediately that it was no accident and it wasn't a far stretch of the imagination to see that Kevlar Gold was involved.

Robert had ran to the door covering his mouth but he couldn't hold it in. He threw up all over his smock. His hands were shaking as he wiped the sweat away from his brow.

"Fuck, John!" Robert exclaimed as he clambered up the stairs to the walkway.

He took off the vomit soaked smock and shoved it in the bin. He staggered along, supporting his weight on the railing, to his and John's shared office.

He picked up the phone and was about to call the police, when a thought crossed his mind. It wasn't his fault that John had gotten himself into this mess, and what was the point of incriminating himself if he didn't need to? He looked at his watch; it was already 4:27AM. The workers were due and, did it really make a difference if it was he or them who called it in? It certainly wouldn't matter to John. And what did he owe John anyway? It's not like they were ever friends.

No, he wasn't going to get himself into trouble because of stupidity on the part of John, not when John had said that he would take care of everything anyway.

As though someone else had taken over his body, he walked across to the safe and typed in the code. It popped open and there was the remainder of the £250,000 that John had put in there 2 months earlier. Robert counted nine £10,000 bundles as he placed them into his briefcase. This was money that never really existed here, John had never entered it into the books, so it wasn't as though he was stealing.

He had pulled his passport from the desk drawer and opened his computer. He booked the next flight to Hong Kong, called a taxi and left the factory for the last time. He felt guilty for leaving Alex in that position, but he didn't owe anything to anyone and Quinn's Meats was not worth giving his life for and quite frankly neither was Alex.

***

Inspector Teri Tilman's phone rang for the umpteenth time that day.

"Yes," she answered curtly, not even checking the caller ID to see who she was speaking to.

"I hope you don't speak to your mother like that," the voice at the other end said.

"You shouldn't be calling me Marcus – it was bad enough when you walked into that interview room yesterday. I almost fell off my chair. How many years has it been?" Tilman said as she ducked into a vacant briefing room, off the hall.

"Too long, Teri."

"What do you want?" Tilman asked.

"It's not a question of what I want; our mutual friend wanted to make sure that you were on the same page – he told me that you hadn't answered him," Marcus said.

"You can tell Luke that I got his parcel and that my best officer is on it now – she'll find the loan sharks – I have faith in her," Tilman replied.

"Look Teri, you can't shut Luke out like that; you've seen what he's capable of – I mean look at what happened to John," Marcus implored.

"Luke swore to me it was an accident," Tilman answered. "I have to keep up the pretence that I'm actually looking into this thing properly and I have a whole team of detectives to misdirect – I don't have time to answer Luke's every whim. Tell him that I got Trudeau off the case; that should keep him satisfied."

"I don't have to remind you, that if any of this gets linked back to Luke and he gets caught, he won't hesitate to air our dirty laundry too," Marcus warned.

"Don't worry – it's under control," Tilman assured him and she hung up the phone.

She had been caught under the thumb of the merciless Luke for years now and felt as though she would never be free. She shoved her phone violently back into her pocket and continued her walk to the Super's office, for the daily update meeting.

'*One bad decision all those years ago and I'm still paying for it now,*' she thought to herself and as she walked along the corridors of the Yard, she thought about all the different ways that she would kill Luke, if she could figure out exactly who he was.

11. WHERE HAVE ALL THE SOLDIERS GONE?

"So what do you think?" Mary asked Baden as they walked back along Black lane together.

They had spent most of the morning with Mrs Watson, listening to stories and remembrances of her two sons. Mary Loxley couldn't help but feel sorry for Mrs Watson – she had lost so much – and her investigation had now become more than just trying to find Emlyn's killer. If Emlyn was on to something, then Mary was determined to find it and give the Watson's the closure they needed.

"I can't get past the missing soldiers," Baden replied, looking at Mary sideways from underneath a wisp of windswept hair. "I heard some stories on the frontlines about soldiers being sent home for recovery and then never being seen again. But it was chaos out there, and with so many people dying and with countless battles on so many different fronts, it was difficult to keep track of everybody. I don't know; maybe the boy saw something and maybe someone shut him up permanently."

"I don't know how we can prove it though," Mary said, stopping to scrape some of the mud off her boots. "If soldiers were going missing from the hospital, then where did they go? What could Cecil have possibly seen that would have gotten him killed? He was eight years old – for Christ's sake." Mary stomped the last of the mud from the edge of her boot and continued, "I saw a lot of soldiers during the war with shell shock and sometimes it manifested into unpredictable behaviours. Maybe Ignatius Finch was guilty and Emlyn just wanted to believe better of him."

"What about Malcolm calling out Cecil's name in his sleep? That has to mean something, doesn't it?" Baden questioned.

"Given that Cecil's murder was three years ago – it does seem strange," Mary replied.

Mary knew what type of man Malcolm was and sentimental was not the first descriptor to spring to mind. He was never the sort to take the blame for anything – even when things were blatantly his fault. But as much as Mary didn't like Malcolm, she found it hard to believe that he had anything to do with this.

"We need to find the files that Mrs Watson spoke about. They were the basis upon which Emlyn had drawn her conclusions. If the files are linked to the hospital, then Malcolm must have them in his office," Mary postulated.

"I still have some contacts in the Army; I can look into the hospital and Malcolm, and see if the military had any complaints or if they knew of any missing soldiers. I'd expect they would have kept a record of the patients that were sent to Loxley Hall; it shouldn't be too hard to find any discrepancies. In the meantime, you can work on finding a way into Malcolm's office," Baden said coming to a halt at the corner of the street.

"I'm going this way – my father is feeling ill today and I promised my mother that I would help her in the store," Baden said, gesturing the opposite way to Loxley Hall. "Oh and I almost forgot," he said as he dug his oversized hand into his trouser pocket and pulled out an envelope. "Here's the forged letter from hospital; the one which dragged me all the way to London, while Emlyn was being, well, you know."

Mary accepted the envelope from Baden and placed it into her pocket. They said their goodbyes and left each other with a clear plan of action. In no time, she had reached the front gates of Loxley Hall and had started to wend her way through the gardens. Her mind was occupied with thoughts about how she could get into Malcolm's office, undetected.

When he wasn't in his office, the door was locked and he kept the keys securely in his top pocket. Mary needed a plan which involved either stealing those keys or breaking in. The office had two outward facing windows – but she would need to climb to the first floor. There was always Godfrey – he held a master set of keys – but could she really trust him not to tell his master if she asked for his help?

Mary reached the front door and grasped the handle of the lion-headed door knocker. She knocked loudly three times and within a minute, the door swung open.

"Good afternoon, My Lady," Winnie said, performing a careful curtsy.

"You can call me Mary," she replied, embarrassed by Winnie's greeting.

"Very good, My Lady," Winnie said, stepping back from the door and allowing Mary entry. "Lovely day outside then, My Lady?" Winnie asked.

"Very nice, thank-you Winnie. Have you seen Addie around today?"

"I haven't seen her yet – but I do sleep in the attic and work my way down with the house keeping – I don't usually see her until around dinner time," Winnie replied.

"If you do see her, can you please send her to my room?"

"Of course, My Lady," Winnie answered.

Mary climbed the stairs and walked along the corridor towards her room. She paused for a moment at the closed door of Malcolm's office. During dinner the evening before, Malcolm had indicated that he had business in Sheffield to attend to for the entire day.

'It couldn't be this easy, could it?' she thought to herself as she tried the doorknob.

Mary could not believe her luck; the door swung open. She glanced up and down the corridor and then peered around the edge of the door into the room. It was empty. She tip-toed across to Malcolm's desk and tried to open the drawers – her luck had run out.

She searched for a letter opener with which to pry open the drawers. It was then that she heard it. Heavy breathing emanated from the couch on the other side of the room.

"Oh Timmy, you naughty boy," giggled Aunt Bett.

Mary slunk silently back towards the door. She was on the precipice of completing her escape, when she heard a great clunk, and the voice of Lord Southby say:

"Mary! This isn't what you think."

Mary spun around, to see a half-naked Lord Southby, who had jumped up from his position on the couch. In doing so, he had hurled Aunt Bett onto the floor, dislodging her wig. The scene was a sad one and Mary wanted nothing more than to leave.

What did she expect from the two of them anyway? She had never known either of them to have any kind of decorum.

Aunt Bett smiled and said, "My dear girl, is there anything that *we* can help you with?"

She emphasised the 'we' in such a manner that it made Mary sick to the stomach at the implication.

"You're double his age," Mary said shaking her head and walking out of the room.

"Love knows no bounds," Aunt Bett called after her.

Mary continued along the corridor and reached the blue bedchamber, trying to erase the picture of the two of them from her mind.

'He'd sleep with a dish full of crabs if he thought they'd get him off,' Mary thought to herself of Lord Southby. *'And she! She would marry bloody Michael Collins if she thought it would make her important.'*

Mary sat on her bed and kicked off her boots. The disappointment of the missed opportunity in Malcolm's office was only now starting to sink in.

To take her mind off what had just occurred, she extracted the letter Baden had given her and studied the envelope. The postmark was definitely from London – she had seen it many times before – and the hospital stationery appeared to be authentic. She moved across to her carry bag and took out her magnifying glass. She removed the letter from its envelope and placed it flat on the table.

Upon examination, one thing was immediately apparent. Mary walked across to the bedside table and this time picked up the note she had received the evening before. She placed the note next to the letter and used the magnifying glass to study the two sheets which now lay in front of her.

From the rightward slant of the writing, to the looped stroke of the 'y' and the excessively long cross of the 't', Mary could see that the note and the letter were written by the same hand.

She dropped the magnifying glass to the table with a clatter. If Addie was the sender, then she was in more danger than Mary could have imagined.

'How did you get yourself involved in this Addie?' Mary thought to herself.

She picked up the sheets of paper, folded them together and shoved them into her pocket. She rushed out of her room – Mary had to find Addie and fast, before there was another dead body hanging from the legacy of Loxley Hall.

***

"Can you please get a move on with those carrots?" Louise Ellis said impatiently as she trundled across the room carrying a pot full of boiling water. "We still have the custard for the Spotted Dick to prepare and the veal isn't going to braise itself," she added, sloshing hot water onto the stovetop.

Martha sighed and visibly increased the rate at which she was chopping the elongated, orange vegetables, which were sitting, peeled and washed in a bowl next to her.

"Why isn't Addie in here helping?" Louise demanded. "She knows how busy we get – especially with the Earl still here – and now that she doesn't have a Lady to wait upon, what else could she possibly be doing with her time?"

"I haven't seen her," Martha replied, her attention still fixed upon the carrots.

Louise Ellis appraised her sister, whose sweat covered face had reddened with the exertion of the day's work. She looked as though she hadn't had a wink of sleep and her hair frizzed out from beneath her cook's hat, as though a whirlwind had just passed through the kitchen. Martha was always so eager to please, and that made Louise feel sick to the stomach. She hadn't raised her to be so weak.

Louise and Martha had lost their parents at a very young age and Louise had taken the responsibility of looking after her younger sister. She had done well for them, considering, and she was now so close to lifting them out of this dank and cramped kitchen permanently.

"Well if you do see her, tell her I want her down here quick smart," Louise said as she added the chicken carcasses to the pot in front of her.

"Who are you referring to?" asked a harried voice from somewhere behind Louise.

Louise swung around, to see Lady Mary standing in the doorway of the kitchen. She could feel her hackles rise as her domain was once again invaded by those who were not welcome.

Whatever happened to good breeding? she thought to herself as she answered, "It's Addie...."

"She had to go away," Martha interrupted.

"What do you mean, she's gone away?" Mary asked.

"Exactly that. Her aunt in London is very sick. We received word last night that it doesn't look good for her and so Master Quinn has given her leave to go and help her family. We don't know how long she will be gone for, but she loves her aunt very much – poor Addie talks about her all the time – and so soon after losing Lady Emlyn too. I can't imagine what that poor dear is going through," Martha bemoaned.

"That is terrible to hear. She didn't happen to leave any messages for me before she left, did she? She was very close to Emlyn, and I was hoping to spend some time with Addie and hear all about her."

"I'm sorry Lady Mary but she didn't mention you at all. She was so concerned about her aunt, that she ran out of here without taking any of her belongings," Martha said, shrugging her shoulders.

The kitchen clock struck three and Louise turned to Martha and said urgently, "You need to start on the veal, otherwise it won't be ready in time for the banquet."

"It looks as though you have enough food to feed an army," Mary commented, leaning against the bench just inside the doorway.

"Master Quinn likes to over-cater, especially when the Earl is here," Martha replied.

Louise gave her a stern look, but Martha had her attention drawn to the pile of veal fillets waiting to be prepared.

"Well, everything looks divine," Mary said. "I won't keep you two much longer, but I do have some questions."

"How can we help you?" Louise asked expertly concealing her exasperation.

Mary turned towards Martha and asked, "You two were stationed here during the war, weren't you?"

"Yes, Lady Mary. We cooked all the food for the soldiers, when Loxley Hall was turned into a hospital," Louise replied wondering exactly where this was leading.

"Do you remember much about Cecil Watson?"

"Nasty business that was," Martha said.

"That Ignatius Finch was one blood thirsty creature," Louise said. "We found the poor boy cowering here in the corner after he was attacked by that monster on the wards. We should have done something about it then, but who could have known that it would have ended up so terribly."

"Did Cecil tell you about anything unusual he may have seen when you found him?" Mary asked.

"The boy was as white as a sheet; he was so frightened, he didn't utter a single word," Martha replied.

"Did either of you tell anyone about Baden and Emlyn's meeting that was arranged for the morning of her death?"

The sudden change in the line of questioning took Louise by surprise.

"How did you know about that? I didn't tell anyone about the meeting," Martha insisted.

"How did you hear it about it?"

"I overheard the two of them talking at the reception Master Quinn had held in honour of Captain Hope's return," Martha replied.

"And you, Louise?" Mary asked.

Louise could feel Lady Mary's steely glare pointed squarely on her.

"I'm not sure what you're talking about," Louise replied turning her back on Mary and stirring the pot in front of her.

"The day that my sister was murdered, she and Baden were supposed to meet under the very same tree that she was found – did you tell anyone about it or not?" Mary asked, her voice rising in sharpness.

Louise heard a loud crash. She turned just in time to see Martha picking up her knife from the floor and wiping it on her apron.

"I'm sorry Martha, it's not often that you hear the word murder, in normal civilised conversation; I didn't mean to startle you," Mary said.

"That's very true Lady Mary. Murder is such a nasty business," Louise intervened. "I'm not in the habit of spreading rumours about married women meeting eligible men in private, if that's what you want to know?" She turned back to her pot and said, "We still have a lot of work to do and standing here gossiping isn't going to get it done!"

"Thanks for your help, I'll leave you both to your work," Mary said and she strolled out of the room.

This was the first time that Louise Ellis had heard anyone mention murder in relation to the death of Emlyn. She hadn't thought that such a thing was possible. It looked just like a suicide and she couldn't see how anybody could make the leap to murder.

She continued to stir the stock which was almost at the boil on the stove as she said to Martha, "If Lady Mary thinks that it's murder, she doesn't have a long list of suspects and you behaving suspiciously doesn't help. Next time, keep a hold of your damned knife. And why did you tell her that you knew about the meeting?"

"She caught me by surprise. I didn't know what to say," Martha replied.

"Look Martha, you know the plans that I have for us; you need to pull yourself together and stop making yourself look guilty, otherwise it could be the gallows for the both of us," Louise warned. "And what was all that guff about Addie? Should I be worried?"

Martha was slouched over the stack of veal fillets as she replied, "Don't worry about Addie and I'll be more careful next time."

"What did you do?" Louise asked.

"She's in with the others, if you must know," Martha answered.

Louise kept on stirring the pot for a lot longer than was necessary. She knew that Lady Mary had a reputation for being much smarter and more determined than everybody else. She wondered if Mary was going to keep digging into things until she found out how and exactly why Emlyn had died. Louise lamented the fact that something which happened in the heat of the war, could still affect her so many years after. At least now with Addie out of the picture, there was one less loose end to tie up.

12. SKELETONS IN THE CLOSET

The train ride to Sheffield had so far been an uneventful one. Matthew, who had spent the previous night upon her couch, had slowly nodded off to sleep and Alex Dewill was left alone lost in her thoughts. Her back ached and her eyes had swollen to the point that she was looking at the world through two narrow slits. John's death was becoming more of an inconvenience than anything else, and she couldn't help but feel resentment towards a man that she had spent the last 12 years of her life with.

From the very beginning, their relationship had been punctuated with half-truths – and not just from John either. If Alex was honest with herself, then it was she who had lied first in their relationship and it was her short-comings which had led to the disintegration of their marriage. It hadn't felt like a big lie at the time; John had wanted her to be a virgin when they were married and so, she had told him what he had wanted to hear.

It was practically true anyway and Alex hated the fact that John was being so old-fashioned – it served him right. However, the lie grew when it came time for them to try to conceive. John wanted a son more than anything, but they were having problems from the very start. He tried to convince her to visit a fertility clinic with him, but she was afraid of what they would find if she did, so she kept avoiding the issue, until eventually, John just gave up.

Alex already knew what the problem was. She had had a relationship when she was in secondary school; they were in love and it seemed as though there would never be anybody else. They only had sex once – but that's all it took. At the time, she had decided to keep the baby and her boyfriend had promised to look after the both of them. They were going to be a family.

The fairy-tale turned sour when she miscarried at 10 weeks. It was an ectopic pregnancy and she just knew that it had permanently damaged her fallopian tubes. Looking back on it all – her lie was the beginning of the end of their marriage and it was all her fault. She closed her eyes and cradled her stomach as the train pulled slowly into Sheffield station.

She looked across at Matthew, who was still sleeping like the baby she never had, and she toyed briefly with the idea of leaving him on the train. He had insisted on coming with her despite her protests. She was meeting John's family for the first time ever and she was bringing another man – it didn't feel right to her. But Matthew didn't see it her way and here he was, all arms and legs and persistence.

"Hey Matthew; wake up, we're here," Alex said as she shook his shoulder gently, conceding defeat to her better self.

He stifled a yawn, stretched his arms into the air – narrowly missing Alex's already battered face with his elbow. He heaved the bags down from the rack above their heads. Alex snatched her bag away from him. She peered covertly into the side pocket; the gun was still exactly where she had placed it. She felt a surge of confidence as she zipped the bag back up and lobbed it onto her shoulder. No one was going to catch her unawares this time.

"Here, let me take that," Matthew said reaching for the straps of her bag.

"No, I've got it," she replied, clasping it tightly with both hands.

The early evening air felt fresh and cool against her skin as she stepped out onto the platform. Light rain fell steadily, but only enough to be bothersome. They stood on the platform and allowed the swarm of people to dissipate. Marcus had assured her that the loan sharks would not follow, but she had been careful since they had started their journey and she couldn't shake the feeling that something was amiss.

They made their way to the front entrance of Sheffield station and exited onto the promenade. Alex admired the impressive water feature as they walked up the incline towards the main road.

"I have something I need to do," Matthew said as they reached the footpath of the busy street. "I can meet you at the Hall later tonight – what's it called again, Loxton Hall?" he asked.

"Loxley Hall," Alex corrected. "I thought you said you didn't want me out of your sight?"

"I thought *you* said that you didn't want me to arrive with you at the Hall?" he countered. "Look – it'll give you some private time with John's family and you won't have to explain to them who I am. I'll come later and you can show me around your new house," he said, a smile stretching across his face.

"What are you going to do?" Alex asked.

"I'm meeting a very old friend of mine," Matthew replied.

He started off along the main road. He turned back as he reached the first corner and waved to her before he disappeared around it. Alex hadn't wanted Matthew to come, but now that he had gone and she was standing there alone in the drizzle, she felt his absence.

She was just about to hail a taxi when she heard a breathless, rasping voice say, "You must be Alex."

In front of her stood an elderly lady, wearing a mulberry coloured, pleated skirt, with a cornflower blue blouse. Her white hair was tied back neatly and although she clearly had some troubles with her eyes, her face was full of life.

"Yes, I am – how did you know?" Alex replied.

"Your face dear. Mr North told me you had had some kind of accident," she answered. "My name is Vanessa. I'm parked over there – you don't mind walking, do you?" she added, gesturing in the direction of the pedestrian crossing.

Alex was happy to walk after sitting on the train for the last two and a half hours. They reached a carpark behind a small set of shops and a beep emanated from a champagne coloured BMW.

"It's a bit gaudy, but John always wanted me to have nice things," she explained as Alex lowered herself into the car.

"John bought this for you?" Alex asked.

"He did. My nephew was always sending us little gifts," Vanessa replied as she started the engine and accelerated, too fast for Alex's liking, out of the parking lot.

Alex felt an anger bubbling away just below the surface at the thought of all the times that they had gone without. John had always told her how much money he was obligated to funnel back into the business and that there just wasn't enough left over for anything more than the bare necessities. Her job in the restaurant helped to pay the bills and as far as Alex was concerned, they had been struggling to stay afloat; and here he was, splashing money around on a family that she never knew, who lived in an estate that she didn't know existed. Bastard.

The car came to a screeching halt at a red light. The sudden, sharp pressure of the seat belt pressing against her sternum, drew Alex away from her thoughts and back into the present. She doubted whether Vanessa should even be driving, given her ailing eyesight, but she didn't want to get off on the wrong foot with her hostess and so Alex held on tight and was thankful that this particular vehicle had all sorts of airbags, covering all sorts of angles.

"Do you know much about the history of our Loxley Hall?" Vanessa asked, as she slammed her foot on the accelerator, in response to the light turning green.

"Nothing at all; I only found out about it and you, yesterday," Alex said, as she felt her entire body forced backwards into the seat.

Vanessa began her explanation, sounding as though she was reciting a page in the encyclopaedia and Alex was thankful to have something to take her mind off Vanessa's wayward driving:

"The village of Loxley was founded by the Loxley family in the twelfth century after the area was used mainly as a hunting ground for the Normans. The Loxleys were granted the rights to work the land by the Earl and it took no time for Loxley to grow into a bustling centre of trade and agriculture.

"Their loyalty to the Earl was rewarded with ownership of a parcel of 40 acres of land. In the 15th century Loxley Hall in its present form was constructed. The Loxleys owned the house and land until 1915, when the eldest Loxley daughter and then owner of the Hall, Emlyn, married Malcolm Quinn, my grandfather.

"Upon her death in 1920, my grandfather took full ownership of Loxley Hall and it has been in my family ever since. It has been passed from father to eldest son through its history with the Quinns, and has now finally, after my nephew's death, fallen to you."

Alex had always wondered why John was so desperate to have a son and now it seemed that she had found the answer; he had been determined to continue the Quinn legacy at Loxley Hall. Alex had a brief moment of satisfaction that Loxley Hall was now under the ownership of a Dewill and she was glad that she hadn't taken on the Quinn name. That had been another source of aggravation in their marriage – but it had been one stipulation that was not negotiable. Even in marriage, she was determined to keep a small piece of her own identity.

Her thoughts were interrupted by their arrival at the front gates of the property. Vanessa allowed the BMW to roll slowly along the winding driveway. Alex was relieved at this change of pace. The garden was overgrown with weeds; it looked as though it hadn't been cared for in a very long time. She imagined that the gardens would have been grand in their day and she decided that if she did nothing else with her time there, that she would do her best to bring the gardens back to their past glory.

Vanessa parked the car and Alex surveyed the imposing building which towered in front of her. It was constructed using the most beautiful, honey-coloured stone and the building looked, with its battlements and turrets, like a fourteenth century castle. The windows, on each side of the entryway, were high and arched; each with eight panes of leaded glass. Above the carved, wooden front doors was a semi-circular pane of stained glass with the image of a pelican, its wings spread, shielding and feeding its children who were perched safely in their nest.

"The garden is unkempt, but it's so big and we no longer have a groundskeeper," Vanessa said as she jingled through a large set of keys. "I hold a separate key for each of the rooms," she added in explanation.

"I'm sure with some hard work I can turn it around; I love gardening," Alex said.

As much as she loved gardening, she also needed a distraction. For most of the night before, Alex had lay awake, keeping watch in case the murderous thugs returned. Although nothing had happened, she had burned enough nervous energy for a lifetime and was looking forward to the rest and meditation which being in the garden provided her.

"We're having a slight inconvenience with the police at the moment – so there will be parts of the garden which are off-limits," Vanessa said as she put the key into the lock.

"The police?"

A large part of her agreeing to come to Loxley Hall was so that she wouldn't have to deal with the police and now here they were invading her new space. She felt her shoulders deflate and her grip tightened on the straps of her bag.

"Found some old bones out the back. Ironically enough, underneath the Killing tree," Vanessa replied as she led Alex inside.

"The Killing tree?"

"That lovely, old linden tree has been called the Killing tree by locals ever since I can remember – I never knew why – and now it has finally lived up to its name."

***

Andy Bliss leaned against the bar. It had been a long day and he was ready for a much-needed drink. After he had spoken to Edris, he had called the Super and explained the situation. True to her nature, Daria had reprimanded him and ordered him to undergo a counselling session when he returned to London. She had wanted to suspend him, but their history had overridden her common sense, and so she had made the necessary arrangements for him to have all the resources that he and Royal needed instead.

Sheffield CID were happy for Andy to take on the case, given it was so cold and they themselves had enough on their plates. There had been a spate of home invasions in Darnall and they required all their senior officers on deck and in the present.

The rest was easy enough. Royal had arrived forty minutes after Andy had called him and Sheffield CID had been accommodating enough to assign a constable – who also just happened to live at Loxley Hall – to the case too. Andy hadn't wanted the extra resource, considering that the perpetrator of the crime was sure to be long dead, and Andy's prime motivation was merely to poke around Loxley Hall without raising the suspicions of the house's occupants. Andy had to admit however, that it was helpful having someone with local knowledge on his team.

PC Eric Pearson rang the bell which stood between a stack of beer mats and a bowl of peanuts.

When no one appeared, he called out, "Hey Jacqueline, you've got customers." He looked at Andy and said, "No wonder she's been losing business like there's no tomorrow."

Andy couldn't believe his luck when Jacqueline eventually emerged from the backroom. Somehow, she looked even more beautiful than she had that morning.

She looked at Andy and then said, "So Eric, who's your new friend?"

"This is Detective Inspector Andy Bliss from New Scotland Yard," Pearson replied, trying his utmost to sound official.

"Dog whisperer and detective hey," she said with a smile and added, "You drink on the house."

"I'll take a whiskey, neat," Andy said, returning her smile.

Her red hair shone in the light as she prepared his drink. She had the kind of figure that could distract a man for days and Andy found his eyes drawn to her and all of her womanly attributes.

Pearson leaned in and whispered, "Trust me – you don't want to get involved with her. Everyone in town has had a ride on that one."

"Including you I take it?"

Pearson nodded.

Jacqueline gave Andy his drink and said, "Anything for you Eric?"

"Still on duty," he replied curtly, gesturing towards his uniform.

Andy followed Pearson to a table in the corner of the room. Pearson sat down heavily across from Andy and gave an audible sigh. Andy wasn't sure exactly what to make of him. He was older than Andy and he had been in the uniform for longer, yet to still be a police constable meant that he was either entirely unambitious or completely incompetent. Andy was yet to discover which one of those criteria fit best.

"How long have you been living out this way?" Andy asked.

"I was born here in Loxley. My parents were farmers and after they died, John and his family were good enough to take me in."

"How did you and John know each other?" Andy asked wondering if Pearson was going to be an impediment to his real investigation.

"John and I went to the same boarding school. We didn't know each other before then – I was always working out on the family farm and we never ran in the same circles here in Loxley. During our first year at Radley, we were both the victims of merciless bullying. We bonded, I guess, over that. I came from a home without as many resources, shall we say, as the other students and they all took it upon themselves to remind me of it – sometimes in cruel and unusual ways.

"One night, when some of the older boys came and dragged me out of the dorm and into the bathroom, John leapt to my defence. It put him in the firing line, but he stood up for me and we got through it together.

"I spent my summers at Loxley Hall after that and I came to know his family quite well. It just seemed natural after my parents died and the farm was foreclosed, that I moved in permanently and I've lived there ever since. He was a good man, John Quinn," Pearson explained, his head bowed.

"When was the last time you saw John?"

"He'd visit for a week every April, without fail. It was the main event here at the Hall; Vanessa always made such a homecoming for him and then the four of us would go hunting," Pearson reminisced.

"The four of you? I couldn't imagine Vanessa roughing it in the forest," Andy replied; although he could easily imagine her stalking and killing a baby deer, after the morning she had subjected him to.

"Not Vanessa – me, John, and his two cousins. You would have met Mark already," Pearson clarified.

Andy felt a buzz in his pocket.

He fished out his phone and answered, "Yes?"

"Hey Andy, you need to get back to the Hall – I've found something."

"I can be there in 7 minutes, Roy."

"As always, I appreciate your precision," Royal answered and he hung up.

Andy finished the last of his whiskey and said, "We have to get back to the Hall; it seems Royal has discovered something."

"Did he say what?" Pearson asked.

"Nope – just that we need to get back there now."

Andy carried his empty glass to the bar. Jacqueline emerged from the back room and took it from him. The tips of their fingers touched and Andy fell into her blue eyes.

"I'll see *you* later," he said.

"I'm counting on it," she replied with a smile.

***

Alex Dewill sat on the salon sofa, immersed in the splendour of the drawing room which was located on the ground floor of Loxley Hall. The red, velour curtains, were held in place by golden, bell-shaped tassels. They hung over the leaden windows and although the curtains were dusty, they intimated towards the grander times of the Hall.

Alex couldn't help but notice an abundance of religious paraphernalia adorning the walls and found it quite odd, considering John had never been religious himself.

'What kind of retreat is this?' she thought to herself as she scanned the room for any kind of clue.

Vanessa entered the room accompanied by the sound of the clatter of dishes coming from the large tray that she was carrying. It was the sound of an elderly lady's shaky hands carrying cups that didn't quite fit to their saucers. Alex went to her assistance and Vanessa seemed pleased to be free of the encumbrance that the tray had represented.

"Sandwich dear? They're left over from the afternoon, but they should still be tasty," Vanessa said as she waved her hand towards the table as if she were a game show model.

Alex wasn't hungry, but out of manners she placed half a tomato and cheese sandwich onto her plate. The juice from the tomato had seeped through the bread, making it soggy and utterly inedible.

Vanessa took the other half of the same sandwich, nibbled at the crust, chewing labouriously, while Alex poured two cups of tea from the teapot. They sat in silence. The only sounds that permeated the room were the ticking of an antique mantel clock sitting above the fire place and a squelching noise that emanated from Vanessa's teeth with every mastication.

Alex leaned forward and put two lumps of sugar and a splash of milk into her Earl Grey tea. She could smell the bergamot overtones as she raised the cup to her lips and took a small sip. It was too hot and so she put the cup back onto the saucer and let it rest on the arm of the couch as she asked:

"Why is it that we've never met before?"

Vanessa smiled slowly, revealing her pearly-white, oversized dentures. Her functioning eye appeared to be looking somewhere into the distance as she replied, "John always did like his secrets; but I must say on this occasion, it was my fault that he never told you about us.

When John first left us to go to London to find his fortune, I was angry. His rightful place was here with us and when he went, I made it clear to him that he could no longer consider himself a Quinn.

"You see – we do good work here and I thought that God intended for all of us to carry it out together. But John had his own ideas and his own mind and I couldn't stop him. We eventually made peace and as it turned out it was God's plan that sent him to London after all – he was doing such great things there," Vanessa said, taking another bite of her sandwich.

Alex wondered exactly what Vanessa meant by 'great things'. The last time she checked, John had been running his meat factory into the ground and with each passing morning she noticed that his features were becoming weaker, his hair was thinning and his waistline thickening; so even his womanising was becoming less successful. Then, on top of all of that, to get himself murdered by two-bit criminals – if God's plan was for John to be an absolute failure, then yes, he was indeed excelling.

"Great things," Alex reiterated and nodded her head.

Vanessa grated off more of her sandwich. The squelch of her saliva had now been replaced by the click of her jaw as she chewed.

"What kind of retreat is this? I'd love to get in some yoga while I'm here, but I have a feeling that you don't offer it," Alex said.

"You're quite right – it's not that kind of retreat, my dear girl. We offer a fresh start for those who have been lost and want to come back onto the path of righteousness – a bit like the work that John was doing in London," Vanessa replied.

Alex was about to question exactly what Vanessa meant by that when a man appeared in the shadow of the doorway; his face shrouded in darkness.

An unexpected jolt shot through Alex's legs and her heart jumped into her throat. She leapt from the place she was sitting and could only find one-word swimming around her head.

She exclaimed, at the man whose height and shape was so familiar to her, "John!"

***

Andy Bliss walked down the embankment and was surprised at the progress that Royal had made since he had left. A tent had already been erected and there were spotlights illuminating the entire area. He felt foolish for sending Pearson into the house to get some torches – of course Royal had come prepared.

Andy ducked in through the doorway. Royal had set up an excavation grid around the site where the child's skeleton lay. He was crouched over the top of something and as usual, he was engaged completely in his work.

"What is it?" Andy asked as he came up beside his old friend.

"Bloody hell, Andy; don't sneak up on me like that!" Royal exclaimed.

"Next time I'll knock, shall I?" Andy retorted as he crouched down beside Royal to get a better view. "What am I looking at?" he asked.

"This," Royal replied as he indicated towards the small hole he had just dug.

Andy leaned forward and saw that underneath the soil was concrete.

"I was hammering a stake into the ground and I hit something solid. When I dug, I found the concrete. I've excavated a few more holes and it seems that the slab is approximately five square metres."

Andy exited the tent and began to stomp his feet around in the long grass. After a few moments, the damp thuds turned into hollow knocks.

"Aha!" Andy exclaimed.

"What is it?" Royal asked.

"We've found ourselves a bunker," Andy revealed as he jogged back into the tent and fetched Royal's shovel.

Andy dug and soon uncovered a rectangular door. He brushed off the excess dirt and yanked on the small, circular handle, but the door wouldn't budge.

"Roy; I'm going to need your help with this."

Royal had a closer look and said, "It's rusted shut."

He ducked back into the tent and emerged again moments later. He knelt beside the door and started to sand the hinges. He pushed the nozzle of a small aerosol can into the metallic couplings and sprayed. Lastly, he struck the edges of the door with a needle-nosed hammer.

"That should do it," Royal said.

"You carry all of that in your case?" Andy asked.

"You never know when you'll need it."

"You sound just like Jordan," Andy said.

"Who's that?" Royal asked.

"Fellow inmate. He carries all sorts of things in his pockets – he rescued me from a splinter earlier today."

"Hmm, I could be just the man to unconvert a converted," Royal replied with a grin as he reached down and effortlessly pulled open the trapdoor.

"I'm sure you are," Andy replied.

Royal switched on his pocket torch and shined it down the hole. There was a rickety, wooden ladder extending downward into darkness. Andy stepped towards it, but Royal stopped him.

"I should go down there first; I am the medical examiner and the resident scientist."

Royal disappeared down the ladder. Time stood still as Andy waited for him to resurface. After ten minutes had elapsed, he knelt next to the opening and called:

"Is everything all right down there?"

Royal appeared at the base of the ladder. His face was ashen and he said with a distinct shakiness in his voice:

"You'd better get down here and see this."

***

John. The word still thundered around Alex's head like a steam train. She sat, cross legged, directly opposite the man who she had just accused of being her late husband. She was embarrassed. Not just at the fact that she had thought she had seen a dead man resurrected, but also at the way she had screamed at him. Her resentment had burst forth in the ugliest of ways and she couldn't take back what she had said in front of Vanessa.

While he was shrouded in darkness, his shape had resembled every bit of John's. Once he had stepped into the light however, Alex could see that although he had some vague similarities, he was definitely not John.

"John would talk about you often when he came and stayed with us and now here I get to meet you in the flesh," the man said, breaking the uncomfortable silence. "I'm Eric, by the way. Eric Pearson. I was your husband's best friend."

He stood up and approached Alex with his hand outstretched and she shook it in turn. Despite his confident display, she could feel that his hand was moist with sweat.

"I'm sorry about my outburst – I don't know what I was thinking," Alex said.

"Don't worry dear; grief strikes us in the most unexpected of ways," Vanessa said. "When my Philip left us, I cut his eyes and ears out of every one of his photos and shredded them." She added, "Eric here does resemble our John – they were always two peas in a pod."

Alex turned to face the doorway as she heard more footsteps enter the room.

"You!" exclaimed Alex as she sprung once more from the couch and approached the room's newest entrant. "John's dead; so if you're looking to conduct one of your witch hunts – then you're in the wrong place."

"Good evening Ms Dewill, no witch hunts on my schedule for today," Andy replied, with an annoying smirk on his face.

"You two already know each other?" Pearson observed from his place upon the couch.

"We go way back," Alex answered, debating with herself as to whether she should slap him in that smug face of his. "I should have known that you would have your nose right into it up here. I would appreciate it, if you could get this over and done with as soon as possible and then you can get back on your high horse and gallop back to Scotland Yard and leave me the hell alone."

"I'm afraid it's not going to be as easy as that," Andy replied coming further into the room and slumping down on the couch.

He was much paler than the last time she had seen him and he had a fragility about him that Alex didn't think was possible.

Andy said, "I need a drink. You got any whiskey here?"

Pearson stood and moved across to a small cupboard which sat on top of the desk at the side of the room. He unlocked it and took out a bottle of scotch.

"Will this do?" he asked.

"Perfect. And you should pour one for yourself while you're at it," Andy said.

"I can't; I'm still on duty," Pearson replied.

"I'm your boss and I'm telling you that you're going to need it," he ordered.

"Why, what is it? What did Doctor Trudeau find?" Pearson asked, dutifully pouring out a second glass.

Alex could feel the heat from the Inspector's eyes as he turned his unyielding gaze upon her.

He said, "How many innocent men do you know, who have the bodies of 42 people buried in their backyards?"

Alex felt her knees weaken and her stomach rolled. Had she just heard him correctly? Forty-two bodies? She had been so certain about John the entire time they were married. She may have fallen out of love with him – but she always knew that he wasn't a bad person. But with all the lies and deception that she was uncovering – especially since his murder – did she really know who this man, John Quinn, was?

She stood up and walked to the door. She couldn't breathe, she needed air. She turned around to see three sets of eyes trained directly upon her. She was so sick of defending a man who had brought her nothing but broken promises and a wasted life.

She said, "I'm tired. I'm going to bed. Do what you will, I'm not going to stop you."

13. LOSING HOPE

Baden Hope had not worn a suit since sometime before the war, and as he adjusted his tie, he realised that it didn't become any more comfortable with age. He had been waiting there, in that very same spot for the last three hours, and with each passing moment it was becoming more and more difficult for him to fight the urge to spring to his feet and demand some kind of action from himself.

The waitress, who for the entire morning so far had kept him hydrated, approached him once again.

"Would you like to order anything else Sir?" She looked up at the clock and added, "It's just past twelve o'clock, if you'd like something for lunch."

He wasn't hungry, but he wasn't fond of being alone with his thoughts either. At least with a plate of food in front of him, he would have a distraction.

Baden surveyed the table next to him and said, "I'll have what that gentleman is having."

"Very good Sir," she said as she scribbled his order onto her notepad and then strode towards the kitchen.

He picked up his glass, which held the final mouthful of the club soda he had been nursing for the past hour, and swirled it gently with his left hand. His mother always used to say that the pings that the ice cubes made as they clinked against the sides of the glass, were the sounds of fairies clapping.

He wanted so badly to blame his mother for everything that had happened. She was at the party the day Emlyn was killed, drinking and gossiping with the rest of the women. If she had just taken an interest in Emlyn; prevented her from going down that embankment somehow, then Baden's one and only love would still be alive.

But he couldn't blame her, nor Malcolm, nor Emlyn herself – as much as he had tried to. He couldn't really blame anyone else at all, when quite clearly, it had been his own choices and mistakes that had snowballed and had caused Emlyn to die.

'I should have just taken her away with me after the war. Why did I wait for so long?' he thought to himself.

The smiling waitress brought out his lunch – what he recognised to be an order of fricassee rabbit. He picked up the pepper and applied it liberally to his meal; not because it needed it, but because he hadn't been able to taste anything since Emlyn had died. And it wasn't just flavours that had eluded him, everything had lost its edge, its colour; everything was dulled.

Baden ate slowly, checking his watch every other minute, trying not to let his impatience get the better of him. He couldn't help but think about the last time he was in London – enjoying his lunch in this very same restaurant – all the while back in Loxley his love was being throttled.

He clenched his fist at the thought of the ferocity with which Emlyn had been killed. He clenched so hard, that his nails dug deeply into the palm of his hand. But he didn't feel pain – not anymore – he felt nothing.

"Good to see that you've eaten something Captain," said a man as he sat down across from Baden and placed a yellow file on the table between them.

"Gus! I was beginning to wonder whether you were coming back," Baden replied.

"We hold innumerable files at the War Office; and they're not all exactly where they should be," Gus replied as he took off his bowler hat and lay it on the chair next to them.

"What were you able to find?" Baden asked.

"In short – nothing," Gus answered.

"And you checked both Loxley Hall and Malcolm Quinn?" Baden asked.

"I even checked on the other names you gave me – the Watsons, Ignatius Finch and Emlyn," Gus explained. "There was a mention of the Cecil Watson incident – but no missing soldiers and no evidence to suggest that anyone but Ignatius Finch killed your young Cecil. The only other thing I found was this," and he slid the folder across to Baden for him to see it for himself.

Baden opened the folder. In front of him lay a commendation from the Directorate General of Army medical services awarded to Malcolm Quinn. It cited the fact that Loxley Hall had the highest success rate of all the home-front convalescence hospitals, in returning soldiers to the front lines fit and ready to fight.

"Quite impressive if you ask me Captain," Gus said as he took the folder back.

"Thanks for trying," Baden said, feeling the weight of his shoulders being pulled towards the floor.

Gus was one of the most brilliant people that Baden knew and he was now working in the British War Office, helping to improve their filing systems for the future. He thought that if anyone could find anything abnormal about Loxley Hall during the war it was Gus.

Baden indicated to the waitress that he wanted to pay and then he gathered himself together to leave. He said:

"I'll walk back with you to the office; there's a couple of things there that I need to take care of."

He paid the bill, leaving a good sized tip and then they started together out the door. As they reached Whitehall, Gus charged forwards and called out:

"Higgie! Hey Higgie, it's Gus and I've got the Captain with me. Hey stop!"

Baden jogged after him and reached Gus just as he tugged the arm of a short, blonde haired man. He swung around and as he did, Gus let go of him.

"Oh, sorry. I thought you were someone else."

"Are you all right?" Baden asked.

"I keep seeing him, you know," Gus replied, staring at his feet.

"Who?"

"Higgie; Higgie Bocastle – you remember him, don't you?"

"He's a hard man to forget," Baden replied. "You do know that it's not possible that you're seeing him."

"But that's just it Captain. I see him all the time. We fought together in those trenches for so long and now here I am back in London and I can't stop seeing his face," Gus explained.

"It wasn't your fault," Baden said simply. "You couldn't have known what was going to happen."

"But he took my watch – it should have been me," Gus replied, tears appearing in the corners of his eyes.

Baden offered him his handkerchief and put a consoling hand on his friend's shoulder. He knew exactly what Gus was talking about, because he could still see the faces of all of those men that he had sent over the top. And now he had Emlyn's face to add to his collection too.

Gus wiped his eyes, blew his nose and said, "Do you ever feel like all of this is a dream – that maybe we're still out there fighting and we're going to wake up right back out there in those trenches again, knee deep in shit, mud and the blood of all of our friends?"

Baden surveyed the busy street; everybody walking around, as though none of it had ever happened. None of the horrors, none of the wasted lives – an entire generation of young men and women cut from the Earth in one fell swoop and nobody gave a damn.

"None of this feels real to me. That's why I didn't come back here in the first place. I couldn't face this," he gestured around at all the other people. "Things are not the same and I can't act as though nothing happened. I can't pretend that I'm not responsible for the deaths of so many people."

"What are you talking about Captain? You're a hero – you saved the lives of half of our troop on more than one occasion," Gus retorted.

"But all those men, those boys, that I sent over the top – I knew that they were going to die – but I just followed my orders anyway. Does that make me any less guilty?"

Gus didn't answer. Instead he said, "All I know is that I don't belong here anymore."

"I thought that my place was with Emlyn – but now that she's gone....... I don't know where I belong either."

*

It was approaching evening by the time Baden's train pulled back into Sheffield station. He was disheartened by the fact that he hadn't found what he was looking for at the War Office, however his trip hadn't been without some success.

Ignoring the old hansom cabdrivers' calls for a fare, Baden set off along the road to Loxley. The sun hung low in the sky and the trees cast long shadows which criss-crossed his path. He wasn't in a hurry to get back to his parents' house and he didn't know how he was going to break the news to them.

After he had escorted Gus back to his working quarters, he had visited the enlistment counter. His meeting with Gus had made him appreciate that no matter how hard he tried, he would never fit in anywhere, especially in Loxley, and without Emlyn, he no longer had anything tangible to live for. He had decided there and then to re-enlist. At least his life would count for something; the lads were already fighting a new war in Ireland and he could use his skills as a soldier where they were needed most.

Baden trudged along, his coccyx still bothering him from his 'accident' a few days before, but he didn't care. He looked at his wrist, which Mary had bandaged together with a splint, and he ripped away it's coverings. It was black and it ached, but it was a punishment that he deserved.

He turned onto his parents' street and there was Mary sitting on a railing, smoking a cigarette. He hadn't seen her for the last two days and she looked decidedly drawn out and pale.

"I didn't know if you'd be back today – but I thought I'd wait for you anyway," she said, jumping down from the rail and stomping on her now discarded cigarette butt.

"You don't look well," Baden said as he approached.

"It's nothing," Mary replied. Her eyes lowered to his wrist and her brow furrowed as she added, "And what have you done there? It took me forever to get your bones back into line."

"It's nothing," Baden said with a smile. "I didn't find anything; I had my best man on the job and all he could find was praise for Malcolm and the hospital."

"It was worth a try," she said as they headed towards Baden's parents' house. "But if I were Malcolm and I was trying to hide something, I wouldn't put it in any official paperwork."

"We're not even certain that Malcolm was involved," Baden replied. "All he did was have a nightmare – we can't hang a man based on that; as much as I'd like to – and even if he was there when Cecil died, he was with the hunting party when Emlyn was killed."

"I do know one thing for sure," Mary said. "Addie is in it up to her neck."

"How do you figure that? Her and Emlyn were more like sisters than the two of you ever were; sorry to say."

Mary told Baden about the note that was slid under her door and the fact that the handwriting matched the letter which drew him away to London.

Baden thought for a moment and then said, "You're only assuming that Addie was the one who slid that note under your door. Maybe someone else wanted to lure you down there and stop you from snooping around."

"We won't be finding out from Addie anyway," Mary said. "It just so happens that she was urgently called away to London to care for a sick relative. Does that sound familiar to you?"

"It is one hell of a coincidence, isn't it?" Baden replied as he reached the front door of his parents' house.

"And I for one don't believe in them," Mary answered.

*

Baden settled onto his bed and kicked off his shoes. He was thankful to be rid of the shirt and tie and he yawned as he adjusted the pillow beneath his weary head. After much deliberation, he had decided not to tell his parents about his re-enlistment. He wasn't due to leave for another month and they were so happy to have him back. His mother had only just recovered from the shock of his sudden return and it didn't seem fair to ruin it for them just yet.

His head sank into the pillow. He hadn't slept at all soundly since the war and so it was with an unfamiliar boat upon which he sailed off into the land of slumber. He couldn't say that it was nightmares that he was having, there were no events or strange happenings, or anything of the like. Instead, his subconscious threw up pictures, still-life pieces of artistry of some of his darkest moments.

There was the time when Johnny Wilkins had panicked and had thrown down his weapon and declared that he was done with all the fighting; he refused to leave the trench when it was his turn to go. Baden couldn't have it. He was in command and if one soldier didn't go – if he wasn't made to go – then Baden knew that he would have a mutiny on his hands. He ordered another soldier to come over and they picked Johnny up and threw him over the top.

The gun fire was immediate and relentless – the enemy bunker couldn't have been more than twenty metres away – and seconds later, Johnny peered back over the edge, his face dripping with blood and half his ear missing, pleading to be let back in. And then bang – Johnny got his wish – a grenade was thrown and his incinerated corpse was blown back into the bunker.

Then Baden had a flash of Higgie Bocastle, whose head was blown off and whose brains had covered most of the troop as they tried to get some rest. And then there was the guy – whose name Baden couldn't even remember, who had screamed and pleaded throughout the night from no-man's land for someone to come and rescue him – anyone at all.

"I'm still alive, help me. I can't feel my legs but I'm here……Help me Captain……Help me, I don't want to die – not like this, not alone. Please Captain, please."

But Baden had kept quiet; he hadn't wanted to give away their position, or anything else to the enemy and instead he spent the night listening to this poor boy's life slowly draining away from him – his tiny voice getting weaker and weaker – and the boy's realisation that his life wasn't worth anything to anyone in that moment; just another pair of boots on the ground. He was only eighteen.

And finally, and most cruelly, his mind showed him what his life with Emlyn could have been, had the war never come, or had he been strong enough to return home after the war and face up to the realities of everything that he had done.

*

It was already light outside when Baden awoke from his fitful night's sleep. His head felt as though it was stuffed full of cotton wool and his eyes were swollen to the point that all he could see was the blurred wall in front of him. It took him a few moments to register that the woman's voice emanating from the sitting room was not that of his mother.

Baden rubbed his eyes and his temples. His wrist which had only been aching the day before, now caused him an inordinate amount of pain. He held it up in front of him. It was every shade of blue and the bones were no longer where they should be.

He dressed slowly, fixed his hair and felt the stubble which had grown upon his chin over the last 24 hours. He hated having to shave every single day. He was thankful that soon he would be ensconced once again in the wilderness of war and wouldn't have to worry about any of these pointless conventions ever again.

Mary was in the sitting room holding a cup and saucer in one hand and her customary cigarette in the other. She was regaling Baden's mother with an entertaining story of some kind and they both laughed as Mary hit the crescendo. It was a moment of candour which Baden appreciated. He had never known Mary to let go of herself so much as to actually laugh and when he saw her eyes, he saw a flash of Emlyn in her that he had never noticed before.

"Mary; what brings you to us this fine morning?" he asked.

"Where are your manners, Baden? It's Lady Mary," corrected Mrs Hope.

"Oh I'm sorry; Lady Mary," he bowed. "How may I be of assistance to you, Your Gracious Highness?"

"It is I who can be of assistance to you, Captain Hope. I heard that you misplaced your last ones," Mary said as she showed him the bandages and splint which she had brought along with her.

He sat alongside her on the couch and offered her his crooked wrist. He wasn't looking forward to the pain of the traction, but he needed his wrist healed if he was going to be fit enough to join the fight in Ireland.

Mrs Hope took one look at the two of them and said, "You'll have to excuse me, I get squeamish around these types of things. I was absolutely useless on the wards at the hospital during the war."

"You volunteered at Loxley Hall?" Mary asked.

"Most of the town – those of us who couldn't be out there fighting – worked at the Hall. As I said, I wasn't much use on the wards, but I counselled some of the more troubled soldiers. I'd like to think that I helped in my own little way," Mrs Hope said.

"Did you ever notice any of the soldiers going missing?" Baden asked, turning his full attention to his mother.

"There was one boy; what was his name again?" she hesitated for a moment and then continued, "That's right, Henry Buckle. He had been refusing his food and had insisted that he couldn't go back and fight – at the very suggestion, he took a knife to his leg and tried to cut it off. He wasn't successful of course. Only a few days after that incident, I went to see how he was progressing and he had vanished. I spoke to Master Quinn and he said that the boy had insisted that he was ready to fight and had been sent back to the frontlines that morning.

"I'm far from a professional, but that boy was not in any kind of state to be sent back, and it made me sick to the stomach at the thought of it. Master Quinn told me that he had spoken to Henry himself and that the boy had decided that if he was going to die – he wanted to die a hero for his country and not as a coward, hiding in a corner."

"I'm sorry Mother. That must have been very difficult for you," Baden said.

"It was – but not as difficult as it was for poor Henry Buckle and his family – wherever they may be," his mother replied.

Mary tugged sharply on Baden's wrist as his mother left the room. The pain was immense, but he breathed deeply and avoided the embarrassment of showing his discomfort. He said:

"Thank-you for coming, it was stupid of me to undo all of your good work. I'm going to need a fully functioning wrist. I re-enlisted yesterday; I'm going to Ireland."

"Good for you," Mary replied. "You need something to take your mind off Emlyn and you are a soldier. I'm returning to Montpellier to study medicine at the university. Loxley is too small for the likes of us."

Baden knew that she of all people would understand. She had seen and endured enough horrors of her own to appreciate what these other people never could.

"I want to stay here until we get to the bottom of all of this and then I'm leaving. I don't think I could live with myself if I didn't at least find out why Emlyn was taken away from me," Baden said.

"Well we have been presented with an opportunity much sooner than I imagined. The Earl and my Aunt Bett are celebrating their betrothal this evening at Clitheroe Manor and Malcolm and I have been invited as their guests of honour."

"Isn't your Aunt Bett a little old for the Earl?" Baden asked.

"She's double his age – but that's not the interesting part. Malcolm has given the staff the night off and we will be gone well into the night. You'll have plenty of time to break into Malcolm's office."

"Me?"

"It's the perfect opportunity – the Hall will be empty. Malcolm's office has two windows – he never locks them because he thinks that they are too high up for anyone to reach. All you need is a ladder and then you're in. I've already been in there; he keeps his drawers locked so you will need to bring something to force them open. It's our best chance to find out what he's hiding," Mary explained.

"All right; I'll do it. What time will the house be clear?"

"Eight o'clock at the latest – I heard the staff are planning an outing to Sheffield for the evening – Godfrey is chaperoning – so you should have at least four hours," Mary said.

"It sounds like a plan," Baden replied.

Mary gave one final pull on his arm. He heard a small crack and she said, "That should do it."

She re-bandaged his wrist and stood up to leave.

She said "I have brought some extra bandages for when you need to change them. If your mother can't stomach it, I'm sure your father can. And Baden, be careful tonight."

*

Baden had realised too late that he didn't have access to a ladder that was tall enough to reach the roof of Loxley Hall. He figured that he would have looked a touch suspicious wondering through town with a twenty-foot ladder under his arm anyway.

By the time he arrived, Loxley Hall was shrouded in darkness and it was only by the measly amount of light provided by the near full moon that he could measure his foot fall. Baden walked around the back of the building and descended the stairs to the servant's entrance. He took the crow-bar, which had been concealed up his sleeve and hooked it into the gap between the door jamb and door. With one swift movement the door sprang open. He was in.

He made his way along the corridor, passing the servants' quarters, the kitchen and finally up the stairs. The house was quiet. Every time Baden had visited the Hall in the past, it had been such a hive of activity. The silence was interrupted by the creak of the stair beneath his foot. He paused instinctively and looked around. He was still alone.

He reached Malcolm's office door; it was locked. He considered prising it open, but with one door already forced, he didn't want to raise any more suspicion. He turned and entered the room behind him.

Baden had been in the sitting room many times throughout his childhood and its familiarity washed over him as he made his way across to the window. It was Emlyn's favourite room and it held the grand piano which Emlyn used to always play. He smiled at the thought of her sitting there playing her self-taught, self-composed tunes. She truly was gifted.

He picked up the golden cushion from the window seat and flung it onto the floor. The window swung open easily and from there he climbed the sloping roof, to the plateau and lowered himself down the other side.

Malcolm's window was unlocked just as Mary had promised. Baden swept across to Malcolm's desk and took out his hook pick and torsion wrench. He settled himself onto one knee and went to work picking each of the four drawer's locks. It was the deepest of the drawers and the final one opened, which held Baden's interest.

In it, he found a stack of files. He lifted out the top one and opened to the first page. It was a file from the Loxley Hall convalescence hospital, for a Corporal James Doyle. The soldier had been suffering from tremors and night terrors. His doctor had noted his refusal to go back to the frontlines and on the second last page was a report on Corporal Doyle's attempt at suicide. They had found him hanging by the neck from his shoelaces, which were tied to the door handle of his room. He was discovered by one of the nurses, unconscious and close to death.

Baden turned to the final page and dropped the file in horror. There staring back up at him was a discharge form, ordering Corporal James Doyle back to the frontline and it was signed by Captain Baden Hope and seconded by another man, whose signature he could not discern.

Baden had signed innumerable forms during his time in the Army – but he couldn't believe that he had ordered such a vulnerable soldier back to the bitterness of war. The poor chap wouldn't have stood a chance and Baden's conscience was running out of storage space, especially for his own errors in judgement.

He examined the sheet and the signature more closely and although it was a very good forgery, it couldn't have been him who had signed it. It was dated July of 1917. For the entire month of July and half of August that year, he and his troop had been cut off from his platoon and they had locked down their position and fought for their lives.

The next file was for a Corporal Cedric Tuppel, who displayed similar symptoms to Corporal Doyle and yet another failed suicide attempt. Baden flicked to the final page and again, there was his signature on the discharge form with orders to return to the front. All the files had his forged signature. He counted through them – there were 27 in all. The final file he encountered was that of Henry Buckle. It was the boy his mother had spoken of and it was exactly as she had said – he did not want to fight anymore, he tried to cut off his leg with a blunt knife and then there was his discharge form and orders.

He folded Henry's file and shoved it into his jacket pocket. With the other files returned safely to their drawer, Baden climbed back out onto the roof. Instead of returning inside, he lowered himself sideways to the old chimney stack. When they were teenagers, he and Emlyn would always sit there together and smoke and kiss and laugh at the world.

He reached into the chimney and pulled out the familiar bundle – a packet of Gold Flakes and Emlyn's father's golden lighter. He lit a smoke. Baden felt a sudden flash of rage. If this was the evidence which Emlyn had found, then she had died thinking that he was somehow involved.

Something was wrong here and someone had dragged his name into it and somehow Emlyn was dead because of it. Baden was now convinced that it was Malcolm who was responsible for all of this – whatever the hell 'all of this' was.

***

Mary Loxley had had a very long night. Having to sit in the same room as Lord Southby had been hard enough at times over the past week – but watching him and a lascivious septuagenarian parading their sham engagement in front of a room full of dignitaries, was too much to bear. She was quite certain that the Earl's father didn't have this in mind when he made it a term of Lord Southby's inheritance that he must be married by the age of thirty-five or he would lose everything.

Mary did have to admit however, that anything that made that old pervert roll in his grave couldn't be all that bad.

'How embarrassing for them all?' she thought to herself.

Mary ascended the stairs and made her way to her chambers. She paused at Malcolm's office door and wondered how Baden's mission had gone. As she pressed her ear lightly against the door, listening for any sign of a disturbance, she felt a light breeze on the back of her neck. The sitting room window was wide open and the curtains were flapping gently in the breeze.

'That's odd,' she thought to herself as she entered the room.

The cushion had been thrown onto the ground. She leaned out of the window and looked around.

"Nice night?" came Baden's inquiring voice from somewhere to her side.

She leaned further out of the window and saw Baden leaning against the chimney stack.

"She died thinking I was heartless bastard," Baden said.

"That's not true," Mary replied. "What are you still doing here anyway?"

"It doesn't matter anymore. Emlyn's gone and she thought I was involved in all of this," he uttered.

"I don't understand – what did you find in there?" Mary asked.

"This," he took the file out of his pocket and tossed it to her.

She caught it, lay it on the window seat and listened as he explained all that he had found.

She waited until he had finished and then she asked, "If these soldiers weren't sent back to you on the front line, then where did they go?"

"I don't know and to be frank, I don't care," Baden said angrily.

He stood up gingerly from his position – clearly still hampered by his bruised coccyx – and he walked across the angled roof. He was within Mary's reach when both of his feet slipped. A look of dismay crossed his face as he tumbled down the steep slope of the roof. He clawed and grabbed but he couldn't maintain a grip on anything until he reached the eaves.

Mary jumped into action.

"Hold on Baden, I'll get something to pull you back up."

She snatched the nearest of the two royal green curtains and yanked on it until it ripped from its rod. Baden's face was already red and sweating from the effort it took him to pull himself up above the level of the roof. Mary rolled the curtain so that it resembled a thick rope and she used the tassels to tie off each end.

"I can't hold on much longer – my wrist," Baden shouted urgently.

Mary lowered the curtain down the slope of the roof.

"Once you get a firm hold on this I can pull you back up," she promised.

The curtain reached him and he seized it between his hands. He wrapped it around his uninjured wrist to give himself more support. Mary pulled with all of her might, but Baden was too heavy for her.

"Hold on, I can get some help!" she exclaimed.

She looked down at him and saw the look on his face. It told her everything that she needed to know before he even spoke. He started to unravel the curtain which supported him as he said:

"Mary, it's too late, I can't do it. I don't want to do it. Maybe it's better this way – now I can be with her."

Mary saw the look of resignation in his eyes and she knew that she wasn't going to be able to save him.

"Emlyn chose you Baden – I read it in her diary, she was going to be with you."

"All I ever wanted was to love her. Goodbye Mary."

The last that Mary saw of Baden was his fingers letting go of the curtain. He was her ally and a friend; but Mary knew that she couldn't have fought the inevitable and as suddenly as she had found him and tried to save him from himself, Baden Hope was lost.

14. DEEPER AND DEEPER SHE GOES

Detective Sergeant Diane Pridis wasn't feeling like much of a detective at all. She had spent the entire day running around in circles and felt as though she had taken several steps backwards in her pursuit of the loan sharks. To make matters worse she was due to give Tilman a report on her day's activities, and Pridis had nothing to give her, despite all her hard work.

It was as though she was searching for a shit in a sewer – they all looked the same and smelled the same – but she had to get her hands dirty, sifting through the cesspool to find the right one, and so far, she hadn't even come close.

Pridis flicked off her computer screen, leaned back in her chair and stretched her arms high above her head. She breathed in deeply and stifled a yawn. She hadn't been home in two days and she could feel the fog of fatigue slowly encroaching upon her consciousness. Pridis opened her drawer and took out her pill bottle. She contemplated the little, blue tablets inside and gently rolled the bottle back and forth across the palm of her hand. Even though she had broken almost all of her promises to Vicki, she was still being careful not to overdo it; not like the last time.

Pridis placed the bottle back and resolved to go home after she had spoken to Tilman – a good, night's sleep was exactly what she needed; a fresh start for the new morning.

Her phone rang.

"DS Pridis," she said wearily into the receiver.

"Hey Pridis, do you have a minute?" came Inspector Bliss' silky voice through the phone.

"For you Inspector, definitely," she replied.

The last time they had spoken, he had promised to help her out with the loan sharks and she was hoping that his source had found something, anything, that she could use.

"It's turned out to be a lot more complicated than I first thought out here and I'm not sure what to make of it just yet. We've found more bones, but I won't know exactly what's going on until Royal finishes his examination. But there's something else that's bothering me and I need you to look into it for me," he said.

"What is it?" Pridis asked, her pen already hovering over her opened notebook.

"The constable who lives here at Loxley Hall – he was best friends with John Quinn. They studied together at Radley college – a boarding school in Oxfordshire. It strikes me as odd, that he went to such an exclusive school on a scholarship, and after more than 15 years on the force he is still a police constable. It doesn't make sense and with these bones turning up – I want to know how deep this all runs."

"You think this PC is involved?" Pridis asked.

"I'm not sure yet – but if you can do a little digging for me – find out why he hasn't progressed further in the force; follow your instincts and see what you can come up with," he replied.

"What's his name?"

"Eric Pearson," he answered.

"I'll get on to it straight away, Inspector," Pridis pronounced.

She was just about to hang up the phone when he said, "Oh and before I forget, I've got my source on the job about those loan sharks. As soon as I hear from him, I'll let you know."

"Thanks Inspector, I've been banging my head up against dead ends all day."

She hung up the phone, just as DC Crocker approached her desk.

"What is it? Did you find Leung?" she asked

DC Crocker shook his head and said, "No not yet, but the missing security guard just walked in the front door and he wants to speak to the person in charge. Tilman is in with the Super, so I thought you might like to have a crack at him first."

"Perfect – put him in interview room one and I'll be there in a few minutes," she replied feeling for the first time that day as if she was finally getting somewhere.

DC Crocker left and Pridis delved back into her drawer. She needed to be fully alert if she was going to get anywhere with this. She placed two Adderall tablets on her tongue and threw her head back, hard. She flicked through her notebook to the interview with the security guard's boss – Rory Hicks – and she refreshed her memory.

Pridis waited until she felt her sharpness begin to return, and then she made her way to the interview room.

*

Jürgen Sampson was nothing at all like Pridis had pictured. He sat there, across the table from her, hunched over and looking at them nervously, through his greasy, blonde dreadlocks. As DC Crocker detailed the formalities of the interview, Sampson anxiously clamped his thumbs in his fists.

After DC Crocker had finished, Pridis began, "So where were you on Wednesday night? Why didn't you show up for your shift?"

With a quivering voice he answered, "I had nothing to do with what happened in that factory. I needed the money and they said that all I had to do was pull a sickie. I didn't know anyone was gonna get hurt."

"Who told you to call in sick?" DC Crocker asked.

Sampson sat there, thumbs still clasped, contemplating the question. He had black bags under his eyes and he looked as though he hadn't slept in at least a week. Pridis couldn't tell if this was a side-effect of his perpetual night shifts or whether his guilty conscience had cast a shadow over his ability to sleep.

Pridis added, "We don't blame you for any of this, we just want to know about the people who encouraged you to take the night off. How helpful you want to be is up to you; but just remember that anything that you give us now will look favourable when it comes time to deal out the charges."

At the mention of charges, Sampson straightened his back, furrowed his brow and laid his hands flat on the table. He cleared his throat and with a steady voice he said:

"I told you I had nothing to do with this. These two guys came to my house on Wednesday arvo, when I was getting ready for work, and they offered me 500 quid to stay home. I didn't ask any questions; it's a lot of money and I figured that there'd be no harm done. I was wrong – but you can't go pinning no charges on me for that."

"Impeding a police investigation, withholding key evidence in a murder inquiry and accessory to murder would be a good start," DC Crocker listed, counting the charges on his fingers.

"What do you want from me? I'll do anything? I can't go to jail," Sampson pleaded, grabbing hold of his thumbs once again and squeezing them so hard that his knuckles turned white.

"Do you have any contact details for these men? How did they pay you?" Pridis asked.

"They came to my house and paid me in cash," Sampson replied urgently. "They just said they wanted space to be able to talk to the guy without interruptions, that's all."

Pridis sighed and asked, "What about a description then? Did you get a good look at them?"

"The older guy had greying hair and a pencil moustache. The other one, had broad shoulders and a tattoo of a red and green snake on his neck. And come to think of it, as they were leaving the younger one called him 'Dad'. They did look sort of similar – they must be a father, son combo," Sampson replied. He took a sip of water and then said with more confidence, "One more thing. I looked out the window to make sure they were gone and I saw them take off in a red Mustang."

"Did you happen to get the number plate?" Pridis asked.

"No I didn't," Sampson said, his face full of apology.

"One last question," Pridis said, "Do you know who could have deleted all the footage from the cameras and the CCTV?"

"Rory Hicks is the only one with all of the codes – so if it wasn't him, then I don't know."

Pridis stood, walked to the door and said, "We'll be in touch – thanks for coming in. The fact that you volunteered will work in your favour."

*

There couldn't be too many father and son loan sharks, who drive red Mustangs,' Pridis thought to herself triumphantly as she made her way towards Tilman's office to give her an update.

Pridis felt bullet proof. Now that she had this information about the loan sharks there was nothing that Tilman could criticize about her performance so far. Pridis approached the office door and heard Tilman in the midst of a hushed and heated phone conversation. She stopped just outside the door and listened:

"We can't keep jumping every time he wants something – it was 8 years ago – we need to find a way out of this; I could lose my job or worse I could go to jail."

Tilman paused, listening to what the caller on the other end of the line had to say. She was sighing intermittently and at times it seemed she was unsuccessfully trying to break back in to the conversation. Then she pleaded:

"I've already let one witness go – who knows what connection he has to John Quinn anyway – and really I don't give a shit. He can't ask us to do this – he's taking it too far – I mean I hate Bliss as much as anyone, but not enough to let *this* happen."

She paused again and then spat, "Well you can tell Luke that I'm out."

Tilman slammed down the receiver. The click-clack of her shoes caused Pridis to retreat down the corridor and duck around the corner. She took a moment to compose herself and then spun around.

Tilman was preoccupied as she walked past Pridis.

Pridis caught her by the arm and said, "You wanted an update?"

Tilman shook her head and said, "Not now, I'm busy," and she ripped her arm free from Pridis' grasp and jogged around the corner and out of sight.

Pridis was still stunned at what she had overheard. Tilman had all but confessed to letting Emily Baribel go before the Quinn case four years ago and now someone was planning something big with Inspector Bliss – so big that even Tilman didn't want to get involved.

She took her phone out of her pocket and tried to call Inspector Bliss to tell him that he was right about Tilman all along and to warn him about the apparent danger he was in – but his phone went directly to voicemail. She left him a message and figured that he was safer in Sheffield working on his bones than being there in London, and by now he'd be surrounded by other police officers and Doctor Trudeau.

Pridis marched into Tilman's office and picked up the phone. She checked the call logs and dialled the most recent number. It rang a couple of times and then a woman's voice answered.

"Marcus North and Associates, how may I direct your enquiry?"

Pridis hung up.

She wondered exactly how Tilman and John Quinn's lawyer were connected, and who could be blackmailing them and why. She was disappointed that she was only able to hear Tilman's side of the conversation, but she ascertained that they were being blackmailed for something which had happened 8 years before. If Pridis could find a connection between Tilman and Marcus North, then maybe she could bring down Tilman once and for all.

*

It was getting late. Pridis had been searching the databases for anything which could connect Tilman and Marcus North and had come up empty handed. She was going to have to think outside of the box on this one. If Tilman had wanted to cover something up, then she wouldn't have left any files on record for just anyone to stumble across. But Pridis had to try.

She massaged the crick, which was still in her neck from falling asleep at her desk the night before. She had promised herself that she would go home that night; if not for the sleep, then at least to have a decent shower and change her clothes. She wasn't looking forward to seeing Vicki – but she couldn't avoid her forever.

Pridis packed it in for the evening and made her way home. The drive was not a long one at that time of the night – most of the traffic had dissipated – and she was thankful that all the lights were off when she pulled up outside of her house. Vicki was either asleep or she wasn't there – either way it meant that Pridis was off the hook.

She opened the front door, careful not to make a sound. Her cat, Pockets, named for the little white patches on her black hips, brushed up against her ankles in greeting. Vicki's shoes were sitting next to the front door, so Pridis knew that she wasn't alone. She entered the kitchen, put on the kettle and tipped some dry food into Pockets' bowl.

Pridis rarely appreciated her flat as much as she did in that moment. It was spacious, reasonably priced and ever since Vicki had moved in, she had added a flair of colour; an art which Pridis had never mastered herself.

The kettle boiled, she flung her green tea bag into the cup and filled it with steaming hot water. Pridis hated green tea, but she figured that the health benefits outweighed the fifteen minutes of discomfort that her tastebuds had to endure every day. Her mind was still racing. She desperately wanted to nail Tilman, pay her back for all the torment of their past relationship – but she still had to wrap up the Quinn murder case and on top of that Inspector Bliss was relying on her to get him the information about PC Pearson.

She finished her tea, had a hot shower and readied herself for bed. Despite her long hours and severe sleep deprivation, Pridis was not tired and she knew exactly why. She should never have taken two Adderall tablets at once – one was normally enough to keep her flying for hours and at this rate she was never going to get any rest.

She sat down next her book shelf and swished her robe to one side.

Since Vicki had moved in the books were in a jumble and she had been meaning to fix it. She removed the books and set about rearranging them by author and genre. The stack of mystery novels sat higher than the rest.

"'C' for Christie, 'G' for George, 'J' for James,' she recited in her head as she heard the door open behind her.

Vicki stood in her blue night dress, holding a glass of water, her blonde hair tousled as if she had been having a rough night's sleep. As their eyes met, Pridis could see the disappointment painted across Vicki's face. Without a single word, Vicki turned her back on Pridis and left the room.

'*Busted*,' Pridis thought to herself as she pushed the book she was holding back onto the shelf.

She considered following Vicki to the bedroom and trying to explain – but she knew it would be fruitless. No excuse would be enough right now to placate her; they had been through it all before and last time Pridis had made all the promises, which in this moment, lay broken and shattered all around her.

It didn't take Pridis long to dress and reapply her make-up before she headed back out to the Yard. This time she brought a spare outfit along with her, so she could give Vicki enough time and space to cool down. She had so much work to do anyway, that being at home seemed like a waste of her precious time.

The computer screen flicked on and she logged in.

She mumbled to herself, "I'm going to find a link between those two, if it's the last thing I do."

After fifteen minutes, Pridis walked across to Inspector Bliss' office. She took a clean coffee mug from his side table and sat down at his desk. His old chair was surprisingly comfortable. She opened his bottom drawer and pulled out his bottle of Chivas Regal. She poured out a double and shot it down in one gulp. The warmth trailed down the back of her throat and into her stomach.

She picked up the bottle and took it back to her desk. She put another pill in her mouth, raised the bottle to her lips and swallowed it down.

'If Vicki's going to accuse me of fucking up, I may as well give her something to be mad about,' Pridis thought as she defiantly took another swig.

15. A SOLEMN AFFAIR AT LOXLEY

Since the night of Baden's death, Mary Loxley had been caught up in a whirlwind of organisation, interspersed with moments of intense grief. It was a feeling that she was not used to and every time that she caught herself in a moment of sorrowful reflection, she chided herself and threw herself further into the work of organising Baden's funeral.

Mary had been accustomed to death. Every day that she had spent on the frontlines she was surrounded by it; covered in the stench of it. And after a time she had come to accept it and all the horrendous ways in which it could arrive. She had been numbed by the endless seas of faceless soldiers who had flooded through her care – most of the time with no hope of survival; their grim fates long ago sealed by the careless decisions of others.

But this time it was different.

In war, death was expected. It was a very part of the fabric of war – young men throwing themselves from the trenches, row after row, in the name of their countries and for their cause. But for Mary, to come home and to stare death right in the face and what's more, to feel responsible for it; was more than she could bear.

And that was the crux of the issue. As much as she knew that Baden was already on his own fast track to self-destruction, she couldn't help but feel responsible for his death.

She knew his state of mind; she knew that he could never have lived a life without Emlyn and still she gave him the tools to finish the job he had started earlier that same week; she sent him onto a God damned roof full of memories. What was she thinking?

She took out Emlyn's snuff box and considered it for a moment. She had given the box to her sister on her seventeenth birthday – Mary had picked it up in London on her way home for her summer break from Rodean. It was the last birthday that they had shared together and it was the last time that Mary had been truly happy.

She took a pinch of the snuff and snorted it deeply. She teetered for a moment and then steadied herself. Everyone else was down at breakfast, but she wouldn't be able to stomach it. Her appetite had already been waning before all of this had happened and since, it had petered out completely.

She stepped into her dress and struggled to reach the zipper at the base of her back. When she finally zipped it up, she noticed that it hung loose at her hips and around her breasts. Had she really lost so much weight since the last time she had worn it?

She picked up Henry Buckle's file, which lay open in front of her. She had been over it again and again – everything Baden had told her, everything in the file – and still none of it made sense. Twenty-seven files, twenty-seven soldiers, all with discharge forms, orders to join Baden's company back on the frontlines and each accompanied by their very own suicide attempt.

Either Malcolm was sending unfit soldiers back to fight in order to plump up his statistics and make his hospital's performance appear better than it actually was, so he could bask in his own imagined glory – or there was something much more sinister going on there; something which Cecil Watson had borne witness to.

There were more questions than answers and Mary was no closer to determining what had happened to Emlyn, let alone Cecil Watson and potentially 27 soldiers. She closed Henry's file, folded it together and shoved it in the inside pocket of her jacket. She would deal with all of that later; today wasn't about any of that. Today was the day that Loxley was to bury a hero, and Mary was to say goodbye to her friend;

the man, who if all had gone as it should have done all those years ago, she would have been proud to call her brother.

*

Mary waited impatiently in the entrance hall for the rest of the household so that they could walk the short distance to the church together. Louise, Martha and Winnie were putting the final touches on the preparations for the wake – which was to be held there at the Hall – and then they joined Mary, to wait for the others. Considering Addie's continued absence and the vast shadow of death which had been cast upon them all, they had done a very good job of it.

Malcolm and Aunt Bett came down the stairs together, followed by Godfrey, Granville and lastly Lord Southby – who was still attempting to tie his own bow-tie, a task which seemed completely foreign to him.

"Oh bugger," he mumbled to himself as his latest attempt failed miserably.

His bride-to-be stepped up to him and said, "Let me do it, my child."

Aunt Bett swatted the Earl's hands away and tied the bow-tie in seconds. She eyed Godfrey disapprovingly for allowing the scene to continue in the public realm without offering any assistance and she pinched the Earl's buttocks as she sent him on his way.

Mary felt nauseated watching the two of them together. She couldn't wait for them to leave and she hoped that it would be sooner rather than later. She was so sick of looking at their smug faces; one gouging her claws into the title and money that she'd always connived to obtain and the other laying claim to his inheritance through a fraudulent marriage to a woman he knew would soon be dead and decaying, deep in the earth.

It was ironic really – the previous Earl had such a penchant for younger things and here was his son, marrying someone old enough to be his grandmother.

The fresh, cool air improved Mary's disposition as they made their way along the winding path through to the front gates of Loxley Hall. The smell of autumn leaves filled Mary's nostrils and calmed her stomach. The sun was low and as she looked upward towards the pale blue sky, a kestrel, with its chestnut coloured plumage swept down into the branches high above.

When they reached the church, Mary noticed a ragtag bunch of fellows had joined together out the front. From a distance she saw that they were all clutching glasses and toasting a lone tumbler which sat filled to the brim in the middle of their circle; the glass that would never again be emptied.

They drank together and then a stocky, unshaven man walked around and refilled their glasses. He called for quiet and as though he were the star of a Shakespearian play, he recited dramatically:

"Together we stood in the trenches of war,
Bound forever over what we fought for,
Soaked in mud and in the blood of others,
The Captain and my band of brothers.

"We fired at the enemy one after another,
Trying to forget that they too had a mother,
Sometimes in the blackness we wanted to shout,
And then we would hear another bullet ring out.

"In the darkness of battle, the fatigue setting in,
Our hope slowly fading, the company wearing thin,
Feeling as though we were lost to the fight,
The Captain led us bravely into the light.

"The Captain, our hero, he was the man upon who,
Without him we would never have made it through,
Battle scarred and weary to England we returned,
Our bond branded on our souls, forever burned.

"As a company of men, here we stand,
Raise it up dear boys, glasses in hand,
Drink up my fellows, our time is short,
Captain's in heaven, holding down the fort."

The young men threw their heads back in unison, drinking the decadently, amber liquid down in one gulp. They clapped rowdily as the stocky man did his round with the bottle once more.

"Savages," Aunt Bett said turning her nose up as they walked past the crowd.

Upon hearing this, Mary strode towards the ring of soldiers.

"Where do you think you're going, young lady?" Aunt Bett called from behind.

Mary ignored her and joined the group. The man with the bottle gave her a glass and filled it. Either side of her she felt the shoulders of Godfrey and Granville. And then came the others. Once they each had a glass, Mary raised it and shouted:

"To Captain Hope – may he have found what he was looking for, in amongst the stars."

Everyone drank and the soldiers clapped. When Mary turned back around, there was Aunt Bett standing alone and indignant. A rush of adrenaline pulsed through her and the whiskey steeled her for what was to come as she threw the glass down onto the ground; glass shards scattered at her feet.

The bells of the church began to toll. They made their way inside; the soldiers jostled noisily through the pews. Once the service began however, they gave their full attention to the reverend. Mary could see the respect which they held for their Captain.

The service was a solemn affair, with prayers and speeches read by family and those who knew Baden well from Loxley town. When it came time for the speech from his army colleagues, the stocky man, who had earlier recited the poem and had happily filled Mary's glass, stepped forward once again.

Considering the amount of alcohol that Mary was sure had already been consumed, he carried himself steadily and resolutely.

He cleared his throat, giving a hearty cough and said, "Captain was a hero. Not just because he won an award or was acknowledged for his bravery by those of you who know nothing of war, but because of the actions that we saw out there every single day. He was our leader. He was strong in the face of impossible battles and he wore the responsibility of our lives like a badge of honour pinned proudly to his chest. He never took a backwards step from anything or anyone.

"We followed him willingly and with all of our hearts into the depths of hell, and he did everything in his power to lead us back from the perils and into the arms of safety, and back to our families and our homes. He did what he had to do in the face of the darkest of times and he did it with integrity. Every one of us who is here today, has him to thank for still being alive. He was a hero and he will never be forgotten."

He looked up to the sky and for the first time Mary could hear a frailty permeate his voice as he said, "Rest in peace Captain, you will remain forever in our hearts."

He stepped down to the wailing applause of the rest of his companions. Mary watched the young man return to his seat. She looked at the soldiers. They were all so young, yet they looked as though they had already lived a thousand turbulent lives. It wasn't fair. How could the world have been complicit in bringing such brutality and depravity upon an entire generation of young men and women? How could God have let all of this happen?

Her eyes shot to the front of the room. On the wall, the crucifix was bearing a particularly pained Jesus, cruelly hung by the flesh of his wrists, tormented and suffering violently at the hands of his subjugators. His face strained upward with such agony cast upon it – and there upon his features, her question was answered; any father who could do that to their own child didn't have the capacity for mercy.

A tear rolled down Mary's cheek. She held her breath and fought to hold back the dam that had welled behind her eyes. The lightest of touches brushed her arm and Malcolm offered her his handkerchief.

She accepted it and dabbed her eyes.

Baden's parents sat in the very front row. Mrs Hope had her face completely covered with a black veil. Mary knew that her eyes would be bloated and her face blotched underneath it, from the hours spent crying and mourning the loss of her child for the second time and barring a divine miracle, the final time.

Her gaze shifted to the town constabulary, which was made up of the lone officer, Sergeant Markson. He had attended Loxley Hall after Baden's death and despite his short comings as an officer of the law, he had restored some kind of order to the place.

Mary had been sitting silently in the corner of the drawing room, trying desperately to come to terms with what had occurred, while Malcolm raged about the house, shouting over and over again:

"What is everyone going to think? Why was Baden even up on my roof to begin with?"

Aunt Bett had said, "Good riddance; the boy was an ignoramus. At one point he asked me for Emlyn's hand. *Him* marry *my Emlyn*; perish the thought."

Mary had exploded and yelled, "At least he loved her, you stupid, old fool. It seems everyone around here has forgotten what that means. And maybe if you had allowed them to marry, they would both still be alive."

"Don't be stupid, girl," Aunt Bett replied. "Marrying Malcolm was the best thing for her – I can't help it that she killed herself."

"But why the hell was he out on *my* roof?" Malcolm had continued, ignoring everybody else and wringing his hands exaggeratedly.

"Reminiscing I expect," Markson had intervened in a quiet and steady voice; his sudden appearance stopped everybody in their tracks. "When I spoke to him after your poor wife's passing, the young captain told me of a time when he would sit out on the roof with your late wife – when they were much younger, of course; before the war, you see." He turned to Mary and asked, "Is that what happened, my dear? He was out there ruminating and then he slipped on his way back inside?"

Markson's voice was slow and he sounded like a dear, old

grandfather who you wouldn't want to disappoint. Mary had wanted to keep the break-in into Malcolm's office a secret and so she had agreed with Markson. It was the truth, she had supposed. She didn't have to tell them that it was she who had sent Baden up there and she who had allowed him to give up his grasp on this life.

Sergeant Markson was quick to classify it as 'Death by Misadventure,' and return as rapidly as he could to the quiet life that everyone in Loxley knew he was so desperately after. He was not long from retirement and he had come to Loxley after the war to see out his tenure – quietly. So far that hadn't worked out so well for him – but he had done his damnedest to ensure that his investigations were as swift as possible.

A few days after Baden's death, Mary had confronted the Sergeant about the possibility that Emlyn was murdered and he had brushed her aside as if she were the town lunatic, escaped from the asylum.

'*Useless*,' Mary had thought to herself within moments of meeting the Sergeant and so far, he had yet to prove her initial assessment wrong.

*

It was the sound of the bells resonating throughout the church hall which pulled Mary from her thoughts and landed her squarely back into the present. A quarter of the troop of drunken soldiers were acting as pall bearers and were already halfway down the aisle with Baden's coffin.

Aunt Bett was busily instructing people to move across to Loxley Hall for the wake. She had Lord Southby clasped by the hand and she wasn't going to let him escape from her grip. Although his demeanour was calm – which was a talent of the aristocracy – beads of sweat gathered at his temples and his pupils were distended. There was only so much that good breeding could account for and he was clearly in supreme discomfort at the fact that he was permanently bound to this woman.

"The rat finally has his cage," Mary mumbled to herself with a broad smile as she watched Aunt Bett drag the Earl along behind her, down the aisle and out the front door.

She turned back around to find a man standing in front of her. He was wearing tortoise-shell glasses and his rounded shoulders told Mary that he was an academically inclined fellow. She recognised him as having been with the group of soldiers and so she asked:

"Why aren't you with the others? I thought it was an honour to carry your Captain out to his final resting place."

"I know this may not be the best time – but the Captain visited me in London and asked me to look into something for him," the man began.

"You must be Gus," Mary said, lightening her tone to make up for her initial severity.

She offered him a cigarette.

He declined and replied, "I am and you're Lady Mary; the one the Captain was working with."

"How did you know?" Mary questioned as she held up a match and puffed on her smoke until it was lit.

"One thing that I've learned over time is that the smaller the town, the bigger the mouths," Gus answered with a smile. "After the Captain left me the other day, I decided to keep digging. The Captain seemed so certain that there was something in those files and I didn't want to disappoint him. There are so many files at the War Office and they are not always so easy to locate."

"And?" Mary said, having trouble disguising her impatience.

"I found something," Gus said, sitting in the pew in front of Mary and continuing in a hushed voice. "The Captain told me that it was Malcolm Quinn who operated the hospital and so when I did my initial search, I kept to the parameters that we set and the names that I was given. But there was someone else who was heavily involved at the hospital – and from the files they did just as much as our Mr Quinn."

"Do I have to start pulling out your teeth?" Mary asked, raising her eyebrows.

"I've always enjoyed an element of drama," Gus shrugged. "I don't get much of a chance for theatrics in at the War Office." He smiled and continued, "Does the name Betty Clovely mean anything to you?"

"Aunt Bett? Volunteering at the hospital?" Mary said, so surprised, that she leapt to her feet and began to pace. "But that's absurd – she's never done a day's work in her life."

"It's all there in the files. She was at Loxley Hall the entire time and she assisted Malcolm in the operations and the finances," Gus answered.

"Ah money; now we come to her real expertise," Mary said. "This does add another dimension to my investigation. Thanks Gus; Baden did say that you were his best."

"I should be getting along now. The lads will be wondering where I've gotten to and they can't start until we're all there."

"You're not coming to the wake?"

"We'll be around – but we have some serious business to attend to first," Gus said as he made for the door. He turned just before he exited and asked, "He really said that I was his best?"

She nodded and he ran out of the door, his shoulders less rounded than they were a moment earlier.

*

Mary walked along the path back towards Loxley Hall. She wasn't sure whether this new piece of information would lead to anything substantial, but it gave her another avenue to explore.

Aunt Bett loved champagne and Mary anticipated that at the wake she would have her fill of it and then Mary could question her in an unguarded state. But first she would need to find a way to wrest the Earl from her Aunt's clutches. Aunt Bett wasn't likely to open up about anything untoward in front of Lord Southby – she wouldn't want to risk her impending matrimony.

'I could always land another knee on that bastard's groin; it's not as though he'll be having children with that dried-up old prune,' she thought to herself.

As she entered the ballroom Mary's thoughts were interrupted by the approach of the stocky man who had been the troop's spokesperson for the day. Once again he was clutching a bottle.

"You give a good speech," Mary said as he came to a standstill next to her.

She could smell the whiskey, fresh and strong on his breath as he replied with a smirk, "Thanks Love. I'm ex-Corporal Georgey Dockrell; fighter, poet, bartender and milkman at your service."

He bent low, took her hand and kissed it gently.

"I don't think that's milk you've been pedalling today," she jibed.

"A little bit of sass – nice to see at such an event. The Captain would've hated such a show of pomp and sorrow, but he's not in a position to have much of a say in it," Georgey shrugged. "Have a drink with me," he said, swishing the bottle in the air and then ripping the cork out with his teeth.

Mary procured a glass and held it out for filling. Georgey obliged. She took a sip of the whiskey; it had a smoky flavour.

"I was there when he died – it was my fault that he was out on that roof."

Georgey replenished her glass, which she had emptied with one big gulp after her admission and he told her: "You listen to me Mary Loxley; he always did everything on his own terms and his death was no exception. He wouldn't have gone out onto that roof if it wasn't his own decision and there would have been nothing that you could have said or done to stop him. He was stubborn all right – you can't blame yourself. None of us do." Georgey sipped his whiskey and continued, "Do you know why he got awarded the Victoria Cross?"

"No, I don't. I suppose he did something awfully heroic," Mary replied.

"He saved my life and the lives of two others," Georgey said. "The three of us had been wounded and were lying, deep in the mud, in no-man's land. He sprung out of the trenches, and dragged each one of us back to safety, all the while, under enemy fire. If it wasn't for him, I would have died out there. He told me later, that bravery wasn't the reason he had decided to jump out of the trenches that night.

"It was your sister. He got a letter telling him that she had married someone else and he realised he had nothing else to live for. When he jumped out of the trench, he had hoped that one of those bullets would find him – put him out of his misery. But when he saw the three of us there, it spurred him into action and from that moment on, he put all his feelings for her into his responsibility for us – his men – and that was what saw us all through the war. It was your sister who had made him the way he was. He would never have been happy in this life without her and now they are together with God."

Georgey's words were little consolation for Mary; she would never be able to forget the role that she played in Baden's death, but it did make it clear to her that he had been suicidal for a lot longer than she had known. Maybe he couldn't ever have been saved.

"Thank-you Mr Dockrell for your kind words, they really do make a difference," she said.

Georgey made a move to leave and said, "The lads and I have a date with a case of whiskey and a bonfire."

"You will be missed."

"I'm sure you'll all get along well without us. It's company tradition," Georgey explained. He was distracted for a moment and then he asked, "Is that Billy Garrot over there? I saw you sitting with him at the service – he sure has done well for himself."

"I think you're mistaken – that's Malcolm Quinn; he's the man who married my sister; the one who stole the Captain's lover," Mary corrected.

"No – I'm sure of it. We lived in the same street in London; I'd know him anywhere," he answered as he waved in Malcolm's direction.

Mary turned to look at Malcolm and by the time she had turned back, Georgey Dockrell had been swept away in a sea of frenzied ex-soldiers who were ready to celebrate the life of Captain Baden Hope and all of those who were alive today because of him.

***

Malcolm Quinn leaned against the wall in the corner of the crowded ballroom. He raised his glass to his lips as he cast his eye across the sea of soldiers. He hadn't seen so many in the one place since he had run the convalescence hospital during the war and he for one, couldn't wait to see the back of them.

'What it must be like to be such inferior creatures,' he thought to himself.

For Malcolm knew that he was more in the hierarchy of man than they and he welcomed the responsibility of it. There were not many who could have done what he did during the war – but nobody appreciated it. Everybody was too absorbed in doting upon the returned soldiers as though they were Gods, to notice the real heroes of the war.

Yes; Captain Hope had been a brave and honourable man – but it was his brute strength and not his intellect which had seen him through the war – and where was the elegance in that?

Malcolm knew that Baden was Emlyn's first great love and he was also shrewd enough to know that women very rarely moved past reminiscences of their first lovers. But Malcolm had never felt threatened by him – not at all. He was glad that Baden was gone however; Malcolm had already been formulating a plan in case Baden had decided not to leave well enough alone. He knew that Baden had been asking questions about Emlyn's death and he couldn't have him poking around the Hall unchecked. But fate had taken care of it for him.

'What was he doing out on that roof anyway?' Malcolm pondered once again.

He hadn't accepted the conclusion that Baden was out there contemplating a lost love. It just didn't stand to reason. Although, he knew it was a place of refuge that Emlyn went to quite regularly. At least now there was one less impediment to him, Malcolm Quinn, attaining the life that he most richly deserved.

He had come a very long way from his humble beginnings in London and after many years of work, he was finally on the cusp of being a legitimate part of high society – a place where he knew he belonged. Aunt Bett and Lord Southby were soon to depart and complete the preparations for their marriage, and with the departure of Mary, Malcolm would finally be free to live the way that he wanted.

His eye was drawn towards Mary as he contemplated his impending freedom. She really did share a resemblance to Emlyn – especially when she wore a dress as she was that day. He then noticed who she was talking to. He had recognised him during the service, but he hadn't thought that Georgey Dockrell would be stupid enough to say anything to anyone around here.

Georgey gave him a wave and Mary looked in his direction. Malcolm returned the smile, but on the inside, he felt a surge of panic. He needed to find out exactly what Georgey Dockrell had told Mary, because if word got out about who he really was and where he had come from – then his entire world would crumble down around him and he would lose everything that he had worked so hard to gain.

16. DEM BONES

The beauty of the sunrise that morning particularly struck Andy Bliss as he stood there, under the pink, hued clouds, which were mixed with wisps of orange and speckled blue. He felt as though he were caught in a beautiful painting, and he admired the way the early morning sunshine was captured in the Hall's windows. The warmth of the rising sun, penetrated through the coldness of the night, which had saturated his bones.

He was beginning to feel the fatigue of a long night without sleep, but he was spurred onward by the grim scene which had met his eyes the evening before. After he had climbed carefully through the darkness, down the old, wooden ladder, he had seen Royal standing there motionless, his torch held aloft, lighting up half of the claustrophobic chamber.

"What's taking you so long?" Andy had said as he reached Royal's side.

The air was thick and the smell of mildew had pervaded his nostrils. Royal stood silently, awe struck by the shelves that towered in front of him. Set upon each of the shelves were rows and rows of bones, all in neat, nest-like piles – each with their own egg-shaped skull in the centre.

The atmosphere had been stifling in that bunker. All the blood drained from his face and he had wanted nothing more than to escape into the fresh air of the night, but he had forced himself to stay in there with the bodies, or what was left of them, of those poor women; women he knew that John Quinn had stolen and abused and had done God knows what else with. This had gone beyond what Andy had ever thought that bastard capable of – he could feel an evil presence melting through every fibre of that crypt.

Andy took a long, deep breath and as he exhaled, he tried to drive the memory of the evening before out of his mind, glad that he was no longer underground. He took one last look at his technicolour sunrise and then he returned to the second tent which he had been using as a makeshift office throughout the night. The operation had ballooned from himself, Royal and Pearson, to an additional team of eight SOCOs, a couple of PCs and a newly minted Detective Constable, DC Cross, all from West Bar CID.

Andy picked up the manila folder which he had been reading earlier and returned it carefully to the safety of its transport container. The pages were already yellowed and the exquisite hand in which it was written, put Andy's own messy scrawl to shame. Andy figured, that in the one hundred years since it was written, it hadn't seen the light of day and he didn't want to be the one responsible for its disintegration.

The entrance of the tent flapped open and Royal marched in, clutching a fistful of loose-leaf papers. He hastily laid them out on the table in front of Andy. Royal had a look of vexation plastered across his face. It was a look which Andy had encountered many times throughout their friendship, and it most usually coincided with cases which caused Royal the highest levels of aggravation.

"I'm trying to work on multiple crime scenes down there and your officer waltzed in and almost ruined everything!" Royal exclaimed with the air of over-caffeination.

"I told the team to leave you to it until we get the all clear from you. I'll have a word with them. Who was it?" Andy asked.

Royal nodded with satisfaction at Andy's resolution and said, "It was that PC Pearson. You tell him from me, that if I see him in my bunker again, I can't be held responsible for what I might do. These scenes are difficult enough to read without him lumbering through them. I'll need his shoe impressions, finger prints and DNA so I can exclude his blunderings from my findings."

"His DNA and finger prints should already be on file – I'll get them sent across. And I'll have a talk to our PC Pearson – there's something I don't like about him and he hasn't been doing himself any favours with his sub-standard work throughout the night," Andy replied. "How's it going down there anyway – when can we start to remove the bones and get started on the identification process?"

"Removal is going to be a problem for some of the older bones. The child's skeleton is already quite degraded and I'm afraid that with further excavation it might disintegrate completely. I've already finished my preliminary report on it," Royal said as he pointed to a paper in the middle of the configuration which he had lain in front of Andy. He picked it up and perused it as Royal continued:

"I can say, with a small amount of confidence, mind you, that this skeleton belonged to a young boy. Normally it's very difficult to determine the gender of a prepubescent skeleton, however the fact that there has been significant degradation of the bones, signifies that they contain a lower mineral density which normally indicates a child of the male gender. Also, its right arm was severed from the elbow, but the bone is too degraded to match the cutting to any kind of tool. Preliminary aging, puts the bones at approximately 100 years of age, but I'll need to take a sample into the lab to get a more specific time frame. The boy himself, based on the skeleton's size, was somewhere between the ages of 7 and 10 years old."

"Your assessment is consistent with the case file that I've been reading," Andy replied. "I had DC Cross look into historical cases of missing children from the region and with the efficiency that I've only ever come to expect from you, old boy, he was able to find what I believe to be the corresponding case hidden deep in the archives from 1917. Surprisingly enough, they were able to get a murder conviction for it."

"What? Without a body? But what about the 'no body, no murder' law – I'm sure that was in play until at least the 1950s?" Royal questioned.

"The man who was found guilty of the murder was in possession of the boy's right arm," Andy said.

"I wouldn't have thought that an arm was sufficient evidence for a murder inquiry back then," Royal replied.

"It was – but given that the man who was convicted was unable to defend himself, it seems to me as though he may have been railroaded. Ignatius Finch was a patient at the convalescence hospital here at Loxley Hall during World War one. According to witness statements, he was completely catatonic and no one had seen him move a muscle until the day of Cecil Watson's disappearance, when he allegedly grabbed the boy's arm. The boy went missing that night and the next day, they found this Ignatius Finch fellow lying in the middle of a field, still catatonic and clutching Cecil Watson's severed arm," Andy explained.

"No; that doesn't hold any water with me," Royal said, his brow furrowed. "Men with a combat stress reaction to the extent of catatonia don't just jump out of bed all of a sudden."

"Maybe he was faking shell shock to get himself sent home and away from the frontlines," Andy countered.

"He wouldn't have gone to all of that trouble, to then risk being hanged for killing this little boy or being executed for cowardice for willingly abandoning his post. And why take the arm? No; I think that someone else killed this boy – whether it was an accident or not and they wanted it swept under the covers as quickly as possible. What better way than to frame up a man who couldn't defend himself and who had interacted, albeit fleetingly, with the child earlier that same day? No, I don't accept that this Ignatius Finch was the killer – there's more to it than that," Royal replied.

"Well, I can't see what *we* can do about it; a hundred years is a long time for any kind of evidence to survive – the best we can do is theorise – but Cecil Watson deserves peace and the least that we can do is try," Andy said.

"That we will do, my friend," Royal answered slapping Andy on the shoulder. "I should have more specifics for you tomorrow – it's going to take most of today to catalogue what we've found and perform some further analysis, but I can tell you a few things from my initial observations."

He showed Andy a hand drawn map of the bunker and said as he pointed to the different areas, "I identified 28 separate skeletons on these two shelves and 12 on another shelf, which was located here. There was also a lone skeleton crumpled in the corner, on the opposite side of the bunker.

"Firstly and most importantly, I've noted the differences between the shelves of bones. The 28 on the much older shelves, were placed in the same order and pattern for each set of remains – meticulous to the point of ritualisation. The 12 others, although still placed in piles, were laid out haphazardly."

"So you think that the bones were put there by different people?" Andy asked.

"It appears so," Royal confirmed. "Also, the preliminary aging of the bones supports that hypothesis too. The 28 seem to be from around the same time as our young Cecil Watson, whereas the 12 are much more recent – but without further testing I can't give an exact age on them. Also, every single skeleton – other than Cecil and the remains found in the corner – have one thing in common; all of the bones are unnaturally clean."

"What the hell do you mean by that?" Andy asked; he could feel his forehead crinkling.

"We couldn't find a trace of anything on them, other than dust. No residue of the flesh that should have decayed away, no remnants of hairs or clothing fibres, no nothing. Normally, at a minimum, the acids in the body fat leave some kind of trace as it did with the boy and the skeleton in the corner – but all of these others have nothing," Royal explained.

"You think someone dipped them in acid?" Andy asked.

"No, it's not acid – I'd be able to tell straight away," Royal countered. "It'll take some testing, but my first impression is that they were boiled."

"Boiled!? In water?" Andy half exclaimed and half questioned. "To get rid of evidence?"

"I won't know until I look further – sorry Andy. But we will get to the bottom of this – I promise," Royal replied.

Andy wasn't sure what to make of it, but he had determined to wait until Royal could give him some more answers and he knew that if anyone could find them, it would be his best friend.

"There is one final thing, for now," Royal added as he reached into the pouch on the side of his coveralls and took out a small, metal box. "I've dusted it for prints and checked for fibres and there was nothing," Royal said as he handed it to Andy.

Andy opened the box and peered inside. "Are you sure these are clean?" he asked taking a pair of gloves out of his pocket. Royal gave him a look of disapproval and Andy said with a smile, "Oh, right, I forgot who I was talking to."

Inside were a number of Polaroids. Andy removed them from the box and sifted through them. Each was a picture of John with his arm around a different woman. Andy didn't recognise the first two, but the third was a photo of Emily Baribel. Andy couldn't help but feel sick to the stomach at how he had let her down. He hadn't seen her since she had gone missing just before the trial four years earlier and he couldn't help but hope to God that she had not been reduced to a pile of bones, sitting forgotten at the base of that son of a bitch's backyard.

He put Emily's photo to the side and continued sorting through them. As he flicked through to the next photo, he felt a sudden jolt in his stomach and he dropped the remainder of the stack onto the table. Staring up at him was a photo of John Quinn, his smile as wide and white as the Cheshire cat's, with his arm around Jarmila. Andy's face ran hot and a rage boiled up from the depths of his stomach.

He hadn't seen Jarmila since that fateful night – the night that he had lost control of his anger – and he hadn't tried to contact her since; he told himself that it was out of respect for her, but he knew deep down in his soul that it was because he was so ashamed of what he had done. The sickening sound of the clatter of her tooth on the ground, had provided the sad soundtrack to the last four years of his life.

"Did you know about this?" Andy asked Royal as he picked up the photo and shoved it towards him.

"I checked the photos and the box for particulates, I didn't look at what was actually on them; that's your job," Royal replied matter-of-factly.

Andy ripped his phone out of his pocket and he dialled Jarmila's number.

"This number is disconnected," came the automated response on the other end of the line.

"Fucking brilliant!" Andy exclaimed as he hung up the phone.

He felt the pulse strengthen in his head. It was drumming as he dialled Pridis' number. It went through to voicemail. As he was leaving instructions for her to track down his ex-wife, he noticed another familiar face on the table in front of him.

He hung up, picked up the photo and said, "The bastard was stalking me – Jarmila and Carla."

"Who's Carla?" Royal asked.

"No one important, she's just a one-legged hooker that I used to know. It does give me some hope though – I've seen her since John was killed, so maybe some of the women in these photos are still alive," Andy replied.

"Maybe these were potential targets – some he abducted and others didn't fit his criteria and so he left them," Royal hypothesised.

A sense of urgency rushed through Andy's veins – he needed to know that Jarmila was safe – but there was nothing that he could do about it now; either she was dead, killed by his own obsession with John Quinn or she was alive and well and Andy was not even present in the most distant of her thoughts.

The flap of the tent rustled once again and Jordan, Andy's fellow 'inmate' at the conversion therapy retreat, entered holding a thermos in one hand and a tray of coffee mugs in the other.

"I heard you boys had been hard at it all night," he said and he placed the thermos and mugs on the table. "I thought you could do with some coffee. There's breakfast inside, if you're hungry. I'm Jordan and who might you be?" he asked honing his attention on Royal.

Andy noticed Royal's face lighten as he said, "I'm Doctor Royal Trudeau – but you can call me Roy," and he offered his hand to Jordan.

It was the first time, in the twenty or so years that they had been friends, that Andy had ever seen Royal shake anyone's hand. Maybe after a night of being exposed to the horrors of the crypt below, Royal had seen the folly of his phobia; we all end up the same way eventually, regardless of how careful we are and choices that we so agonise over.

Andy said, "I think I need to go inside and freshen up; it's been a long couple of days. Why don't you take a break Roy?"

Andy gathered up the Polaroids and walked out into the fresh morning air, leaving Royal and Jordan to their cups of coffee and each other's company. Maybe something good could come out of this after all.

***

Alex Dewill had had a horrid night's sleep. It wasn't just because of the unavoidable noise of the police tramping through the estate, nor was it individually due to her mattress being as hard and uneven as a piece of corrugated iron, or the permanent kind of coldness which had entered the unheated room and had been absorbed by her body gradually through the night. All of these circumstances, which had conspired against her intentions of sleep, still did not outweigh the fact that every time she closed her eyes, every time she approached the land of dreams, all she could see in her mind's eye was John covered in blood with a maniacal look in his eyes.

Not that she had ever seen John like that before – but it was the power of suggestion, a seed planted in her sub-conscious by that damned detective the night before, that had sent her imagination whirling into the realms of absurdity. John was a lot of things, but Alex still believed that her husband was not a murderer. There must be another explanation for the discovery down that embankment and

Alex had determined to find it.

It wasn't necessarily that she didn't think John capable of doing what he was accused of, but she couldn't live with the fact that if he was guilty – then that, in her mind, made her equally as responsible. She would have noticed something off about him, wouldn't she? Even with their different schedules and their increasingly separate lives, she would have known. They shared a bed for God's sake.

Alex reluctantly pulled herself out from under the covers. She shivered with the cold and gathered her clothing together. She entered the bathroom – which was across the hall – and she turned on the shower. She allowed it to run for a full 5 minutes, before she conceded that there was to be no relief from the cold that morning.

"Old houses," she mumbled to herself as she switched off the faucet, which had been spewing out ice cold water and then she changed into her outfit – unshowered and unimpressed.

Alex made her way down the stairs and into the entrance hall. She could hear the clanking of plates coming from her left and so she deduced that was the most likely location of the breakfast buffet. She wasn't feeling particularly hungry, she was even a little nauseated, but she needed something hot to warm her body up, before she succumbed to hypothermia.

Vanessa was in the room, clearing some dishes. At the end of the table sat Eric and Inspector Bliss. They hadn't noticed her entrance and so unchecked, Eric had said defensively:

"Look Inspector; it's my house and I wanted to see it for myself."

Inspector Bliss straightened his back and replied tersely, "Well, PC Pearson; it's my crime scene and you can't go roaming around where ever you like. I'm assigning you to the front gate from now on."

"You can't just cast me to the side like that, I used to be a detective. You need all hands on deck – I saw how many bones were down there," Eric replied sounding stung.

"The media is sure to hear about this soon and I don't want them coming in here. I need someone on the gate and your actions have proven that you can't follow orders – so that's what you get; you're lucky I'm not writing you up for this – although the only place you could be demoted to, is out of the force. One more thing, before you go to the gates, I need you to give one the SOCOs an impression of your boots."

Eric stood up, forcefully thrusting his chair backwards. He looked as though he wanted to say more, but instead he just said, "Right, Inspector; whatever you say," and then he walked towards the door. As he passed Alex, he whispered, "He's a right twat, that one," and she gave him a nod in agreement.

Alex didn't acknowledge Inspector Bliss. Instead she went directly to the buffet table and picked up a plate. Even just looking at the food, especially the scrambled eggs, made her want to vomit. There was some porridge in a pot at the end of the line and given the way her stomach had responded to everything else, she figured it to be a safe bet.

She ladled some onto her plate, drizzled it with honey and sprinkled cinnamon over the top of the mound and then sat at the table.

Vanessa re-entered the room and said, "Good morning dear, did you sleep well?"

"I did," Alex lied.

"I must apologise about the heating last night. The fire in the boiler went out and none of my boys were here to fix it for me. My dear Mark has recently returned however, so the heating and hot water should be back on presently," Vanessa informed as she placed more dishes onto the trolley and wheeled it slowly out of the room.

Alex spooned the porridge into her mouth and swallowed hard. She regretted putting the cinnamon and honey on it immediately, as she felt a lurch from deep within her stomach.

"You look pale – are you all right?" Inspector Bliss asked from across the table.

She stood, feeling woozy and said, with as much vitriol as she could muster, "Like you really care, Inspector. You can save your insincerity for someone who gives a shit."

"Of course I care," he replied. "It's only ever been your husband that I've been after."

"Yeah, well I suppose you're getting your jollies now, aren't you?" Alex spat.

"You think this is a joke? You think that I'd be taking any joy out of the murders of all of these women?" he said as he threw a stack of Polaroids across the table. He held up one of the pictures. "That's my fucking wife!" he exclaimed punching the table so hard that it shook.

"I had nothing to do with any of this," she said, turning from the table and making for the door.

"While you were ignoring your husband, he was out there murdering women – and when he finally got caught red-handed, you did everything in your power to hinder us."

"You had no evidence – you can't go putting your shit police work on me; you're the ones who lost the fucking witness," she shouted as she left the room.

Alex ran back up the stairs and made it to the bathroom just in time to throw up into the toilet. The bandaging on her face made it harder to clean herself up and so she ripped it off revealing her swollen, purple nose. She rinsed out her mouth; pain shot up the bridge of her nose as she spat the water into the sink, and she fixed her hair in the mirror. Her eyes were still blackened and they were bloodshot from her lack of sleep. Her face was even paler than her usual pallid complexion.

She heard the jingling of keys in the corridor outside and she steeled herself for a second encounter with Inspector Bliss. He had all but accused her of being responsible for John's actions and although she may have held herself to that level of accountability, Inspector Bliss had no right to place that kind of judgement upon her.

She burst out of the door and standing with key in hand was Matthew. Alex didn't know what came over her – it had been such a harrowing time for her since he had left her at Sheffield station. She ran to him and threw her arms around him. She felt his muscles tighten.

"I'm so glad you're here – when did you get in?" Alex asked.

"This morning," he answered shortly.

Alex stepped back and took a look at him. Something was different about him. She asked:

"What have you done to your hair?"

He put his hand through it and then said, "Gel."

She grabbed his other hand and took a closer look; it was covered in grease.

"Have you been doing some handy work?" she questioned.

"It's nothing – car trouble. Look, I need to straighten up – I'll be out in a few minutes," he replied and he unlocked the door and sidled quickly into the room.

She put her ear to the door and could hear Matthew bumping around the room.

"Always knees and elbows," she smiled to herself.

She called through the door, "I've got so much to tell you Matthew; it's been crazy here."

The door opened after a few more minutes and Matthew re-emerged. He had changed his clothes and had managed to lessen the effects of the gel on his hair.

He put his arm around her and said, "I'm glad you missed me," and he leaned in and kissed her forehead.

Although she still had her nose packed with gauze and her eyes were sore to the touch she took his head in her hands and she kissed him softly on the lips. He kissed her back, hard. She took his hand and lead him towards her bedroom. As she unlocked the door, she could feel him pressed up against the back of her, the writhing of his groin telling her everything that she needed to know.

Yes, she had just lost her husband, she was sleep deprived and she still felt nauseated, but she needed comfort, she needed warmth and most of all she needed the strong presence of a man deep inside of her.

17. CLOSING IN ON THE QUINNS

The morning after the wake for Captain Baden Hope saw everyone who had attended with a decidedly sore head. Aunt Bett had been left in charge of the ordering and had ensured that there was a much higher ratio of alcohol to food than was usual for such events. But the evening had not spun out of control until the arrival of Baden's company men, who had finished with their bonfire and whiskey and had come to see what else was on offer at the Hall. Their arrival had transformed a dull and depressing affair, into a real celebration of Baden's life.

Mary Loxley had retired to her bedchamber at first light that morning, after having out drunk most of the attendees and having had numerous unsuccessful attempts at trying to isolate and interrogate her aunt about her activities at the hospital during the war. She awoke after a short slumber, having quelled most of what was sure to be a monstrous hangover.

She propped herself up on the bed using her pillows. She felt queasy as she surveyed the room. Her dress from the day before had been flung across the chair which stood in front of the dresser. Her shoes were tossed haphazardly, with what she was sure was good intentions, towards the closet, and hanging on the back of the door was her blazer. The corner of Henry Buckle's file peeked out of the inside pocket.

She sipped from the glass of water which stood like an oasis on her bedside table and enjoyed the coolness of it, as it entered her overheated and dehydrated body. Once the water hit her stomach however, she immediately regretted her decision as a wave of nausea washed across her. She closed her eyes and used all her focus to overcome the unsettled feeling which swept through her body.

There was a feather-light knock on the door. Mary ignored it in the hope that whoever it was would give-up and go away. Moments later, there was a heavier, more urgent rapping on the door. Clear that this intrusion was unavoidable, Mary alighted from her bed and walked gingerly to the door. She opened it a crack and peered out into the corridor, leaning her head wearily against the door jamb.

Godfrey stood in the doorway looking as fresh as the new morning suggested he should be – however Mary had memories of Godfrey working the party until late into the night, and he would have risen early that morning to ensure that the house was in order before the new day. Godfrey descended from a long line of butlers, all of whom had served at Loxley Hall before him, and it had always been an honour for him to carry on his family's tradition. His professionalism was beyond reproach and it was on display in all its glory that morning, reflected in the crispness of his suit and in the shine of his shoes.

"My Lady, how are you feeling today?" Godfrey inquired.

"I'm holding up, dear Godfrey," she replied. "Although I could do with some more sleep," she added, her subtlety akin to a butcher taking to a side of beef with a meat mallet.

"Yes, sleep will do you some good – you've been very pale lately, just as your sister had been before she….," he hesitated, bowed his head and then said, "I have a confession that I must make to you."

"This sounds ominous," Mary replied. "Would you like to come in and sit down?"

"No thank-you, My Lady; I'd just as happily stand."

"At least come in so that I can sit down – I'm feeling very unsteady this morning," she said backing into her room and motioning for Godfrey to follow.

"As is your will, My Lady."

Mary perched upon one of the chairs in the alcove, tucking her legs beneath her.

Godfrey looked at her earnestly and said, "Since Lady Emlyn died, I have been questioning where it is that my loyalties should lie. Now with the final Loxley leaving the Hall, I feel that my time here is coming to an end. It has never been the history of the building itself that was the honour of serving here at Loxley Hall, it was serving the family who had occupied it for as many years as my forefathers had served them. I'm afraid that I realised this too late and that I surrendered my loyalty too easily to Master Quinn."

"If you want my blessing to leave this damnable place – then you have it, my dear Godfrey. You should take Granville far away from here and build a life that doesn't involve servitude to others," Mary said.

"That's not exactly what I meant. I wouldn't know what else to do – I have been in the service of others since I was but a boy," Godfrey answered. "No, I, wanted to tell you that I am the one who is responsible for your sister's death and I am willing to accept whichever punishment you feel necessary."

Mary went to speak – to impress upon him that it wasn't possible – but Godfrey put up a hand to silence her and continued, "You see, I saw her in Master Quinn's office while he was away doing business in London. I had no intention of telling him – but when he returned and opened his desk, he noticed that some of the files had been moved. He accused me of stealing and he threatened my position here at the Hall. I panicked. I couldn't bear the thought of being the first of our line to be thrown out of Loxley Hall, disgraced; and so, I told him what I had seen; I chose my place here at the Hall over being loyal to a true Loxley – I can't ever forgive myself."

"And you think that Malcolm killed my sister because of this?" Mary asked.

"No, however, I fear that the repercussions may have been what caused Lady Emlyn to kill herself. I heard the two of them arguing the night I told Master Quinn of her misdemeanour, and I'm afraid that he was quite vicious. The next morning, he insisted that they sleep in separate rooms. Master Quinn isn't completely innocent in all of this either – it was his mistreatment of Lady Emlyn which caused her depression; and he who invited the damned Earl back to Loxley Hall – we all know what that man's father did to Lady Emlyn all those years ago. To dig up such skeletons…."

Godfrey balled his hands into fists and a flicker of rage crossed his eyes. Mary could relate to his feelings of hostility towards the Earl and his family. She had experienced first-hand that the apple hadn't fallen far from the tree when it came to Lord Southby.

Godfrey lowered his voice conspiratorially, "While I'm making my confessions – there is one other thing. At the time, I didn't know what to make of it, but with Captain Hope slipping – I mean he was very athletic and sure footed wasn't he? It just doesn't seem right."

"What is it Godfrey?" Mary encouraged.

"Winnie noticed some of her wax missing from her cleaning products – I audit them once a week for the books – and she couldn't explain where an entire quart had disappeared to. On that very same day, the day before Lady Emlyn died, I saw Master Quinn climbing back in through the window of the sitting room, the very same window through which Captain Hope had climbed and fallen."

Despite feeling rough around the edges and a whole lot softer in between, Mary felt a sudden jolt into action. She hadn't thought that Baden's death had been anything but an accident turned suicide until that moment, and she wanted to examine the roof for herself.

"So you believe that Malcolm had a hand in Baden's death?"

"I think he put wax out on that roof – but I can't see how he could have known that Captain Hope would venture out there," Godfrey replied.

"Don't you see? That was always my sister's place of refuge; Malcolm must've known that," she said jumping to her feet.

Godfrey's eyes connected with Mary's. There was a distinct sadness streaking through them. He was so pitiful in that moment, that Mary's heart couldn't help but break for him. Godfrey was a man who was questioning everything that he had ever known and he appeared as though he had been strung through a wringer multiple times. But he had been nothing but a loyal and a good man and she couldn't help but hate Malcolm Quinn more than ever, for turning this man into what he was in that very moment.

"My dear Godfrey, thank-you for telling me this; you have more than confirmed my suspicions of Malcolm. I still don't know how he did it, but I am certain he had a hand in Emlyn's murder and I'm going to need your help to get to the bottom of it."

"But he was out on the hunt when Lady Emlyn died; I saw him for myself, he couldn't possibly have been in two places at once," Godfrey replied with exasperation.

"Well then he must've had help," Mary said forcefully. "And I'm placing my bets on Addie. I really must speak to her."

"She's still in London, with no expected date of return," Godfrey countered. "The Ellis sisters told me how quickly she left – she didn't even pack a bag."

"You didn't see Addie leave for yourself?" Mary asked.

"No – it was the middle of the night and according to Martha Ellis, it all happened so fast that she hardly said a word to anyone."

"I have a feeling that Addie won't be coming back anytime soon," Mary postulated. She thought for a moment and then asked, "You carry a key to Malcolm's office, do you not?"

"I do, My Lady. What exactly are you thinking of doing?"

"Meet me at the door to his office in half an hour and bring a knife."

"I don't know about this, My Lady."

She clasped Godfrey's hand, pressed it gently to her cheek and said, "After our parents died and Emlyn and I were left with Aunt Bett, it seemed as though our world had ended. But you were always there for us, you were like a father to Emlyn and me. And now Emlyn needs someone who is there for her again – someone who can be her advocate now that she can no longer speak for herself. I need your help, my dear Godfrey – I need you to help me to be Emlyn's voice; are you with me?"

Godfrey raised his head and stood to attention like a soldier reporting for an assignment that he knew he would not return from.

He said, "If it's as you say it is, then let's nail that blasted weasel."

****

Detective Sergeant Diane Pridis felt as though she had the wind at her back, filling her sails to their fullest extent as she continued drilling into the computer, searching for any link between Tilman and Marcus North. She had tried every single search parameter that she could think of and more, yet she had arrived at the morning completely devoid of anything. But that didn't discourage Pridis, not at all, it only served to make her more determined.

She drank from her coffee mug, which was now filled to the brim with boiling hot coffee – thanks to DC Crocker – and she massaged her eyes, which had become dry from staring at the computer screen for an inordinate number of hours. She certainly didn't need the caffeine, but it was a habit that she couldn't deny. It also provided strong cover for the whiskey which sat on her breath from the evening before.

DC Crocker had arrived early that morning and had finally located Robert Leung, alive and well. Pridis had truly thought that Leung would show up in a dumpster, or chained to a rock, sunken somewhere in the Thames. Instead, the silly bugger had done a runner, not just from the loan sharks but from his family as well, and he had landed back in his native land; Hong Kong.

DC Crocker had interviewed Robert over the phone and had ascertained that after he discovered John Quinn's body, he panicked and drove directly to the airport. Leung couldn't offer anything of much use, other than a description of the older loan shark, which had matched Jürgen Sampson's description all the way down to the pencil moustache and the Red Mustang.

"I've finished my report – what do you want me to follow up on now?" DC Crocker asked.

Pridis tapped her fingers on the desk and considered the young officer who stood in front of her. His face dripped with eagerness. He had ambition and a want to impress. He never wore a tie and when he sat cross-legged, his purple and orange socks were exposed, which were at complete odds with his, boring, blue trousers and white shirt.

"How well do you know Inspector Bliss?" she asked.

"As well as most I suppose. He does like to keep himself to himself. I've worked a few cases with him. I wouldn't say that his reputation is deserved. He does enjoy a drink here and there, but I've never seen it affect his work," DC Crocker replied, apparently unfazed by the abstruse question. "I do think that you're hitching your wagon to the wrong horse however."

"I'm more than capable of handling the direction of my career thanks Constable. Let's just wait and see how working with Tilman goes for you, before you start questioning my decisions," she retorted. "Anyway, I need you to track down Inspector Bliss' wife for me – well his ex-wife," Pridis stated.

DC Crocker eyed her warily as if she were setting him up for a fall and he couldn't quite get the angle yet.

He replied, "So he's already got you running personal errands for him, has he?"

"It's nothing like that. Trust me, it's related to the case. He hasn't seen her for four years and he needs to know that she's safe. From the sounds of it, I'd say you're better off getting a set of eyes on her rather than trying to speak to her; apparently they didn't leave it on good terms – he just needs to know that she's safe, he doesn't want her to be alarmed."

"I'll get on it. You got an address or anything that you can help me out with?" he asked.

"Nope – only that her name is Jarmila and he said that she's most likely gone back to her maiden name – Hollant," Pridis replied.

"Jarmila Hollant," he murmured as he wrote her name down into his notebook. As he was leaving he turned and said, "I didn't mean to be presumptuous. I just hate watching a good officer go to waste."

Pridis waved him off and turned her attention back to her computer. DC Crocker may not have meant to be presumptuous, but he certainly had been. He would find out soon enough that Tilman was not the upstanding officer that everyone thought she was. The seven months that they had spent as partners, at work and in each other's beds, now seemed like an eternity ago; and the very thought of it made Pridis sick to the stomach.

It was shortly after 8am and she had been at the computer now for so long that she needed a break. She picked up the phone, opened her notebook and dialled the number which she had noted down during her research, the evening before.

A woman's voice answered, "Radley College, how may I help you?"

"This is Detective Sergeant Diane Pridis, from New Scotland Yard CID. I have some questions regarding an old student of yours – an Eric Pearson. He would have attended your school around twenty years ago."

"The records of our students are held strictly under the 'Data Protection act' – I'm afraid that you'll have to send us through a warrant," the woman replied.

"I don't require access to his record, only some general information about his performance during his time there – I'm sure that's within the realms of the law – I don't need specifics. If you could please have a look through his file and let me know if there's anything that stands out? It would really help to further our investigation."

The woman breathed heavily into the mouthpiece, ruminating over her options and then she said, "I'll place you on hold and I'll see what I can do."

After ten minutes of listening to a mix of what could be confidently termed golden oldies, to anyone under the age of fifty, the woman returned to the line.

She said, "I flicked through Eric Pearson's file and I can safely say that there is nothing remarkable in there. He had average marks, no behavioural problems – he was very good at keeping his head down; not like some of the others we've had come through here."

The incongruity of the information caused Pridis asked, "I wonder – how did such an average kind of boy, who came from such an average kind of background, earn a scholarship to your prestigious scholastic institution?"

"I don't know," the woman answered. Papers rustled in the background and then the woman added, "I can tell you that it was an old collegian called Jeremy Quinn who recommended him for the scholarship and vouched for him, if that helps."

Pridis thanked the woman for her assistance and she hung up the phone. It was no coincidence that the man who had helped Eric Pearson matriculate at Radley was a Quinn – she just wanted to confirm exactly how Jeremy Quinn was related to the Quinn's of Loxley Hall before she jumped to any further conclusions.

She was just about to begin a search for him on her computer, when her phone rang.

"DS Diane Pridis," she answered.

"Hey Prid, it's Bridge," came the quick and hushed reply.

"That was quick," Pridis said.

She had only sent Detective Sergeant Bridget Ives an e-mail request at 3am – not expecting her to read it until the morning and now here she was, Pridis hoped, with a response.

"I pulled his file and had a look. You were right, PC Pearson was once DC Pearson; he was demoted after gross negligence on a case, which lead to the death of a young woman," DS Ives elucidated. "I've e-mailed a copy of his file through to you – I'd appreciate it if you deleted it after reading – I'd hate for it to get out that I'm being fast and loose with the personnel files of South Yorkshire's finest."

Pridis had attended the College of Policing with DS Ives and their careers had advanced together in parallel. They had come to know each other well over the years and DS Ives was someone that she could trust. At one point Pridis had even considered testing the waters in advancing their relationship somewhere beyond the realms of a working friendship – however DS Ives had illustrated time and time again that she was not on that side of the fence.

Pridis opened the e-mail and delved into the file for herself, while DS Ives regaled her with stories of her private life since the last time they had spoken. To Pridis, it seemed that the stories she told were always the same, just with new names filling in the blanks each time.

Pridis interrupted a particularly amusing anecdote about a date night mix-up where she ended up having to entertain two men in her flat – both of whom seemed partial to the idea of a ménage à trois.

She asked, "Do you have a copy of the case file – the one he was working on when he was demoted? I see the report on his conduct during the case, but not the actual details of the case itself."

"It's not in there?" DS Ives asked. Pridis could hear the tapping of keys and then, "I see that it's not; and it's not in the system either. Do you think it's important?"

"Not sure yet – but my gut tells me that it could be," Pridis replied.

"All right then – I'll have to dig the hard copy out of the archives. It'll take some time – but I'll scan it through as soon as I find it. And Prid; you're gonna owe me for this," and with that ominous statement, DS Ives hung up.

***

Andy Bliss had managed to steal a couple of hours sleep without interruption. Before he had attempted such a feat, he had handed DC Cross the Polaroids and given him access to the list of missing women that he had assembled over time using Edris' algorithm. His task, although not an easy one, was to identify the women in the photos, pull their dental records and obtain DNA from the closest relatives that he could find – if it wasn't already on file. This constituted the very beginning of the long and arduous identification process – especially when the remains were in a state such as they were.

He switched on his phone, which was in a perpetual state of dwindling charge and checked the messages. There were only two, both from Pridis; the first confirmed what he already knew of Tilman and he didn't much care to waste his time on conspiracy theories – he was on the cusp of nailing John Quinn and that was all that mattered. It was the second message which interested Andy more; in it Pridis had declared that she had made good headway into investigating PC

Pearson. John Quinn's father had played a large role in securing his scholarship to Radley College, yet according to Pearson himself, he hadn't met the Quinns until after he had begun studying at the school. Why had Pearson wanted to cover up his connection to the Quinns? What was he hiding?

Andy rested against the window sill, taking in a view of the vast grounds of the Hall. Below, standing on the terrace, Alex leaned on the balustrade. She appeared paler than she had done that morning and if Andy wasn't still angry at her from their confrontation, he might have been concerned for her health.

Mark strode out onto the terrace with two glasses in hand. He gave one to Alex and kept one for himself. They turned together to look out across the gardens. Mark softly elbowed her in the side and she laughed. Andy figured that someone as inconceivably maddening as Alex, would get along with someone as twisted as Mark.

He checked on the time. It was fast approaching one o'clock. He decided that he had allowed his quarry enough time to sleep in. He knew her habits well enough from the times that she had bunked in with him at his Middlesex apartment and after the way they had left things, he was sure that she wouldn't be happy to hear his voice regardless of how long he allowed her to sleep.

He dialled her number and she answered, "You! I should have blocked your fucking number."

"Probably; but you didn't," he answered. Before she could continue in her negative vein, or worse, hang-up on him, he continued quickly, "Carla, I know what I said to you was shit, I want to apologise – it was in the heat of the moment and I should never have treated you like that."

"Okay, I'll listen; what do you want?" she asked.

His line of enquiry required a certain level of delicacy. Carla was very secretive about her clients but if he could just push the right buttons, then who knew what he could find out?

He said, "I would have called you sooner, but just after our last liaison, I was assigned a major case which has taken me out to

Sheffield."

"You're in Sheffield?"

"I am; and I don't know how long I'm going to be out here. The case I'm working; it's a big one, it's been in all the papers – maybe you've seen it?"

"I don't read the papers, Love."

"A fellow called John Quinn was murdered in his factory there in London; pretty grisly stuff – you haven't heard of it? It must be in all the news," he continued.

The phone clattered and Andy heard the awkward fall of her uneven footsteps. Her door creaked open and then there was silence. A few minutes later, the door slammed shut and there was a whirlwind of paper and hurried footsteps steaming back towards the phone.

Carla said in a carefully controlled voice, "How did you know?"

"How did I know what?" Andy asked.

"You know full well what I'm talking about."

"I swear – I truly don't – please tell me what you mean," he pleaded.

"That fucker – the one in the papers – John Quinn – he's the reason I'm a cripple. He's the reason I lost my leg."

18. BRIGHTER THAN GOLD

It burned through her nostrils as she snorted it up from the counter. She tossed the rolled-up piece of cardboard into the bin by the door, screwed the top back onto her jade-green pendant, and tucked it into the tight nook created by her cleavage. The burn intensified and her nose began a steady drip.

Detective Inspector Teri Tilman pulled out her handkerchief and she dabbed at her nostril. Normally the anaesthetic properties of the coke would have cut in and stopped the severe burning that was now, not only in her septum, but draining down the back of her throat and into her oesophagus.

This was the last thing that she needed. She had spent the past 24 hours trying to come up with a solution to the mess that she was mired so deeply in. As much as she had tried however, she had come up empty handed and the only thing that she could count on, was that Andy would not be stupid enough to fall into Luke's trap and get himself killed.

Yes; Tilman supposed that she could warn him, but if Luke ever caught wind of it, then she and Marcus would be hung out to dry. Not that she gave two stuffs about Marcus North – he was the reason that they were both under the thumb of a merciless blackmailer – but she hadn't worked so hard and sacrificed so much to get where she was, to just give up on everything now. Not without a fight anyway.

But that was the problem – she was willing to fight, to scratch, nail and claw her way out of this – but she still couldn't be sure who this Luke even was. She knew that the name was an alias, and she had her suspicions as to who it could be, but she had never been able to get close enough to be certain.

Tilman cleared her throat and spat the blood and mucus into the white sink. The bleeding wasn't subsiding and so she leaned forward, tipped her head over the basin and allowed the blood to run freely from her nose. The contrast of the bright, red drops against the white background, made her blood appear much more oxygenated than she was sure that it actually was.

The first time that she had heard from Luke, she'd thought nothing of it. It was 6 months after the 'accident' on Marcus' boat and she had received an anonymous call, threatening to tell the world the truth about what had happened that night, unless she 'lost' a crucial piece of evidence in a case that she was working.

Tilman was in Vice Squad back then and it was a simple case of solicitation gone wrong – the stupid pillock hadn't realised that the hooker was only 16 when he'd made his play for her services in a back alley in Soho. She didn't take the threat seriously – no one other than Marcus could truly have known what had happened that night – and so she called his bluff.

When she hadn't heard back from Luke within a week and the case had hit the courts, she thought that it was over. Someone had tried to start a game with her, that she wasn't stupid enough to play; or so she had thought. Late one night she had arrived home to find her wire door hanging open. The light was on – which was not unusual in itself – but the way it caught the small, glinting, rectangle of plastic attached to the wooden door made her stop in her tracks.

What she found, made her gag. She threw up; her face submerged in the hydrangeas. In front of her – nailed to the door at her eye level, as if Luke had somehow measured her height with a tape measure while she was sleeping – was the driver's licence of Mandy Jones.

Mandy's hazel eyes stared out at her, sparkling with the joy of someone who had just attained the freedom of independence on their birthday, by means of a licence to drive. She looked so vibrant and beautiful – not like the last time that Tilman had seen her; limp and colourless, except for the blood dripping from her nose and the yellow vomit dribbling from her mouth, sprawled on the deck of Marcus' damned boat.

Tilman clawed at the plastic until she ripped it from the door. Her phone rang from within the darkness of her house. She knew that it would be Luke and she wanted to know how he knew. But that was still one of the many questions that she didn't have the answer to – not even now – eight years later.

From that moment on, she had taken care of things for Luke. It was self-preservation – she was a survivalist and the only way she was going to come out of this unscathed was to submit to him. Over the years all that he had wanted was quite simple stuff really – lose a piece of evidence here, misfile a report there. The higher her rank became, the easier it was to bury these transgressions – including her own. She had scrubbed any record of the 'accident' from the Crime Reporting Information System.

A sharp pain stabbed underneath her jaw and shot down her neck. The white basin was filling with blood. It felt as though someone had wrapped a rubber band around her chest and was pulling it, hard, from behind. The face which stared back at her from the mirror didn't feel like her own. It was blurry and smeared with blood and her hair was moving as though it had a life of its own. She clutched at her chest and sucked in as much air as she could.

When Luke had told her to lose a witness, she hadn't wanted to do it – she knew that John Quinn was guilty and Andy had been baying for his blood too. Andy had been all over the case and if she did as Luke wanted, then she would lose her reputation forever. As luck had it however, all the blame for losing Emily Baribel had fallen upon Andy. It was on his watch that she left and he was passed out drunk. Only Tilman and Andy knew the truth, and as his alcoholism became more pronounced, fewer people believed his account of that evening's events.

When John Quinn showed up dead, Tilman knew that she'd hear from Luke. But she was pleasantly surprised when he had handed her the culprits. He wanted them caught and she was more than happy to oblige. Case closed in record time and a chance to bolster her success rate – how could she lose? She'd put Pridis onto the loan sharks as soon as she had heard from Luke and she knew that Dee would deliver soon enough.

But that wasn't enough for Luke; it never was, and from what Tilman had learned – it never would be. He'd changed his mind. He needed the Golds for one final job and she was to leave them out of it. Tilman had guessed what that job was – to sort out the mess in Sheffield, including Andy.

Pridis wasn't stupid though and to suddenly pull her off the loan sharks and give her another angle, would all but guarantee that Tilman's corruption would be uncovered. Tilman had told Luke that he'd have to find another way to complete his plan, and so he had threatened her once again and now here she was, in the bathroom at the Yard contemplating her options, and as it looked, there was nothing else that she could do. She was not going to end up in jail.

She fished in her cleavage again and unscrewed the pendant. She poured out the remainder of her tainted stash onto the bench in front of her and divided it into three neat lines. She fashioned a small piece of cardboard into a straw. A drop of blood fell onto the surface as she snorted it deeply and defiantly, tasting a mixture of metal and gasoline.

Instead of the instant high, the rush that her body so craved, the stabbing pain in her jaw intensified and a shooting pain radiated up her left arm.

She stared into the mirror as her vision began to fade into black. Her knees weakened and her hands lost their grip on the sides of the basin. She took a breath, and for the first time in 8 years she felt a kind of freedom. As she fell to the floor, in a final act which seemed to take an eternity to complete, she thought to herself:

'I'm going out my own way.'

And as the back of her head smashed painfully against the tiles, everything around Detective Inspector Teri Tilman faded into blackness.

***

Detective Sergeant Diane Pridis snapped her fingers and looked around the room for someone, anyone, to share the moment with. After dedicating plenty of grunt work to the task, she had finally found the names and potential location of the loan sharks, who had literally turned one of their customers into mincemeat. She wondered whether this was the first time that the, 'make mincemeat of someone' idiom, had been turned into a gruesome reality.

Upon reflection, she mumbled, "Probably not," to herself, thinking about all the lowest forms of dredged-up excuses for human beings, who she had been exposed to over her years in the force.

The Golds, Kevlar and Josephus, also known as Sparks, had rap sheets longer than time itself, and their descriptions closely matched those that Pridis had received from both Jürgen Sampson and Robert Leung. Adding to that, a red Mustang registered to one Kevlar Gold, and Pridis could almost taste the champagne that she knew Tilman would gift her once the case had been solved.

She rose from behind her desk and looked towards DC Crocker's alcove. He was gone; probably still out chasing down the whereabouts of Inspector Bliss' ex-missus. She checked the duty roster to see who was available – she didn't like the idea of going out on the job with DC Harper; his breath was always rank and he had a propensity to get close to people when he spoke – an unfortunate combination.

Pridis strolled towards the bathroom, she had been holding it in for a while now and if she took long enough, then maybe DC Crocker would rematerialise, and she wouldn't have to confine herself in such a small space with Harper and his rancid exhalations. It felt good to stretch her legs; she'd been sitting at her desk for so long that her hamstrings had begun to tingle.

She leaned into the door of the lady's room. It opened an inch and then hit an obstruction causing Pridis to bounce off the door. She propelled her shoulder into it, this time, braced and ready for the impact. There was a loud, metallic crash and the door swung fully open.

It took Pridis a few moments to process the scene which met her eyes. It wasn't the blood, which was smeared on the mirror and the sink and shimmering in a puddle on the tiles beneath Tilman's head that was the worst, nor was it the fact that it was her ex-lover and current boss sprawled out, unmoving on the floor. It was the way that she was lying there. Her legs seemed to protrude at the most unnatural of angles. And there, out in the open, lying upon her left bosom, was her pendant – opened and emptied and exposed for everyone to see.

Pridis snapped into action. She dove at Tilman and checked her pulse and her breathing – she couldn't feel either, but her body was still warm. She took the pendant and quickly tucked it back into Tilman's shirt – not to hide evidence, it was way too late for that – but she just knew that Tilman would have not wanted the world to find out about her addiction like that.

She phoned for an ambulance. They advised her to begin CPR; the paramedics were only a few minutes away. Pridis jumped to her feet and ran to the door.

"Somebody, help! I need help!"

In a flash, Redvers O'Dell was in the corridor, his eyes wide, full of adrenaline and ready for action – reminiscent of a man who missed being out on the beat.

"In here – she's collapsed, I need help."

Redvers limped past Pridis, sank to the floor – his knee encroaching on the pool of blood at Tilman's head. He picked up her limp wrist and then dropped it to the floor. He measured the appropriate distance beneath her sternum and then, with his two hands clasped together, he began compressions. Pridis wiped the blood from Tilman's nose and mouth with the handkerchief she found next to the body and gave Tilman two full breaths after every count of fifteen.

"What the hell happened?" Redvers asked as he stopped to check her vitals again after the first four cycles.

"I don't know," Pridis replied. "She was like this when I found her – I called an ambulance and then I called for help."

They continued CPR for what felt like forever. Redvers counting the compressions aloud and Pridis giving Tilman the gift of her breath after every fifteen. It had a rhythm to it that gave Pridis something to focus on, instead of having to face the reality of the situation. Although she had her issues with Tilman, she didn't want her to die like this. She had loved her at one point. Or what Pridis had thought was love.

The door burst open and through it ran the paramedics. Redvers moved aside and one of them took over.

"Who called it in?"

"I did," Pridis replied.

"Do you know what happened? Do you know how long she's been out?"

"I don't know."

With the help of Redvers they lifted Tilman onto the stretcher and one of the paramedics mounted her and continued giving CPR. Tilman's arm dangled lifelessly from the side of the stretcher and her cuticles were tinged with blue. As the paramedic thumped down on Tilman's chest, the rest of her body shuddered with each movement – not of her own accord, but as though she were an abused blow-up doll.

The stretcher was set and they were about to wheel her away, when Pridis felt her stomach burn. It was as though there was a lump of red-hot coal sitting right there in the base of her enteric system. She thought for a moment about the repercussions of what she was about to say and decided that Tilman couldn't begrudge her trying to save her life – even if it would destroy her career. Pridis grabbed the arm of the paramedic and whispered:

"I don't know if this makes a difference, but she's on cocaine."

***

Andy Bliss had had a shit of a day and he was ready to turn himself over to the elixir which had so often rescued him from his over active mind. He was still reeling from the discovery of his wife's photo mixed in with those of potential victims and to hear Carla's explanation for her own photo being in John Quinn's possession, did nothing to quell his sense of disquiet.

Jacqueline had been in the process of closing when he had arrived at her establishment. She had allowed him entry and as he found a seat at the bar, the latch clicked behind him.

"What'll it be, Detective?"

She had that sexy kind of way of moving, and with a flick of her head her fiery locks formed a sensual frame around her face.

"Surprise me," he said and he watched her go to work, mixing this spirit with that, wondering if she was choosing the bottles on the higher shelves so as to show off the more pleasing aspects of her figure.

Jacqueline shook her concoction, took down two tall glasses, dropped three cubes of ice in each – clinking the sides of the glass as they fell – and then poured. She reached beneath the counter and fumbled through the bottles in the fridge below, giving Andy ample time to enjoy the view down her top and into the valley created by her two mountainous breasts.

He felt a pulse of heat enter his loins and knew exactly what he wanted to do – needed to do – to take his mind off his troubles. She straightened and added a dash of cola and a slice of lemon to each glass.

"Long Island ice tea," she declared as she walked around the bar and sat on the stool next to him. "You look as though you've had a rough day. You want to talk about it?"

Jacqueline leaned towards him and put her hand on his thigh. The last thing that he wanted to do was talk about his day. He put his drink down on the bar in front of him and turned to face her. She gave him an inviting smile as she stroked his leg. That was all the encouragement Andy needed.

He grabbed her, pulled her from her chair and drew her close into him. At the thought of what he was about to do to her, he could feel his cock harden against her. She reached her hand down and caressed *It* gently and then she thrust herself towards him. He knew that she wanted him to take her, have her, any way that he pleased and Andy was ready to oblige.

He stood, lifting her with him and carried her – as she was mounting him and rubbing her heat against him – across to the corner booth. He laid her on the table and she reached down and unbuckled his belt. He ripped away her blouse, taking no care in the fate of the buttons.

Jacqueline unzipped his trousers. She teased him with the slowness of her movements, when all he wanted to do was rip and tear and thrust and burn.

And then his phone rang. He took it from his pocket and was about to answer, when Jacqueline snatched it from him, rejected the call and threw his phone under the table.

"They'll be none of that tonight," she whispered, already panting and staring up at him with her big blue eyes.

He was just about to protest when she took his cock into her mouth and he felt the tip in the back of her throat. From that moment, he had forgotten what a phone was, or even who he was and instead he succumbed to the animalistic pleasures and let go of all the worries of the world.

***

Edris Bliss was a juggler. That was what he was so good at. He had one ball here and one there and another seven high above his head, but he always made sure that he didn't lose track of any of them even when a gust of wind, such as his brother Andy, interfered.

He had built a reputation for himself and was proud of what he had achieved. He was organised and he was well connected – all without the help of anyone except for his brothers in the crew. He was known as a Mr Fix-it and if anyone in the underworld had any kind of problem, they knew that they could call him and he would sort it all out. He had an uncanny ability to make problems disappear.

On the night that John Quinn had gotten it, Edris had fielded a panicked call from Kevlar Gold explaining that he was showing his son the family business and that Sparks had made a mess of it; how much of a mess, he didn't realise until he had come to the factory to have a look for himself.

To accidently shoot a guy was one thing – there were plenty of people in his line of work who had gotten over zealous and discharged their weapon unintentionally – but to mince a guy's arm like that, was taking it to another level. Edris had imposed himself upon the situation and had organised for the CCTV footage which showed them all in the area to be erased. He did all of this for a fee of course – but he was always happy to help a fellow crim out of the invariably sticky situations which surfaced in their line of work.

His brother rarely called him and when he did it was hard for Edris. He and Andy were tight growing up, but when Edris found the place where he belonged, a place that he could call home, he had to leave Andy behind. Who knew that his lack of influence would cause the little tacker to turn straight on him though? The rest of the family were trouble, their mother especially – in and out of the clink – Edris could never understand how Andy turned out so straight laced.

When Andy did call him, he always felt compelled to help – not only because it was a rarity, but because deep down Edris felt guilty about abandoning his little bro so many years ago. He couldn't tell Andy the extent of his reach and his influence in the underworld however, and so Andy only ever reached out to him when there were low level crooks involved and he was desperate for a lead. If he knew, for example, that Edris had just had lunch with Jimmy Adams, one of the UK's most wanted criminals, then Andy wouldn't just call for a favour, he would place Edris under arrest.

Edris already had the information that Andy needed when he first called – he was there when John Quinn was given exactly what karma had set out for him – but he was concerned. Edris rarely got his hands dirty and although he'd gotten rid of the CCTV from that night, there were still two witnesses and he wanted to ensure that the Golds didn't put him in it. He wanted to know their plans and if he needed to be worried or at least prepared.

His driver announced that they had arrived at the Duke of

Wellington in Dalston not long after 10pm. Their arrival had surprised him as he had expected the traffic to keep them a lot longer on the drive back to town from Cambridge, where he had been seeing to business, on behalf of Jimmy Adams.

The Duke of Wellington was the local hang out of the Gold's, and when they weren't out pestering people for repayments or handing out loans to people who could never afford them, they were normally throwing back ales and picking up slappers at the Duke.

He entered the pub and there propping up the bar was Sparks. He sat, drinking a pint and he had a woman on the barstool next to him, who wore a Lycra skirt and a tank top with layers of flab oozing out at every opportunity. Her make-up was so thick and dark around her eyes, she looked as though she had been punched, and she was drooling over Sparks' wallet, which bulged thickly in his pocket.

"A bit early to get on the mingers, isn't it?" Edris quipped as he pulled up the stool on the other side of Sparks.

He swung around with a mean look in his eyes, until he saw who it was. "Ed, buddy," he said putting his arm around him. "What're ya doin' here?" he shouted as he pushed the woman away, and she retreated to the corner of the room like a nervous crab, looking to lunge at her next drunk and unsuspecting victim.

Edris hated being called Ed but for the sake of his fact-finding mission he took it in his stride.

"Just in the neighbourhood," he lied. "How are you getting along anyway? I hear that business is booming."

"Yeah; Me dad's pretty happy with all of it. He's round 'ere somewhere," Sparks uttered looking around the room. He quietened his voice and added, "Hey Ed, thanks for the help out – I thought I'd fucked it all up. Fuckin' up a mark first time out, coulda been the end for me. Lucky our client has other plans in mind."

"You were doing a job for someone else?" Edris probed.

"Yeah; normals we do it for ourselves – but this one was special. Some guy called Luke. I think me dad owed 'im one," Sparks said.

As Sparks divulged this piece of information, Kevlar appeared from a back room. He had a satisfied smile on his face, and about five seconds later, he was followed by another spandexed creature, who was wiping her mouth surreptitiously on her sleeve.

He sat down on the other side of Edris and called across him to Sparks, "Take a note son, that one gives excellent head – uses the teeth, she does – but not too much." Kevlar took one look at Edris and said, "What the fuck are you doin' 'ere?"

"Just in the neighbourhood," he repeated. "I heard the coppers are looking into the John Quinn death – it wasn't ruled an accident as we had hoped," Edris said conversationally.

"Don't worry about that Ed; the coppers are useless, they won't get near us," Sparks replied.

"And if they do?" Edris questioned.

Before either of the Golds answered, Kevlar's phone rang. He answered it, listened to the other end and then replied:

"Luke, I was just thinking of you."

He hesitated once more and then said, "That sneaky sow – Sheffield you say." Kevlar paused and then continued, "Tomorrow night? You want us to neck the copper too? Yep. Good. We won't let you down." He hung up and said to Sparks, "Pack your guns, we're going to Sheffield – you have a chance to redeem yourself."

Kevlar turned to Edris and said, "Don't worry about the cops – our client said he has it under control. And besides, I ain't no grass and neither is me son."

The two of them left in a hurry, eager to get the preparations underway for their new job. Even though Edris hadn't heard their plan, it appeared that they meant business. Whoever this Luke person was, he really wanted his money and it appeared that he would go to any lengths to get it. Edris picked up his phone and called Andy. He wanted to warn him that the Golds were coming and that they were packing heat – but it went straight through to voicemail. Edris didn't leave a message – he never did; didn't like to leave a trace. He'd reach him in the morning – he'd let his brother sleep in peace for now.

***

Luke paced around outside wondering exactly how everything had started to spiral out of control. He was starting to get cold, but he didn't really care. It was air that he needed right now, not the cosiness of a fire, or a blanket and a pillow – that would take away from his focus – and it was focus that he needed right now too.

He thought that he had formulated the perfect plan, until the imbecilic Golds ruined it for him, and now he could feel it all slipping away. John was supposed to just sign the papers and all of this would have been over. Killing him was never a part of the plan.

Luke had adapted however, after he had heard the bad news of John's death. Initially he wanted to kill the Golds themselves, mince them into oblivion, but then he realised that maybe they had done him a favour. He would never have gotten everything that he had wanted with John still around and so he had forgiven them. But then his plan to keep Alex exposed and vulnerable out at Loxley Hall had backfired as well and he needed the Golds to ensure that his new and much more complex plan worked.

The fact that Inspector Bliss had found the skeleton of the little boy – something which Luke could never have foreseen – and then the further explosion into a full-blown investigation was difficult enough, but with the media starting to get their hooks into the story, it had made things damn near impossible. That was when Luke had decided that it was the Golds who had gotten him into this mess and so it was the Golds who were going to get him out of it.

He slipped his phone back into his pocket, happy that Kevlar sounded enthusiastic about his new project. Luke blew on his hands to warm them and then buried them deep in his jacket pockets. He was finally going to get what he had always deserved and what should have been his in the first place. His new plan was all falling into place quite nicely and he couldn't wait for all the fireworks to begin.

19. FINAL FAREWELLS

Godfrey's uneven footfall hurried along the corridor as Mary Loxley changed out of her night clothes and into her trousers. The revelation that Baden's death was no accident had been enough to blow the cobwebs created the previous evening, clear from Mary's head. She had always known that Malcolm Quinn was not a particularly good man, but she had never thought him capable of murder.

She lamented the fact that she had allowed her sister to marry him in the first place. Mary had returned briefly from her nursing studies to Loxley Hall for the wedding, before she was deployed to France and the Great War. It was the first time that she had met Malcolm and she remembered feeling her skin crawl as Aunt Bett had fawned all over him. Of course, it was that infernal woman who had pushed Malcolm onto Emlyn in the first place and she who had encourage their courtship in Mary's absence.

Mary had to concede however, that Emlyn had appeared to be happy with Malcolm, and in a time of war, happiness was a rare jewel to find. Mary had truly doubted that Baden would return from the front lines and she didn't wish the heartache of waiting for his return on her sister, only to be met, not with the unbounding promises of a love fulfilled, but with the earth-shattering sadness of a telegram.

She had considered protesting against their impending matrimony – she had even imagined herself jumping up during the ceremony, declaring her dissention and then whisking her sister away to safety.

But then came the fateful event which put all thoughts of objecting to Malcolm becoming her brother-in-law out of her mind; her revulsion replaced by gratitude.

On the night before the wedding there was a grand celebration at the Hall. It was in the early days of the war and so there were no real restrictions or curfews in place – the lights were all a flare and the feast was bountiful. It was in a time where the ferocity of the war had yet to take a hold. They were still so innocent to the ways in which it was going to rip them all apart – ignorant to its savagery.

Lord Southby, who had escaped the clutches of the War Office, with what Mary could only gather was a counterfeit condition concocted by the Earl's personal physician, had over indulged on all that there was to offer.

Mary had taken to her chambers for the evening and had only just turned out the lights, when the door creaked slowly open. She strained her eyes to see who it could possibly be – but the room was thick with darkness and she was surrounded by black. Maybe one of the maids hadn't noticed that the room was already occupied and had come to light the fire.

"Who's there?" she whispered.

She was met only with silence. Quiet footsteps approached her bed.

A mass weighed down on the side of her mattress, which caused her body to turn towards it. It was the hands that she felt first; large, sweaty hands, clutching clumsily in the dark for her breasts. She slapped them away and tried to sit up, but he threw his entire body on top of hers and ripped at her nightclothes. She tried to call out, but he clamped his hand down hard upon her mouth. He was pressed violently against her and she could feel his erection pushing into her – her underclothes, her only protection.

She fought hard in the dark that night, scratching and biting, but she wasn't strong enough. He had overpowered her; her arms pinned high above her head, her arm bones pulling at the shoulder sockets, his hands crushing her wrists against the bedhead and she had resigned herself to the horror of what was to come.

The door burst open and Malcolm charged into the room carrying a lantern in one hand and a truncheon in the other. He tore the Earl off Mary and threw him powerfully out of the room. The sudden relief, both physically and mentally, caused Mary to break down into tears and she threw her arms gratefully around Malcolm's shoulders.

If it wasn't for Malcolm entering the room when he did, Mary would have been turned into a murderer that night – because she knew in her heart of hearts, that if Lord Southby had been allowed to go through with what he had intended, she would have tied him down where he slept later that night and slit his throat by a thousand paper cuts.

She shrugged off the memory and finished her glass of water, thankful for the refreshment and she pulled on her jacket. Even though she still owed Malcolm for saving her from Lord Southby that night – it would never be enough for Mary to allow him to get away with murder; especially of those who she cared most about in this world.

Mary inhaled some snuff, slipped the box into her pocket and rushed out of the door towards the sitting room. She felt apprehensive about returning to the room where she had watched an honourable man give up on life and knowing now that it wasn't just some horrible accident made it all the more difficult.

Her heart pounded and her palms felt damp to the touch. The walls felt as though they were closing in on her; claustrophobic, she found it hard to breathe. The remnants of the ripped curtain still hung from above and brought with it a myriad of bad memories.

'The room holds no power,' she thought to herself as she approached the window. *'It's all in your mind.'*

She swung open the window and breathed in the cool, morning air. The vast lawns that trailed off towards the embankment were covered with dew, and the first glimpses of the morning sun caused a low mist to sweep across the grounds. The remains of the soldiers' bonfire, still smouldered in the western corner of the gardens.

'Godfrey is not going to be happy with that,' she mused.

Mary surveyed the room. Standing by the fireplace was exactly what she needed. The poker was her weapon of choice; with its length and pointed end, it fit her purposes perfectly.

As she lifted the poker from its stand, Mary caught sight of herself in the mirror which hung above the mantelpiece. She looked pale and fatigued. She paused for a moment, leaned against the arm of the red, velvet sofa and lit up a cigarette. She took her first puff for the day. The first was always the most satisfying.

She studied the glowing ash of the cigarette as she wondered how it had all come down to this. She had been living the life that she had wanted to in Montpellier and now here she was, dragged back into this small-minded, unambitious, little town, cast in the shadow of death, which she had thought she had left behind when the war had ended.

Mary returned to the window, rested her smoke on the left side of her lip and leant as far out as she could without having to look downward. It was not as though she was afraid of heights, that phobia was not logical to Mary; it was that she didn't want to look upon the place where Baden had lived his final moment. And besides, after the night she had endured, she couldn't trust that her stomach would keep its contents to itself.

She thrust forth the poker as far as she could reach, and scrapped its point along the roof tiles at the exact place where Baden had lost his footing.

A hand pushed against her back. The cigarette fell from her mouth as she tried to regain her balance. It rolled down the slope of the roof, just as Baden had. Adrenaline pumped through every muscle in her body as she was yanked backwards; the poker clunked to the ground.

"Godfrey! You gave me a fright," she exclaimed.

"Me? You were about to climb out onto that roof — I can't lose you too," he replied.

Mary picked up the poker and said, "I was using this. I wasn't going anywhere."

She studied the sharp tip of the poker and rubbed the residue that had been lifted from the roof between her thumb and forefinger — it felt as though she had melted a candle directly onto her finger tips. The substance was smooth and thick and her fingers glided easily back and forth. She raised the sample to her nose. It smelled of beeswax and turpentine.

The smell was not only familiar to her, but she had smelled it very recently indeed. She rifled through her pockets, unable to extract what she was looking for quickly enough. At the very bottom of her inner jacket pocket lay the damning piece of evidence. At Baden's funeral, she had just wanted to cover her tears before anyone noticed them. She didn't feel as though she deserved to cry for Baden – not like his mother.

It hadn't crossed her mind when Malcolm handed over his handkerchief. The odour hadn't fully registered with her, her thoughts were deep in more important considerations. But now, here she was, in the sitting room holding Malcolm's handkerchief, and its odour was the most important thing of all. He had used it to wipe his hands clean after he had placed the wax on the roof – and regardless of who it was intended for, Mary finally had proof of his sins.

"We have him," Mary said as she strode out of the room and towards Malcolm's office.

Godfrey followed close behind.

"What is it?" he asked.

She showed him the handkerchief and said, "This proves that he put the wax on the roof and now I'm going to get him to admit it." Mary nodded at the door and said, "Open it."

Godfrey did as she asked.

"You keep watch out here. If anyone comes, get rid of them. Do you have the knife?" Mary asked.

He nodded, handed over a small pocket knife and said, "It may be small, but it's sharp and it does the job."

Godfrey stood guard as she moved across to Malcolm's roll top desk. She folded the knife's blade out of its casing and prised it into the space between the desk and the drawer. With only a modicum of force, the lock popped open. If she could just find something about these soldiers, something which she could hold over Malcolm's head, then she could get a confession.

She picked up the first. The name was Cedric Tuppel and as she scanned through it, it was almost identical to that of Henry Buckle. If she hadn't have had confirmation from Baden's mother that Henry was a real person, then she would have thought that Malcolm had been duplicating the records to receive more rations than he and the hospital were entitled.

She reached the final page – the discharge form with orders to return to the front line – and there it was; the very thing that she had been looking for, and she couldn't believe that she hadn't recognised it straight away, when she had been talking to Geogrey Dockrell the day before. He had insisted that Malcolm was a man called Billy Garrot. Mary had assumed that he was mistaken and she now regretted the fact that she had dismissed his claims so quickly. It could be no coincidence that the co-signature on the discharge forms was the very name that Georgey Dockrell had attributed to Malcolm.

She rushed towards the door and called to Godfrey, "Are the soldiers from the wake still here?"

"I saw the last of them out this morning. It was the fellow who did all the speaking and most of the drinking. He had a train to catch," Godfrey replied. He looked in on Malcolm's study and said, "Are you going to tidy that up?"

"No; let him see it," she replied as she dashed towards the stairs. "We must stop Georgey from catching that train."

"Why? What does he have to do with all of this?" Godfrey questioned looking baffled.

"He's the one who can tell us exactly who Malcolm Quinn really is."

***

Betty Clovely stood there sandwiched between her old friend Malcolm and her husband to be, Lord Southby. Granville had finished stowing their luggage in the automobile and it was time to bid farewell to Loxley Hall forever. She was starting to get nervous as she didn't have any inclination to see her niece Mary.

She had promised Malcolm that she would leave and never come back and in return he had given her a sizable sum of money and the information which would ensure that Lord Southby, the Earl of Lancashire, would stay by her side in holy matrimony for as long as she dictated.

Betty had truly only come for the weekend and the promise of a grand party – so she could recover from the rejection which she had suffered in Constantinople – but the death of dear Emlyn had set in motion a much larger series of events which had culminated in her current and most favourable position.

Betty understood why Malcolm wanted her gone. She was a reminder of his life with Emlyn and as he had put it, he needed to move forward. Mary would soon disappear again, back under the rock where she had crawled out from and without the spectre of the old Loxley family around, Malcolm would be able to forge ahead with new ways and new traditions – which was exceedingly important, especially in the post war world.

Malcolm had promised her the money and had told her all about the night that Lord Southby had tried to take advantage of a young Mary. Malcolm and Betty both knew that the Earl could do without the scandal – especially having strict morality clauses in his father's will, which if broken would result in the loss of his title regardless of their marriage; a title which was very important to Lord Southby.

Betty was not naïve either; the Earl could throw her out on her ear at any time once he fulfilled the marriage clause in his father's will and secured his inheritance. This information was her insurance policy and she was forever grateful to Malcolm for supplying her with it. They had made a great team over the years; firstly, with the orchestration of his marriage to Emlyn and then with the fortunes that their teamwork had netted them throughout the war using the hospital and now her crowning glory; her marriage into the aristocracy – exactly where she belonged.

She squeezed Lord Southby's hand and smiled up at him. He

returned her smile and then looked longingly towards the automobile.

Betty bade farewell to Malcolm and then both she and Lord Southby entered the vehicle. The driver started the engine – one of those brand-new push button starters – and was about to set-off when Mary appeared at a jog out of the front door of the Hall, followed closely by Godfrey. Mary lunged and opened the door as the vehicle began its roll.

"I need to go to the train station and I need to talk to you," Mary said holding Betty's livid gaze.

"We're not going anywhere near the station," Lord Southby intervened, with a dismissive swish of his hand.

"You are now," Mary retorted, her eyes not leaving Betty's.

"To Sheffield station then," Betty called through to the driver.

"Yes ma'am," he replied.

"What is all of this unpleasantness in aid of?" Betty asked, her hand resting gently on Lord Southby's left thigh.

"The convalescence hospital, during the war," Mary began.

"Yes, what about it?" Betty replied.

"What was your involvement?"

"I worked there, mainly in the realms of administration," Betty answered cautiously.

"And what exactly was in it for you?"

"What do you mean by that?" Betty replied.

"I mean, that you've never done a thing in your life without you receiving some kind of benefit," Mary clarified.

Betty felt a pinch in her throat.

She retorted, "I gave up my life for the two of you. After your parents died, I came here and looked after you as if you were my own."

"You did nothing of the sort. Godfrey was more of a parent than you ever were. We didn't just need a presence, we needed someone who was there emotionally – someone who actually loved us and wanted to see us for who we really were and not what you wanted us to be."

"What did it matter to you? You were never there, you were off at that boarding school of yours – you didn't care about us, about your family. When did you last speak to your sister? She killed herself and you weren't even there," Betty retorted viciously.

"You brought in your friend to marry her and take control of Loxley Hall and now he's returned the favour and handed you the Earl. The entire thing makes me sick – but I'm not here to talk about that – I want to know why the hospital was sending unfit soldiers back to the frontlines? What was in it for you?" Mary interrogated.

Lord Southby cleared his throat and when Betty looked at him, he indicated, red faced, to his thigh. She loosened her grip, which had become vice like. His leg was definitely going to bruise. She regarded her niece for a moment wondering whether she could trust her with the truth about what she had done during the war.

She decided that if she didn't come clean now, then Mary would never stop digging and would never give her any peace.

She said, "We were struggling to keep the hospital afloat. Our resources were stretched and more and more soldiers were being sent to us. We couldn't cope. That was until Malcolm found a way to procure extra rations. I don't know where he sourced them, but I worked the black markets with the surplus and I was able to trade them for medical supplies. Now, if we happened to skim a small amount off the top as a fee," she shrugged her shoulders, "Well, that's the way the world works, isn't it?"

"Where the hell did he find the extra rations?" Mary paused as if in thought and then continued, "Was he falsifying records, increasing his numbers, so that they would allocate more food?"

"That's not possible – we were filled to the rafters and I would have known. He told me that he'd found a source. I didn't push him, because to be quite honest, I didn't want to know. I was comfortable – we had food, shelter, and a purpose, while the rest of the world was crumbling. I'd like to think that what I did – getting us those medical supplies – even though I had to get my hands dirty doing it, truly helped. If you want to know how he did it, you're going to have to ask Malcolm and the Ellis sisters; they must have known something, working in the kitchen. All I know is that after he found his source, there was always extra meat – more protein for the soldiers."

The vehicle came to a halt at the station. Betty reached across to Mary and put a hand on her knee.

She said as gently as she could, "I'm sorry about Emlyn and I'm sorry that you feel this way about the time we spent together as a family. I tried my best."

Mary opened the door, left the cabin and replied, "I know you did, Aunt Bett and I'm sorry too."

Mary walked away, into the crowded station.

Betty swallowed hard. Mary had been right about her. She had spent her life always looking for ways to improve her own position, to climb the social ladder. But she had never comprehended the impact that she had had on others until that moment. She leaned into the Earl and felt his body tighten. What was she doing with a man who could barely stand to look at her?

The sunlight caught her diamond ring and all those sentiments were forgotten.

"To Clitheroe Manor," she commanded and they sputtered off towards her new life as Countess Betty Southby, wife of the Earl of Lancashire.

***

"I've been searching for you everywhere."

Granville stood there, his eyes still blackened from the recoil of the rifle. He held a large suitcase in his hands. Everything had moved so fast for Godfrey that morning that he was in a daze. He had gone from confessor, to defender, to observer, as Lady Mary had put herself in the Earl's vehicle and the wheels had spun her away towards what Godfrey hoped was Sheffield station.

His son, who had now come to stand directly in front of him continued to speak.

"I wanted to tell you, before I left, that I will make you proud."

Godfrey stretched his brain to figure out what his son was talking about. A moment later, Winnie emerged also carrying a suitcase.

"What in the name of Moses is going on here? Where is it that you two think, you are going?"

"I have given them to the Earl as a wedding gift," Malcolm said.

Godfrey felt as though he had been punched in the stomach. "You can't do that. These are people – you can't just give them away."

"I can and I am. I pay for you all and I can do as I please with you and I am giving them to Lord Southby. Clitheroe Manor can use them more than me, especially now that Emlyn is gone."

"But Sir, he's my son," Godfrey implored.

"You're more than welcome to go with them – I won't be requiring your services any longer either," Malcolm replied without even looking at him.

Godfrey felt as though the air had been sucked from the atmosphere around him. He had never known anything but Loxley Hall. He had been born there and he had always figured that it was the place where he would die, just as those of his family had done before him. He considered his son. Granville's expression was full of hope and expectation. It showed a great deal of faith in him, that Master Quinn would send him to live with and work for the Earl. And Winnie, she looked up at Granville with a look that could only come from a devotion borne in teenaged infatuation.

On one hand, Godfrey wanted to help Lady Mary. It was his duty to see it through to the end; he had promised her that much and Lady Emlyn indeed deserved a voice, someone to speak for her. If it was Master Quinn who took that away from her, then he deserved punishment; retribution. However, Lady Mary had also told him that he should leave the Hall, have a fresh start and this new beginning could be precisely that.

He looked at his old Master and said, "I will pack my things," and he trudged off towards his room.

As the horse and carriage pulled away from Loxley Hall, Godfrey took one last look at the old building. He couldn't believe that all the years of sacrifice, through all the generations of his family, had come down to this moment. He and his son had been given away like a rotten piece of meat to a leprous beggar. Godfrey spat out of the window, onto the driveway towards the place where Malcolm Quinn had stood.

"The place is going to the dogs anyway," he said and then he sat back in his seat and settled in for the long ride to Clitheroe Manor.

20. TAINTED LINES

Alex Dewill flicked through the pages of an old and tattered magazine as she sat in a white walled room, which was adorned with blue and red Tachisme style paintings. The smell of antiseptic, mixed with a pine scented air freshener infused the air and pervaded her very senses. Her stomach swirled like a washing machine as she checked the time on the large, rectangular clock, which hung opposite her. Her appointment was set for 4pm and it was already twenty-six minutes past the hour.

'Why did they even bother to offer appointments if they were never able to keep them?'

The ticking of the clock became louder and louder, as though someone stubborn was trying to drive a crooked nail into an impenetrable wall. She turned the page of her magazine and staring back up at her was a photo of Princess Di – *'How old was this magazine anyway?'* Alex checked the cover, 'Woman's Weekly,' June 1996 – *'Twenty-one years old, I should throw it a party,'* she thought to herself.

Instead, she threw the magazine back onto the stack and gazed towards the automatic doors that led back out onto the street. What was she doing there, really? Her stomach had been playing up since John had been killed and she had felt inexplicably tired, but was that reason enough to bother a doctor with her problems? It was probably just a reaction to the medication that she was taking for her broken nose.

The day had started off well enough; Alex had awoken in Matthew's arms – warm and secure – the water had been hot when she had taken her shower and when Alex had reached the breakfast table, she had found that the ridiculous Inspector had already left for the day. But then two things had happened. Firstly, when Matthew came down the stairs, he acted as if he didn't recognise her. She had hoped that he wasn't going to be the kind of man who got what he wanted from a woman and then found someone else; shinier, newer and less accessible to fawn over.

He didn't bother to join her at the table – he crept in, saw that Alex was talking to Vanessa – and without a word, he left the room and sauntered back up the stairs. Alex tried to ignore him; tried to forget about the fact that they had just had sex the entire night and that in the throes of orgasm he had even told her that he loved her.

Vanessa had explained that since the only legitimate retreat guest, Jordan, had absconded with the police medical examiner the evening before with all his belongings, she was going to London for the evening.

"The conversion business isn't what it used to be," Vanessa had said.

"That's because what you offer a cure for, isn't really a sickness," Alex had replied.

And that, Alex had come to realise, was the catalyst for the second unpleasant occurrence of the morning.

Vanessa shot up and stood towering over Alex. She wasn't a tall woman, but she could be imposing when she wanted to be and with her defective eye, the entire effect was quite striking.

She pointed to the painting of Jesus, which hung over the fireplace at the end of the room and shouted, "You dare to say in front of our Lord, that homosexuality is not a disease, not a plague upon mankind? You don't think that these people, feeble of mind, choose to sin – choose this abomination? I can tell you right now that you are an ignorant, naïve, little girl. Their Leftist agenda has brainwashed you; it has brainwashed everyone. Telling you all that it's normal, that people are born that way – it's all just an excuse for their sexual deviancies."

Alex was in shock. She had been raised in a conservative household, but even her parents had never been so backward. She felt frustration and anger build in her chest.

"You don't think that I'm going to allow this place to continue operating once I sign the paperwork for the Hall, do you?"

"My John said that no matter what happened, he would allow me and my sons to continue living here – Mr North told me that you have to let us stay."

"You can live here Vanessa, but I won't tolerate you spreading your hatred; not from my house, you won't."

"Hatred?!" Vanessa exclaimed. "I'm trying to help these people. I'm trying to get them their ticket into the kingdom of Heaven. There is no greater gift that I can give these poor, wretched souls. I'm a charitable Christian – there's not one ounce of hatred in me."

"If you're such a good Christian, then why do you spend all your time judging other people and their actions? If your book is to be believed, isn't it the job of your God to judge us all when that day arises, not you? Nobody put you in charge."

"I don't understand how John married you. He was a most pious young man; and to marry a non-believer?" Vanessa sighed and moved off towards the door. She turned back to Alex and said, "I offer a service here and if people want my help, I give it. I don't force anyone to come – all those who ask me, are disgusted with themselves. They want to change for themselves and they want the opportunity to turn back to the Lord and his forgiveness."

Alex felt as though she would be better off speaking to a cement, telegraph pole. It was always the people who thought that they were backed up by a big, invisible being in the sky, who seemed to be the most confident in their arguments and the most stubborn. John wasn't even religious, but growing up in a house such as this, Alex supposed that he had to at least put up a façade until he could escape to London.

She went back upstairs without eating, not that she had been hungry in the first place and she found Matthew coming out of the bathroom. She took one look at him and his smiling face and said, "I'm going out – I've had enough of this place and of you."

*

A call came out of nowhere, bringing Alex back from her thoughts, "Ms Dewill. Alexandra Dewill."

She looked up from the carpet, which she had been staring at blankly in her daze and observed the woman who had just summoned her. She was middle aged, her hair was ragged, and she looked as overworked as she was underpaid – the very personification of the entire NHS all rolled into one poor doctor.

Alex followed her down a narrow corridor, into a small consulting room. The antiseptic smell was so strong, that it did Alex's stomach no favours.

The doctor indicated for her to take a seat next to her desk and as she sat, she said:

"My name's Dr Stark, what can I do for you today? I see that you've had some kind of mishap."

Alex reflexively put her hand to her face and said, "Oh, I'm not here about my nose, although it has been aching."

Dr Stark made a note on her computer and then nodded for Alex to continue.

"I've been having the strong urge to vomit for about the last week or so and I'm exhausted all the time; it's as though someone has hung weights off every part of my body. Everything is so difficult, I feel as though I'm wading through mud."

"A week is a long time to be feeling nauseated. Is there anything specific that brings it on? Or is it a constant feeling?" Dr Stark asked.

"It comes and goes – but it's triggered by strong smells and of course food has been a real problem for me. I haven't been eating consistently, if at all – I just haven't felt all that hungry. I thought that it was a part of the natural grieving process." Dr Stark gave her a quizzical look, so Alex elaborated, "My husband was killed last week;

murdered."

"I'm so sorry to hear that," Dr Stark replied, shifting uneasily in her seat. "Clearly it's a stressful time for you and this can cause the symptoms that you're referring to – however I would like to run a few tests, just in case."

Dr Stark began to type, using only her two index fingers – which was a point of irritation for Alex. When she had finally finished, she handed Alex a small plastic jar.

"Fill this up to the halfway mark and give it to one of the nurses at the pathology desk. They can get started on the analysis while we do some other tests in here."

As Alex walked out of the room, Dr Stark called after her, "Middle stream please."

Alex did as she was asked and then returned to the consulting room, where Dr Stark poked and prodded her and subjected her to several tests.

"Is that amount necessary? I'm already feeling faint," Alex asked as she watched Dr Stark draw blood steadily into a third vial.

Dr Stark nodded to the affirmative and gave her a comforting smile as she gathered the vials together and left the room. She returned about ten minutes later, holding a sheet of paper. She untangled her reading glasses from the top of her head and she studied the results.

Eventually Dr Stark asked, "When was the last time you menstruated?"

That question threw Alex off balance. It wasn't something that she paid much attention to as she had given up on the idea that she could bear children a long time ago, and it was always so inconsistent that there was never a pattern to it.

"Maybe 4 or 5 weeks ago," she guessed. "But my cycle is usually all over the place – so that's nothing unusual," she clarified.

Dr Stark handed over the sheet of paper and said, "These are the results of your urine test and it seems that the reason you've been feeling sick isn't only because of your grief. See that high hCG hormone count on the list – that number tells me that you're pregnant.

Your nausea is morning sickness."

Alex felt her hand go weak as she dropped the sheet of paper that she had been holding. If she had been standing, she was sure that her knees would have given way from underneath her. Her mouth hung open but no words came out. She and John had tried for so many years and they had never been able to conceive – she had just resigned herself to the fact that a baby was something that she would never be able to have. And now that he was dead and she was finding out about who John really was, she wasn't sure if she wanted any part of him inside of her, let alone a daily reminder of him, bound to her for the rest of her life.

"I can't be pregnant – it's not possible. We've been trying for years and we've never come close," Alex breathed.

"Were you seeing a fertility doctor before? Someone who is aware of your history?" Dr Stark asked.

"I had an ectopic pregnancy when I was younger and I lost the baby. It was quite violent and my body didn't respond well. I just assumed that everything down there was broken; that I was defective," Alex replied.

"Well, with hCG numbers like this it is almost certain that you are pregnant. We'll confirm it with the blood test and have the results for you in a couple of days at the very latest."

Alex thought about it and calculated that she and John had had their habitual, fuck a month, about three weeks before he had died. She put her hand to her stomach and rubbed it – trying to feel if it was any bigger than she could last remember.

She had always felt the burden of not being able to give John the child that he had wanted and now it turned out that she had tortured herself over nothing. She had spent all those years feeling guilty because it was the one thing upon which she had lied to John, and it was the driving force behind the gradual dissolution of their marriage.

She left the doctor's surgery at a loss that afternoon – she was confused, afraid. Here she was, in her mid-thirties, widowed, alone and she had the baby of a potential monster growing inside of her. She hated John Quinn more than ever in that moment. He had lied to her, left her at the mercy of those merciless loan sharks – who had already inflicted bodily damage upon her, and he had knocked her up with something that she could never love.

***

"Did you know about this?" Superintendent Daria Zukowski asked before she had even announced her presence.

Detective Sergeant Diane Pridis had been expecting this moment; dreading it. She had spent half the night mulling over all the different answers which she could give and how each would affect herself and Tilman and she was yet to figure out her best course of action. The truth was not an option –

"Of course I knew that my senior officer was on coke – we were fucking and she got me hooked on Adderall too."

But then Pridis couldn't anticipate what Tilman would say, when or if she woke up. Would she incriminate Pridis to get back at her for telling the world about her love of cocaine? Or would she be unselfish for once in her life and take the hit on her own? Tilman was vindictive, but there would be nothing to gain if they both lost their careers and Pridis did save her life.

"I had my suspicions," Pridis replied keeping her gaze fixed steadily upon Tilman's comatose body.

"There's going to be an investigation – they'll want to talk to you. The doctors say that the cocaine was tainted," the Super said. She massaged her own left shoulder, sighed and continued, "Inspector Bliss tried to warn me about her – but I never listened. I always assumed that he was trying to draw my attention away from his own shortcomings. She was my best detective and she was running around Scotland Yard, coked up to the eyeballs; you'd think one of you other detectives would have noticed before it came to this."

"Some people wear their addictions well," Pridis answered, still averting her eyes from her superior officer.

"Do you think you can take the lead on the Quinn case? Inspector Bliss has his hands full in Sheffield and you're performance has been exemplary so far. I see no reason to bring someone else in on it – do you?"

Pridis looked up from Tilman's bed; the heart rate monitor beat irregularly in the background. She was ambitious and she had been waiting for an opportunity to demonstrate what she could do.

"We already have two suspects and I've sent DC Harper and a couple of uniforms out to pick them up. We should have the case closed out by the end of the day if everything goes as it should," Pridis said.

"Good. Has Tilman's family been notified?" the Super asked.

"She doesn't have anyone," Pridis replied with a sigh.

"It figures." The Super took a seat next to Tilman's bed and asked, "When was the last time you slept?"

"I can't remember," Pridis said, using all of her will power to control the steady shaking of her left hand.

Since Tilman's overdose, Pridis had sworn to herself that she was never going to take another pill – and so for the second time within the week, she had tossed her entire supply of Adderall out and she was now submerged deeply in the throes of withdrawal. She had hoped that she could hide herself at the hospital until the worst of it had passed, but all she wanted to do now was swallow an entire bottle of Adderall to halt the torment of the anxiety, hunger, and exhaustion, which had been crashing over her since early that morning, when her body had discovered that it wasn't going to get the hit that it so desperately craved.

"You should go home, have a shower, freshen up and get ready to close out your first case as the lead. I'll stay here; keep watch. I can't have one of my officer's waking up alone, even if she has disappointed us all," the Super said.

Pridis gathered her things. On her way down the corridor, she buttoned up her jacket to cover the smudge of Tilman's blood which adorned the front of her shirt. She hadn't slept for at least three days and without her chemical help, her body was crashing fast. She checked her watch; it was just after 5pm. Vicki would still be at work, so she'd have time enough to head home and shower without confrontation. She started her car, found her parking ticket, took out her credit card and drove towards the exit. She dialled Inspector Bliss' number once again. She hadn't been able to get through to him the previous evening or that morning and she wanted to update him on Tilman, the Quinn case and speak to him about PC Pearson.

It went straight through to voice mail. She hung up. She wasn't going to leave another message – he would call her back when he had time. With so many bones up there, he certainly did have his hands full.

As she hung up, her phone vibrated in her hand. She answered.

"I hear you're the new boss," DC Crocker said.

"Geez, news sure does travel fast around here. I just heard about it myself," Pridis replied.

"The canteen was aflutter with talk of Tilman's demise and it seemed to be the natural progression," DC Crocker answered.

"What have you got for me? Have you found Jarmila yet?" Pridis asked as she pulled out of the carpark, heading in the direction of her apartment.

"I haven't been able to track down Bliss' missus, but Rory Hicks has come in with his mother – he said that she's having a bout of lucidity and that she wants to talk about the night the CCTV was tampered with. What should I do with them?"

Pridis checked her mirrors and swung her car around immediately.

"Put them in with the sketch artist; don't show them any photos of the Golds, I don't want her biased in any way – she's our only eyewitness – I'm coming now."

This was the breakthrough that Pridis had been waiting for. She had descriptions of the Golds from both Jürgen Sampson and Robert Leung and the circumstantial evidence had certainly piled up, however there was no direct connection between the Golds and the night of the murder, other than the CCTV. If she could put the Golds in Rory

Hicks' house, then Pridis had them dead to rights. She just hoped that Mrs Hicks would remain lucid enough for them to get what they needed.

*

The sketch artist sat clutching his notepad, showing Rory Hicks and his mother the resultant drawing, when Pridis entered the room.

"Are you sure that's him Mum? Do you remember anything else?" Hicks asked.

"Yes Dear, that's him," she replied with an airy voice.

"I'm sorry mate, we've wasted your time," Hicks said as he helped his mother from her chair.

"Why what's wrong?" Pridis asked, startling everyone in the room.

"That's the spitting image of my father and I can guarantee that he's still dead," Hicks said with frustration. "She was so with it earlier. It was as though someone flicked a switch and I had my mother back for a while. I'm sorry."

"Don't be. You tried. It must be hard seeing her like that," Pridis said.

Hicks nodded.

"I'll walk you out," Pridis offered. She turned to Hicks' mother and said, "Thank-you for coming in today."

As they reached the front of the building, Mrs Hicks broke away from her son and walked slowly towards a man who was leaning against the wall, a smoke hanging from the corner of his mouth.

"Tom, darling!" Mrs Hicks exclaimed.

The man took a drag on his cigarette and gave her a mystified look.

He said through a cloud of smoke, "Sorry lady, I think you have me mixed up with somebody else."

Mrs Hicks began to protest when her son grasped his mother's elbow, apologised to the smoker and lead her back to where Pridis was standing.

Hicks said, "I'll let you know if she comes back to me any time soon. I hope you catch the bastard who did this. Breaking into my house like that, it makes my blood boil."

"We'll get them, Mr Hicks; don't you worry about that."

***

Edris Bliss finished his cigarette, crushed it beneath his black, leather boot and entered enemy territory. New Scotland Yard was the last place that he wanted to be, but he hadn't been able to get through to his bro and time was now of the essence. He hadn't expected to see that little, old lady again – he had put her to bed the night that he had wiped the CCTV – as mad as a hen in a snake pit, she was, insisting that he was her husband. He had played along with it – he wasn't in the habit of offing the innocent, especially someone as vulnerable as she was, and no one would take her claims seriously.

"I need to get a hold of Inspector Andy Bliss, it's urgent," Edris said to one of the receptionists.

"I'll call up to him," the receptionist replied.

"He's not here – he's in Sheffield," Edris snapped. "If he was here, I wouldn't have a fucken problem, would I?"

"Watch your language," came a woman's voice from over his left shoulder.

"What's it to you?"

"It'll be money out of your pocket if you're not careful," the woman said.

"Look, we're wasting time – I need to speak to my brother!"

"You're Edris?" she asked.

"How the hell did you know that?"

"I'm Detective Sergeant Diane Pridis – I'm your brother's partner. Doctor Trudeau mentioned your algorithm."

"I need to warn Andy. The Golds are going to Sheffield – they're carrying and they're going to get Luke's money whichever way they can. I've been trying to call him all day; he's not safe," Edris said in a rush.

Pridis' phone rang. She excused herself and answered it out of Edris' earshot.

She hung up and as she ran off with a renewed sense of urgency towards the elevators, she called to him, "Don't worry, I'll get it sorted."

21. LOCKED AWAY

"You've no evidence to incriminate me." Malcolm Quinn breathed onto the lenses of his spectacles and polished them with the handkerchief which Mary had just flung onto the desk between them and continued, "The Captain slipped – you saw it for yourself."

"I find it evidence enough, that you haven't directly denied my allegation," Mary replied snatching the handkerchief back from him and placing it carefully in her pocket.

"You don't expect that I give enough credence to this allegation to answer to it, do you? A spot or two of wax on my handkerchief and you're ready to hang me," Malcolm sneered.

"Maybe you will take me seriously once I include Sergeant Markson in our conversation," Mary answered.

She lit her cigarette with the silver desk lighter. Malcolm took advantage of the distraction, walked across to the decanter. He returned with two glasses, each half filled with a honey coloured liquid. Mary assumed it to be whiskey, however after one sip she could taste the tell-tale sweetness and spices of Drambuie – which contrasted well with the smoky undertones deposited on her tastebuds by the cigarette.

Malcolm gave her a look of half apology and half pity which was usually given after someone had made a fool of themselves.

"I'm sorry that I haven't been here for you Mary. To find out that Emlyn had died and then to be present when our poor, young Captain fell off the roof, must have been very difficult," Malcolm said.

"It has been a trying time and it hasn't been made any easier by you. It hasn't slipped my awareness that you've been avoiding me," Mary responded, inhaling on her cigarette and disposing of the ash into the alabaster ashtray.

"I tend to distance myself from others when there are times of such difficulty; especially when people I care about are involved. It has always been a coping mechanism of mine – I need to detach myself from it all. I can't be seen to be emotional – it's not becoming of someone in my position. And your resemblance to Emlyn is something else; it brings my memories of her flooding back," he explained.

"It's just the two of us here now; you never really cared about Emlyn, you were just after a house to go with all of that new money of yours," she accused.

"What are we going to do with you Mary? You never wanted me to marry your sister – I shouldn't be surprised about your antagonism towards me now that she's dead. But so you know; I truly did love your sister. It's just a shame that she never fully gave me her heart. I married her knowing that she still had feelings for Captain Hope – I didn't realise how much she loved him until she killed herself. Seeing him again overwhelmed her and she couldn't face another day with me. I will never forgive myself for not being enough for her."

"You can stop with your false sentiments; I know that Emlyn was looking into the disappearance and murder of Cecil Watson and I know that she found evidence of wrong doing at your hospital in the process. The child knew about the disappearing soldiers and Emlyn had found out about it too and now they're both dead."

"I don't know what you're talking about. I had a nightmare about a month ago and Emlyn told me that I had shouted Cecil's name. That was the first that I had thought of him in a very long time. I do feel responsible for his death – I should never have allowed that Watson woman to bring her child into the hospital that day. A war hospital is no place for a child – as I'm sure you are well aware. It was a mistake and one which will haunt me for as long as I live. Ignatius Finch was my responsibility and so were his actions." He paused for a long moment, contemplating the contents of his glass and continued, "This doesn't have anything to do with Georgey Dockrell, does it? I saw you two drinking together at Captain Hope's wake. He hasn't poisoned you against me, has he?"

Mary had spoken to Georgey at the train station earlier that day. She had caught him just before his train had left the station. In the brief moments that they had to converse, he hadn't been able to give her anything more than a short history of the early years of Billy Garrot's life. He was the son of a prostitute and a conman, who had started teaching Billy the tricks of the trade at a very young age. They were well known around the neighbourhood and Georgey learnt not to cross Billy's path if he could help it. But there was nothing more than evidence of a man who had had a rough start in life and who had wanted to shift his wicket.

She decided to change tack.

"Where did you get the extra rations from during the war? Aunt Bett told me about the abundance of meat," Mary asked.

"It was through good management – I found a way to stretch what we already had; utilise more fully what wasn't reaching its potential," Malcolm replied.

"If your management was so superior, then why were you signing the discharge forms for some of the mentally infirmed soldiers, approving their placement back on the frontlines?" Mary motioned towards the files which lay strewn across Malcolm's desk. "If they were as ill as those files indicate then they shouldn't have been discharged at all. Sending them back to the front in that condition is tantamount to murder."

"I didn't," Malcolm replied.

"Georgey told me all about you, Billy. You can't tell me that it's a coincidence that Billy Garrot is the same name which appears on those forms. And then to bring Baden into it – he told me that he hadn't sent those orders, that someone else had forged his signature. I can only guess that if it all went awry, you were prepared to blame everything on him. I suppose you assumed that he would die out there – like so many others? And then when Emlyn started digging, you killed her – didn't you?"

"Mary, I know how you feel, and it is easy to lash out at someone when tragedies such as these happen. But we need to accept the fact that Emlyn wasn't happy and she let the darkness pull her down. I loved her so very much and when we found her swinging from that God forsaken tree...," he paused and sighed heavily, "...you are so lucky that you didn't have to see her like that Mary. I can't get the sight of it out of my head. And what she was doing down there – away from the other wives – I will never know.

"At first I thought it was murder. What else could it have been? But when Sergeant Markson explained how she had done it herself and the doctor had said that there were no signs of struggle – I had to accept the truth, as hard as it has been."

The door burst open and Louise Ellis ran into the room.

Out of breath, she exclaimed, "Sir, you must come quickly!"

"What is it, Miss Ellis?" Malcolm asked.

"It's Addie – she's down by the linden tree. She has a rope and she's threatening to hang herself," Louise explained.

The three of them ran towards the embankment; Mary leading the way. Hanging from the tree, was a mass. It swung slowly in the breeze.

"My God, she's really done it!" Louise exclaimed shrilly.

Mary flew down the embankment and grabbed a hold of Addie's legs. They were as cold as ice. She looked up at Addie's face. It was purple and dried blood was caked in her hair and down her cheeks.

She let go of Addie and walked slowly towards Malcolm.

"She's been dead for at least a week," Mary shouted.

Malcolm rushed suddenly towards her. She stepped backwards to avoid contact, but instead of feeling the safety of the ground beneath her feet, there was nothing but air. She hadn't noticed that the entrance to the bunker had been wide open. She fell in slow motion, a thousand thoughts running through her head.

Her ankle hit the ground first with a snap, jolting her leg and throwing her to the ground. An agonising pain stabbed along the entire length of her right leg. It was broken – in how many places, she couldn't be sure. There was an unbearable odour which hit her nostrils with a suffocating thickness; it was a smell that she knew very well from the frontlines; the smell of unrestrained death.

Two figures peered down at her from above and the voice of Malcolm echoed, "You couldn't leave well enough alone, could you?"

He slammed the trapdoor shut and she heard the lock click into place. The darkness swallowed her.

She shouted as loudly as she could, "What is the meaning of this? You did it, didn't you? You killed Emlyn. Murderers!"

Malcolm's muffled voice came floating through, "I admit that I'm a murderer – but I never hurt Emlyn."

"What are you going to do with me?" she said – the desperation of her situation beginning to sink in.

"I gave you the opportunity to leave, return to Montpellier and yet you decided to continue pushing. This is your own fault," Malcolm shouted.

"If you're going to kill me too – then I at least deserve some answers," Mary implored.

She was met with silence and she thought that they had abandoned her; left her to rot. She wondered why Louise was helping Malcolm. Had he fallen in love with the help? Was all of this because he wanted to be with Louise Ellis? He had brought the Ellis sisters with him from his previous posting at Humbleton House and Emlyn had not wanted them – but Malcolm had employed them anyway.

The sound of voices arguing floated through the trapdoor and then there was a damp thud from above and Malcolm said, "I'll give you your answers."

Mary thought for a moment, she didn't really have a choice other than to keep Malcolm talking. It was her only hope. She said:

"All right, but I want to know everything – start from the beginning – start from the day that Cecil Watson disappeared," she replied as she fumbled in her pocket for her notepad and pencil.

"If you want to know everything, then I'm going to have to go back much further than Cecil Watson – I need to start from my childhood, back when I was known as Billy Garrot," Malcolm began.

****

It was getting late. The sun had sunken away and the sky was now dark, revealing the sparkling stars which had been hidden by the light of day. Andy Bliss sat in his car and took a moment to reflect on his harrowing day. He had set off from the warmth of Jacqueline's bed early that morning, unable to sleep as he was still troubled by his phone call with Carla and he needed to speak to her face to face. The drive to London had been punctuated with traffic along the way, but he had made it in good time.

Carla was in her usual spot – leaning casually against the wall of The Shacklewell Arms, waiting for either her first customer of the day or for the pub to open – whichever came first. The stillness of the day, caused the smoke from her cigarette, to linger around her. He wound down his window and called to her. She had a lightness in her face, which he hadn't seen in a very long time; it disappeared the moment she saw that it was him.

"What the fuck are you doing here? You said you were in Sheffield, you lying son of a bitch. Fuck-off, before you scare away my clientele."

"I'm not here to make any trouble Carla – I just want to talk. After our phone conversation, I needed to know that you're all right. I drove all the way from Sheffield to make sure. Tell me about your leg; what does it have to do with John Quinn?" Andy asked.

"It's a little late for your concern, isn't it? You've had so many chances to ask me about it. You're only asking me now because it benefits you," she retorted.

Carla made a move to return to her place upon the wall. Andy grabbed a hold of her wrist. She swung around; annoyance filtered across her every feature.

"Let go of me!" she shouted as she yanked her arm free.

"Tell me about John Quinn and then I'll leave you alone – forever, if that's what you want."

She looked like a defeated woman. She sighed and said:

"It was around ten years ago. Back then I was either high on coke or looking to score. That's why I got into this business in the first place; sell my body, to feed my soul. John Quinn found me when I was at my lowest and he preyed on that weakness.

"He offered me fifteen grand for my leg and another five thousand on top of that for my silence. I'd never seen that much lolly before in my life and at the time I thought – what the hell, I don't need my leg to fuck, right? He put me to sleep and when I woke up, my leg was gone and so was he.

"The money didn't last long. I snorted it and shot it into my veins as quick as I could, and then I was left with nothing – a cripple."

"Did he tell you why he wanted it?" Andy asked.

"No, and I didn't care. All I wanted was drugs and the only way to get them was to get my hands on money – and he offered me what felt like a lifetime supply of it. Twenty thousand pounds; that's plenty of Johns that I didn't have to fuck. I felt like the fucken Queen – well at least for that 6 months; at least until the cash and the drugs ran out. I should have overdosed. I tried once. But I just woke up in a pool of my own vomit, with a man at the end of my bed, zipping up his trousers."

Andy couldn't understand what John Quinn wanted with Carla's leg – but that seemed to be a problem best saved for another day.

He breathed in the cold night air as he crossed the road and entered Jacqueline's pub. He had driven for at least nine hours that day and all he wanted was a whiskey and a woman. The pub was empty inside, as it had been on his previous visits. Andy wondered how Jacqueline kept such a liability afloat.

"Jacqueline?" he called through to the back, when she hadn't appeared after a few minutes.

There was no reply.

He walked around the bar and helped himself to a drink. A beep echoed from the corner of the room. He walked to the booth – a place that held pleasant memories. Beep. His mobile phone lay under the table from the evening before. He had been so concerned about Carla, that he hadn't noticed its absence.

A dog barked. Andy went to stand up and hit the top of his head on the table.

"Ah shit!" he exclaimed as he stood up, rubbing his head.

Jacqueline's small terrier, the one who had found Cecil Watson's femur, came trotting happily into the room. With its tail wagging, it lay down and started licking the carpet. Andy approached and saw that there were drops of blood spattered on the ground. He cleared the dog away and took a closer look. The blood was fresh.

"Jacqueline?!" he called, with much more volume and urgency than before.

The dog took fright and ran back behind the bar. Andy pursued it. He was beginning to think that the dog was a harbinger of death. He searched the office and back room – there was no sign of her.

He glanced at his phone. There were countless missed calls from Pridis and Royal and even one from the Super, but nothing from Jacqueline. He opened his text messages. The first was from Edris.

'The loan sharks are heading your way and they're packing heat – someone called Luke is pulling the strings. Watch yourself little bro.'

Andy raced to his car. Loxley Hall had been at the centre of everything so far and chances were that he would find Jacqueline there. And as much as he didn't like Alex, he didn't want to leave her vulnerable to the loan sharks. They had already broken her face, and Andy didn't want her murder on his conscience.

As Andy sped towards the towering, front gates, he saw a crumpled mass lying on the ground, and the gates, which had been routinely locked and guarded by PC Pearson during the evenings, were gaping open.

Andy burst from his car; the cold air slapped him in the face. He ran to the lump that was sprawled on the ground. PC Pearson's jacket lay ripped and bloodied. Andy knelt and examined it – blood was spattered across the back and there were some heavy droplets apparent on the dusty surface of the road.

He sprinted, faster and faster along the driveway, guided only by the dull shine of the moon. His heart raced. He wended this way and that, and as he rounded the final bend he could see that the front door was wide open.

The adrenalin pumped through his veins and his breathing was heavy and laboured. A dim light radiated from the dining room. He exploded through the door, ready for action.

The gun sat on the table, next to a bottle of bourbon. It glinted in the dim light of the candles. Andy leapt towards the table.

"Come any closer and I'll use it," Alex said, as she swept her long brown hair out of her face.

The tears gleamed upon her cheeks. She picked up the gun and pointed it at Andy.

"I didn't think that it was possible – we tried so many times and never had any success and now he's dead." She took a swig from the bottle and turned the gun towards her stomach. "I should off the monster now, before it's unleashed on this world. If it's anything like its father…."

Her sentence trailed off and she drank once more.

"Do you have a cigarette?" she asked pointing the gun back towards Andy.

"Sorry Ms Dewill, I don't. You know, I'd feel more comfortable if you just put that down," he said motioning towards the gun and taking a step closer.

"Wouldn't you now," she replied. "The mighty Inspector Bliss, afraid of a little gun. John told me how you beat him in the interview room. He wouldn't give you what you wanted and so you thought you would take it. Maybe you should have hit him harder, beaten his skull right in – you would have done us all a favour."

"You're right. I should have killed that son of a bitch when I had the chance – but I didn't and I have to live with the lives of all those women that he took. But I'm not going to allow him to take another life." Andy stepped even closer and said, "Please, give me the gun –

we can talk about this – I can even find you some smokes."

She leapt from her chair and backed away from him. Andy lunged towards her and knocked the gun out of her hand. It slid under the table and she clawed at his face. He grabbed Alex's wrists and restrained her.

"Let go of me!" she exclaimed, but he held onto her tightly.

"Funnily enough, you're not the first woman to say that to me today," Andy replied.

There was a click and Andy felt something solid sticking into his back, right between his shoulder blades.

"I'd let the broad go if I were you."

Andy spun around. There were two men, one standing in the doorway and the other holding a gun, which was now trained directly on Andy's head.

"Where's Jacqueline?" Andy demanded.

"Who the hell's that?" the man in the doorway answered.

"The woman who runs the pub," Andy responded.

"I don't know about her – but we took good care of that copper on the gate," the man replied.

"He was easy. I can't believe that coppers still don't carry guns," the other one added as he waved his in the air.

"On a date, are we? Moved on quick from your dead husband, din't ya?" the man said, now entering the room.

"Firstly, this is *not* a date, far from it actually; and secondly who are you people?" Alex asked.

"I thought you'd recognise us from your little stoush with the door. I'm Kevlar, and this is me son, Sparks. We told you not to skip town, and yet here we are."

Andy peered sideways, towards Alex's gun which lay under the table. It was in diving distance, but he was certain that if he tried for it, he would get both he and Alex shot; and he couldn't be sure that it was loaded – where did she even get it from?

"Look, Kevlar, I didn't take your money. Apparently that was my husband and according to yourselves and your note, you're the ones who killed him. If you wanted your money so badly, I'm pretty sure that best business practice in your line of work is to injure, not kill," Alex said.

"Very astute young lady – but sometimes it don't work out that way," Kevlar replied.

"I'm sure we can sort this out without having to resort to violence," Andy implored.

"Who the hell are you anyway?" Sparks shouted. "We're not here to talk to you; so you can sit the fuck down and shut the fuck up."

"Watch ya language in front of the lady," Kevlar chided. He reached into his inside pocket and took out a piece of paper. "There's still one way out of this. Our client has said that we can pardon your debt if you sign this piece of paper right here, right now. We can make all of these troubles disappear," he added.

"My lawyer's in the process of getting your money. I don't need to sign anything," Alex said.

"Luke wants you to sign it, so sign it you will," Sparks said now pointing the gun at Alex.

Kevlar gave Sparks a disgruntled look and whispered, "You don't use the client's name, ever. We can't bring Edris in every time you fuck something up."

Sparks grunted.

"Go ahead, shoot – just aim for my stomach – you'd be doing me a favour," Alex challenged, slurring her speech ever so slightly.

"You stupid bitch," Sparks shouted as he took a menacing step towards her.

Andy heard two loud pops. He instinctively dove on top of Alex. When he noticed that neither of them were shot, he turned to see both Sparks and Kevlar prone on the ground. Blood was oozing from the backs of their heads, forming devilish halos. They lay motionless.

Alex sprang to her feet and ran towards their saviour, "Matthew, you're amazing."

"That's Mark," Andy corrected. "Thanks mate, I thought we were done for."

"You're both right. Hey Mark, show yourself," Matthew said.

"You're twins?" Andy asked redundantly.

"You're John's, what? Cousin?" Alex questioned. "But why?"

"I wanted to get the job in your kitchen on merit. I didn't want you to feel like you had to give me the job because I was related to John; I wanted to earn it," Matthew explained.

"Why didn't you say anything when we came here? Or even after John died?"

"I couldn't find the right words and anyway, I love you Alex. I didn't want to make things weird between us."

"And this isn't?" Alex questioned.

Andy could hear Mark in the entrance hall. He was speaking on his phone.

"Matthew burst in and shot them………Yes, with the hunting rifle………No, she didn't sign it and no, they're not dead………I told him to wait………. Well, I can do it now………..What do you mean I've got to switch the guns?……….We'll throw them in the bunker. Don't worry Luke, we'll sort it out."

Andy reached for Spark's gun, which had jolted out of his hand when he had hit the floor, but Matthew was too quick. He picked it up and pointed it at Andy.

"I'll take care of this problem now," he shouted through to Mark.

"Luke said to wait. We need to put them in the bunker – something about the guns we need to use and the gunshot residue," Mark replied.

"You don't have to do this," Andy said. "Alex said she can get the money and I'm sure she'll sign whatever it is that you want."

"Speak for yourself," Alex retorted. "Do either of you at least have a cigarette?"

Matthew handed Sparks' gun to Mark. He took a cigarette out of his pocket, lit it and gave it to Alex. Mark pointed his gun at Andy's head and ordered him and Alex to the bunker. They ducked beneath the crime-scene tape and passed the tents. It was late and the SOCO team had called it a day, after completing the arduous extraction of all the bones. When they reached the trapdoor, Andy entered first and then helped an unsteady Alex, down the ladder. Mark slammed the trapdoor shut and Andy could hear a metallic clicking sound. Enveloped in the darkness, Andy and Alex were now at the mercy of the mysterious Luke.

22. THE GOSPEL ACCORDING TO LUKE

"What the hell are we going to do?" Alex said in a panicked whisper.

She struggled for air; the gauze in her nose seemed to be packed tighter than before. Her heart beat through her chest and to make matters worse, it was completely black in there, as though night itself had come to rest in the bunker. She stood rooted to the spot. All she could hear was Andy banging around haplessly in the dark

Her body was shaking and her head was spinning. Why was Matthew doing this to her? He had shot those two men as if it were nothing, and he had allowed Mark to lock her away without any protestation. An overwhelming sense of urgency flooded her veins. She needed to get out of this place – get away from John and his family and any part of his history. She was being suffocated by the weight of him and his sins.

She had to do something. She charged through the darkness; she was strong, she'd break through whatever came between her and her freedom.

Bang. She ran straight into Andy, and they landed with a thud onto the floor.

"What are you doing?" Andy asked as she untangled her legs from his.

She separated herself from him and found the nearest vertical surface to lean against.

"I don't know," she replied, hanging her head between her knees.

"I'm going to get us out of here," Andy said; determination permeating his voice.

Alex heard him regain his feet and start to stumble around the room again. He picked up the cigarette which Alex had dropped on her way down the ladder. The tip brightened as Andy took one drag and then another. She heard a soft hissing sound and saw the path of the tip as it moved downward and then there was light.

As her eyes adjusted, she saw Andy standing there holding a lantern.

"I thought that's what I'd laid my hands on just before we had our little tangle," Andy said. "Lucky that you're craving nicotine – although I wouldn't recommend it for the little one."

Alex instinctively caressed her stomach and just as quickly felt sickened by the thought of what she had growing inside of her.

The light emanating from the lamp was powerful enough to illuminate the entire room. It was Alex's first time in the bunker and to her it seemed quite empty; devoid of anything except for a table. She would never have thought that it had been the tomb, the final resting place of so many. It saddened her.

Andy climbed back up the ladder and used his shoulder to push against the trapdoor. It didn't budge.

"No use," he said.

He climbed back down and pounded on the wall. He moved across a step and then pounded again.

"I'm looking for a hollow sound," he informed. "The trapdoor hadn't been opened in years until we found it – there must be another access point. Some of the bones we found in here were very recent."

"Brilliant!" exclaimed Alex, jumping to her feet. "Now we just have to find it."

Alex noted that two of the walls were made of brick and the other two of wood and so it stood to reason that the exit would be concealed somewhere behind the wooden panels. They both continued banging and banging but all they kept finding were dull thuds. Hope was beginning to fade when suddenly Andy's fist produced a large hollow boom.

"This is it!" he exclaimed. "There must be a lever or some mechanism around to open it – otherwise I'll have to kick it down."

Alex brought the lamp closer and they both examined the wall. There was nothing obvious and so she looked around the room for anything which appeared out of place. A brick protruded from the adjacent wall by a couple of inches. She pushed it and then pulled on it. It sprang loose, almost landing on her foot. The door hadn't opened, but there was a leather pouch tucked away in the nook behind the wall. She reached in and carefully extracted it.

The pouch was old and covered in an age worth of dust. Alex walked across to the table, set the brick down and opened it. It was full of papers – all handwritten and discoloured. The ink was preserved however, most likely due to the fact that they had not seen the light of day and had not been exposed to the humidity of air or the oily skin of human contact.

Andy picked up the brick from the table and said, "Perfect – I can use this to knock through the wood," and he walked back to his position and started to bash it on the wall.

Alex rifled gently through the papers. There were notes and letters but the one piece which stood out was filled with a rushed scrawl, headed in big block letters – 'THE CONFESSION OF MALCOLM QUINN'.

Alex scanned the piece of paper and said to Andy, "I think this is the key that you've been looking for."

"Does it tell you how to open the door?" he asked.

"Not the key to the door, the key to the story of your skeletons," Alex replied with a hint of annoyance.

"I think we have more pressing issues at hand right now – I could do with some help on getting this door open," Andy pleaded.

She handed the leather pouch to Andy and examined the wall. She could see the outline of a doorway.

"Do you have your wallet?" Alex asked her hand already outstretched.

"Yes," he said, eyeing her suspiciously as he laid it on her hand.

She rummaged through it and took out his credit card. She turned her back to him and in a moment the door clicked open.

"You might need a new card," she said with a smirk, as she handed him back his wallet.

"Well at least we got the door open."

"We?" Alex exclaimed.

"It was my card," Andy shrugged.

Andy led the way cautiously through the tunnel. He appeared uncertain – he had a look on his face which was a cross between concentration and confusion. It didn't fill her with any confidence.

In the distance, she could see a light. From the direction that the tunnel had taken, Alex was sure that they were returning to the Hall. Her thoughts were first and foremost on retrieving her gun from the dining room floor. The light became brighter and brighter as they approached. As they emerged from the tunnel, she heard a familiar voice say, "I wondered how long it would take for the two of you to figure it out – I've been waiting."

*

They had surfaced into an industrial style kitchen. It was fitted-out with stainless steel surfaces and there were oversized appliances and cutting implements spread throughout the room. A cauldron-shaped pot, bubbled away on the stove. Against the wall opposite to where they now stood were four black, leather chairs and right above them hung a banner, giving the room the feel of a bizarre clubhouse kitchen. The banner had the image of the four horsemen, weapons drawn, and riding in on a cloud, ready to enact their doom upon the Earth.

All four chairs were filled – three were facing them, but the forth had its back turned.

"What the fuck happened to you?" Andy barked.

Pearson ignored him and said to Alex, "The offer that I expressed to you through the Golds, still stands; sign these papers and I will let you go, debt free."

"So, you're Luke. I thought you were John's best friend – why the hell did you want him dead?" Andy questioned.

Pearson nodded at Mark; he pointed the gun directly at Andy. Now that Alex saw the twins together she could see the subtle differences between the two of them. At least she could understand the reason why she thought Matthew had been so cold to her – not that it mattered much now.

Matthew brought the papers across to Alex. He removed a pen from his pocket and gave it to her.

As she perused them, Matthew said in a hushed voice, "Just sign them Alex and then we can get out of here."

"Is that what all of this has been about?" she questioned, ignoring Matthew's plea. "You want me to sign Loxley Hall over to you? It doesn't make sense – you already live here, what difference does it make if you own it or not?"

"John promised the Hall to me – it was my birthright and he knew it. Then the bastard changed his mind," Pearson said, a dark look shadowing his face. "He told me that it was his duty to have a son – to carry on the Quinn name and he wanted to leave a legacy; his business was in the toilet and he wanted to leave something everlasting for his son. When he told me that he was going to get you pregnant, that was it."

"Well you killed him for no reason – we couldn't have kids; we've been trying for years."

Her statement was true for what she had known up until that morning and it was true for what John had died believing.

"That's not exactly the truth," Pearson said, a broad smile breaking out across his face. "John never wanted children – they weren't a part of his plan. He only married you in the first place because we had all decided that you would provide a good cover for his afterhours activities."

"Then why did he keep insisting that we try?" she asked in exasperation.

"John loved torture. He took pleasure in the pain that he saw in your eyes every time you failed to get pregnant," Pearson answered. "He'd been feeding you the morning after pill, crushed and mixed with your food. He would give you one every morning after you'd fucked. He liked that he was controlling your body and he wanted you to think that it was all you – that you were a failure as a woman."

It happened, before she realised what she was doing. The hand which held the pen, had thrust itself towards her stomach, towards her womb. She didn't want that thing growing inside of her. She was going to dig it out, any way possible.

A strong hand gripped her wrist and pulled the pen away. Matthew checked her stomach and when he was satisfied that she hadn't penetrated her flesh, he sat back down next to Pearson – the pen held firmly in his hand.

The tears felt hot running down her cheeks.

"I'm glad you killed him," she spat.

She felt faint. But she was determined not to show any weakness in front of them. She grit her teeth and pulled her focus inward. Andy stepped towards her and Mark cocked the gun.

"Going somewhere?" Mark asked casually.

"Can't you see that the lady's in distress?" Andy replied.

"Inspector Bliss to the rescue," Pearson said sarcastically. "Give me a break."

"I still don't understand why you want the Hall?" Alex said, regaining her composure.

"I can answer that," Andy replied. "Jeremy Quinn was your father, wasn't he?"

"How did you know that? I thought I guarded that secret exceptionally well."

"He sponsored your scholarship to Radley – there is no reason, other than paternity, that would incline such a toff be interested in the education of a dirt, poor farm boy," Andy stated.

"Great detective work Inspector, but you left out the part where my mother was raped by Jeremy Quinn and that he allowed me to be born into squalor. I didn't just grow up poor – my mother's husband knew that I was the product of his wife's rape and he treated me accordingly. I was beaten and starved and my real father knew about it and all he did was throw money at the problem. I found out about it by the time I was ten years old – and I resolved to take back what was mine.

"And now it's my turn. I'm going to throw my father's own sister out on her ear and she can see what it's like," Pearson said belligerently.

"You can't just turn our mother out onto the streets – she's never known anything but Loxley Hall," Mark argued.

"What do you care? You've always wanted away from this place – I'm setting you free, boys," Pearson replied.

Matthew added, "It is what you've always wanted, Mark. I can help set you up in London. We can continue John's work. We can take whoever we want, whenever we want and we don't have to be at the mercy of anyone. Not Mother, not John – and we'll have Alex to come home to, just as John did."

"I'm not a fucking piece of meat – I'm not your prized possession. And if you think that I'm going anywhere with you, you're just as delusional as……What am I saying? – you're all fucking delusional," Alex replied.

"You're not going to have any say in it. Have you been down into your basement lately? Our John had been working on a project and I think that you'll find it more than comfortable down there. He was planning on moving our base of operations to London – it was always so much work for him to bring the women to us – and so he was going to bring us to the women," Matthew said.

Hostility boiled through her and the only thing preventing her from releasing it was the fact that they held all the guns.

"Tell me about the women?" Andy asked. "Why did John take that hooker's leg, why not kill her?"

"John always did the cutting work," Pearson said calmly. "The whore was his test subject, just as she's going to be mine," he said as he spun the forth chair around to face them.

Alex felt the tension in Andy's body as he charged forwards. Bang. He fell in a heap on the ground. Smoke trailed from the nozzle of the gun held aloft by Mark. He had shot Andy squarely in the stomach. He writhed on the ground, hunched in the foetal position. Alex's first instinct was to go to his aid.

"Move and you get one too," Mark said, his gun now trained on Alex.

Andy raised his head from the ground and spat through gritted teeth, "Jacqueline! You won't get away with this Pearson."

"Ah, but I will, my dear Inspector. You and Alex were sitting down to dinner, when the bloodthirsty Golds arrived – who had already murdered Alex's beloved husband – and they shot you. Upon hearing the shots, our young hero – Matthew – ran towards them and with the family hunting rifle in hand and in self-defence of course, he shot the Golds. I was knocked out by the gates and Mark was never even here. And Jacqueline – there'll be nothing left of her to find. After your unfortunate murder, people will believe it reasonable that she left town – she does have a history of disappearing."

"What about the bones?" Andy asked with a strained whisper.

"A shot to the stomach is one of the most effective and extremely painful deaths imaginable, I find it admirable you can still talk," Pearson said arrogantly. "We all took a piece of each of the women – but now that John's dead, I think he has the least to lose if we pin it on him. He selected them, drugged them, brought them to us, and he was the one who put the bolt through their temples and prepared them."

"Prepare them for what?" Alex asked, not sure if she really wanted the answer.

Pearson pointed to the huge pot, which bubbled violently, upon the stove.

"Why is it, do you think, that the all bones are so clean?" Pearson drawled, moistening his lips.

Mark arose from his chair and approached Alex, the gun still at the ready in his hand. He advanced until he was toe to toe with her – towering over her small frame.

He said, "We found a letter in the bunker, beside the heap of bones in the corner. It was a letter, written a hundred years ago by someone called Addie. It's what has given the four of us our meaning. It described the deeds of our forefathers, during and after the first World War. It showed us, who we truly are and it described the unusual habit of those who came before us. Would you like to take a guess at what that might have been?"

She was frozen to the spot, paralysed by a combination of fear and disgust. He leaned down and he slowly licked her cheek. She shuddered. He smelled like cheap aftershave and yesterday's garlic. Her nausea returned tenfold and she couldn't help but vomit right there on the spot.

Mark laughed and said, "I couldn't help myself, I just had to have a taste." He leaned in and whispered, "Have you ever craved the taste of meat?"

He waited for her to answer and so she reluctantly replied as she wiped away his saliva, "Yes."

"We're not just talking about any meat. We're talking about flesh; the flesh of an animal which is at the top of the kingdom, at the top of the tree for intelligence and ingenuity." Mark cocked to his head to the side, "Can you guess just yet, what our little secret is? The reason why all the bones are so clean?"

Alex wretched; there was nothing left inside of her stomach but her body still tried to purge itself. She knew exactly what Mark was referring to and the thought of it turned her entire body upside down.

"You're lucky, you know? The only thing that saved you on the night you met John, was that you didn't accept his invitation upstairs to his apartment. You could've ended up here, all those years ago. Instead he married you. You intrigued him," Mark said.

Alex was completely numb. She could no longer feel anything at all. The man who she had once loved and who she had spent the last twelve years with, was a murderer and a cannibal. She was no longer in her own body; it was as though she were watching all of this unfold from a safe distance, and that it wasn't her life, but the life of some poor, unfortunate soul who she would never know.

Mark stepped back, raised the gun once again and pointed it at Alex. "Now sign the papers," he demanded.

"You can put your gun down, I'll sign. I don't want anything to do with John or this place and I certainly don't want anything from any of you," Alex said.

"You didn't really think that we'd let you go, did you?" Pearson pronounced rising from his chair. "Either you sign now and get a quick one in the head. Or you resist and you get a slow, painful death like him," he said pointing at Andy.

"You promised that she wouldn't get hurt," Matthew said menacingly.

"Did I now?" Pearson replied.

There was a scuffle. Matthew lunged at Pearson's neck with the pen. Mark spun around and shot his brother in the back.

Alex took her chance.

As Mark turned back towards her, she kicked him as hard as she could in the crotch. He dropped the gun and doubled over in pain – a look of anguish stamped across his face. He tried to straighten himself up as Alex nimbly bent down and picked up the gun.

Crack. Something whistled past her ear. She was showered in a fine mist of warm, sticky blood, which had splattered the room from the point in Pearson's head where the bullet had penetrated his skull. She spun around, her newly acquired gun cocked and ready for anything.

"Police, don't move. Drop your weapon or I'll drop you!"

Alex released the gun which she had just picked up, raised her hands and got down on her knees. Mark did the same, although his features were still twisted with pain. She had never felt such an enormous sense of relief in her life. She went from a state of severe tension to one of near total collapse.

Andy slowly sat up and looked across to Alex. He appeared to be in pain, but she noticed that there was no blood. He lifted his shirt and extracted a silver hipflask, which had been tucked into his belt. Embedded in the flask was a crushed bullet and on his stomach, she could see the beginnings of a bruise. He unscrewed the lid and offered her a drink. She took a swig and coughed at the strength of the whiskey – but she enjoyed the instantaneous effects of the alcohol which surged into her weakened system.

Andy raised himself slowly and untied Jacqueline, who was sitting unconscious in the chair.

"How did you know where to find us Roy?" Andy asked as he threw Royal a set of hand cuffs and he in turn affixed them to Mark's wrists.

"It was Edris," Royal said.

"Who's Edris?" Alex asked remembering the name from earlier that evening.

"No one," Andy replied and prompted Royal to continue as he checked Jacqueline's pupils.

"He told Pridis about the Golds and then she discovered somehow that Pearson was the one who had hired them. We tried calling you, but no one could get through. So Pridis told me to get on my bike and check on you. I had just parked out the front when I heard a gunshot. I raced into the dining room thinking it had come from there and I found this little beauty under the table." Royal showed them Alex's gun. "I heard shouting coming from the floor below. And the rest is history."

"Your timing is impeccable. Where've you been anyway?" Andy asked.

With a sly smile across his face, Royal said, "I have to go to the car and get my equipment. I called the cavalry after I heard the gunshot. There'll be officers bumbling all through my scene before I know it."

*

Royal was right. In no time at all, the room was swarming with police and SOCOs and Alex's statement was taken and then she was swept aside by the wave of activity.

She pressed her hand to her stomach and still couldn't feel any connection with the life that was growing inside of her. How could she ever love something that came from such a man? How could she spend another second with a piece of him inside of her? She was such a fool.

John had never deserved her loyalty. She realised that she had always trusted the wrong men; first John and then Matthew and she had even preferred Pearson to Andy.

She took off her wedding ring. She had not removed it since John had placed it on her finger all those years before. She had no idea why she was still wearing it. It was all a sham. He had never loved her and even if he had at some point – she could never accept the love of such a vile creature. She placed it on the bench underneath the banner of the four horsemen and she simply walked away.

23. THE LAST OF THE LOXLEYS

"Everything I did, was for the greater good. Before I tell you anything else – I need you to understand that," Malcolm said.

He had just finished telling Mary about his early days as a confidence man and how he had convinced Aunt Bett that he was the right man to marry Emlyn. Malcolm had promised to tell her about Emlyn, Cecil Watson and the soldiers, as long as she understood that his motivations were purely for the good of King and country.

Mary couldn't see how murder, under any circumstances, was good – especially after experiencing firsthand what war did to people – but she needed the truth and so she agreed to see it from Malcolm's perspective.

"By 1917, there were so many sick and wounded soldiers coming in, that Loxley Hall was running well beyond its capacity. We were running out of resources; running out of food and medicine – without much hope of resupply. There was so much pressure to get the men back up and fighting and onto the front lines. It was then that I had to make some very difficult decisions.

"We needed resources and there were those who didn't deserve them. They were weak of mind and weak of constitution and I couldn't have them taking up space for the real heroes of the war. So, I decided to do something about it.

"I took the cowards, the ones who had tried self-harm, or had refused to return to the frontlines and I rid the hospital of them. I marched them out to the linden tree at dawn and I executed them for cowardice. I did the world a service. These weren't men, they were nothing."

"Without a trial? Without the proper authorisation?" Mary questioned.

"Their medical records were evidence enough – you saw them for yourself. Weak, inferior and only good for one thing – the barrel of my gun. They didn't deserve our resources, we needed the meat. Then that boy saw and he had to go too."

"He was an eight-year-old boy, who had a propensity towards telling tall stories. No one would have believed him. There was no need to kill him," Mary argued.

"He saw what we were doing with the bodies and I couldn't have it getting out. The hospital had started to thrive. Aunt Bett had found a source for medicines, one who was happy to take extra rations, and I found a way to make those cowards go to work for their country. I got them back to the frontlines all right.

"The boy was easy enough to take care of – all the pieces had fallen into place when Ignatius Finch latched onto the boy. I coaxed him out of his house that evening on the promise of sweets. He trusted me. I think he was happy to have someone who listened to him. He told me what he had seen and I knew then that I had to take care of it. You see, he didn't know that I was involved – because it was Addie who he had seen carrying the incriminating piece of evidence.

"I led him out to the linden tree. He was quite a small child for his age, surprisingly light. I grabbed him by his ankles and I swung him against the tree until his brains splattered the trunk. I couldn't risk the child's body being discovered – not in the shape that I had left it and so I lopped off the boy's arm and I planted it and Ignatius Finch in the field.

"I thought that it had all gone away after the war had finished and the hospital had finally closed down. It was a relief really, to be away from it all. I altered the paperwork to ensure that anyone who enquired after the 27 soldiers would see that they had been returned to fight. What were 27 more young men, when so many had already been lost to the battle? But then one morning, only a month ago, Emlyn told me that I had shouted Cecil Watson's name in my sleep. I truly thought that I had left it all behind me.

"She wouldn't stop digging – she kept asking questions and she visited the Watsons. When I discovered that she'd rifled through my desk and found the files; what else was I to do? She had to be silenced.

"We found out about her meeting with the heroic Captain and it set the wheels in motion. Addie wrote the letter that I sent to the Captain from London, purporting to be from the hospital. It was easy enough to obtain the letter head. And we ensured that I had an iron-clad alibi for the time of her death.

"It all went perfectly to plan, everybody was adequately convinced that it was a suicide and I played the part of widowed husband perfectly – until you showed up. I knew that it spelled trouble the moment you arrived. I should have thrown you out then, but instead I welcomed you into my home and now I'm going to have the blood of the last Loxley on my hands."

Malcolm paused for a moment. Mary could hear the sound of muffled voices once again and then he said, "Make yourself comfortable down there, I have some urgent business to attend to up at the Hall."

And then silence.

*

Mary was mad with rage. She could not believe what he had done. Executing the soldiers for cowardice was one thing – but to murder an innocent child so brutally and to conspire to kill his own wife to cover it all up, was beyond abominable. And not just Malcolm; somehow both Addie and Louise had gotten themselves caught up in all of this, and all Addie had to show for it was a caved in skull.

She took a deep breath – her nose not yet used to the rancid odour which filled the room – and she tried her best to calm herself. Malcolm had left her, but he could return at any time and he would be coming to kill her.

Adrenaline shot through her veins and although her leg was shattered, she pulled herself up and felt her way around the room. She found a small shelf protruding from the wall. She ran her hand across it and found what she was looking for – a lantern.

She lit it and inspected the room. The scene that met her eyes was ghastly. There was a sea of bones adorning the shelves in front of her. There were so many piles, and the dark pits in the skulls, where the soldiers' eyes used to be, were staring upon her. She felt the weight of their deaths upon her shoulders. She knew who had killed them and she didn't want Malcolm Quinn's confession to die with her.

The walls were covered in dried, brownish splatters, which she knew to be blood and the atmosphere was oppressive. She leaned against the table which was in the centre of the room, took out her leather pouch, pencil and a piece of paper. She wrote:

THE CONFESSIONS OF MALCOLM QUINN

Mary wrote as fast and as much as she could and when her hand started to ache, it motivated her to write even faster. He was not going to get away with this. When she was done, she searched for a place to hide her pouch. Near the corner of the room was a loose brick. She hurried across and removed it. She reached behind and pushed her leather satchel to the very back of the hole. She had just replaced the brick in the wall, when she heard heavy footsteps pounding on the ground above.

She considered retrieving the brick from the wall and using that as a weapon – but she didn't want to risk the discovery of the package which she was trying so hard to conceal, and with the damage to her leg, she wouldn't be able to swing it as hard as would be necessary to inflict enough damage upon Malcolm's skull.

There was the clink of metal; Malcolm was coming to finish what he had started. A surge of adrenaline caused her body to respond more quickly and nervously to her every movement. In a flash, she was back at the table where she had been scribing Malcolm's words. She used it to support most of her weight and then she reached into her pocket and took out the knife. She unfolded the blade. The knife was small, but a wound to the right place would be enough to incapacitate him and even kill.

She held it securely in her hand; poised and ready to strike as the trap door swung open. Heavy, brown boots made their way, one rung at a time, down the ladder. He jumped down the last few rungs and swung around to stand directly in front of her and well within her reach.

"I never meant for any of this to happen – what I did during the war was for Britain, to help the war effort and I couldn't let that boy jeopardise my hospital; and then Emlyn and now you – both stubborn and digging into business that never concerned either of you."

He approached slowly. It was now or never. Mary lunged at him and plunged the knife as hard as she could towards his neck. She couldn't tell how much penetration she was able to get, but it had lodged in his flesh. She heard a pained groan as she pushed past him and started to climb the ladder, adrenaline pushing her through the pain produced by her lame leg.

She emerged from the trap door into the light of the day. In the blink of an eye, a long piece of wood swung towards her and she felt a sharp pain in the side of her head as she lost her grip on the ladder and she fell. The last thing Mary felt was her shoulder and then her head hitting the solid ground.

*

Mary opened her eyes. Her sight was blurred. The fresh air was a relief. She couldn't be sure as to how long she had been unconscious, but the sun was now setting over the crenellations of the Hall. As she began to regain her senses, she saw that Louise Ellis was attending to Malcolm's wound as he sat on the bench. She chided him for being so careless.

Addie's body now lay limp next to the open trapdoor – discoloured and decomposing. Mary tried to move, but her arms and legs were bound.

"What are you going to do to me?"

Both Malcolm and Louise turned to face her. Malcolm was pale and looked a sorry sight. It was Louise who answered.

"We're going to string you up just like we did to your meddling sister."

Louise approached Mary, looking at her as though she were an injured animal.

She knelt over her and whispered, "We're going to put you out of your misery."

Mary struggled against her binds, but they were too secure. She squirmed and wriggled and tried with all of her strength to break free, but it was no use. Louise slipped a noose around her neck and then she took a hold of the other end of the rope – which had already been hung over the branch.

"Everybody knows that suicidal tendencies run in families," Louise said as she tugged on the rope.

Mary felt the noose tighten, but the force wasn't enough to lift her from the ground.

"You're going to have to try harder than that," Mary said defiantly.

Louise called over her shoulder to Malcolm, "I'll need your help to pull this one up – when you feel ready – there's no rush. She's not going anywhere."

Louise yanked the rope again and squealed gleefully, "I know they say not to play with your food – but I always find that it's half the fun."

She tugged once again – this time much harder and the noose tightened enough to cause Mary to gurgle.

"She's been snorting Emlyn's snuff – I don't think that it would be wise to have her. The oleander has most likely leached into her flesh by now," Malcolm stated.

"Another perfectly good carcass going to waste!" Louise snapped.

Malcolm moved across to where Louise stood.

"Let's get this over with," he said as his hands encompassed the thick rope.

The pressure on Mary's neck felt like the weight of the world. Black spots impeded her vision and she felt the veins in her forehead pop. Her body left the ground; the weight of her own body crushed her larynx.

She wasn't ready to give up though; she wasn't ready to die. Mary had always been so fascinated with the mysteries of life and with living, that she had always thought herself immune to death. She had survived the Great War and had only begun to live her life with Rosaline in Montpellier. She was going to climb mountains and discover new worlds and now here she was dying at the hands of a greedy, unimaginative cook, in the place that she had worked so hard to escape from.

As the last ounce of consciousness was flowing from her body, she heard the bolt being drawn back on a rifle.

"Stop it now; or I'll shoot," Godfrey shouted.

Her vision was fading slowly to black. She had no air, no capacity for speech. She wanted to scream. She wanted to tell them to drop her, let her breath – but she couldn't. They lowered her and as she hit the ground the noose loosened enough for her to say,

"Thank-you Godfrey, I thought you had left."

"I made you a promise," he replied. "I couldn't leave you here at the mercy of....."

Clang. Godfrey fell to the ground. Standing behind him was Martha, holding a skillet.

"He fell more easily than when I hit Addie. I guess he's older. What did I miss?" Martha said casually going to join them.

Any kind of relief that Mary had felt, dissipated. The tugging began again and she knew that this time there was nobody coming to save her.

***

Malcolm stepped back and admired their handy work. He hadn't understood how difficult it was to haul up a body and hang it from a tree. He had a sudden appreciation of the work that had been done to

kill Emlyn – something which he had only helped to plan.

"We've already been telling everyone how depressed she's been. Ever since she was there when the Captain died and she wasn't able to save him," Martha stated breaking the silence.

Malcolm watched Mary's lifeless body swinging from the thick rope which now wrapped around the lowest of the branches of the old, linden tree. He had a sudden flashback to when he and his hunting companions had returned from the forests behind Loxley Hall to see Emlyn dangling from the very same place.

He added in a monotone, "I noticed that she hadn't been eating much either. I'm sure the others did too."

"I suppose we'll have to get that idiot Markson out here again," Louise sighed as she kicked Addie's body and then Godfrey into the bunker.

"I suppose we will. I wouldn't call him an idiot though – he has been our saviour," Malcolm countered as he put his arm around Louise and kissed her cheek.

"If he was any smarter than an idiot, then he might have actually investigated some of these deaths," Louise observed.

"The Captain was an accident," Malcolm protested.

"If you call rubbing wax all over the roof with the hopes of making someone slip and fall an accident?" Martha replied facetiously.

"Yes, well – it's better that Captain Hope's out of the way too. He might've started asking more questions if he was here to see Mary's 'suicide'. No, it's much better that he's gone," Louise said decisively.

The three of them made their way back up to the Hall.

"I'll fix us some tea and bring it up to your study and then we better bring in Markson," Louise said as she walked towards the passageway which eventually led to the servants' area. She turned and added, "When can I bring my things upstairs, Mr Garrot?"

"Soon enough, Mrs Garrot; but not until we clear up the business of Mary's suicide," Malcolm answered tenderly.

She took her aged wedding ring out of her cleavage and gave it a kiss. She had hung it from her necklace – ready to place it back on her hand on the day that Malcolm could finally be free.

Louise and Martha left the room. He sat in his chair and he took out a cigarette. He lit it and inhaled deeply – he coughed. It had been a while since he had smoked, but with the day he had had, he certainly needed one.

For his entire life all he had ever wanted was to find a place where he belonged. Having a woman of the night as his mother – his father pimping her out and running all kinds of schemes – had always taken its toll and had left him with so much uncertainty. Throughout his entire childhood he always felt like an outsider; displaced from society. Becoming Malcolm Quinn had been the making of him, and even though his life had been built on stealing the identity of another, he felt as though he had used the credentials well and been able to build the kind of life that he deserved.

He was never a killer – it was the war that brought it out in him. He never wanted to hurt anyone, but it was justified. He did what needed to be done and he ran the best hospital in all of Britain. Those men would never have returned to fight and so he executed them and put them to good use. He never meant for any innocent people to be killed – but he needed to protect himself and everything he had built.

He'd married Louise as a young man and she and Martha had always supported him in all his endeavours. And finally, he could make her Lady Louise Quinn and give her everything that she deserved.

Louise entered with a pot of tea and some biscuits and sat down opposite him. She poured him out a cup and looked at him with longing in her eyes.

"Martha's begun preparing that meat loaf you liked so very much during the war. Who knew that old fool Godfrey would come in handy for something?" Louise said.

They drank their tea in silence and when they had finished, Louise said, "All right my love, let's do this."

She readied herself to go and fetch Sergeant Markson.

Malcolm declared, "Yes, my love, I think that we should get married, well re-married, in the spring."

Louise flung her arms around him. Malcolm was relieved that everything was finally over and he sank down in his chair, happy in the knowledge that natural justice had won out in the end.

Louise said, "I do prefer Mrs Garrot – but I suppose Lady Quinn will just have to do."

Malcolm smiled and nodded and he rested his hand on Louise's stomach; on the life that they had created together and on the future of the new Quinn dynasty.

24. HALCYON DAYS

"I wanted to thank-you," Andy said. "If you didn't send Royal to check on me, I'd be dead."

"You don't have to thank me; what are partners for?" Pridis replied from the open doorway of Andy's office.

"The way I left the Yard that day – I wasn't the kind of partner to you, that I want to be. Sometimes I get caught up in things, especially when it comes to John Quinn and what he did – but it doesn't excuse the fact that I was a complete bellend," Andy said apologetically.

"You were right though; about John Quinn and Tilman," Pridis replied.

"Being right isn't everything – although it is nice to see Tilman finally get what she deserves," Andy said.

"When is her hearing?" Pridis asked.

"It will be a while before she's out of the hospital and they need time to check through all of her cases. It'll be more work for us – either way. I knew that she wasn't a good person, but I didn't think that she was corrupt. I thought she was selfish and ambitious and incompetent – but never corrupt."

"She had secrets that she wanted to keep hidden," Pridis mused.

"How did you piece it all together?" Andy asked.

"When I found out that Tilman and Marcus North were being blackmailed, I tried to find a connection between them. I had almost given up, when DS Ives scanned me the file on the case which led to Pearson's demotion. It was the missing link.

"Pearson had gone in to speak to a young woman who was under suicide watch at the hospital – she had OD'd on a yacht and she'd been listed as suicidal. The report said that when he left the room to take a telephone call, he left his pen lying on her side table. When he returned to the room, she had already bled out from a stab wound in her neck.

"The yacht was Marcus', and Tilman was listed as being present. They denied any knowledge of Mandy Jones or the drugs. They claimed that she had stowed away and that they found her passed out when they went below deck. My theory, is that Pearson found out what really happened that night and was using it against them."

"It wouldn't surprise me if Pearson stabbed her in the neck himself and staged the suicide," Andy postulated.

"With Pearson dead, we'll never know. Tilman tried so hard to cover her tracks. She had cleared off all the reports of Mandy Jones and any link she had to her – but she couldn't get her hooks into the hard copy. It made sense that Pearson was Luke, and when your brother told me that it was Luke who had hired the Golds – it all fell into place," Pridis explained.

Andy sighed, "Tilman did all of this to cover up her drug addiction and then it all came out anyway. I don't understand what drives people sometimes. Carla sold her own leg for a 6 month high."

He opened the bottom drawer of his desk and took out his bottle of Chivas.

"Sorry Inspector; I may have raided your supply while you were gone," Pridis admitted.

"I don't need this shit anymore," he said as he threw the bottle into the bin. "It's never done me any good, and I hate being at its mercy."

"Good for you." Pridis smiled and made to leave, "It's time I finally went home."

The paperwork was piled high on Andy's desk. It had been two days since the incident at Loxley Hall and the Super had been on his back for the report. The bones were still being identified by Royal and his team in Sheffield and it was going to take a long time to wade through the mess.

Andy looked at the list of names that he had compiled using Edris' algorithm. He wondered how many he could have saved if he had been more capable. He could blame Tilman all he wanted – but Andy knew in his heart that if he hadn't been drunk, then she wouldn't have had the opportunity to lose Emily Baribel. If he hadn't been so drunk, then Jarmila would be safe and would still be his wife.

He finished typing up his report. It seemed ridiculous. The amount of humanity lost underneath that damned tree. He'd read the confession which Alex had found hidden in the wall; the murders of the soldiers, of Cecil Watson and the Loxley sisters. The military was sending a representative in the coming days. Back then, cowardice executions were condoned – something that Andy still couldn't comprehend. He wondered how they would sweep this one under the carpet.

It was late. He dropped the report on the Super's desk and he made his way home.

*

"Nice to see you're still alive," Edris said as he emerged from the shadows of Andy's front porch.

"Not by much, brother," Andy replied. "You coming in?"

"I have somewhere to be," Edris answered. "You wanted to see me?"

"How are you involved in all of this?" Andy asked.

"You know I don't talk about my work – especially with you. Let's just say that the Golds made an error and I helped them out using my skills and expertise. I pressed the button on one of your old problems."

"So, you got rid of John Quinn and the CCTV? Pridis told me that Hicks' mother recognised you as her husband – the same as with the person who put her to bed that night."

Edris nodded his head. He was never one for verbal admissions.

"And the police run cameras?" Andy asked.

"I'm not going to give you all my tricks, little bro."

"What if I took you down to the Yard? Would that jog your memory?" Andy threatened.

"I wouldn't count on it being the only thing that got jogged. You really don't remember the night that Jarmila 'went away' do you?"

At the mention of Jarmila, Andy felt his stomach tighten. DC Crocker still hadn't located her and Royal had not yet identified all of the bones.

Edris continued, "You called me. You were incoherent. You said that you'd hit her and she wouldn't get up."

"You're saying I killed her?"

"I'm saying that I came and helped you that night. I cleaned up your mess, packed her bags, got her out of there and got her help. You broke her skull, little bro, and while you were passed out in the corner, I fixed it for you. I still send her money; every month," Edris explained.

"Where is she?" Andy asked.

"She's moved on. She doesn't want to see you and I don't blame her."

Andy's insides squirmed. He needed to throw up. He had spent all this time obsessed with John Quinn; sickened by him and everything that he had done to those women. Andy pushed past Edris and stumbled inside. He fell to the ground, clutched his head and pulled his hair. The realisation had finally settled upon him, that he was no better than John Quinn.

*

"On behalf of the Rosaline Stern Foundation I would like to thank-you for your hard work. My mother was a very stubborn woman. She tried to tell the authorities that Mary Loxley didn't kill herself, but no one ever listened. It was hard enough being a woman back then, but to be in love with another woman was much harder," Mary Stern said.

"I'm happy that we could finally give them some justice. I'm just sorry that neither of them are here to see it," Andy said.

"I spent a very long time, resenting my mother. She spent her life chasing lost causes, when all I wanted was someone to look after me. But at my age, you come to learn that there are things worth fighting for."

Mary Stern wheeled her chair out of his office. Her children had waited for her outside. Her mother, Rosaline, had campaigned for many things over the years, spurred on by the memory of a lost love and by the injustice that she had suffered at the hands of the authorities because she was different.

He reread the letter which he had just shown to Mary Stern. The letter had been found next to the crumpled skeleton of Addie, by John and Eric when they were home from Radley one Summer. It was the letter which John Quinn had used to justify his actions and it was the letter which had shocked the nation.

Dear Lady Mary,
I have held onto my silence for long enough. I need to warn you, that you are in grave danger and from sources upon which you would not expect. I can no longer stand back and watch more innocent blood be spilled. I want you to understand that I only did as I was told, and before I had realised I had sunken beyond any hope of redemption.

I worked in the kitchen at Loxley Hall during the war. We were running short on supplies. In early 1917, the Ellis sisters told me that they had found a meat supplier. I didn't know who and I didn't ask any questions.

When the meat arrived in the kitchen, it was hacked and mutilated. I couldn't tell what kind of meat it was, but any kind of protein for the soldiers was a Godsend. It wasn't until the day I saw Louise emerge from a hidden doorway carrying a package filled with flesh, wearing a blood smeared apron, that I began to question exactly what was going on.

Eventually they let me in on their secret, and to this day I wish that they hadn't. Once every two weeks they would pick out a patient from the wards – one who Malcolm deemed unfit to be a soldier – and he would shoot them. The Ellis sisters would then extract the meat as best they could and boil the bones for stock.

I was petrified. I couldn't believe that the meat I had been stewing and preparing was human flesh – I had thought that it was an exotic meat, maybe cat or dog. But they justified it – What did a few lives matter, when the hospital and our efforts were saving so many?

Everything unravelled the day that Cecil Watson ran into the kitchen and hid in the corner. By that time, we were not so careful. We took entire limbs into the kitchen and I helped with the butchery. That was what Cecil Watson saw. I emerged from the secret passageway carrying a severed leg and from there his fate was sealed.

I wanted to come clean – tell the authorities. If what we were doing was really for the good of the war effort and these soldiers were truly cowards, then I thought that we could confess and be pardoned. But Malcolm and the Ellis sisters took it into their own hands and little Cecil Watson was killed. I know that I should have said something then. But I wasn't strong enough.

I thought it had all ended after the war had finished and everything went back to normal. If only Lady Emlyn hadn't started looking into the death of Cecil Watson. It was only a matter of time. It was Malcolm's idea to hang her, but it was I and the Ellis sisters who did it. I will never forget the exaggerated look on her face and the puff of her eyes and her bluish lips. It has been imprinted on my soul forever.

I've been having nightmares and I haven't been able to sleep. I don't think that I can live with myself any longer and I think Martha is suspicious. We only killed Lady Emlyn to save ourselves from the gallows but there has been too much blood spilled and I don't see it ending any time soon.

I have decided to go on the run. You can do with my letter what you will, but you need to get away from here as soon as possible – otherwise I fear for your life and I can't guarantee that you will be safe,

I am sorry for everything,
Yours in guilt and in sin,
Addie.

Andy folded Addie's letter and returned it to the evidence file. It had been almost three months since he had left Loxley Hall. In the meantime, he and Pridis had worked to unravel the events that occurred in Loxley during the war. In conjunction with Malcolm Quinn's confession and the other papers which Alex had uncovered –

they had been able to piece together a credible timeline of events.

It had been much harder work to verify the information, as it was now almost a hundred years ago, however Pridis and the team had performed exceptionally and they were on the verge of having all of the older bones identified. Royal had finished identifying the recent bones and the families of the 13 women had been able to lay their loved ones to rest.

Andy had also reclassified the deaths of Emlyn Quinn, Mary Loxley and Baden Hope, to murder. And if that wasn't enough, they had uncovered and solved the most heinous of war crimes ever to have been committed on English soil.

Andy checked his watch. It was a quarter to seven and they needed to leave if they were going to arrive at the restaurant on time. He stood up, grabbed his jacket and left his office. Next door, the lights were still on in the conference room, and there was Pridis head first in a stack of papers. The room was full of boxes and he could not envisage the end of the infinite amount of paperwork.

"Hey Pridis, let's go. It's time for the party."

"I don't know Inspector; I've still got so much to get through here and Vicki and I are going so well for now – I think I should just get home," Pridis replied.

"The paperwork's not going anywhere. I won't take no for an answer and I'll make sure that you get home safely," Andy declared.

"Okay then," Pridis said typing furiously on her computer.

Andy Bliss studied his partner. In the beginning, he wasn't so sure that their partnership would last – but he was wrong. She had proven herself to be a fine and loyal officer and he was glad to have her by his side.

"Did you see that Loxley Hall sold for 10 million pounds?" Andy said as he leaned on the side of Pridis' desk. "They said in the paper that it went for double the price because of the chamber of horrors underneath the Killing tree."

"People are morbid," Pridis replied.

"Alex didn't look pregnant in any of the pictures," Andy said.

"It would have been a difficult decision – but I can understand it," Pridis said as she switched off her computer.

The cold air slapped against Andy's worn-out face as they exited the Yard. Tilman was huddled against the wall, smoking. She had gained weight and it was the first time that Andy had seen her without make-up.

"I'll catch up," he said to Pridis and he made his way across to Tilman.

Her disciplinary hearing had been in full swing and Andy had heard that she was already going to rehab.

"Hey Andy, I wanted to tell you how sorry I am about everything. If I'd not been so selfish, then some of those women would still be alive," Tilman said.

Andy stopped her before she could continue and said, "I spent so much time blaming you for things, when maybe I should have looked a little harder at myself. Nobody's perfect Teri, no one makes the right decisions all the time; we're all human."

"I'm still sorry," she said quietly.

"And you'll face up to the consequences of your actions and that's all that we can do," Andy replied. "Do you want to come to Royal and Jordan's engagement party with me?" he asked, placing his hand gently on her arm.

"I'd like that," she replied.

As Andy and Tilman raced to catch up with Pridis, he was glad that something good had come out of all of this.

ABOUT THE AUTHOR

Marijka Bright is originally from Australia; however, she has been living in Berlin, Germany, for the past four years. She has degrees in Biomedical Science, Psychology and Accounting and relinquished a very secure job at a large firm, to pursue her dream of becoming an author. 'Underneath the Killing Tree' is the first of two novels to be released this year, with her second novel – 'The Never After' in the final stages of editing. Marijka had her short story, 'The Glooms' published in 'The Wild Word' magazine and she has a collection of short stories which will be released at the end of 2018.

Printed in Poland
by Amazon Fulfillment
Poland Sp. z o.o., Wrocław